Hannah Dennison was born in England, relocating to Los Angeles with her daughter and two cats in tow to pursue a career in screenwriting. Along the road to publication she has served as an obituary reporter, antique dealer, private jet flight attendant and Hollywood story analyst.

Hannah is currently serving on the judging committee for the 2012 Edgar Allan Poe Awards for the Mystery Writers of America. She teaches mystery writing and social media at UCLA in Los Angeles and still works full-time for Davis Elen Advertising, a west coast advertising agency.

Although California is where she currently lives, Hannah's heart will always be in the English countryside. She enjoys hiking, horse riding, skiing and seriously good chocolate. Hannah is married to a fellow writer.

Website: www.hannahdennison.com

Blog: www.hannahdennison.blogspot.com

Twitter: @HannahLDennison

Facebook: www.facebook.com/VickyHillMysteries

Vicky Hill's Facebook page: www.facebook.com/pages/
Vicky-Hill/84329298565

Exposé!

HANNAH DENNISON

ROBINSON

Constable & Robinson Ltd
55–56 Russell Square
London WC1B 4HP
www.constablerobinson.com

Published in the US by The Berkley Publishing Group, a division of Penguin
Group (USA) Inc., New York, 2009

First published in the UK by Robinson,
an imprint of Constable & Robinson Ltd, 2012

A copy of the British Library Cataloguing in
Publication data is available from the British Library

ISBN: 978-1-78033-063-1 (paperback)
ISBN: 978-1-78033-064-8 (ebook)

Printed and bound by CPI Group (UK) Ltd, Croydon, CR0 4YY

1 3 5 7 9 10 8 6 4 2

For Dad,
I hear you in the wind and see you in the stars

1

People like to believe that an investigative reporter never sleeps. It certainly seemed the case this morning when my mobile woke me at a ridiculously early hour.

'Are you Vicky Hill?' a woman said in a low voice.

'It depends,' I said crossly. It's not often I dream of the elusively gorgeous Lieutenant Robin Berry but when I do, I resent being woken up at *the* crucial moment.

'Don't you do the funerals?'

When I mumbled that I did, she said, 'You've got to get to St Peter's. It's urgent.'

'*Now?*' I glanced over at the clock on the nightstand. It was barely six thirty. 'You must be mistaken,' I said. 'Reverend Whittler is away on holiday and everything is on hold until he gets back.' In fact, Whittler had left strict instructions with Dr Frost and Coroner Cripps that bodies from *any* deaths arising whilst he was in Disney World were to be kept in cold storage at Gipping morgue.

There was a long pause on the other end of the line.

'Who is this?' I said.

'Don't bother. I'll phone the other girl—'

'No. Don't do that,' I said quickly, knowing full well that the 'other girl' could only mean my nemesis and rival, Annabel Lake. 'I'm on my way. Hello? Are you still there?'

The phone was dead. I immediately hit one-four-seven-one only to be told by an infuriating mechanical voice that the 'number you have called is not in service.'

As I dragged on the jeans, sweater, clean underwear, socks and sneakers I always left folded and ready on the floor next to my bed (childhood memories of nighttime police raids die hard), I wondered who on earth could have died and why I was only finding out about it now.

Frankly, I was grateful to the mystery woman. In the one hundred and forty-odd years of being in existence, the *Gipping Gazette* had never once missed sending a reporter to the church to record the names of all the mourners. The thought that I almost broke the tradition was too horrible to bear.

I hurried down the stairs surprised that my landlady, Mrs Evans, was not in the kitchen listening to Radio Two. It was unusual for her to sleep in. I was sorely tempted to grab a quick cuppa and slice of toast but the tone of the caller implied it was urgent.

Donning my helmet and goggles, I set off on my red Yamaha SRI25. Within minutes, 21 Factory Terrace was far behind me. I headed north toward Upper Gipping, taking the shortcut through the narrow country lanes flanked by green, luscious hedgerows.

It was a gloriously sunny May morning. Lambs frolicked in the fields; late-blooming daffodils and primroses sparkled in the early dew. I couldn't help thinking it was a lovely day for a funeral.

With practically no traffic at this early hour – apart from the odd tractor en route to a field – I reached St Peter's the Martyr in record time.

Turning into Church Lane, the twelfth-century grey stone Norman church peeped between the treetops a quarter of a mile further on. I entered the gravel car park and discovered two cars were parked outside the wooden lych-gate.

One was a hearse – and an unconventional one at that.

It was an American Cadillac – the sort seen in old movies from the sixties. Faded black, scalloped curtains hung in the large picture windows. Embellished in gothic-styled lettering on the side panels was GO-GO GOTHIC – OUR PASSENGERS GO ALL THE WAY.

This hearse certainly didn't belong to Ripley and Ravish, Gipping-on-Plym's funeral directors – DUST TO DUST WITH DIGNITY – who owned a very smart fleet of Peugeot DA3's. Besides, they had taken Whittler's absence as a chance to close their facilities for refurbishing.

I'd heard about rogue funeral outfits such as Horizontal Taxis and Hearsedriver.com available on the Internet. Hatch, Match and Dispatch was a common sight in the less affluent areas of Plymouth, but I never expected to see such a tacky sight in Gipping-on-Plym.

As I pulled up behind the Cadillac, I was astonished to see a sleek black Audi RS Avant with the registration plate DF 007. I recognized it as belonging to Douglas Fleming, the managing director of Gipping-on-Plym Power Services.

Thanks to my usual daily dose of funerals, I prided myself on knowing the domestic state of all my readers. Douglas Fleming had been married to Scarlett, an American from Atlanta, for more than forty years. As far as I knew, they had no children or relatives on this side of the Atlantic so the presence of his car at this early hour was most intriguing.

What's more, Douglas Fleming came from an old Devonian family and was unlikely to flaunt convention. Besides, Scarlett was as ostentatious as her namesake from *Gone With the Wind*. Everything she did had to be bigger and better than everyone else. From hiring a team of gardeners so she could win the Best-Garden-of-Gipping prize, to training with a French pastry chef and snagging the Best-Victoria-Sponge trophy at Gipping Church Fête.

Taking out my Canon Digital Rebel, I ran off a few quick snaps of the American Cadillac both inside and out. The hearse had none of the gleaming brass and burnished wood fixtures that any of the Ripley and Ravish Peugeots boasted. I even spied an empty wine bottle, a half-eaten egg-and-cress sandwich and a copy of *Land Ahoy!* a well-known guidebook to Plymouth nightlife.

My curiosity was piqued.

Passing through the church lych-gate, I took the shortcut diagonally across the cemetery, taking care not to trample on late-blooming daffodils. Within minutes my sneakers were soaked through with early morning dew.

The churchyard was enormous. I scanned the rows of lichen-covered headstones for any sign of life – no pun intended – and then recalled that the Flemings kept a family vault in the posh part of St Peter's.

Known locally as Albert Square, the private enclosure had been created in the late nineteenth century during Queen Victoria's reign when Gipping-on-Plym had a thriving wool and textile industry.

Located in the sheltered southwest corner, Albert Square was enclosed by a beautifully clipped yew hedge and accessed by a six-foot-high, wrought-iron gate flanked by stone angels. The gate stood ajar.

As I drew closer, I noted paper streamers and dead flowers were woven through the railings. One stone angel even wore a cone-shaped party hat – all remnants from another grand Devon family funeral held a few weeks earlier.

Ninety-five-year-old Samuel K. Larch's tragic passing had been a true celebration of an eccentric life – or death – depending on how well you knew him. Everyone from the newspaper was invited to the post-service shin-dig and we all got plastered on scrumpy and cheap sherry, which was more than I could say for this morning's sad event.

It was one of the reasons that I took my job as funeral reporter

4

extremely seriously. Someone had to record a life – however insignificant – for posterity. Someone had to make that life *count*.

I pushed open the gate and stepped inside. Albert Square housed four marble tabernacles adorned with winged, trumpeting angels, a pyramid – Sammy Larch's final resting place – made of granite guarded by two small sphinxes, three identical miniature Greek temples with ornate porticos, and a Gothic chapel choked with brambles behind rusting iron railings. All were crammed into a space not much bigger than Gipping's village hall and knee-deep in weeds. The place seemed deserted.

For a horrible moment, I thought I must be in the wrong location until I spotted wheeled track marks – presumably left by some kind of trolley – in the tall grass hugging the yew hedge boundary.

I set off, surprised to find a further overgrown area tucked away around a corner. Albert Square was more of an L-shape and not a square at all.

Two figures and a hospital trolley stood next to the entrance of a stone burial vault carved with gargoyles. No doubt, pallbearers were an extra charge.

I recognized Douglas Fleming immediately. He was smoking a cigarette with a man wearing a Victorian frock coat, pinstripe trousers, and top hat who had his back to me.

'Morning gents!' I called out and walked over to join them.

Douglas Fleming saw me, gave a start of surprise, and dropped his cigarette into the tall grass. 'Why, it's Vicky! Goodness,' he said, grinding the butt under his heel. 'What a piece of luck. I was going to come and see you later.'

The Victorian frock-coated gent turned to me and said, 'Neil Titley, Esquire. Nice to meet you.'

'Hello.' I tried hard not to stare at the ghoulish-looking man before me. Kohl pencil-rimmed dark brown eyes with white face powder gave him a deathly pale complexion. His large Roman

5

nose lay slightly bent and flattened as if someone had punched him full in the face and he hadn't bothered to see a doctor.

'Allow me to introduce Vicky Hill from our local newspaper,' Douglas Fleming said.

'*Gipping Gazette,*' I said, offering my hand.

'Delighted.' Neil Titley took it in his leather-clad own and held it just a little too long. I caught a whiff of cigarette breath. 'Here's my business card,' he went on, withdrawing a small white card from inside his frock-coat pocket. It was the cheap print-your-own variety, available at any railway station. 'Funerals are only one service we offer—'

'Thank you, Mr Titley,' Douglas Fleming snatched the card out of his grasp. 'Hardly the right time to tout for new business.'

'Sorry, sir.' Neil Titley did not look sorry. He promptly withdrew *another* card and pushed it into my hand whispering, 'We accept cash only. No credit cards. Tell your friends and I'll give them a good price.'

'Goodbye,' Douglas Fleming said coldly.

'Good day to you both.' Neil Titley touched his top hat and, with practised skill, collapsed the hospital trolley with a snap. 'May your poor wife rest in peace.'

'Your *wife*? Goodness. I *am* sorry!' I was stunned. I'd seen Scarlett Fleming only two weeks ago picking up first prize for Gipping's Bottled Jam Boil-Off. She'd been in rude health judging by the fight she picked with Mayor Rawlings after her preserves had been initially placed third.

'Was it an accident?' I said gently.

Douglas Fleming's eyes filled with tears. 'It happened so quickly. One moment she was alive and the next . . .' He shook his head with despair. 'I just can't believe it.'

Nor could I.

Something wasn't right. Pete Chambers, our chief reporter, had a hotline to Gipping Police Station, Fire Station, and morgue for accidents and fatalities. We also had informers dotted around

Devon eager to earn fifteen pounds for any gossip worth printing.

Given Douglas Fleming's stature in the community, it was astonishing that this tragedy might have passed by unnoticed had it not been for that mystery phone call this morning. It also occurred to me that whoever made that call was not here, either.

'I've written a short paragraph for your newspaper,' said Douglas Fleming. 'I know there will be some people who won't be happy that we didn't have a big bash, but' – he wiped away a tear – 'this is exactly what Scarlett wanted – a quiet funeral with no fuss.'

'Of course,' I said, thinking a lot of Gipping churchgoers would feel incensed about being cheated out of a slap-up meal especially since Scarlett Fleming was regarded as a local celebrity.

'My Scarlett led a very simple life,' Douglas Fleming went on. 'She didn't like to draw attention to herself.'

I stifled a snort of disbelief. Were we talking about the same person? My landlady, Mrs Evans, ran a cleaning business called Doing-it-Daily and counted the Flemings as one of her clients. She always enjoyed gossiping about Scarlett's glamorous lifestyle. The twice-weekly manicures in Plymouth to keep her acrylic nails in peak condition, the private yoga classes with a trainer rumoured to have worked in Los Angeles, and her brand-new Range Rover Vogue SE with the personalized number plate, SCLTT.

'Scarlett always said that if she died before me' – Fleming swallowed hard – 'a quickie burial was her only request. Even her coffin is plain. Would you like to see it?' He withdrew a heavy ornate key from his pocket. 'I can unlock the vault.'

'No thanks.' I studied Douglas Fleming's expression. His face was etched with grief. This was not the time to question him further about the gory details. He was obviously still in shock.

'Perhaps I should come to your house this afternoon?' This would give me a chance to ring emergency services and get the real scoop on Scarlett Fleming.

'I'm going to the office,' he said. 'Being alone at Headcellars with all those memories is more than I can bear. Come before we close, just before three.'

Mr Fleming escorted me back to the car park in silence. It was only when we reached the lych-gate and he stopped to usher me through, that he spoke again. 'I know I should have called you about this but I couldn't face it,' he said. 'How did you find out?'

'I got tipped off. A woman phoned but wouldn't give her name. I was going to mention it earlier but somehow, it didn't seem the right thing.'

'Tipped *off*?' Douglas Fleming frowned. 'Who on earth . . . oh, dear.'

'Do you know who it could be?'

'I'm afraid I might.' Douglas Fleming turned pale. 'Good God!' He lowered his voice and whispered, 'Look no further. I believe your answer is over there.'

A silver Ford Fiesta was parked on the far side of the church car park in the shadows.

I was flabbergasted. 'Doesn't that car belong to Eunice Pratt?'

It was a well-known fact that she remained wildly infatuated with Douglas Fleming, her childhood sweetheart, but how she found out about this morning's burial so quickly was anyone's guess.

'Forgive me. I must go.' Douglas Fleming grabbed my hands and squeezed them tightly in his own. 'Please, Vicky. I can't deal with her now. Would you mind?'

And with that, he hurried to his Audi and leapt in, just as a slight figure with a lavender-coloured perm scrambled out of the Fiesta shouting, 'Dougie! Dougie! Wait!'

Mr Fleming appeared not to hear. He gunned the engine and tore past her at high speed as if his life depended on it.

Eunice scurried toward me, her face shining with excitement. 'It's true isn't it?' she cried. 'Scarlett Fleming is dead. Dougie is mine at last!'

2

Eunice Pratt engulfed me in a warm embrace. Her pale blue twinset and beige skirt smelled strongly of lavender water and mothballs. She was so thin I feared she might snap in two.

Mrs Pratt was not one of my favourite people. She was a bitter woman in her sixties with a nasty temper. She was also the love of my life's – Lieutenant Robin Berry – aunt. Given that Robin adored her, it was important I keep on her good side. Of course, Robin and I hadn't actually gone on our first proper date yet but it wasn't for want of trying. On the two occasions we'd made dinner plans, he'd had to cancel at the last minute, due to 'top secret naval business'.

'I can't thank you enough, dearest Vicky,' Eunice Pratt cried.

'I didn't do anything,' I said, gently extricating myself.

'Of course you did.' She beamed. 'You gave me hope. If you hadn't told me how Dougie felt, I'd never have dared to dream.'

How horribly awkward! A few weeks ago, I *had* inadvertently hinted that the embers of her school day romance with Douglas Fleming may not have grown cold, but it was just a passing remark to make her feel special. Unfortunately, given the speed with which Douglas Fleming had peeled out of the church car park, it would appear that as far as he was concerned, those embers had definitely fizzled out.

'I had no idea Scarlett was ill,' Mrs Pratt chattered on happily. 'I wonder what she died of – probably her heart. She had high blood pressure, you know – and of course, that dreadful temper. Poor Dougie. Good riddance to bad rubbish is what I say.'

I hadn't expected heartfelt sympathies but Mrs Pratt's callous remark got me thinking. 'By the way, thank you for telephoning this morning.'

She looked blank. 'I don't know what you are talking about.'

'Don't you remember?' I said indulgently. I was used to dealing with these senior lapses of memory. 'You told me to get a reporter to St Peter's immediately but didn't want to leave your name?'

'Are you implying I made an *anonymous* call?' Mrs Pratt said, appalled.

'Someone phoned—'

'It was certainly not me,' she snapped.

The funny thing was, I actually believed she was telling the truth. Even if she had forgotten she'd made that phone call, Eunice Pratt would always leave her name.

Rather like her dead rival, Mrs Pratt basked in the limelight and never missed an opportunity to plug her latest petition, no matter how inappropriate the circumstances. At Sammy Larch's funeral I caught her handing out inflammatory flyers condemning the British government's plans to add loudspeakers to the numerous CCTV cameras that were now installed throughout the country. 'A shocking invasion of privacy!' Eunice claimed and I had to admit she could be right.

I wondered what prompted Douglas Fleming to suggest his former love had been the caller. 'How did *you* hear about today's sad event?'

Mrs Pratt turned a mottled shade of red. 'I was just passing by and recognized Dougie's car.'

'Really? That was lucky.' *Hardly passing by.* Church Lane was off the main road and dead-ended in a field.

A peculiar feeling came over me. Surely there wasn't anything sinister about Scarlett Fleming's death? *Good grief!* What if Eunice and Douglas Fleming were having an affair? What if they'd knocked Scarlett off and he was only *pretending* to dislike her to throw me off the scent? Now I thought about it, Fleming's hasty get-away exit from the car park had seemed staged.

'A lot of people are going to be disappointed that Mrs Fleming wasn't given a traditional funeral,' I said slyly. 'Don't you think that odd?'

'Why? She wasn't very popular.' Nor was Sammy Larch, I thought, and people turned up in droves for his official departure. 'I assume she'll still get her fifteen minutes of fame on page eleven?' Eunice added.

'Yes. I will be writing Mrs Fleming's obituary,' I said. 'I'm going to see Mr Fleming this afternoon.'

'Good. I must pay my respects, too. I'll come with you and bring one of my homemade cakes.'

'I might just phone him instead,' I said quickly.

'I've been learning to cook. She was a good cook, you know. But I shall be better.'

I checked my watch and gave a yelp of horror. Every Thursday morning, Pete held a Page One meeting. I was going to be late. 'Sorry, Mrs Pratt, I'd love to stop and chat but I have to dash.'

'Do call me Eunice,' she said, grabbing my arm. 'Tell you what, why don't you come for supper tonight and we can talk about this more?'

I hesitated. The thought of sitting amongst live chickens in a kitchen that smelled of damp dog, listening to Eunice fantasizing about a future with Douglas Fleming was not my idea of fun. But sometimes one had to make sacrifices to get the truth. I was quite certain my heroine, Christiane Amanpour, had endured far worse meals out on the battlefield.

'I'd love to,' I said with as much enthusiasm as I could muster.

'It's formal attire. Come at six.' She gave a happy nod. 'I'm making monkfish medallions with tomato lemon coulis followed by snow eggs with pistachio custard and chocolate drizzle.'

'It sounds delicious,' I said – and alarmingly ambitious. Still, better than the usual liver and onions I got every Thursday night at Chez Evans. 'Yes. I'm having a practice run,' Eunice said. 'And of course, Dougie *loved* fish Fridays at school.'

As I sped back to the *Gazette,* my mind was spinning. A mysterious phone call, a much-loved wife practically buried in secret, a dubious funeral company, and an old flame so anxious to reunite with her former lover that she admitted to taking up cooking!

Call me suspicious, but I wondered if Douglas Fleming and Eunice were up to something. The question was could it involve murder?

3

It was well past nine by the time I rushed into reception. 'There you are,' cried Barbara Meadows, our sixty-something you're-as-old-as-you-feel receptionist. Dressed in her usual shapeless, purple hand-knitted cardigan over a crimplene polka-dot dress, Barbara was perched on the edge of one of the hideous brown leatherette chairs. It looked like she was wrestling with an extremely large, deflated exercise ball. 'Annabel has rung down twice wondering where you were.'

'Plym Bridge was closed. I had to go the long way around. But Pete knows.' I'd sent him a text and left an explanation on his mobile. Experience had shown that I couldn't rely on Barbara or Annabel to pass on messages. The former genuinely forgot – and the latter pretended to.

'Hair, dear. Take this.' Barbara reached into her cardigan pocket and withdrew a tortoiseshell mirror and comb. She always wore her iron grey tresses scraped into a tight bun. 'You look like you've just got out of bed,' she went on, with a knowing wink. Barbara always had sex on the brain.

I pretended not to hear. 'No time,' I said, hurrying past.

Ignoring her cries of 'You really should grow it,' and, 'Men love long hair,' I left reception and tore upstairs.

The other reporters were already in Pete's office judging by the angry voices coming from behind his closed door. Someone other than me was in the hot seat this morning.

I hovered outside – not eavesdropping, of course – just waiting for the right kind of lull so I could make my entrance.

'Find yourself another sports writer,' I heard Tony Perkins yell. 'I'm through!'

Pete's door flew open, narrowly avoiding knocking me off my feet. Tony stormed out and slammed it behind him, hard. His thin, pointed face was white with rage. With his lank, shoulder-length brown hair, a growth of stubble on his chin, and dressed in a tattered, old grey sweatshirt emblazoned with the logo GIPPING GROWLERS – our local football team – Tony looked even scruffier than usual.

I was just about to rap on Pete's office door when an ominous voice stopped me in my tracks.

'What's all this caterwauling?' Wilf Veysey, our reclusive editor, emerged from his corner office. Dressed in his trademark brown tweed jacket and corduroy trousers, he cradled his Dunhill pipe in his hand. His one good eye zoomed in on Tony, giving me the chance to duck behind my desk out of Wilf's range of vision.

'Tony?' said Wilf sternly. 'Come into my office and close the door.' I waited until Tony had done just that, then darted into Pete's. This was bad. No one liked to disturb the great man.

Pete was standing by the window, shirtsleeves rolled up, wearing ancient jeans and gnawing on the end of a pencil. I hated this room. It was small, cramped and stuffy and still smelled of stale cigarettes despite the fact Pete had given up smoking months ago.

'Well, good afternoon,' Pete snapped. 'Glad you decided to stop by.'

'Sorry I'm late,' I said. 'I left a . . . never mind.' *Blast!* Pete's mobile was recharging on the top of his filing cabinet.

'Don't get so stressed you silly thing.' Annabel was sharing the tartan two-seater sofa with Edward Lyle, our court reporter. Today, Annabel was dressed simply in a plain cream V-neck T-shirt dress that accentuated her curves. Gold chains hung around her neck and she wore espadrilles that laced up to her knees.

'I told Pete it wasn't like you to be late,' she said, adding with a nasty laugh, 'I expect you were on the trail of some new scoop.'

'I was, actually.' The words flew out of my mouth before I could stop them. Annoyance flashed across Annabel's face.

'Let's get on with this week's edition – and in the future Vicky, don't go off without permission when you know you're supposed to be *here,* at *nine* on Thursday mornings!'

'Sorry.' I refused to look at Annabel, but I heard a snigger. 'Edward, budge up or get up,' she ordered, patting the tartan two-seater sofa. 'Where are your manners?'

Without a word, Edward got to his feet and went to lounge against a bank of olive green filing cabinets against the back wall. Dressed in his usual smart khakis and pristine white trainers, today's yellow polo shirt bore the helpful word *Thursday.*

'Well?' Pete demanded. 'Did Tony leave? Stupid idiot.'

'He's in Wilf's office,' I faltered.

There was a universal gasp of horror and a 'Bloody hell,' from Edward who rarely cursed.

'Wilf? *Wilf?*' Pete regarded me with utter fury as if I had physically put Tony there, myself. 'That sneaky bastard!'

'Wilf came out of his office,' I said gingerly. 'He wanted to know what all the caterwauling was about.'

'Oh, great. That's just bloody great,' Pete threw his hands up in despair and went and sat in the chair behind his desk. 'That's all I need.'

'Wilf is a fan,' Annabel whispered.

'Of what?' I said.

She gestured to Pete who was sifting through a stack of

16

photographs on his desk. He selected one and held it up. It was an eight-by-ten photograph of a garden snail labelled SEABISCUIT. A plaque with the number one was stuck to the snail's shell.

'This, believe it or not, is our lead story,' said Pete grimly.

'Snails? You're joking!' I shrieked, expecting to be joined by a chorus of ridicule.

'Let me explain, Vicky,' said Annabel. 'Hedge-jumping ends on April thirtieth. From May until the end of August, it's officially snail season.'

'*Snail* season?' I'd thought hedge-jumping was strange enough. Would I ever understand these bizarre country pursuits?

'Something to do with birds nesting and nature recovering,' Annabel went on. 'Call it an enforced detente between the hedge-jumpers and cutters. Gives the men something else to think about. I must say I'm surprised you didn't know this.'

'Thank *you*, Annabel,' said Pete. 'We kick off with the GSRF—'

'The Gipping Snail Racing Federation, Vicky,' Annabel put in, adding in a low voice, 'Tony accepted the role of scrutineer this season. Pete feels it's a conflict of interests.'

'Are you finished?' Pete snarled.

'Sorry,' said Annabel. 'But Vicky keeps asking questions.'

'Actually, that's—'

'You can ask me afterwards. I'm the bloody chief reporter, got it?' Pete said. 'As I was saying, the Gastropod Gala is tomorrow night. The first race of the season will be on Sunday at the Three Tuns. Wilf has written some very exciting features on breeding and training. We'll finish up the interviews with the owners today. Those will appear on pages eleven and twelve since there aren't any funerals – thank you very much, Reverend Whittler.'

I raised my hand. 'Actually, there is one obit—'

'Edward, what's the latest on the Larch Legacy?' said Pete.

Annabel whispered in my ear, 'The Larch Legacy—'

'I wrote Sammy Larch's obituary,' I hissed. 'I know what it is, thank you.' Once a year this highly coveted award – and five hundred pounds cash – was given to one of the dozens of local societies deemed worthy of recognition. With no guidelines or prerequisites, it was more a case of finding favour with the now – thankfully – deceased old man.

'The winner will be announced at the gala,' said Edward. 'Being as it's the last one, his daughter, Olive, wanted to make a big deal about it.'

Pete frowned. 'That's too late to get into this Saturday's edition. By next week, it'll be old news.' Pete slammed his hand down on the table. 'Someone's got to know who gets the award? Christ! Larch has been dead for weeks.'

'I already asked Olive,' said Edward. 'She said the winner's name is in a sealed envelope in the safe and she doesn't even know who, herself.'

'Goddamit! Wasn't last month's Gipping Guessing Game calling on readers to vote on who might win?'

'Barbara won't talk,' said Edward. 'She padlocked the voting box.'

'Bollocks.' Pete slammed his hand down on the table again. 'I need something else beside bloody snails on Page One.'

'I thought my CCTV report was going on the front page,' said Annabel in a sulky voice.

'Haven't seen it.'

'I tried to give it to you last night.' Annabel batted her eyelashes. 'Remember? When we were working late?' Annabel leaned over giving Pete an eyeful of cleavage, and pulled out a manila folder from yet another new handbag – Gucci, this time. She flipped through her notes and began to read, 'New cameras have been installed on Plym Bridge, the industrial estate, the market square—'

'Yeah, but what's your angle?' Pete said.

'Angle?' Annabel looked blank. 'Um – well – there are a lot of cameras.'

'Latest statistic I heard was there are 4.2 million – and rising,' Edward chipped in. 'That's one CCTV camera for at least every fourteen people.'

'But not in Gipping.' Annabel glowered at Edward.

'I think it's an invasion of privacy,' I said. 'They're talking about introducing loudspeakers, as well. Can you imagine – a voice coming from the void like God, ordering people to pick up their litter! Shouting at shoplifters.'

'That's stupid,' said Annabel. 'You're making it up.'

'No, she's not. Do your bloody homework,' Pete declared. 'Talk to the man in the street. Is the level of surveillance in this entire country becoming a nationwide Big Brother?'

'You told me to focus on Gipping-on-Plym,' Annabel whined.

'There's a whole wide world out there! Do I have to tell you everything?' Pete rolled his eyes. 'What's your headline?'

'How about, CCTV? REALITY TV?' I suggested.

'Yeah. I like it. Good one.'

'I was going to say that,' Annabel snapped.

'Bloody hell!' Pete jumped to his feet. 'Morning, sir.'

'Carry on, carry on.' Wilf walked in, followed by Tony looking smug.

Annabel and I stood up. She gave Wilf a flirtatious wave but was rewarded with a scowl as his good eye zeroed in on her short dress and lithe, tan legs.

'No need to get up,' Wilf said. We promptly sat back down. 'Tony tells me we're all set for this week's Gastropod bumper edition.'

'Tony said that, did he?' Pete's eyes flashed with fury. 'Thanks for doing my job.'

'He had an excellent idea about running a weekly column about the challenges of being a scrutineer,' Wilf said. 'Readers can phone in with their questions and Tony will answer them.'

Tony looked pointedly at Pete. 'Should ramp up the circulation. People like to see their name in print.'

'And who is going to man the phones?' Pete said. 'Barbara doesn't have the time.'

'What about Vicky?' Annabel suggested. 'With Whittler away, there's nothing for her to do.'

'As a matter of fact, I went to a funeral this morning, which was why I was late. Scarlett Fleming died.'

'Good God!' Wilf's jaw dropped. 'Wait a minute. You say the funeral has already taken *place*?'

'She was buried this morning in the family vault.'

Wilf swung round to face Pete. 'When did she die? Why weren't we informed?'

'No one told me,' Pete said with a shrug.

'But young Vicky seems to know all about it.'

'One of my informers tipped me off,' I said. 'I'll get the full details later on today.'

'Isn't Whittler still in Florida?' said Wilf.

I nodded. 'Yes. But Douglas Fleming said she'd always wanted to be buried quietly with no fuss. He seemed in a hurry.'

'There'll be a backlash from the traditionalists.' Frowning, Wilf clamped his pipe between his teeth. 'Old Fleming comes from a big Devon family. I suppose Ripley took her to St Peter's?'

'No,' I said. 'They used one of those new for-hire companies called Go-Go Gothic.'

'Well, I'll be damned!' Wilf's pipe clattered to the floor. Annabel darted forward to pick it up and passed it back to him with a grimace. Surreptitiously, she wiped her hand on the side of the sofa.

'I never thought I'd live to see the day,' said Wilf. '*Here!* In *Gipping*!'

'Awful, isn't it, sir,' I said.

'Isn't that kind of thing illegal?' said Annabel.

'Not if they are following the rules implemented by the Funeral Planning Authority,' Edward declared. 'Anyone can do it and frankly, with the economy as it is, I can't say I blame them. Death comes to all of us and people tend to forget how expensive these things are. When my dad died, it cost Mum thousands of pounds to give him the whole shebang.'

'I was thinking about doing an exposé on these new, cut-price services,' I said slowly. I hadn't been, but it suddenly seemed a good idea. 'It's bad enough with big superstores like Tesco moving in and putting the corner shops out of business.'

'We've got to move with the times,' said Edward. 'It won't be long until there'll be virtual undertakers handling all the arrangements from Mumbai.'

'They're called funeral directors, nowadays,' I pointed out.

'Not on my watch,' growled Wilf. 'The *Gipping Gazette* is a traditional newspaper with traditional values.'

'How about this for a headline – GRAVESIDE GUERRILLAS: GREED OR GRIEF?' I said, warming to my theme.

'Good idea, young Vicky. Let's have a full report. Get to Plymouth. Find these guerrilla undertakers. Get photographs. Take them to lunch if you have to. See how they get their business.'

'Internet,' said Edward.

'A lot of the elderly don't have computers,' I said.

'Don't you think it strange that old Fleming should hire someone like that?' Annabel chipped in. 'Sounds a bit fishy to me. Wasn't Scarlett only in her sixties? What if her old man knocked her off?'

My thoughts exactly! *Blast!* I knew I should have spoken up.

'This is not the *Plymouth Bugle,* Annabel,' Wilf said coldly. *Thank God I hadn't spoken up!* 'We don't want to start rumours. Dougie Fleming and I went to school together. He's a decent chap. I was an usher at their wedding.'

Annabel turned a lurid shade of beetroot, which clashed horribly with her Nice 'n Easy natural copper red hair. Wilf really disliked her and it showed.

'You can help Barbara in reception, Annabel,' Wilf said. 'Once you've gone home and got dressed properly.'

'Actually, I'm not going to be in the office much,' Annabel said quickly. 'Am I, Pete?'

'That's right,' Pete said. 'She's working on a big story.'

Wilf swung round to Pete and gave him the full force of his good eye. 'And you think she's got something?'

'That's what she told me,' he said with a shrug.

'Facts? Photos? Evidence?' Wilf swung back to Annabel. 'Well? What is this big story?'

'I'd rather not s-s-say,' she stammered.

'We work as a team or not at all,' Wilf said.

'I just don't want to put anyone in danger,' Annabel mumbled.

'I suspect Annabel has an informer to protect,' I suggested.

Annabel shot me a grateful smile, 'Yes. That's right. I do.'

Wilf merely grunted, turned on his heel, and left the room.

'Right, let's get on with our bloody day.' Pete's face was grim. 'Annabel, this scoop you are working on had better be good.'

'Oh, it's good, all right.' Annabel gave a smirk. 'It's not really a scoop, I'd say it was more of an exposé.'

I wasn't worried about Annabel's so-called exposé. It was totally obvious she was lying to get out of fielding phone calls with Barbara.

We got to our feet. Annabel gave her dress a self-conscious tug and turned to me. 'Vicky, can I talk to you somewhere private? It's really important.'

As I followed her into the ladies' loo, I suffered a flash of intuition. I immediately guessed what was so 'really important'.

Annabel was still desperate for her elusive front-page scoop. With two nationwide exclusives to my name, she had become increasingly devious in her attempts to steal my thunder. Twice,

I caught her following me on assignments and once she even tailed me to the dentist on my day off.

Annabel was going to try to muscle in on my investigation. I was *sure* of it! Fat chance!

I'd soon put her straight.

4

'Honestly, I am *not* going home to change,' Annabel said from behind the locked toilet door.

'I really can't hang around,' I said. Call me prudish, but I hated conducting conversations in the ladies' loo.

'Wilf is so transparent. It's obvious that he fancies me. Men are like that. The meaner they are, the more they like you.' There was a rustle of toilet paper. 'Did you know that seventy-five per cent of sexually transmitted diseases are caught from toilet seats?'

'No, I didn't. What's so important?' To distract me from her ablutions, I took a closer look at the pale beige Gucci bag that Annabel had left on the wooden chair next to the hand washbasin. To my surprise, it was a designer knock-off, which was definitely a first. She usually only carried the real thing.

'I wanted to apologize.' Annabel started to pee. It was a delicate tinkling noise that made me cringe with embarrassment. 'I know I've been a bitch to you from the start and I'm really sorry.'

This was completely unexpected. I didn't know what to say mainly because I'd fantasized about Annabel apologizing to me for months, but not through a toilet door. She flushed, shouting, 'Did you hear what I said?'

'Yes!' I shouted back.

'I want us to be friends.' Annabel emerged from the stall to wash her hands. 'I suppose I was jealous of you. Silly really.' She turned on the taps and studied her reflection in the overhead mirror as she pushed the soap dispenser and lathered up. 'After you saved my life, I had this revelation.'

It was true, but it had been weeks since I'd rescued Annabel from almost certain death – weeks of having to put up with far more than her usual sarcastic comments.

'I know, I know, I should have said something sooner,' Annabel went on. 'I was trying to pluck up courage.'

I was stunned. *Who would have thought!* 'Is that why you've been following me?'

Annabel watched me via the mirror. Her green eyes widened with surprise. 'Guilty as charged.' She laughed. 'Now that we've got that out of the way, you're coming to the gala with me tomorrow night.'

'Are you joking? It's hideously expensive.' It was also black-tie and I didn't have anything to wear.

'Come on, we'll have a laugh. I quite like the idea of flirting with Wilf actually – just to get him riled up.'

'What about Dr Frost?'

'He's working. As usual.' Annabel pulled a face. 'He bought the tickets and told me to take a friend. You were the very first person I thought of.'

'I don't know what to say.' I had to admit I was quite pleased.

'Just say yes. *Please*,' Annabel cried. 'We're both alone in the world, Vicky.'

I hesitated. She was right. It might be fun, plus it would be a good opportunity to see just how sincere her offer of the proverbial olive branch was. Besides, Dad always said, *'Keep your friends close, but your enemies closer.'*

'Okay. I'd love to.'

'Excellent!' Annabel stepped closer and looked into my eyes. 'Do you mind if I do something?'

'It depends,' I said instantly on guard. Topaz Potter, my so-called High Street spy and owner of The Copper Kettle café – was the last woman who had uttered just those words and she had tried to kiss me.

'I've been dying to do this.' Annabel reached for her handbag and pulled out a pink floral makeup bag. She grabbed a pair of tweezers. 'Do you mind if I pluck your eyebrows? I'd love to make up your eyes, too. They're the most incredible sapphire blue.'

'You've got nice green eyes,' I said lamely.

Annabel laughed. 'They're tinted contacts, silly. Seriously. People must compliment you all the time. Let me show you how to make the most of those cute little peepers.'

'Okay,' I said reluctantly. 'But I've got a lot to do this morning.'

'Sit down there and just trust me, okay?' Annabel moved her fake Gucci handbag and set out her brushes on the narrow shelf.

As she plucked, applied shadows, powder, and mascara, we chatted about Wilf and Tony's obsession with snail racing.

Annabel made me laugh. True, it was usually at someone else's expense but, for those few minutes in the ladies' loo, upstairs at the *Gipping Gazette*, I felt I had a friend at last. Maybe she really *had* suffered a revelation? It was only fair to give her the benefit of the doubt.

'Just a touch of blusher and lip-gloss and . . . voilà!' Annabel stood back to admire her handiwork.

I gasped. The face that looked back at me in the mirror was actually quite attractive. 'Is that really *me*?' I couldn't stop staring at myself.

Annabel whipped out her mobile phone. 'Mind if I take a picture?' And before I could protest, she'd taken a quick snap. 'Of course, if we had more time I could have done something with your dreadful hair.'

'It's illegal to ride a moped without a helmet,' I said defensively.

'You really need to buy a car,' said Annabel as she deftly touched up her own makeup.

'I'm saving up.' *Not everyone has rich boyfriends.*

'Now we just need to revamp your wardrobe. That safari jacket has got to go. Who do you think you are? Christiane Amanpour?'

'It's comfortable,' I mumbled. There was no question of me giving up my jacket. It had taken me months of traipsing around the flea markets in Newcastle, my hometown, to find one just like Christiane's.

'Being fashionable is not about being comfortable,' Annabel scolded. 'Anyway, I've got lots of clothes I never wear. I was going to donate them to the Salvation Army but you can have them. Thing is, they might be too big on top.'

As if to prove her point, Annabel plunged her hand down her neckline and started rearranging her breasts in her bra.

'Mrs Evans is good at sewing,' I said hopefully.

'Why don't you come over tonight?' she went on. 'We could try on clothes.'

'That would be great!' I cried. 'No, wait. I can't.' I felt really disappointed. What a pity that I had this new look and no one was going to enjoy it.

'Hot date?' Annabel joked.

'I've already got plans.' For a second I fantasized that Lieutenant Robin Berry was not on manoeuvres in the English Channel and that I was devouring him on a bed of monkfish medallions and drizzling chocolate sauce all over his—

'Are you all right?' Annabel said. 'You've got a peculiar look on your face.'

'I was just thinking we could go to your place tomorrow lunchtime instead,' I said quickly.

'No can do.' Annabel picked up her handbag and brushed imaginary dust off the bottom. 'I've got business in Tavistock.'

'Whatever for?' I said, puzzled. 'Tavistock isn't Gipping turf.'

'It doesn't have to be. As Pete says, there's a whole world out there. And anyway, I'm aiming for the big time,' Annabel declared. 'You did it. Twice!' She paused in the doorway. 'Oh! I take it you'll be writing the obit for Scarlett Fleming?'

'Yes, why?'

'It might be an idea to look into why Fleming picked that weird limo company. Sounds suspicious.'

'I was going to,' I said.

Annabel smirked. 'Don't worry, Fleming's all yours. I've got my hands full with this other thing.'

'If you need a sounding board—'

'I just might.' She flashed a beautiful smile and left.

I was flummoxed. What a turn-up for the books! How strange that all this time Annabel had been jealous of me. The Gastropod Gala tomorrow night was going to be fun – especially if she agreed to do my makeup again.

I studied my reflection one more time. Surely it wasn't that difficult to put kohl pencil around my eyes. After all, Neil Titley from Go-Go Gothic had done a good job of it and he was a *man*.

The assignment Wilf had given me was something I knew I'd enjoy – especially since he said, 'Take them to lunch if you have to.'

For the first time I felt like a real investigative reporter. What's more, if Douglas Fleming had hired Go-Go Gothic for sinister reasons, it would provide the perfect guise to discreetly ask some questions.

I pulled Mr Titley's business card from my safari-jacket pocket. There was a Plymouth area code and a post office box number. I didn't expect him to answer so I just left a message telling him that I was interested in his services.

Next, I needed to prepare for my meeting with Douglas Fleming. He might think that a 'short paragraph' about his wife was acceptable, but I knew otherwise. The obituary pages in the

Gipping Gazette were read with great relish by the old biddies in the town and I wasn't going to let them feel cheated.

The Flemings had been enthusiastic members of the Gipping Bards, our local amateur dramatic society. Since Barbara was heavily involved and fancied herself as the next Helen Mirren, I decided to start with her.

5

'You remember Sammy Larch's daughter, Olive, don't you?' Barbara said, pointing to a pair of thin, jean-clad legs attempting to clamber into the Gazette's front window display. Olive's slight body was completely masked by an enormous inflatable yellow snail.

There was a muffled cry of sorts. Barbara rolled her eyes in exasperation and shouted, 'Just push it in, Olive. It won't bite.'

'You can't let her do that by herself!' Olive Larch was the same age as Barbara but quite frail. 'We should help her.'

'My toe is playing up.' Barbara gestured to the counter that was covered in streamers and limp balloons. A helium tank stood on the floor. 'We'll never get this finished tonight at the rate she's going.' She lowered her voice. 'She's so slow.'

What sounded like an indignant retort was muffled by the snail's shell.

I hurried to Olive's side and helped push the ungainly object through the narrow opening. Suddenly, it shot forward with a loud bang. Olive gave a shriek and toppled after it. She lay facedown without moving. For a moment, I thought she'd knocked herself unconscious, but with a supreme effort, she rolled over onto her back and lay there panting heavily.

Are you all right?' I felt annoyed with Barbara. 'Couldn't one of the men have done this?'

'We've got to build up Olive's strength,' Barbara declared. 'This is the *new* Olive. She's got to learn to live a little. Get *wild*.'

Olive gave me a look I could only describe as a silent appeal for help. But she did *appear* different from the last time I saw her at her father's funeral. Her usual frizzy perm had been cut out. Her silvery grey hair now sported several heavy-handed black streaks. One was rakishly swept across her high forehead and secured with a butterfly barrette.

Gone were the dreary baggy skirts and shapeless tops that looked as if she'd served in the Chinese Republican Army. Today, Olive wore denim jeans, a bright red, short-sleeved shirt, and matching red pumps with bows.

I helped Olive out of the window and sat her down on one of the two ugly brown leatherette chairs that were a constant reminder that, where décor was concerned, the *Gipping Gazette* was stuck in a seventies time warp.

'Are you feeling dizzy?' I said. 'Can I get you a glass of water?'

'Just a little out of breath,' panted Olive. 'I'll be all right in a minute.'

'Do you like her new look, Vicky?' Barbara said, seemingly unconcerned about her friend's health. 'I persuaded her to spend some of that money. It's not doing any good rotting away in a bank.'

'Barbara, please don't,' Olive whimpered.

'You look lovely, Olive,' I said.

'She's got a lot of catching up to do,' said Barbara. 'And I'm going to help her.'

I'd heard that Olive was an only child and ten years old when her mother died. Her father had forced her to keep house and kept her on a tight rein. They lived in virtual squalor despite the fact that Sammy Larch was worth millions after selling acres of marshland to a property developer. Unfortunately, the identical matchbox houses sank an inch a year. The residents fondly referred to their community as Little Venice but it was commonly known as The Marshes.

'Hair. Makeup. New clothes,' Barbara went on. 'What have you done to your eyes, Vicky? Did you use eyeliner? Look at them, Olive. Aren't they just something?'

There was also something very 'Annabelish' in the way Barbara was taking charge of poor Olive. It was as if I was looking at myself forty years on. I wondered if Olive had ever had a proper boyfriend, too.

Swiftly changing the subject I said, 'Where did you find the inflatable snail?'

'It was a prop when we did the musical version of *The Magic Roundabout*,' Barbara said. 'I found it in the Gipping Bards storage unit on the industrial estate. I'm glad to see we now have CCTV cameras installed over there. We've already had one break-in this year.'

'Speaking of the Gipping Bards,' I said, 'I wanted to talk to you about Scarlett Fleming. She was a very active member, wasn't she?'

'Still is,' Barbara parked her ample rump on the arm of Olive's chair. 'Unfortunately, Scarlett always hogs the plum roles. She was far too old to play Cleopatra.'

'Actually, I've got—'

'Scarlett is a very good actress,' Olive protested. 'She and Dougie have been very kind to me ever since Daddy—' Olive's eyes filled with tears. 'They're like family.'

I wasn't quite sure how to break the news especially in light of the fact that poor Olive had only lost her father a few weeks ago. 'I'm glad you are both sitting down because I've got something very upsetting to tell you.' I paused to take Olive's hand. Squeezing it gently, I said, 'I'm afraid Scarlett Fleming has died.'

Barbara's jaw dropped. 'Scarlett Fleming is *dead*?'

Olive gasped and began to pant heavily. Her eyes widened in panic as she struggled to breathe.

'Oh, no! She's having one of her episodes!' Barbara flew to Olive's side and grabbed her hand. 'Breathe in . . . breathe out . . . breathe in – Vicky go and get some water – breathe out.'

I scurried downstairs into the basement kitchenette. By the time I'd found a clean glass and returned, Olive seemed to have suitably recovered. She held a silver hip flask in her hand. Her cheeks were flushed and her eyes bright.

'I remembered the brandy,' said Barbara, waving the glass away. 'I always keep it under the counter if ever you need a quick nip.'

'I shouldn't really,' Olive said, taking another sip. 'Daddy didn't approve of me drinking.'

'He didn't approve of most things,' said Barbara darkly. 'But you're free of him now.'

'Barbara!' cried Olive with dismay.

'Well, it's true,' said Barbara. 'You were like a virtual prisoner in that house. Time to live a little. Time to have some fun. You might even fall in love! Wait a minute . . .' Barbara paused for thought. I could almost hear her brain cells turning. With a cry of delight she said, 'What about Dougie Fleming?'

Olive turned pink. 'Oh!'

'Don't you think it's a bit soon for that?' I said hastily. 'He only buried his wife this morning.'

'We'll wait a few weeks, of course,' Barbara said, beaming. 'Life's too short to grieve.'

Olive's pink flush deepened to a dark red. 'Scarlett *did* always say if anything ever happened to her, she'd like me to take care of Dougie.'

'You never told me that.' Barbara's voice was heavy with accusation.

'I just thought she was being nice.'

It looked like Eunice might have a few rivals in her bid to win back her old flame.

'When's the funeral?' Barbara said. 'It'll be a big one, mark my words.'

'Mr Fleming buried her this morning. It was a very quiet affair.'

Olive's face crumpled. She began to cry. 'Scarlett loved peonies.'

'I don't believe it!' Barbara cried. 'You must be mistaken.'

'Mr Fleming said she'd insisted on a no-fuss funeral.'

'No fuss? Since *when*?' Barbara scoffed. 'She told the Bards she wanted an open casket and a thirteen-pan steel band.'

'And a big party with lots of champagne,' Olive chipped in.

'*And* a slide show of her life—'

'Like we're having in Daddy's honour tomorrow night at the Gala.'

It all sounded very expensive to me. 'The cost of funerals has really gone up,' I said. 'Perhaps their financial circumstances had changed and he just couldn't afford it.'

Olive pulled out a handkerchief and dabbed at her eyes. 'Do you know what happened?'

'I bet it was a car accident,' Barbara declared. 'She drove far too fast on these twisty lanes. Perhaps she met a combine harvester—'

'No!' squealed Olive, flapping her hands wildly. 'Don't tell me the details!'

'I'll find out this afternoon,' I said.

'I heard she was going on a yoga retreat,' Barbara said. 'So they can't have been that financially strapped.'

'Have either of you ladies heard of a company called Go-Go Gothic or seen an American Cadillac driving around the area?'

'Here? In Gipping?' Barbara said, adding wistfully, 'Jimmy Kitchen had a convertible. One night, we drove to the beach with the top down.'

Fortunately, the front door buzzed open, sparing us from Barbara's infamous Jimmy Kitchen the-one-who-got-away reminiscences. Olive screamed and leapt out of her chair.

'Oh!' She clamped her hand over her nose. 'What's that terrible smell?'

I knew that smell very well. Boiled cabbages.

Barbara darted back to her post behind the counter and grabbed a box of Kleenex.

'Morning ladies!' Ronnie Binns, Chief Garbologist of Gipping County Council, strolled in clutching a cheap-looking bouquet of pink carnations and a large manila envelope.

Dressed in a pair of pristine gabardine overalls and thigh-high waders, Ronnie's face and hands looked unusually clean; even his bald pate shone. But it would appear that even soap and water could not erase his customary cabbagelike aroma.

'Can I help you, Mr Binns?' Barbara said, holding a tissue over her nose.

'I've got a date with Annabel Lake,' he said shyly.

'She's not here.'

Ronnie scratched his head. 'I suppose I could wait.'

'You'll have a long one,' Barbara said. 'She's gone all day.'

'But she promised to take me to lunch.' Ronnie's shoulders slumped. Even his carnations seemed to droop. Presumably the flowers were for Annabel, which I thought rather touching.

'At ten thirty in the morning?' said Barbara.

'I've been up since four,' Ronnie sounded indignant. 'I changed my rounds for her.'

Olive started to titter nervously and Barbara certainly seemed to be enjoying Ronnie's pain.

I stepped forward. 'Perhaps you got the day wrong, Mr Binns?' It was obvious that Ronnie was smitten with Annabel, and as my mum says, *'You can't choose who you fall in love with.'* Even so, I couldn't imagine Annabel ever agreeing to a date with Ronnie.

'No. She phoned.' He pulled a scrap of paper out of his

pocket. 'See? I wrote it down. Said she had something very important to ask me.'

I took the crumpled – and grubby – note. He was right. The date and time were correct. 'Perhaps she meant your office, not this office?'

Ronnie brightened up. 'Oh, yes. More private, like.'

'You'd better hurry up in that case,' said Barbara. 'What's in that envelope? A love letter?'

Olive tittered again.

Ronnie scowled and slapped the envelope down on the counter. 'Tony said you needed headshots for the newspaper.'

'Oh! Is it Rambo?' Olive cried with delight. She scurried over, her face alight with enthusiasm. 'Let me see. What's his form?'

Ronnie pulled out an eight-by-ten photograph of a garden snail. 'We've got a good crack at the championship this season. Now that – no disrespect—' he touched his forehead at Olive, 'your father – God rest his soul – is not racing Seabiscuit.'

'Dougie is going to run Seabiscuit now,' Olive beamed.

Ronnie's face darkened. 'I thought Fleming was banned for another season for cheating.'

'It was all a misunderstanding,' Olive said quickly. 'Dougie appealed to the committee and his name was cleared.

'Excuse me,' I said. 'How can one cheat at snail racing?'

'Each snail is handicapped,' Olive said. 'Small weights are sewn into their racing silks.'

'So, he's going to succeed as Chief Marshall, after all?' Ronnie grumbled.

'It's what Daddy wanted and you know that Daddy always got his own way.' Olive made another silent appeal to me for help.

'Thank you for coming in, Mr Binns,' I said smoothly, stepping forward and snatching up the photograph. 'Can I talk to you for a minute?'

I took Ronnie's arm and propelled him toward the front door.

'I wondered if you saw an American Cadillac on your rounds this morning,' I said, trying not to inhale.

'A what?' Ronnie seemed momentarily taken off guard.

'Today is Thursday. Don't you usually do Upper Gipping on Thursdays?'

'Mondays.' Ronnie squinted down at me and readjusted his overalls. It suddenly occurred to me that Ronnie might have made the mystery phone call. With thigh-high waders that snug his voice could easily go up an octave or two. 'I might have seen something,' he went on. 'It depends.'

'It's just a question,' I said. 'There is no money involved.'

'In that case, no.'

Ushering Ronnie out of the front door I watched him – and his pink carnations – climb into an old blue Ford Escort parked a few yards down the High Street. Glancing across the road, I noted The Copper Kettle was open for business.

Of course! Topaz was bound to have heard some gossip about the Flemings. What's more, it was the first Thursday of the month and I was positive that several of the Women's Institute often popped in for a quick cuppa after their weekly knitting meeting.

Given that Scarlett Fleming had also been a member of the Women's Institute, I could almost guarantee news of her death would cause quite a stir.

6

The Copper Kettle was part of a row of Queen Anne terraced houses that flanked the High Street. It was a former charity junk shop that Topaz – whose real name was Ethel Turberville-Spat – had converted into a café on the cheap. If it hadn't been so conveniently located directly opposite the office, I doubt I would have ever have been tempted to step inside since the food left much to be desired.

I pushed open the door and stepped into the gloom. With its low-beamed ceiling, faded wallpaper and dismal prints of dead game hanging on the shabby walls, the place was always so depressing. Along the original shop counter, Topaz had arranged a selection of copper kettles that she swore were used by her aristocratic ancestors.

There was no sign of the Women's Institute members – or any other customers for that matter. Topaz was perched on a stool behind the cash register, deeply engrossed in a book. She was dressed in her usual olive-green serge medieval dress and white-lace mop cap.

'Where is everybody?' I said.

Topaz gave a yelp of joy. 'Oh! *Just* the person I want to see.'

She slithered off the stool and hurried to greet me waving her book. I noted the title, *Haunted Devon*, and my heart sank. For some time now, Topaz had been convinced Gipping-on-Plym was riddled with UFOs and paranormal happenings. For weeks she'd been begging me to ghost write – no pun intended – her research on local hauntings. Topaz harboured unrealistic expectations that this would propel us to stardom as in, 'We'll be on *Oprah*!' and 'We'll get our own reality TV show!'

Frankly, I didn't mind what she did as long as it distracted her from bugging me about becoming an official staff member of the *Gazette*. I could never find the right time to tell her that our arrangement was strictly – and secretly – between the two of us.

Topaz flipped the door sign to CLOSED and rewarded me with her usual gummy smile. 'So I can give you my undivided attention,' she added with a wink.

I'd gotten used to Topaz's flirtatious behaviour and still wasn't sure which way her sexual preferences lay, but as long as I kept her at arm's length, she usually didn't cause me too many problems.

'I'm here on business,' I said.

'Goodie. What's going down, boss?' Topaz watched too many American police dramas. 'Wait. You look different.' She stepped closer and studied my face. I shrank back. 'Your eyes look frightfully pretty. Did you do them yourself?'

'Yes,' I lied, knowing that Topaz loathed Annabel and the feeling was mutual. 'Come along, Topaz. This is work.'

'Sorry, boss.'

'I thought the Women's Institute met here on the first Thursday of the month.'

Topaz scowled. 'Apparently, they prefer The Warming Pan because it has a better menu.'

This didn't surprise me. I'd seen Topaz buying cakes from the past-sell-by-date section at Tesco Superstore. She was notoriously stingy with her portions and I'd seen her reuse tea bags until they were nothing but pale limp pads.

'But I don't care,' she went on. 'I'm working on a new menu myself. You'll never guess what it is.'

'I don't have a lot of time for a guessing game this morning,' I said, but since I'd had to skip breakfast, I was hungry and could easily devour a bun, stale or otherwise.

There was a tap on the front door. I recognized the face pressed against the window as one of my mourner regulars, Hilda Hicks, from Gipping Riding School. She gestured at the CLOSED sign.

'Ignore her.' Topaz grabbed my arm and pushed me toward the red and plastic fringe that led to the kitchen. I'd long grown used to Topaz's appalling customer service. She only opened the café when she was in the mood. It was just as well she received income from her tenants who farmed The Grange estate she'd inherited from her Aunt Clarissa. Topaz would never make a living in the catering industry.

I sat down in one of the two, tatty old Victorian armchairs, noting the kitchen was even more untidy than usual. The draining board that flanked the stone sink held clumps of earth and what looked like shells.

There was also a peculiar smell that took me back to one of the rare family holidays I'd spent in a small fishing village in Cornwall. It seemed to be coming from a large pot, bubbling on one of the gas rings in the corner.

'What are you cooking?'

'Snails!' Topaz looked hugely pleased with herself.

I was appalled. 'You can't be serious.'

'It's snail season. We should have them on the menu,' Topaz beamed. 'I've purged them. It's a frightfully complicated process, you know. Would you like to try a bowl?'

'No thanks.' Recalling how lovingly Ronnie Binns had spoken about Rambo, I said, 'I'm not sure if they'll be that popular.'

Topaz's expression was stubborn. 'Why?'

'A lot people regard their snails as pets,' I said. 'It would be like eating Slipper.' I gestured to the ancient old Labrador sleeping in the basket by the fireplace.

'Don't be silly,' Topaz said. 'It's completely different. Besides, the French eat snails.'

'French snails are specially bred for restaurants on snail farms.' I dreaded to ask where Topaz had found hers, but judging by the mounds of earth, suspected it was someone's garden.

'Did you know that in my grandfather's day, snail racing used to be a sport for the aristocracy?' Topaz said with a snooty sniff. 'The lower classes are taking over everything. No offence, Vicky, but you know they are.'

I hated Topaz pulling social rank. She made me feel like a servant. 'In that case why don't you serve jellied eels?' I said sarcastically.

'I couldn't. Aunt Clarissa would turn in her grave.' A timer went off. Topaz took the steaming pot off the gas flame and poured the liquid containing the pathetic creatures into a colander to drain over the sink. The smell was enough to make me gag. She ladled a heap of snails into a bowl and took the other chair. 'Are you sure you don't want some?'

I shook my head. Topaz pulled out a fork from a hidden pocket in her serge apron and began deftly withdrawing the slimy grey meat from each shell.

I'd completely lost my appetite. 'Aren't you supposed to slather them with garlic sauce?'

Topaz swallowed one whole and turned a shade of green. 'These aren't quite ready yet.' She leapt to her feet and darted over to the sink, spitting the contents out of her mouth with disgust. I only just managed not to laugh. She dumped the remaining snails from the draining board into a large rubbish bin muttering, 'I think I'd better start again.'

I tried to sound sincere. 'Are you all right?'

'Fine. Let's get down to business,' Topaz said, wiping her mouth on her apron. 'How can I help?'

'Make me a cup of tea and I'll tell you,' I said. 'And I'd like a fresh tea bag, please.'

'I love it when you're bossy.'

Minutes later, I sipped on a scalding cuppa and nibbled a stale cinnamon bun. 'I've got some sad news. Scarlett Fleming died unexpectedly and I'm working on her obituary. Did you know her at all?'

'I'm afraid I'm not sorry.' Topaz wrinkled her nose with distaste. 'She was a frightful snob. The ones who have no money and pretend they do are the worst. There'll be a ghastly vulgar funeral, of course.'

How interesting. Barbara had said the same thing. I would never rely on hearsay, but it certainly confirmed my hunch that something wasn't quite right. 'How do you know?'

'I overheard Scarlett telling Ruth Reeves she'd purchased some kind of funeral plan.' She gave a shudder. 'She had a list of the most ridiculous requests. One was a thirteen-pan steel *band*! Here! In Gipping!'

'I heard that, too.'

'She wanted an excerpt from *Romeo and Juliet* read over her open casket. Let me think—' Topaz clutched her hands together and said in a dramatic voice, '"Eyes! Look your last! Arms, take your last embrace!" Act five, scene three. I studied Shakespeare at St Helen and St Katherine, Abingdon. Where did you go to school?'

'Well, Mrs Fleming didn't get any of that,' I said neatly changing the subject. I always felt inadequate whenever Topaz mentioned her school days. There was no fancy independent school for me. We were always on the move.

'What are you talking about?' said Topaz.

'It's too late. Scarlett Fleming was quietly buried this morning.'

'This *morning*?' Topaz's eyes widened in surprise. 'I thought she was in Spain.'

'Spain? Why?' My stomach flipped over. I couldn't help it.

Of course, no one knew my parents were on the lam in Spain, but whenever that country was mentioned, I felt ill.

'She'd booked herself into a fancy yoga retreat,' Topaz said. 'If you ask me, I think she was going to get plastic surgery. Maybe something went wrong and she died under the knife. It happens all the time.'

I felt inexplicably disappointed. But it certainly explained why the *Gazette* wasn't notified through the usual channels. It would explain why Douglas Fleming wasn't forthcoming about how she died, either. He was obviously embarrassed. Perhaps he was trying to protect her reputation? Using a quickie burial company meant he didn't have to deal with the endless gossip at the graveside, particularly now it seemed that Scarlett Fleming wasn't as popular as I'd first thought. However, it still didn't explain why I got the mystery phone call this morning, but perhaps that no longer mattered?

'I thought Whittler had put a hold on all funerals,' Topaz said with a frown.

'Douglas Fleming hired a cut-price company called Go-Go Gothic.'

'Never heard of them. Sounds horrid and so nouveau riche – though I'm not surprised. The Flemings were always living beyond their means. They were flat broke.'

'How do you know?'

'The Fleming clan has been selling off land for decades. Aunt Clarissa told me.'

I wanted to point out that the same had been true of Topaz's ancestors and how she was always coming up with schemes to keep The Grange afloat. Even now a large poster hung on the wall of the café saying, BEAUTIFUL MANSION AND STABLES AVAILABLE FOR SHORT-TERM LET. ASK TOPAZ POTTER FOR DETAILS.

Currently the house stood empty while Topaz pretended to live in London as Ethel Turberville-Spat but actually occupied the poky flat above the café.

'Of course, the Flemings were originally in trade,' she went on scornfully. 'And before you say anything, yes, I know Uncle Hugh was in wool and textiles, but not my side of the family. The Turberville-Spats go back to the Wars of the—'

'Roses. Yes, I know, you've told me.' I was tired of hearing about Topaz's distinguished family tree. 'Didn't you want to see me about something?'

'My special project. Oh!' Topaz clapped her hands with excitement. 'You'll be writing Scarlett Fleming's obituary, won't you?'

'Yes, why?'

'That means you have to go to Headcellars, yes?'

'I'm going to Mr Fleming's office,' I said. 'Why?'

'Tell him you'll go to his house instead.' Topaz did a little bunny hop on the spot. 'Oh! Oh! Please let me come with you this time. You keep promising and—'

'Sorry, Topaz,' I lied. 'I haven't had a chance to talk to Pete about bringing you on board officially, yet.'

'I'm not interested in obituaries, silly.' Topaz retrieved a cardboard box that was sitting on top of a case of Heinz baked beans. She brought out a tattered book that bore the title, *Reformation Horrors! Tales Beyond The Grave*, and flapped it in my direction. 'Headcellars is listed in here. I've been *dying* to look inside.'

'I don't think it's a good time,' I said. 'He's just lost his wife.'

'Can't you just ask him? Pleeeease?' she said in a little girl's voice. 'It's for our special project. I've done tons of research already.' Topaz seemed so excited she was actually trembling.

'Go on,' I said with a sigh.

'Goody. Headcellars is one of the few remaining homes in Devon with an original priest hole!' Leafing through the book, she began to read aloud, 'When Henry VIII abolished the monasteries to become head of the Church of England, dozens of important Catholic families built special secret rooms to hide their priests from the bloodthirsty killings of the king's men. Rumour has it that Father Gregory sought refuge at the medieval manor house, Headcellars.'

Topaz gave a theatrical shudder and continued in a dramatic whisper, 'When the king's men raided the house they tortured and killed the family – probably gouged out eyes and stuff. But even though they never found the priest, rumour has it that Father Gregory starved to death and haunts the corridors of the house begging for food.'

'He actually *talks*?' I did not believe in ghosts. 'I wonder what he asks for? Apple pie?'

'That's what I want to find out,' Topaz said darkly. 'And you're coming, too.'

I knew better than to turn Topaz down flat and got to my feet. 'I'll think about it.'

Topaz flung her arms around me. Fortunately, I'd anticipated the move and ducked down to pat Slipper. Her kiss landed below my left ear.

'What are you going to wear to the Gala tomorrow night?' she said.

Blast! 'You're not going, are you?'

Topaz laughed. 'Of course I am, silly.'

'I didn't think it was an Ethel Turberville-Spat kind of thing.'

'You're quite right. It's not. Ethel wouldn't be seen dead at one of those frightful events,' Topaz said. 'That's why I'm going as me. Wait. Topaz, I mean.'

'Not Topaz-the-vigilante, I hope?'

'The Caped Kitten, actually,' Topaz said. 'That's my official name now.' Recently, Topaz had begun to believe she was a female Peter Parker and had started prowling the streets at night trying to 'keep law-abiding citizens safe'. I'd given up trying to understand her eccentric behaviour long ago.

'Why?' I said. 'Are you expecting trouble?'

'With it being the final year for the Larch Legacy, feelings are running high.'

'Any idea who's the favourite?'

'Rumour has it the hedge-jumpers are in with a chance. It's all so frightfully *political*.' She gave a heavy sigh. 'Shall I pick you up at six in the Capri or should we get a taxi? We'll be drinking.'

'Topaz, there is something—'

'Surprise!' Topaz pulled two tickets out of her apron pocket. 'You have no idea what I had to do to get them.'

'I'm afraid I'm already going.'

Topaz's jaw hardened. 'With whom?'

'The thing is . . .' I couldn't believe it. I was actually nervous about telling her. 'I have to go with Annabel.'

'Annabel? You're going with *Annabel*?' Topaz turned an ugly shade of red. 'How could you? What about *us*?'

'It's work,' I said hastily. 'Honestly, it is. There's nothing going on between Annabel—' I snapped my mouth shut. What on earth was I saying?

Topaz snatched the mug out of my hand and threw it into the rubbish bin on top of the dead snails.

'The kitchen is off-limits for *customers*,' she hissed. 'Please leave.'

I got up without a word. There was no point arguing when Topaz was in one of her moods. I had more important things to think about.

If Scarlett *had* died in Spain, there was no connection with Eunice Pratt or Douglas Fleming. It was just a tragic accident. If Scarlett Fleming was a victim of cosmetic surgery gone bad, her death should be handled with tact and compassion.

But for now I resolved to focus my energies on the guerrilla grave service report that Wilf had asked for.

I picked up an egg-and-cress sandwich at Tesco Superstore – I was still hungry – and returned to the *Gazette* where Barbara was showing Olive how to answer the telephone in a professional manner. Judging by the odd word I heard on passing, Olive had been recruited to help out with the reader phone-in.

Upstairs, back at my desk, I left a second message on Neil Titley's answering service, then got cracking on surfing the Internet for similar funeral outfits. I visited various websites and took copious notes on services offered – some were quite classy and, I would have assumed, far more suited to Scarlett Fleming's flamboyant personality.

I spent ages searching Go-Go Gothic on Google, as well as Neil Titley, and even the phrase, *Our passengers go all the way*, but drew a blank. I pored through the yellow pages, called directory assistance and the Funeral Planning Authority, but to no avail.

It was most puzzling. If I couldn't find Go-Go Gothic, how could Douglas Fleming, and why would he choose Titley anyway?

My suspicions deepened. I was determined to find out.

7

It was two thirty p.m. when I stopped outside Gipping-on-Plym Power Services offices in Thrift Shop Row – a full half hour before they closed. It gave me plenty of time to have a chat with Douglas Fleming and perhaps even wangle an early cuppa. The vision of one of Scarlett Fleming's delicious homemade biscuits flashed before me. Any woman was going to find it difficult to step into her shoes.

The cylindrical blue-and-white-striped, barber-style revolving pole turned cheerfully in the sunshine. I half expected the Venetian blinds in the windows to be edged in black, but it looked like it was business as usual.

Douglas Fleming said it was always quiet in the afternoons and he was right. The spotlessly clean office with its three pale blue desks and row of blue plastic chairs was devoid of customers. His plump assistant, Melanie Carew, was talking to someone on the phone. In her midforties with cropped red hair and bright red lipstick, Melanie was nibbling a carrot. I caught snatches of her conversation. 'That's illegal . . . she's a tramp . . . Viagra.'

Experience had shown I might wait for hours for Melanie to

finish her personal conversation. I marched up to her desk and flashed my press card. Gesturing toward Douglas Fleming's closed door, I said, 'He's expecting me.'

Melanie held her forefinger up – presumably, it translated to 'Wait one minute' – while she nodded and listened intensely on the phone. I didn't have all day, but it occurred to me that Melanie might have some information on Go-Go Gothic. Maybe she booked them? Better still, perhaps it was Melanie who had called me this morning?

I nodded and smiled but didn't go and sit down. Instead, I took in my surroundings.

It was hard to miss the magazines and self-help books littered on Melanie's desk: *Weight Watchers*, *A New Sexy You* and *Cooking for Love*. More pieces of chopped carrots and sticks of celery were in plastic bags next to her computer. Rumour had it that Melanie was married to a burly Welshman who worked on the oil rigs out in the North Sea but no one had seen him for years. She bore all the outward signs of the newly divorced.

Behind Melanie's desk, three CCTV monitors sat under shelves filled with blue office binders. One camera was trained on next door's building supplier, a second overlooked a row of storage units on the industrial estate, and a third gave an excellent view of the G.O.P.P.S. car park. I noted that Douglas Fleming's Audi was parked next to Melanie's Vauxhall Astra.

'Got to go, Madge,' Melanie said. 'Be brave.' She put the phone down. 'Sorry. My sister's having marital problems. None of our husbands are as wonderful as Mr Fleming.'

'Awful news about his wife, isn't it?' I said.

'Tragic,' Melanie said, not looking remotely distressed. 'He told me yesterday.'

'Only yesterday?' I said surprised. 'I was under the impression that she died a few days ago in Spain.'

'That's right. He was prostrate with grief,' she went on. 'Couldn't bring himself to tell anyone. Grief makes people act funny.'

She could say that again! 'I suppose you helped with the funeral arrangements?'

'No. Mr Fleming wanted to do everything himself,' she said. 'It'll be a grand affair, mark my words. She liked to do things in style, did Mrs Fleming.'

So, Melanie was none the wiser, either. 'I'll just pop in and see him.' I brought out my notebook. 'Just a few questions for the obituary.'

'Wait!' Melanie swivelled around in her chair and grabbed an envelope from the counter behind. 'Mr Fleming asked me to give this to you,' she said, staring at the CCTV screens.

'Thanks.' I retreated to one of the plastic chairs and opened it. There was a photograph of Scarlett Fleming wearing a crown and sash saying Miss ATLANTA 1946. Douglas Fleming had scribbled a headline, MY SCARLETT, GONE IN THE WIND. LOVED BY MANY, MISSED BY ALL.

Scanning the contents, I sensed that Douglas Fleming's one-paragraph effort must have been written when he was consumed with grief. True, he'd listed her culinary prizes, her proficiency at Tae Kwon Do, and all the starring roles she'd played for the Gipping Bards – most notably their partnering in *Antony and Cleopatra.* But overall it was bland, boring and unprintable – at least, according to my high standards. There was absolutely *no* mention of her accident or how she died.

Judging by the comments I'd already received about the lack of a decent burial service, post-service party, and blatant disregard of Scarlett's requests, if I printed this sorry offering, the *Gazette* could have a riot on its hands.

When I wrote obituaries, I liked to get a feel for the person who had just passed away. Not a dreary born-lived-died account of their lives. I liked to inject characteristics, hobbies and personality flaws – even family feuds, whenever possible. Some-times it prompted a few telephone calls from outraged readers, but for the most part, the responses were complimentary – 'You captured old Mrs Rockwell's dirty laugh' and 'You're right,

Dickie Knole should have been locked away years ago with that nasty habit.'

Returning to Melanie's desk, I noted that she was riveted to the monitors.

'Excuse me,' I said.

'Hang on!' Melanie peered closer at the screen and held up her forefinger once more. 'Wait a minute . . . Oh! I don't believe it!' She let out a snort of laughter, reached for the phone and hit speed dial. 'Madge! You'll never guess who I just saw . . .'

Melanie's fascination with CCTVs was just as I feared. Eunice Pratt was right. Big Brother had come to town, and privacy had gone out the window.

Without further ado, I slipped past Melanie and headed straight for Douglas Fleming's office, ignoring her shrieks of, 'Don't go in! He doesn't want to be disturbed.'

I knocked on Mr Fleming's door, counted to ten, and opened it.

Douglas Fleming was sitting at his desk, seemingly mesmerized by a photograph he held in his hands. In fact, as I took in my surroundings, every available surface held pictures of his dead wife. I'd only been in his office once before. Back then there had been just the one photograph of Scarlett on his desk.

Mr Fleming seemed to be converting his starkly furnished office into a shrine.

I'd had a lot of experience with grief, but his behaviour was unusual. Of course, 99 per cent of the obituaries I wrote dealt with senior deaths or farming accidents. True, there had been a couple of murders, but even those hadn't evoked the almost catatonic state I saw now in Douglas Fleming.

I felt out of my depth. For a moment, I was tempted to leave him to it, but Wilf was expecting the obituary. The newspaper needed it.

Sometimes it wasn't easy being a journalist.

I approached his desk and gave a delicate cough. 'Mr

51

Fleming?' I said softly. 'I'm sorry to bother you at this time, but I have a few questions.'

The mourning widower slowly raised his tortured eyes to meet mine. 'Didn't Melanie give you the envelope?'

'I just need a few more details. Mind if I sit?' I perched on the edge of the chair opposite him and took out my reporter notebook. 'It will only take a moment.'

Douglas Fleming gave a heavy sigh. 'Vicky, dear, I know you have a job to do, but I'd rather not.'

'The problem is' – I tried my best smile – 'the news of poor Mrs Fleming's passing is flying around the town like wildfire. Your wife had many friends anxious to know what happened.'

'I hate to say this, but it's really none of their business, is it?' he said. 'They're just gossips.'

'You wouldn't want them getting the wrong idea, would you?'

'What's that supposed to mean?' he said sharply, and sat bolt upright.

I was tempted to mention Topaz's theory that his wife had booked in for plastic surgery and died under the knife, but thought better of it. Perhaps Scarlett had been planning on surprising him? 'As you say, they're gossips and tend to spread the most malicious rumours,' I said. 'So it's important to nip those in the bud.'

'Are you implying . . . ?' A peculiar look came over Mr Fleming's face. If I hadn't known otherwise, I would have said it was fear. 'Good God, Vicky! I'd never hurt her. Never. I adored her.'

'Of course not!' I said quickly. 'Everyone knows you were devoted to each other.'

'I wasn't even with her when it happened.' His voice cracked with emotion.

'Do you think you can talk about it?'

'She was on her way to a yoga retreat in Spain.'

'A car accident?'

52

He nodded. 'Those foreign roads are treacherous. The Spanish drive like *lunatics*!'

'I'm sorry.' I reached across the desk and gently touched his arm, but he threw it off and strode over to the window.

'Scarlett left Gipping late Saturday afternoon,' he said, staring out into the distance. 'She took a flight from Plymouth to Barcelona.'

Spain! Although my parents had relocated to the coast – the Costa Brava to be exact – it wasn't that far away from the city of Barcelona. 'Where was this yoga retreat?'

'Somewhere in the Pyrenees.'

Good. Not the Costa Brava! 'Do you have the name of—?'

'Does it matter?' he said desperately. 'I got a phone call on Sunday night saying she never arrived. Her hired car had blown a tire and gone off the road into a ravine.'

'That's awful,' I said. 'She was lucky to be found at all.'

'Oh, God!' Douglas Fleming hurried over to my side and put his arm around my shoulders. 'How could I be so insensitive?'

'Excuse me?'

'Your parents! That car accident in Africa and . . .' He squeezed my shoulder. 'The lions . . .'

I squirmed in my chair, wishing with all my heart I hadn't cooked up such a gruesome demise for my poor parents, who were obviously still very much alive. 'I'd rather not talk about it.'

'So, you *must* understand why I can't, either?'

I nodded. Douglas Fleming slammed his fist onto the desk, making me jump. 'If *only* I'd gone with her, she'd be alive today! Why didn't I stop her? *Why?* I'll never forgive myself.'

He turned away from me and went back to his post by the window, thrusting his hands savagely into his jacket pockets.

'How did you learn of the accident?' I said timidly. 'Was it through the FCO?'

Douglas Fleming looked momentarily confused. 'The what?'

'The British Foreign and Commonwealth Office.'

'I don't remember. Wait. Yes. No. It was the Spanish police. Señor something or other.'

'The Spanish police?' I couldn't disguise the surprise in my voice. 'Are you sure?' This was unheard of – especially over something as routine as a car crash. I didn't mean to sound callous, but the roads in Spain *were* treacherous and fatal accidents were an everyday occurrence. Even though the Policía Nacional collaborated with our police forces and Interpol all the time, any incident involving a British citizen always went through the FCO.

I made a note on my pad – *find name of yoga retreat, airline, car hire firm and Spanish copper.*

'Why are you writing all that down?' Douglas Fleming said, jingling his keys in his jacket pocket. 'I'm not a suspect, am I?'

'Of course not. These are just routine questions,' I said. 'When did you fly to Spain?'

'I didn't fly to Spain. I – I have an alibi,' he said suddenly. 'I was with Olive Larch all Saturday afternoon and most of Sunday. We were discussing the Gastropod Gala. I have been appointed the new Chief Marshal.'

'Congratulations.'

'Thank you. I got to her house at nine in the morning and left around five. You can check if you like.'

What an extraordinary thing to say! Why would he need an alibi? If Scarlett Fleming had not been killed in Spain, I would have felt extremely suspicious.

'Any idea why you chose Go-Go Gothic?'

Douglas Fleming began pacing around his office. 'Reverend Whittler was away. I wanted it over and done with. They were the first company I called.'

'You called Go-Go Gothic?' If Neil Titley hadn't given me his business card, I'd never have found their number. 'Was it a referral?'

'Yes. No. Yes.' Douglas Fleming was beginning to get

flustered. He clutched his head as if in pain. 'I forget who told me. Actually, Vicky dear, I'm not feeling so good. I need to go and lie down.'

'I *am* sorry,' I said, getting to my feet. *Honestly, sometimes, being a reporter is a thankless task.* 'We can talk about this another time.'

'Thank you, dear. I know you are just doing your job. Scarlett always said you were a journalist with a heart.'

I followed him to the door. 'Oh, but there is just one thing . . .' I'd almost forgotten about Topaz's request. 'A friend of mine wondered if she could have a look around Headcellars?'

'What on earth for?' Mr Fleming looked startled.

'She's interested in the supernatural, and apparently Headcellars harbours a famous ghost.'

'Ghost? Utter nonsense.' Douglas Fleming added a deep Vaudeville-sounding laugh. 'Ha-ha-ha-ha.' He really *did* need to lie down. The man was close to hysterics.

'Doesn't Headcellars have secret passages and priest holes? Remnants from the Reformation?'

'I'm afraid your friend is misinformed. I've lived at Headcellars for years and I can promise you, there is no ghost.'

'I'll tell her.'

There came a cry of outrage from reception. 'I'll call the police again!' yelled Melanie.

'I only want to give him these, you silly bitch,' snapped a familiar voice. My heart sank.

I caught a flicker of alarm in Douglas Fleming's eyes. He took a deep breath and threw open the door to reveal Melanie's legging-clad bulk filling the frame. She gripped the doorjamb for dear life.

Over Melanie's shoulder I could just see Eunice's hand, waving madly. 'Dougie! Dougie!'

'No need for that, Melanie. I'll take care of this,' Mr Fleming said wearily. 'Hello, Eunice.'

Melanie stood aside and cracked her knuckles – I recalled

she often played with the Gipping Growlers when they were a man short.

'Hello, Vicky.' Eunice had changed her clothes since I'd seen her at St Peter's church this morning. Dressed in a pale lemon suit and matching pillbox hat. Eunice looked as if she was going to a garden party at Buckingham Palace. In her hands was a plate of chocolate chip cookies covered with plastic wrap. 'I baked these myself.'

'Very kind of you,' Douglas Fleming said, taking the plate. 'I'm a bit busy at the moment talking to Vicky.'

'I can wait,' Eunice said.

'He said he's busy,' Melanie snarled. 'You know you're not supposed to be here.'

'It's none of your business,' Eunice hissed. 'Anyway, with Scarlett gone, it doesn't matter.'

'You heartless tart,' said Melanie. 'Mrs Fleming isn't even cold and—'

'He's not feeling too well.' I took Eunice's arm and drew her to one side, whispering, 'Why don't you go home and I'll tell you all about it tonight.'

'You're right. Of course, he's still in shock.' Eunice nodded, then spun round to Melanie who was studying her with ill-concealed contempt. 'I can see myself out.'

Head held high, Eunice left without even a backward glance.

'Thanks for coming to my rescue,' Douglas Fleming said. 'I'm afraid I don't know what to do about Eunice. But she seems to like you. Would you mind having a word with her?'

'About what?'

'We were childhood sweethearts, you know,' he said. 'I think she's under the impression that . . .' He shook his head sadly. 'It was so long ago. People change.'

Men! How typical. I distinctly remembered his reaction only a few weeks earlier on being told that Eunice was still besotted. He'd been flattered. Now that Douglas Fleming was available and free to marry again, his fantasy of the 'one who got away' was over. Poor Eunice, she'd kept her flame burning for forty years in the hope she'd get another chance.

As I sped back to the *Gazette* on my moped, my mind was awhirl with theories.

Yes, Scarlett Fleming had died in Spain and even though Fleming had a cast-iron alibi in the timid Olive Larch, his reactions to some of my questions were just plain suspicious.

Had Fleming hired a hit man to murder his wife? The more I thought about Neil Titley and his broken nose, the more I was positive he was just the hit man type. But the question was, why kill Scarlett?

Mum always said that no matter how happy a couple seemed to be, no one knew what went on behind closed doors. But in this instance I was lucky enough to be able to call upon someone who might – my very own landlady.

I checked my watch. It was well past four. Mrs Evans was bound to be back at Factory Terrace by now. Since I wasn't expected at Dairy Cottage until six, I might as well pop home and ask her a few questions.

8

I let myself in the front door and tossed my house keys into the basket on the hall table along with Mrs Evans's lucky rabbit's-foot key ring.

Apart from a strange creaking sound coming from the ceiling above my head, the house seemed eerily quiet.

'Mrs E!' I shouted out. 'Hello?'

I walked into the kitchen. Two plates of half-eaten Victoria sponge sat on the table along with a full cup of untouched tea. A second cup contained just a splash of milk. Both chairs had been thrust back, as if someone had left in a hurry. On the floor lay a red fluffy mule. I stared at it, not sure if I should be alarmed.

Halfway up the stairs, I saw the second mule, lying on its side. Muffled voices were coming from behind Mrs Evans's closed door. My face turned hot. *Good grief!* Was my landlady having an affair?

I wouldn't blame her. Her husband Leonard was hardly the life and soul of the party. I'd lived here for a good six months and discovered he spent all his days doing something – God knows what – in the shed at the bottom of the garden. When he joined us for breakfast or dinner, he rarely uttered a word.

Good for you, Mrs E.! As my mum would say, *'Who should begrudge her a bit of love in her twilight years?'*

As I tiptoed past her bedroom door, it suddenly flew open. Mrs Evans stood there dressed in a red satin robe embroidered with dragons, fiddling with the sash. Her face was flushed – though whether from her physical exertions or acute embarrassment, it was hard to tell.

'Oh! It *is* you, Vicky.' Mrs Evans retied her robe allowing me a glimpse of pale flesh. I hastily averted my eyes. 'Lenny thought he heard your voice.'

Over her shoulder I saw a sight I hoped never to see again. Leonard Evans was standing there in nothing but a pair of bottle green socks. Our eyes met. We both looked mortified. I looked down at my feet trying to forget what I'd seen. He was a scrawny man in every sense of the word.

'Sorry.' I searched for something suitable to add, but drew a blank. Frankly, I felt a bit betrayed. Mrs Evans was always complaining about her husband. In fact, she was often downright nasty – especially when it came to their wayward daughter Sadie – yet, here she was, indulging in rampant sex on a Thursday afternoon.

Mum was right. No one *did* know what went on behind closed doors – though in this case, I had a very good idea.

'We were just about to enjoy an afternoon cuppa—' Mrs Evans stepped out onto the landing, neatly blocking my escape. 'When Lenny said—'

'"How about a bit of crumpet?"' He hooted with laughter and grabbed Mrs Evans from behind. She squealed with delight as he jiggled her spare tire that was clearly visibly through the tightened fabric.

Mrs Evans clicked her dentures. '"*Crumpet!*" said I. "You'll be lucky." Because I'd just made a Victoria sponge. So *he* said—'

'"Fancy a bit with jam!"' The two of them cracked up at some secret joke.

'Really? How funny,' I said with a forced grin. Honestly, had they no shame? What seems hilarious to the young sounds utterly perverted coming from a pensioner, although I got a quick flash of the coquettish young woman Leonard Evans married all those years ago.

'Please, don't mind me.' I gestured to their bedroom. 'Carry on.'

'No, no, we're done for now.' Mrs Evans herded me ahead of her. 'Come downstairs and have a slice of sponge. The tea will still be hot in the pot.'

'Just like my Millie,' quipped Mr Evans.

I shuddered. If I hadn't needed to talk to Mrs Evans about the state of the Fleming's marriage, I would have made my excuses and fled but truthfully, her Victoria sponge was legendary. I was also pretty certain that tonight's culinary feast at Dairy Cottage would end up in the small plastic bag I intended to take in my pocket so as not to hurt Eunice's feelings.

We sat at the kitchen table. Mrs Evans stayed in her red satin robe though, thankfully, Mr Evans donned his usual corduroy trousers and blue checked shirt. Every time she walked past him, he'd slap her firmly on the rump. She'd shriek, then pinch his cheek, cooing, 'You're a devil, you are!' It was absolutely horrible but luckily short-lived.

'I'll be off, Millie.' Mr Evans drained his cup and got to his feet. 'Have you got it?'

Mrs Evans handed her husband a large plastic bag filled with lettuce and shooed him out the back door.

'Lettuce?' I said.

'For his snails, dear.' She sat down heavily in the chair. 'He exhausts me at this time of the year, but I shouldn't complain.'

'I didn't realize he was a snail fan.'

'Not just a fan and a competitor, but this season's bookie, too!' Mrs Evans said proudly. 'Bullet's a favourite.'

'*Bullet?*' Rambo? Seabiscuit? Bullet? I tried not to giggle.

'Oh, *yes*. Lenny's pride and joy. He's in with a real chance this season. More cake?'

I nodded. It was delicious. 'Of course, he's got a few youngsters in training. They're all in that garden shed. I'm sure he'd love to show you his boys.'

The garden shed! Ever since I'd moved into chez Evans I'd puzzled over what he did in there day in, day out. Now I knew.

'Lenny isn't an easy man to be married to,' Mrs Evans chattered on. 'But for the next three months, he's almost human and of course, with Sammy Larch dead, he's in very good spirits.'

'I'd heard Sammy Larch wasn't very popular,' I said, recalling the jubilation and festive atmosphere in Albert Square on the day he was buried.

'Dreadful man. Rich as Croesus, but they lived in squalor. That poor Olive . . .' She shook her head. 'Treated her like a slave, he did. She practically froze to death last winter when we had that cold snap.'

'She does seem very frail,' I said.

'Her father didn't believe in central heating unless it was for his snails. Lenny told me there was no expense spared especially when it came to Seabiscuit.'

'I heard Mr Fleming was racing him this season.'

'*No!*' Mrs Evans sat back in her chair with her arms folded. 'Lenny is not going to be happy about that.'

'Actually, I wanted to talk to you about the Flemings.' I took a sip of tea. 'Did you know that Scarlett Fleming died?'

'Scarlett Fleming? *Dead*?' Mrs Evans jaw dropped so low her dentures almost fell out. '*No!* When?'

'Last Sunday. She had a car accident in Spain.'

'Spain? *Spain*?' Mrs Evans cried. 'How can she afford to go to Spain?'

I shrugged. 'She was going on a yoga retreat.'

'Yoga? Another of her fads that wouldn't have lasted five minutes.' Mrs Evans's eyes flashed with fury. 'Well, that's very nice isn't it? She tells me they can't afford to pay me anymore and then clears off on some fancy holiday to Spain.'

'Perhaps she'd already paid for her holiday ahead of time?' I suggested.

'I've never known anyone live so high on the hog.' Mrs Evans seethed on. 'That new Range Rover cost a bomb, and of course she wouldn't let anyone else drive it. Not even Mr Fleming.'

'When were you asked to leave?'

'Last Wednesday. I've cleaned Headcellars ever since my Sadie was five years old. Scarlett used to bake butterfly cakes just because they were Sadie's favourite,' she said, adding in a hard voice. 'It was a horrible house. Haunted, you know. And what's more, I left my best ostrich feather duster with the mahogany handle in the upstairs guest bedroom. When I went back on the Thursday morning to get it, they'd changed the locks! Imagine!'

'Really!' This came as no surprise. Mrs Evans's clients always changed the locks when she left. No doubt Douglas Fleming had caught her snooping and they'd tactfully decided to get rid of her by pretending they were economizing.

'The reverend isn't back until next Tuesday,' Mrs Evans said. 'They'll have to wait for the burial. It'll be a big flashy do, money or no money, you mark my words.'

'Actually, she was buried at St Peter's this morning,' I said. 'Douglas Fleming hired some cut-price freelance funeral service called Go-Go Gothic.'

'*No!*' Mrs Evans shook her head with disbelief. 'That'll put the cat amongst the pigeons. Those old biddies from the Women's Institute aren't going to be happy, and what about her relative from Atlanta?'

'I didn't know she had family.' Douglas Fleming certainly hadn't mentioned it. Taking out my notebook I scribbled down, *Relative. Atlanta.* 'I'm writing the obit. What was their marriage like?'

'Scarlett definitely wore the trousers,' Mrs Evans declared. 'She bossed him around, but he liked it. They seemed happy enough, though she was always complaining that they didn't have enough money – but who does in this day and age?'

'I hear they did a lot of amateur dramatics.'

'That's right. You should have seen them in *Antony and Cleopatra*,' said Mrs Evans. 'They were just like Laurence Olivier and Vivien Leigh. The death scene with the asp was very realistic. One of Barry Fir's kids loaned them his mechanical snake.'

Mrs Evans got to her feet and gave an almighty yawn. 'Well, I think I'm going to nip upstairs for a quick nap. I take it you'll be home for liver and onions tonight?'

'Sorry. I've actually got plans.'

'A date?' Mrs Evans cried. 'Is that why your eyes are all made up?'

'No. It's work.' Even if I had a date I'd never tell her, though it was gratifying to know that Annabel's makeup skills had been noticed.

Upstairs in my bedroom, I changed into a clean pair of jeans and long-sleeved sweatshirt. Mrs Evans's insights on the Fleming marriage had only thrown up more questions.

It was highly likely that Scarlett Fleming had a hefty life insurance policy that Douglas Fleming now stood to inherit. Wasn't murdering for money one of the oldest motives in the book?

I left a *third* message on Neil Titley's answering machine, but this time, I mentioned I wanted to write a day-in-the-life of a limo driver for the newspaper, which sounded innocent enough – and true. Wilf wanted the lowdown on these blokes and he was going to get it.

Thoughts of Titley brought me back to Eunice's coincidental arrival at St Peter's and the evening ahead.

If Eunice had made that phone call, why would she ask me to go to the church?

As I headed for Dairy Cottage, I resolved to get the truth out of her – one way or another.

9

Eunice was not coping very well in the kitchen.

Dressed in a floral apron, splattered with what looked like most of the tomato coulis, her face was bright red. Beads of sweat trickled down her forehead. The room was stiflingly hot and there was the most ghastly smell of overcooked fish.

'I've brought you a box of Black Magic chocolates,' I said, giving her my best smile.

'Don't give them to me now!' Eunice shrieked, brandishing a spatula. 'Can't you see I'm cooking? Mary! Mary! Come here, *quickly*! Our guest has arrived!'

Smoke started to billow from the Aga. Eunice gave a cry of dismay as it rapidly filled the kitchen.

'I'll open a window,' I said, flinging the nearest one wide. As the air slowly began to clear, the sepulchral form of Eunice's sister-in-law, Mary Berry, clutching a wrench, drifted toward me. I noted she had a smudge of grease on her forehead and wore a housecoat over a calf-length, black evening dress.

'It's dreadful in here,' she said grimly. 'If we don't die of suffocation, we'll die of food poisoning.'

Mrs Berry peered at the chocolates, muttered, 'Eunice hates

Black Magic,' and slunk back to the pine kitchen table, which I now saw was strewn with several pieces of farm machinery.

I stood in the midst of chaos. Dirty pots and pans were scattered haphazardly over every available countertop. Five live chickens huddled under a small desk along with stacks of old newspapers. Laundry was piled in a heap in the corner next to a rusty, dilapidated washing machine. I changed my mind about taking off my safari jacket and just undid the buttons. There was nowhere to hang it.

In the end, I left the chocolates balanced on top of a row of empty milk bottles on the window ledge. 'Can I do anything to help, Eunice?'

'Take in the starters. Oh!' My hostess flipped my safari jacket open with her spatula and scowled at my jeans and top. 'I said formal attire.' Peeping from the hem of her floral apron, I saw a shimmering electric blue skirt.

'I came straight from the office,' I lied, stepping neatly away from the spatula. I didn't want to get food on my favourite – and only – jacket. 'It was a busy day.'

'It's too late to change now. Mary!' barked Eunice. 'Leave that wretched tractor alone!' She gestured for me to come closer and said in a low voice, 'We'll talk later, but what did Dougie say about me?'

'Well, he's obviously still in a state of shock,' I said. 'I think—'

'Sssh! Not *now! Later.*' Eunice hissed as her sister-in-law trudged toward us hefting an old car battery. 'Mary always goes to bed early.'

'I'll take that,' I said, bounding toward Mary.

'She can manage.' Eunice pointed her spatula at a wall of outdoor coats. 'Go through that door into the hall. The dining room is the first room on the right.'

'Where are the starters?' I said, stifling the urge to snatch the spatula out of Eunice's hand and beat her about the head.

'Mary will open the hatch.' Eunice waved her spatula – *again*

– at a side table weighed down by stacks of mouldy-looking pamphlets emblazoned BAN CCTV! NO PRIVACY! Above them was a sliding frosted-glass window, underneath stood a mound of moth-eaten blankets and a half-chewed dog bone.

'Where's Jenny tonight?' I tried to sound casual but my stomach churned with fear.

'In the barn,' said Eunice.

Thank God! I'd have to get over my inherent terror of dogs, if Robin and I were to ever have a future.

Having dumped the car battery on the floor where anyone could trip over it, Mary Berry grasped the door handle and, after much heaving and groaning, the hatch shuddered open to reveal a gloomy room beyond.

'Pop around, Vicky dear,' Mary Berry said. 'This is such a waste of time.'

I slipped out of the kitchen and into the hallway. To my delight, the interior walls still retained their original oak-panelled wainscoting. These days most of the Devon long-houses had been ruthlessly modernized. Dividing walls were knocked down to let in more light and inglenook fireplaces were bricked up to stop drafts and keep in heat.

It would appear that Dairy Cottage had retained all of its seventeenth-century features including beautiful flagstone flooring that shone like glass from hundreds of years of wear. It made me want to stop for a second to consider my own mortality.

But there was no time for that tonight. I pushed open the door to a dingy dining room. The ceiling was so low I could reach up and touch the beams without standing on tiptoe. At the far end stood a vast inglenook but no fire burned merrily in the grate. Even though it was May, the place was freezing. It probably faced north. The smell of mildew and dust was overpowering. I suspected it must have been years since this room had last been used.

I went straight to the diamond-paned, leaded-light casement

windows and forced one open. Unfortunately, the stench of manure from the cowshed outside was even worse. I tried to close the window again, but it jammed. The evening was rapidly turning into a disaster and we hadn't even sat down to eat what promised to be a somewhat challenging meal.

I took in my surroundings. Imprints on the faded red-patterned carpet showed that at one time there must have been far more furniture here than just the heavy oak sideboard, refectory table, and high-backed chairs. The yellowing walls had lighter rectangular patches where paintings had probably once hung. Presumably, they'd been sold.

I felt sad. I knew that ever since Mary Berry's farming husband had been fatally electrocuted while trimming a roadside hedge, the two women had been struggling to make ends meet. I'd even persuaded Topaz – Dairy Cottage was on Grange land – to allow the ladies to live there rent free, but even so, it can't have been easy for them. This lavish dinner must have cost Eunice a lot of money. I resolved to pretend to love every mouthful.

The refectory table had been laid with what I guessed was their best china – a complete set of matching plates and tureens carrying the Asiatic pheasant pattern – and polished sterling-silver cutlery. There were three chairs on either side with an elbow chair at each end.

Instinctively, I was drawn to a beautiful silver centrepiece of a male and female mallard swimming in a lake of solid silver. Out of habit, I picked it up, carried it to the window where the light was better, and turned it over. I could just make out the four distinguishing marks – Britannia and the lion's head were fairly standard – though I couldn't read the exact date mark or maker. This piece was definitely valuable and was most probably a family heirloom that had been passed down from generation to generation. I felt a quiver of excitement. Hadn't something similar to this sold at Sotheby's last year for thousands and thousands of pounds?

Dad would be thrilled to hear about this treasure, but I could never tell him. Although I shared his passionate love of silver, I had no desire to join the family business and couldn't even begin to imagine stealing this from my poverty-stricken hosts.

All thoughts of the silver mallards vanished when I realized the table was set for four. I knew some widows still laid a place for their deceased loved ones. I hoped I didn't have to conduct an imaginary conversation with Gordon Berry as in 'He'll always be with us in spirit.'

'What are you waiting for?' shouted Eunice. Her ferrety face peered through the hatch, then disappeared from sight.

I hurried over. 'Coming!'

'Mary! Hand her the herrings!'

Mary Berry passed me two plates of gelatinous-looking roll-mop herrings. Each one was garnished with a tiny sprig of what looked like chickweed. 'No one can eat this muck,' she muttered. I had a sinking feeling she might be right.

I set the plates down on place mats depicting various hunting scenes and returned for the other two. 'Who is our fourth guest, Mrs Berry?'

'Call me Mary,' she said. 'Eunice bullied Robin into coming. She wanted a man's opinion on her cooking.'

Robin was here! I swear I nearly dropped the china. My hands literally began to tremble. I should have dressed for dinner but at least I was wearing eye makeup.

The evening had suddenly improved, especially now that I was officially on first-name terms with my prospective mother-in-law!

'I thought he was at sea?'

'Robin never tells me anything.'

'Do we have any nice candles?' I said brightly. 'It would make the table look so romantic.'

'Doubt it,' said Mary. 'You could try looking in the side-board. We might have a couple of stumps we keep for power cuts.'

I found three, tucked behind several dusty bottles of homemade sloe gin. The candlesticks were tarnished but they'd have to do. I even found some Swan Vesta matches – though most had been used and put back into the box.

I'd been fantasizing about enjoying a candlelight dinner with my handsome lieutenant in full naval regalia for weeks. True, tonight we'd be joined by his mother and aunt, but it was a start and far better than trying to talk in a bar filled with noisy punters.

I needed to check my reflection and wash my hands. I went back to the hatch and was about to ask where the downstairs loo was when I was struck dumb.

Robin had entered the kitchen.

'Ahoy there matey!' Robin scooped up his mother and gave her a big kiss on the cheek. 'Hmm. Lovely smell of old lightbulbs. What's cooking?'

'Dead fish,' said Mary dryly.

Not wanting to miss a single minute, I trotted back to the kitchen and stood in the doorway just staring at the most handsome man I had ever met.

'Why aren't you in dress uniform?' Eunice scolded, still clutching that wretched spatula. I had to admit that Robin didn't look as attractive in plain denim jeans and a red-checked shirt. Out of uniform, I noted he had a very small bottom and short, rather thin legs.

'I hope you're not going to dine in that dirty apron, Auntie,' he teased. 'Oh, wait! What's that you're wearing underneath? Is that one of my favourite dresses?'

Eunice gave a twirl.

Mary saw me watching and rolled her eyes. 'Aren't you going to say hello to our guest, Robin?'

Robin turned around, rewarding me with a brilliant smile and a nautical salute. 'Oh! It's Vicky! You look pretty tonight – but not as beautiful as you, Auntie.'

'I thought you were still in the English Channel on manoeuvres,' I said, recalling our last disjointed conversation transmitted from HMS *Dauntless*. Fortunately, he managed to cancel our date before I reached the Three Tuns. There's nothing worse than being stood up in a bar packed with farmers, which was what happened the other time we'd tried to make plans.

'Manoeuvres?' Eunice declared. 'You told me you were doing shore-based drills this month. I wrote it down on the calendar.'

'Change of plan, Auntie. You know how it is,' Robin said smoothly. 'What's everyone drinking?'

'I thought you'd never ask,' Mary said. 'I'll have a large one.'

'Don't give her a double,' said Eunice. 'You know she can't take it.'

'Auntie? Dry martini?' Robin said. 'Do we have any olives, Mum?'

'No olives.'

At the mention of the word, I felt uncomfortable. Should I mention Olive's interest in Douglas Fleming? Sooner or later the subject was bound to come up. I resolved to do it later. Eunice was bound to be more affable after a drink.

'If there are no olives, I can hardly have a martini, can I?' Eunice snapped.

'In that case, gin and tonics all round,' said Robin cheerfully.

'A weak one for me,' I said. 'I'm driving.' I hated gin. It depressed me.

Robin disappeared into the walk-in larder and emerged with an enormous bottle of Gordon's gin and Tesco tonic water.

'Ice? Lemon?' he said.

'No ice. No lemons,' said Mary.

'Never mind.' Robin searched for a space to put down the bottles. 'Mum, mind if we shift some of this stuff?'

'I'll help,' I said. Between us, Robin and I managed to move the tractor drive shaft under the table. Our fingers touched, twice.

Eunice produced four grubby glass tumblers and darted back to the Aga as a loud hissing sound signalled that something had boiled over.

Robin deftly mixed the drinks. I took a sip and practically keeled over. It was pure gin. 'Is there a splash more tonic?'

'I can't taste anything.' Mary picked up the gin bottle and added a generous slug.

Robin sashayed over to Eunice who was just in the process of removing the tinfoil from a fish kettle. The smell was beyond nauseating. He handed her a tumbler and they clinked glasses. 'What's on the menu, Martha Stewart?'

Eunice laughed with delight. 'Monkfish medallions with tomato lemon coulis followed by snow eggs with pistachio custard and chocolate drizzle.'

'Good Lord! We are in for a treat!'

'Or a visit to emergency.' Mary took a large draft of gin and gave a happy shudder as it went down.

'What's the occasion?' said Robin. 'Whose birthday?'

'It's a practice run isn't it, Eunice?' Mary said. 'Douglas—'

'Shut up!' said Eunice.

Robin frowned. 'Auntie? You're not up to your old tricks again, are you?'

'She most certainly is.' Mary took another sip. 'Not even a restraining order can stop your aunt, now that old Scarlett Fleming is dead.'

Restraining order? I recalled Melanie's comment earlier during the day. Hadn't she said, 'I'll call the police, again?'

Robin looked genuinely concerned. I caught him shooting his mother a look of alarm but Mary just shrugged and knocked back her drink.

'Well, if it's a practice run,' he said, rubbing his hands with forced glee, 'we'd better get started!'

The food was worse than I feared, probably because the entire dining room smelled of cow manure, but the others didn't seem to notice. Robin kept up a cheerful banter, praising his aunt's nonexistent culinary skills.

The roll-mop herrings felt and tasted of rubber. The monkfish medallions were more of a blob than the flat, perfectly rounded

72

shape illustrated in the cookbook that Eunice had proudly shown me earlier.

As the evening wore on, Eunice became more subdued and Mary kept leaving the room with her glass in hand, on the pretext of having a weak bladder – obviously, topping up her gin.

Robin and I tried to cheer Eunice up. He told dreadful jokes but she didn't laugh. I even committed a professional no-no by giving her the heads-up about this week's article on the pros and cons of her current favourite subject, CCTV cameras, but to no avail. Yet, without intending to be unkind, Eunice's misery was my joy. I really felt Robin and I were bonding in our effort to boost her spirits.

When we were finally confronted with dessert, I wasn't sure if I could brave a single teaspoon. The snow eggs had curdled and the pistachio custard with chocolate drizzle looked like something the cat had thrown up.

'Well . . .' Mary said, finally, as she pushed her untouched plate aside. 'You're not going to win hearts with your cooking.'

'I imagine it was a complicated recipe,' I protested, trying to retrieve my spoon that was, quite literally, stuck in the pistachio custard. 'It's all delicious. Thank you.'

'You'll just have to practise some more, Auntie,' Robin said, giving Eunice a playful nudge.

'That's it!' Eunice flung her spoon and fork down with a clatter. She leapt to her feet and fled from the room.

'Auntie! It was a joke!' Robin put his napkin down, adding, 'I'd better go and see if she's all right.'

'I'll just nip to the loo.' Mary stood up unsteadily and weaved after them. I was left all alone and in a bit of a dilemma. It was only seven forty-five. Was the evening over? What about the conversation I needed to have with Eunice about Douglas Fleming? And, what about my Robin? Was he going to be stuck to her side *all* evening? At one point – after he had told a hilarious knock-knock joke – I'd fantasized about Eunice saying, 'Run along you two lovebirds,' and how Robin would take my hand. We'd go for a moonlit walk through the muddy farmyard and enjoy a goodnight kiss. He'd look deep into my eyes and say, 'My mother and aunt adore you, and so do I.'

I decided to wait. Perhaps he'd gone to tuck her up in bed? I suddenly felt incredibly maudlin. It must be the gin. Mum called it a 'mother's ruin' and never touched the stuff. I should have followed her example.

I waited until the candle stumps had all burnt out and the room was in complete darkness. I thought everyone had forgotten I existed until I heard voices coming from the kitchen and went to investigate.

Despite the summer evening, Eunice was dressed to go out in a heavy blue wool coat and headscarf.

'I'm taking Auntie up to the Three Tuns for a plate of scampi,' said Robin. 'You don't mind keeping Mum company do you, Vicky?'

'You go with them. Don't mind me.' Mary scowled. 'I'm sure I'll have time to clear the plates, wash up, and clean the kitchen before I have to get up at four to milk the cows tomorrow morning.'

I hesitated, torn between an evening with Robin trying to make his aunt laugh or getting into his mother's good books. Judging by the near-empty gin bottle that Mary clutched to her chest, I chose the latter. I was curious about this so-called restraining order.

'Of course I'll stay with Mary,' I said. 'I wouldn't dream of leaving her with all the washing up.'

As Robin ushered Eunice out the back door, he whispered in my ear, 'I'll make it up to you at the Gala. Save me a dance.'

What incredible luck! As I turned to face the messiest kitchen in Christendom, I reflected that the evening had worked out, after all.

Was it really any of my business to speculate or gossip about Douglas Fleming's future? Perhaps I might tell Mary that Douglas Fleming had other admirers. Surely, it was far kinder for Eunice to hear this kind of news from a family member.

But that aside, I really wanted to talk to Mary about Robin. There was so much I didn't know about him. I was sure that she'd soon realize I would make the perfect daughter-in-law.

10

'No, I do not want to talk about Robin,' Mary said firmly, opening a bottle of sloe gin labeled 2003. 'I hear it from Eunice day in, day out.'

'He's devoted to her, isn't he?' I began to restack the draining board and put the dirty plates in some kind of order before tackling the washing up. 'Shall I wash and you dry?'

'Oh, just leave the dishes. Let Eunice do them tomorrow. It's her mess.' Mary sat down heavily at the kitchen table and poured two glasses. 'Eunice thought she'd hidden this.' Mary took a sip and pulled a face as if she'd just sucked a lemon. 'Try it.' She handed me a glass.

'No thanks. I'm driving.' I knew all about the local sloe gin. It was even more lethal than scrumpy, the famed Devon cider. I'd helped Barbara make some gin one day last winter at work. She brought in a plastic shopping bag full of the hard, black, oval-shaped berries, picked from hawthorn hedges down at Penny moor Jump. It took hours to prick each berry with a needle. The prepared berries were put into empty screw-top bottles, covered with sugar, and, filled to the brim with neat gin. The bottles were left to steep for as many months as possible.

'Go on. It's my birthday,' Mary said.

'All right.' We clinked glasses. After the initial burning sensation, it was surprisingly good. 'Is it really your birthday?'

'No.' Three enormous sloe gins later, the real Mary Berry began to emerge. Out of the shadow of her overbearing sister-in-law, Mary was an extremely intelligent woman. She was remarkably informed on subsidized farming in the European Union and the price of wheat in Kansas. She'd taken evening classes in automotive engineering and was restoring an ancient Garrett steam traction engine that she planned on exhibiting at Gipping Church Fête in her husband's memory. 'I've called it The Gordon.' She went on to say that she missed him very much but one just got on with it and she wished Eunice would, too. 'And now with that wretched Douglas business,' Mary said, 'I can see she's headed for another nervous breakdown, if he doesn't marry her.'

'Surely, she can't really believe they have a future. It was so long ago.'

Mary poured herself another glass of sloe gin. 'Ever since you told her that he still had feelings—'

'I didn't actually say that.' The problem was, I couldn't quite remember my exact words. The sick feeling in my stomach came back again.

'You didn't have to. Give her an inch and she'll take a mile,' Mary said.

'Surely, she wouldn't do anything stupid.' *Like murder, perhaps?*

'Eunice was devastated when he married that Scarlett. Took an overdose of sleeping pills.'

'God. That's awful.'

'Oh, yes. She had to have her stomach pumped out. Right *here*!' Mary slammed her hand down hard on the kitchen table. 'Dr Jolly did it with a rubber tube from the lambing shed.'

'Isn't Dr Jolly a podiatrist?' I said fighting back the image of

Eunice being laid out like a fish on a slab being poked at with Jab-it-Jolly's clumsy fingers.

'That was before Dr Frost's time, of course,' Mary said. 'She tried again after marrying that idiot Pratt on the rebound when he left her.'

'What happened?'

'She kept calling him Dougie and his name was George.'

Mary turned the empty sloe gin bottle upside down and gave a sigh of disappointment. 'Eunice is always threatening to kill herself. Every time one of her petitions is rejected she has one of her tantrums. I never take any notice but Robin gets upset.'

'How could she do that to poor Robin?' I said, appalled.

'She doesn't care. He found her once, lying facedown in the bath. Another time she threatened to jump from the top of the old water tower in Trewallyn Woods. I wished she had.'

'Has she ever seen a doctor?'

'She doesn't like taking her medication but there are other ways to handle her,' Mary said darkly.

'You mentioned a restraining order.'

'I told Eunice to leave Douglas alone, but she wouldn't listen. She said he kept phoning her and inviting her over, but when she got there, he denied it and then Scarlett would call the police.'

'Do you think she imagined it?'

'What do *you* think?'

It sounded like Eunice was not only mentally unstable, but delusional, too. I felt terrible. *My God!* Could Eunice's current state of mind be all my fault?

I had to ask. 'Has Eunice ever been to Spain or does she know any Spaniards?'

Mary looked puzzled. 'She's never left Devon. Doesn't even have a passport. Why?'

'I just wanted to rule her out,' I said. 'It's not common knowledge yet, but Scarlett Fleming died in Spain.'

Mary's eyes widened. She actually smiled. 'You think Eunice might have *killed* her?' She added hopefully, 'How many years would she get? Life, perhaps?'

'But you said she didn't leave Devon,' I quickly pointed out. 'Did you know I saw her at the church this morning? How could she have known that Scarlett had died?'

'Because I told her.'

'*You?*' I was flabbergasted.

'Oh, yes.' Mary nodded. 'I saw one of those big fancy American cars from gangster films. It looked like a hearse.'

'When? Where?' *Idiot Vicky!* Why hadn't I thought to question Mary about Go-Go Gothic?

'At Headcellars,' Mary said calmly. 'Our lower meadow runs along the Fleming's drive. I always put the cows out there after milking.'

I took my pencil and notebook out of my safari jacket and flipped it open. My heart was pounding. 'What time was this?'

Mary paused and closed her eyes. When she didn't speak for at least a minute, I feared all that sloe gin had sent her off to sleep. Suddenly, her eyes snapped open. 'It was just before six.'

'That's early,' I said. 'Are you absolutely positive?'

Mary closed her eyes again. A deep frown creased her forehead. 'An undertaker dressed in a Victorian frock coat helped Douglas load the coffin into the hearse.'

'The coffin was *in* the house?' I scribbled down *Body back from Spain?* Perhaps Go-Go Gothic provided that service, too?

Mary's eyes snapped open again. 'And then Douglas waved.'

'He *waved*? To whom?'

'Me.'

'Why?'

'I often saw Scarlett that early in the morning. She liked to practise her yoga on the front lawn.'

The revelation hit me hard. What if Scarlett Fleming had never even got to Spain?

What if her husband killed her, right there, in her home?

Wasn't it true that most victims were killed by people they knew? Yet, why would Douglas Fleming wave?

There were two possible explanations. One, it implied he was guilt free and just being friendly. Or, knowing Mary passed by every morning, he hoped she'd tell Eunice. It could have been some kind of prearranged secret signal like 'the dastardly deed is done.'

But, wait! 'How did *you* know that Scarlett had died, Mary?'

'I didn't. I just told Eunice I saw a coffin.'

I knocked back the rest of my sloe gin. It certainly helped to clear my head. 'Was it you who called me this morning?'

'You? Why would I?' Mary gave an enormous yawn. 'I think I need to close my eyes for a moment. Sorry dear. I'll just put my head down on the table.'

Within seconds she was fast asleep, snoring gently.

As I left Dairy Cottage, my head was spinning. Robin would be devastated if Eunice turned out to be involved in Scarlett's murder.

I felt sorry for them all and made a vow to be the kind of fiancée who truly cared for Robin's family, warts and all. If Robin could love his mad aunt, then so could I. Perhaps I should offer to keep an eye on her when he was away at sea?

I imagined drifting up to the farm carrying a wicker basket filled with warm crusty bread, cheese and pickles. In my fantasy, Mary was already dead and Eunice would be bedridden, living in the dining room downstairs and close to death herself.

I'd sit with her awhile, reading poetry aloud because she'd recently gone blind.

Or perhaps, read one of the many letters Robin wrote to me daily from HMS *Dauntless*. Naturally, I'd emphasize the parts where he praised my goodness and said how deliriously happy he was that we were to be married. In her final days, Eunice would give me a personal gift – the remaining family silver heirlooms. She'd have a huge stash upstairs. I'd hand them over to Dad, who would then forgive me for not following in his footsteps. Dad would cheerfully throw Robin and me a lavish wedding in an Italian castle, and we'd live happily ever after.

Satisfied with that little picture, I decided I would tell Robin that from now on, his aunt would be in my capable hands and that he no longer needed to bear the burden alone.

Tomorrow night's Gala loomed before me. With Douglas Fleming escorting Olive Larch, Topaz could be right that feelings were going to be running *very* high indeed.

I also realized I had nothing suitable to wear and checked my watch. It was just after nine-fifteen – not too late to take Annabel up on her offer of loaning me an outfit.

I had never been to the house she shared with Dr Frost in Blundells Court, Middle Gipping. Annabel had been living with him for as long as I'd been lodging with Mrs Evans. For a moment, I hesitated, as the memory of my landlady cavorting with her naked husband filled my mind in a kaleidoscope of ghastly graphic images. What if I caught Dr Frost and Annabel having sex?

I decided against calling Annabel ahead of time. She just might say no, and I really needed to borrow a dress.

Turning into the narrow lane leading to Blundells Court, I whipped off a quick prayer to Our Lord and Saviour that Annabel would be home and, most important, fully clothed.

11

Located behind Blundells Manor – one of the oldest Elizabethan houses in Gipping-on-Plym and now a school – stood three identical, neat, redbrick houses with window boxes filled with red geraniums.

Annabel's silver BMW and Dr Frost's silver Saab 9.3 were parked on the driveway outside number one. Downstairs, the curtains were open and the lights were on. I could see a figure moving about.

Encouraged, I parked my moped, removed my helmet and goggles, put them in the pannier, and knocked on the front door.

'Vicky! Is everything all right?' Tall, silver-haired Dr Frost stood in the doorway dressed in a pair of navy checked pyjama bottoms and a grey GIPPING GROWLERS sweatshirt. Wearing thick-rimmed glasses – he obviously wore contact lenses for work – and minus his white coat and stethoscope, the man had zero sex appeal. In fact, he looked positively nerdy.

'I tried to call Annabel's mobile,' I lied. 'I'm sorry. I should have phoned the house.'

Dr Frost produced his white coat from behind the door and pulled it on. 'Is anyone hurt?'

'Oh, no,' I said. 'Nothing like that.'

He heaved a heavy sigh of relief. 'With Whittler gone and this flu bug going around, the morgue is full. I fear you're going to be very busy when he returns from America.'

'Perhaps that's why some people are considering do-it-yourself burial services.' I hadn't thought of asking Dr Frost's opinion and whipped out my notebook.

Dr Frost frowned. 'I'm not sure I follow.'

'Some people are hiring freelancers to avoid the backlog.'

'But that's terrible! Are you sure?' Dr Frost shook his head with dismay. 'I'm a Devon man and tradition is tradition. For many of the old folks, the country funeral and reception is the highlight of their week.'

'Mind if I quote you on that?' I asked, pencil poised. 'I'm writing a report on these new cut-price funeral outfits and the impact they may have on the local community.'

'Please do. Surely, we've not had one in Gipping?'

'Have you heard of Go-Go Gothic?'

'No. I have not.' Dr Frost's voice was heavy with disapproval. 'This is most worrying. There are a lot of legal formalities, you know. You can't just go and pick a plot and start digging.'

'That's what I'm looking into.' I scribbled *legal formalities* on my pad. 'Didn't Annabel tell you about Douglas Fleming's wife?'

'We make it a rule not to discuss work at home,' he said. 'What's wrong with Scarlett?'

'She had a fatal car accident.'

'Good Lord. When?' Dr Frost ran his long fingers through his silver hair. 'Why wasn't I informed?'

'It happened in Spain last Sunday,' I said. 'She was buried in Gipping this morning.'

'Buried this *morning*!' he cried. 'But that's not possible.'

'Are you saying she couldn't have died in Spain?' I said sharply.

'No. She was very excited about some yoga retreat,' he said. 'Scarlett came for a checkup last Friday. She was having problems with the downward dog position . . .' He fell silent at the memory.

'Why wasn't it possible?'

'Scarlett was an avid churchgoer,' said Dr Frost. 'We sang in the choir together.' I duly scribbled this down, glad to add little touches of colour to Scarlett Fleming's obituary.

'Scarlett had something called a pre-need funeral package,' Dr Frost went on. 'She was very clear about what she wanted when she died.'

'The open casket? The thirteen-pan steel band?' I ventured. 'Did she tell you about it?'

'I signed the paperwork with Dougie,' said Dr Frost. 'Ripley and Ravish have a copy in their files.'

I made a note of that, too. 'It sounds expensive.'

'Cherry oak caskets lined in red silk *are* expensive,' the doctor went on. 'But I believe payment plans are available.'

So why did Fleming go against his wife's wishes!

Dr Frost dramatically cleared his throat and said loudly, 'Are you here to see Annabel?'

I spun round to see a masculine-looking woman in her late sixties, trying to keep up with her pale brown boxer who was straining at the leash.

'Good evening, Ms Willows,' Dr Frost called out. 'How's that knee?'

Ms Willows just scowled and hurried past.

'You'd better come inside.'

I stepped into a meticulously tidy hall. A cream-painted table with a hollowed-out skull – used from what I could see for keeping keys – stood in the hallway. Framed abstract prints hung on walls painted a safe shade of magnolia. The carpet was a beige Berber twist and spotlessly clean. An empty wastepaper basket stood on the floor next to a pair of gold sandals.

This was nothing like Annabel's last home at Beaver Lock

Lodge, which had been filled with girly knick-knacks, scraps of lace and fluffy cushions.

'Annabel's upstairs.' Dr Frost bent down and picked up the sandals. 'Please ask her to put these back in her cupboard.' I took them, surprised that her feet were so large. Poor Annabel! She had to take at least a size ten.

'Third door on the right,' the doctor went on. 'You can't miss it.'

The third door on the right was, indeed, hard to miss. It was covered in angel stickers and the word *Annabel* was stencilled on the outside in fancy twirls. How odd! Did this mean they kept separate bedrooms?

Tapping lightly on the door, I opened it and stopped dead. Annabel sat on the floor with her back toward me surrounded by cardboard boxes filled with designer handbags, still in their protective plastic bags.

I couldn't believe it! I'd caught her red-handed!

My new best friend was a thief!

12

Mesmerized, I watched from the doorway as Annabel stuffed pink tissue paper into a Chanel handbag to plump it up. She was crooning, 'You're a beauty,' and 'Yes, yes, lovely,' as if the purse were a living object.

On the floor beside her was a large notepad. She picked up a pencil with a pink fluffy pom-pom stuck on the end, and made a tick against a list.

Were these handbags fakes or the real deal? They looked very similar to the stolen merchandise my dad's friend, Chuffy McSnatch, distributed from his hideaway in London.

The criminal world was a small one. Even the remotest possibility that Annabel and Chuffy knew each other filled me with such terror, I began to feel physically ill.

With a supreme effort, I composed myself and knocked on a wooden bookcase covered with a lace mantle. 'Anyone home?'

Annabel spun around. Her face was deathly pale.

'Just brought these up,' I said, waving the sandals by way of a greeting.

She looked awful. Dressed in black leggings and a plain white T-shirt, Annabel's auburn hair was scraped back in a high ponytail. She wore wire-rimmed glasses and, without makeup, it looked as if she had no eyebrows at all.

'Out! Out!' Annabel screamed. She leapt to her feet, snatched the sandals from my hands, and bundled me out of the bedroom.

'I came to borrow a dress,' I protested. 'You said I—'

'I know, I know,' said Annabel. 'Just wait here.' The door slammed in my face, hard.

Did she seriously think she'd hide all those boxes and pretend I didn't know what she was up to? I calculated there had to be a street value of hundreds of pounds – if they were fakes – and possibly thousands, if they were real.

I waited outside on the landing thoroughly unsettled. Did Dr Frost know about Annabel's business on the side? Given that he had no qualms in distributing a fake aphrodisiac to the vulnerable senior citizens of Gipping-on-Plym, the two of them seemed well suited.

I put my ear to the door, expecting to hear furniture being moved around or even the sound of a hammer banging nails into the floorboards in an attempt to seal a secret compartment. But, all was silent. What on earth could she be doing?

I took in my surroundings. The door next to Annabel's room was ajar. Quickly, I slipped inside. The curtains weren't yet drawn and, thanks to the streetlight outside, I could see a double bed flanked by matching lamps and nightstands. One held books, the other magazines. Dad always said you could tell a lot about a person by what they read.

I hurried over to inspect them. One nightstand held *You Are What You Eat*, by Dr Gillian McKeith, and *The Abolition Of Britain: From Winston Churchill to Princess Diana,* by Peter Hitchens. I'd heard of the latter bemoaning the end of the British Empire and all our traditions from education to immigration. I'd seen a copy on Wilf's desk, and even my dad – who was more of a John Grisham type and rarely read nonfiction – had urged me to take a look, saying, *'It's official. England has gone to the dogs.'*

'What are you doing in here?' Annabel was watching from the doorway. She flipped on the light.

'I was looking for the loo,' I said quickly.

'It's at the end of the hall,' she said. 'Isn't this room boring? The decor is so yucky.'

I was about to tactfully agree but was distracted by Annabel's new appearance. She had taken off her glasses and put in contact lenses. She'd also completely made-up her face – right down to applying a pale, shimmering lip gloss. Her scruffy jeans and T-shirt had now been replaced by a Juicy Couture sweat suit in a dark shade of plum.

'You didn't have to change for my benefit.'

'I never allow *anyone* to see me without my makeup,' Annabel said with a sniff.

'Dr Frost must have seen you tonight,' I pointed out, neatly changing the subject.

'He doesn't notice anymore, so why bother?' I detected a note of sadness in her voice. 'Anyway, I don't care. Hurry up and go to the loo. I've already decided what you can borrow for tomorrow night.'

Back in Annabel's bedroom, I was surprised – and pleased – to find the boxes of handbags had not been moved after all. It suddenly occurred to me that Annabel had been far more worried about being seen without her makeup.

'Wow!' I said. 'What great handbags. Can I have a look?'

'It's a little business I have on the side.' Annabel gently picked up a cream-coloured Louis Vuitton purse with its trademark chocolate-leather-and-gold *LV* monogram. 'Isn't she a beauty?'

I went to take it but she snatched the bag away. 'Did you wash your hands?'

'Of course I did.' I held them palm up for her scrutiny. 'Where did you get all this?'

'A secret.' She smiled, then sat down on the bed. 'Come sit.'

I moved aside a red heart-shaped cushion with huggable

arms. 'You're not doing anything illegal, are you?' I unzipped the Louis Vuitton bag to inspect the lining inside. Relief washed over me. This was definitely a fake – and not even a good one at that.

Annabel laughed. 'Don't be silly. There's nothing wrong with a little harmless copying.'

She gestured to a small pink-painted desk where her laptop lay open. 'I put them up for auction on eBay. Pick one and I'll give you a good price.'

'I don't need one.' I refused to touch dodgy property. It was a matter of principle.

'You can't keep everything shoved in that tatty old jacket pocket.'

'Why not?' I happened to be very fond of my Christiane Amanpour safari jacket. 'You should be careful, Annabel.'

'Everyone who buys them knows they're fake,' she said.

'Those handbags are made in sweatshops using child labour,' I said. 'The profits are used to finance terrorism and organized crime.'

'Nonsense. My contact said a percentage of the profits goes to charity.'

'And you believed him?' Annabel could be so naive! 'There's a huge clampdown on counterfeit goods,' I went on. 'Haven't you heard of the Anti-Counterfeiting Group?'

Annabel shrugged. 'Maybe.'

'The ACG works closely with law enforcement and HM Revenue and Customs. They watch UK ports. There's also the Border Agency, too. I'm warning you. You're playing with fire.'

'How come you know so much about it?' said Annabel suspiciously.

Of course I did! I made it my business to know. Even though Dad dealt primarily in silver and jewellery, he had many friends in the import-export business.

'It's part of being an investigative reporter,' I said sternly. 'I make a point of keeping up-to-date on current issues.'

'Yes. You're right, and I'm wrong,' Annabel sighed.

'If money is going into your bank account, you're effectively receiving money for counterfeit goods. You could go to prison.'

'Prison!' Annabel's eyes widened. She smiled. 'Of course! *Prison!*'

'It's not funny,' I scolded. 'I know people say that serving time these days is easy, but that's not true.'

'I read somewhere that being in prison was like being in a hotel,' said Annabel. 'You can even take a degree.'

'It depends on what category it is.'

'What are categories?' Annabel cocked her head.

'There are four – A, B, C and D. Category A is for prisoners whose escape is highly dangerous to the public or national security; B is for those who do not require maximum security, but for whom escape needs to be made very difficult.' Dad had been in a category B.

'And C? Go on,' said Annabel. 'This is fascinating.'

'C is for prisoners who cannot be trusted in open conditions, but who are unlikely to escape. Category D is more of an open prison. Some can even work in the community if they have an ROTL.'

'A what?'

'A Release on Temporary Licence.'

'I had no idea you knew so much,' said Annabel. 'What category is Wormwood Scrubs?'

'Why?' I began to feel uncomfortable. Wormwood Scrubs in London was one of several prisons where Dad had done time.

'Just wondered. It's always on the telly,' said Annabel. 'What about our local prison in Dartmoor?'

Dad had been in Dartmoor, too. I didn't want to discuss prisons. It was too close to home. 'Gosh. Is that the time?' I stood up. 'I'd better go. I'm keeping you up.'

'I thought you wanted to borrow a dress?'

'I do. Yes. Thanks. I almost forgot.' I sat back down again.

Annabel got off the bed and sauntered over to a mirrored built-in wardrobe. She opened the sliding doors. It was stuffed with clothes. There were shelves stacked with brightly coloured tops and racks of shoes. I had a small, old-fashioned freestanding wardrobe that made my meagre selection of clothes smell of mothballs.

'Jack put in extra shelves just for me,' said Annabel.

'Do you sleep in here?' I was glad to change the subject.

'Sometimes. But really, I just keep all my lovely things here,' Annabel said. 'Jack doesn't like clutter. He says this room is mine to do whatever I want with. It's like my own boudoir.'

Annabel brought out two dresses and laid them out on the bed.

'This is a lovely colour,' I said, picking up a cobalt blue halter-neck, floor-length dress. It still had the price tag on it – though I noted it had been heavily reduced.

'I've never worn it,' said Annabel. 'I don't know why I bought it. Its price was knocked down because of a stain on the hem.'

I inspected the hem. There was a tiny black mark. 'You can't really see it.' I held the gown up to my face and looked in the mirror. The blue really emphasized the colour of my eyes. It was a magnificent dress and, with the low cut back, I could just imagine Robin's hands itching to wander over my bare flesh.

'I'm not sure it will suit you after all.' Annabel snatched the dress away. 'Frankly, you need to have bosoms to really carry off a halter-neck. Try on the black sheath instead.'

'I'll change in the bathroom.' My undies were still drying in Mrs Evans's airing cupboard and I was wearing my emergency underwear.

'Don't be silly. I won't look.'

The dress was strapless and held in place by an elasticized smocked bodice. It dropped to the floor, ending in a pool of excess material around my ankles. I felt swamped by the dress and disappointed.

I knew I was being childish, but Robin would have loved me in the cobalt blue dress.

I fiddled with the bodice. 'It'll never stay up.'

Annabel slapped my hand away. 'Use a safety pin.'

'It's too long,' I whined. 'You're so much taller than me.'

'Wear high heels.'

'I really liked the blue—'

'Dress it up with jewellery.' Annabel went over to the pink painted chest of drawers and opened one. She retrieved an Egyptian-looking disc-shaped necklace and matching earrings. 'Try these. Now, this is where your short hair will look good. People will see the earrings.' She leaned in closer. 'What funny little ears you have.'

I caught sight of both of us standing side by side in the mirror – Annabel was actually pouting at her own reflection – and felt a wave of insecurity. She was a tall, voluptuous, beautiful redhead – even if she did have large feet – and next to her, I looked like a boy in drag.

'Are you disappointed that Dr Frost isn't coming?' I said.

'He doesn't like big social events. I think it's because men hit on me and he gets jealous.' Annabel gave a heavy sigh. 'I can't help being attractive to men, Vicky. You don't realize how lucky you are.'

'Speaking of all your admirers,' I said, ignoring the back-handed compliment. 'Did you get the message that Ronnie Binns expected to have lunch with you today?'

'Ronnie Binns?' Annabel's eyes widened. 'The *dustman*? Wanted to have *lunch*? With me?' She started to laugh. It was the fake kind I'd heard many times in theatre pantomimes. I was instantly suspicious.

'No. He didn't *want* to have lunch,' I said coldly. 'He was adamant you'd invited him. He even brought you flowers. *Those* flowers!' I pointed to the pink carnations on her desk.

'Jack bought me those.' Annabel turned red. 'For heaven's sake, does it matter? Do you want the dress or not? I've got things to do this evening.'

'Yes. Please.' An uneasy silence fell between us. I knew she was lying about meeting Ronnie Binns. I *knew* those were his flowers, but couldn't think why.

Annabel shoved the dress into a plastic bag, and I followed her downstairs where we found Dr Frost – wearing his white coat – checking his reflection in the hall mirror. A black leather doctor's bag stood on the floor by the front door.

Annabel's face fell. 'You're not going out, are you?'

'Olive Larch,' he said. 'She called in a frightful state. She can hear someone moving about the back garden.'

'It's probably a fox,' Annabel said, exasperated. 'That's *twice* this week. Can't she phone a friend or something?'

'It's my job, dear.' Dr Frost put his arm around Annabel and gave her a hug. 'With her father dead and gone, she's all alone.'

'But, I'm alone.' Annabel scowled.

'I can't risk her having another of her episodes.'

Annabel folded her arms across her ample breasts. 'What time will you be back?'

'I'm not sure.' He kissed her gently on the forehead. 'Don't wait up.'

Annabel and I watched Dr Frost get into his Saab and drive away. When I turned to say my goodbyes, too, I was surprised to see Annabel's eyes had filled with tears. She wiped them away angrily. 'Honestly, sometimes I think he loves his patients more than he loves me.'

'Do you want me to stay?'

'I'm used to it.' Annabel sighed. 'Men! Sometimes I think you did the right thing choosing to be celibate.'

Celibate? I knew Pete and Annabel called me the Ice Maiden of Gipping behind my back, but now I was *celibate,* too?

'According to *Cosmopolitan*,' Annabel went on. 'It's quite fashionable these days to wait until marriage.'

93

'*Finally,* the world is waking up to the importance of being celibate,' I said dryly. 'You should try it.'

'What on earth for?'

'My mum once said that one's sexuality is the most precious gift you can give a man.'

'How quaint,' Annabel said, ushering me out of the front door. 'But pointless. If a man doesn't get it from you, he'll just go elsewhere.'

'Mum says . . . used to say that, too.' I sighed. *'Men!'*

'Yes! *Men!* We're both alone in the world, Vicky,' Annabel said with a brave smile. 'I'm so glad we're friends.'

Placing the plastic bag in my moped pannier, I sped back to Factory Terrace. The more I got to know Annabel, the more I realized she was actually quite vulnerable. I knew she never heard from her mother who ran off with the local vet when she was just a child. Her father was in the navy and according to rumour he hadn't seen her in years, either.

It was no wonder Annabel had a penchant for older men. She was searching for a father figure – married, or otherwise. It sounded like life with Dr Frost was not all hearts and flowers. He wasn't accompanying her to tomorrow night's Gala *and* he was spending nights away from home.

With my borrowed black dress and jewellery safe in my moped pannier, I felt extremely cheerful.

Robin was going to fall madly in love with me. I couldn't wait for tomorrow night to come.

13

As I pulled into the parking area behind the *Gazette* office the next morning, I was surprised to find Dave Randall's Land Rover idling in the alley.

He beeped the horn twice and wound down the window. 'I've been waiting for you,' he shouted, flapping a large brown envelope. 'Got some great news!'

'I love news!' I parked my moped and strolled over. 'What have you got?'

Dave looked as if he hadn't slept or shaved for a week. His usual dark curls were matted and stuck to his head.

'I've been driving around England drumming up support,' he beamed, hardly able to contain his excitement. 'We're going to the Olympics!' Dave had harboured a lifelong ambition to have hedge-jumping accepted as an Olympic sport.

I was genuinely thrilled for him. 'That's wonderful!'

'The Olympic committee want to meet me in London next week. I can't believe it. Do you remember when this was all a dream?'

I did. Dave and I were at the Three Tuns. I also remembered never to drink scrumpy again as that was yet another night when I narrowly missed surrendering my virginity to Mr Wrong.

'If we're quick, we can try to get you in tomorrow's paper. Wilf and Pete don't go to the printers until noon.'

'I know it's top secret, but . . .' Dave beckoned me to step closer. He smelled of earth and damp leaves. 'The jumpers are getting the Larch Legacy. It'll be announced tonight. That's what clinched it! Good old Sammy!'

'Are you sure?' I recalled the winner's name was kept in a sealed envelope.

'I'm sure, all right,' said Dave. 'Sammy tipped me off. We've named a new jump in his honour – the Larch Leap. It's an updated version of the 1950s Western Roll. Not as streamlined as the Fosbury Flop but—'

'That's amazing!' I knew once Dave got started rhapsodizing over his pet subject, I'd be there all morning. 'You should come and tell Pete.'

'No need. It's all in here.' Dave thrust the brown envelope at me.

'He might have some questions.'

'No thanks. Webster and his cronies are hanging out front.' Dave laughed triumphantly. 'I can't wait to see his face when he hears about it. Webster thought he had the Legacy in the bag.'

It was no secret that Jack Webster – one of Devon's champion hedge cutters – and Dave despised each other. Since the former lovingly cut and laid hedges and the latter systematically destroyed them, it was easy to understand why.

Congratulating Dave on his exciting news, I cut down the side alley and came upon a wall of people – Jack Webster among them – waiting for the *Gazette* doors to open.

Even the morning rush-hour traffic was slowing down so drivers could try to get a look at Barbara's window display. I had no idea that an inflatable snail from the Gipping Bards prop department could have generated so much interest.

The air was festive. Faces were pressed against the window

and money was changing hands amid cries of 'Killer's slime looks good,' 'Rambo's got excellent form,' and 'Wow! Seabiscuit is out of his shell.'

The front door was locked. I rapped smartly on the glass and Barbara – clutching a bottle of wine – darted forward to let me inside and promptly locked up again.

'We're not quite ready for them yet,' she declared. 'How are we doing, Olive?' Barbara rolled her eyes and whispered, 'She's so slow.'

Olive Larch was carefully arranging green plastic cups in a straight line along the counter with painstaking precision.

'I need a quick word with her about this year's Larch Legacy.'

'I wouldn't bother. She doesn't know anything, dear,' said Barbara. 'Glass of dandelion wine? It's one of Phyllis Fairweather's home brews.'

'Isn't it a little early to start drinking?' It was only eight forty-five, plus, I knew from experience that Phyllis's wine was lethal.

'It's a Gipping tradition. Snail season officially kicks off today. Once the door opens, we'll be taking bets in the nook for the first race on Sunday at the Three Tuns.'

'The punters already seem to be doing that outside.' I noted the corner nook had been made into a betting cubicle. The brown-spangled curtains were swept back to reveal a ballot box standing atop the plastic circular table.

Olive stepped back from the counter and admired her handiwork. 'The cups are ready now.'

Barbara started to pour the urine-coloured liquid into each one. 'Olive? A snifter?' She passed her a cup. 'Go on. Live dangerously.'

'I shouldn't really.' Olive took a dainty sip and pulled a face. 'It's a bit strong,'

Someone hammered on the glass front door. Startled, Olive screamed and spilt most of the liquid down her white capri pants.

'Five minutes.' Barbara held up five fingers at the figures

97

crushed against the glass front door. I recognized a couple of my younger mourner farmers – forty-something Bernard J. Kirby and his wife, Lily. Both wore green tops emblazoned with the logo GSRF. I also recalled the pair were serious hedge-cutters and Lily had come to blows with Dave on more than one occasion. No wonder he hadn't wanted to come to the front door.

'You've been very busy, Barbara,' I said, gesturing to the walls and ceiling.

The reception had undergone a huge transformation. Coloured bunting in green, silver and black was suspended from the crown mouldings. Helium-filled green and silver balloons bobbed along the ceiling. GIPPING-ON-PLYM SNAIL RACING FEDERATION was written in giant letters on a green-silver-and-black-checkered banner that stretched along an entire wall.

Barbara beamed. 'Olive and I finished decorating late last night.'

'How late?' I said, recalling Dr Frost's assignation. I'd left Annabel's at around nine thirty.

'We were here until ten. Of course, Olive had to come home with me and sleep in the spare room.' She lowered her voice, saying, 'Hates being alone.'

Good grief! Was Dr Frost having an affair?

'Time to get the party started,' said Barbara, knocking back her cup of wine.

After promising to send Tony back downstairs to help with the betting, I made my excuses and escaped to the reporters' room.

I couldn't wait to see Pete's face when I told him Dave's exciting news.

14

I stepped into Pete's office. 'You'll never guess,' I said, waving Dave's brown envelope.

'I don't do guessing games.' Pete didn't look up, being too busy stuffing papers into a surprisingly smart leather briefcase.

'The jumpers are getting the Larch Legacy.'

'Bloody hell!' He looked up sharply. 'How did you find out?'

'I have my ways,' I said modestly, and handed him the envelope. 'It's all in there.'

Pete tore it open and tipped the contents onto his desk. 'We'll have to use it next week.'

'You said you wanted something other than snails on Page One,' I said.

'There's no time to go through it *now,* is there?'

'I thought you didn't leave for Plymouth until noon.'

'Wilf wants to put the paper to bed early today. Get back for the Gala. Christ. I hate those fancy dos,' Pete grumbled. 'Had to hire a bloody tux. The Larch Legacy can wait.'

'Did I hear Larch Legacy?' I stepped aside as our illustrious editor – already wearing his fedora and ready to go – hastened over to Pete's desk. Wilf picked up Dave's press release. 'What's all this?'

Stop the Presses! Stop the Presses!

Gipping Hedge Jumping Society was awarded the coveted Larch Legacy at the prestigious Gipping Gastropod Gala last night.

As a gesture of our gratitude, GHJS created a new jumping style in Sammy Larch's memory. The Larch Leap will join other famous names such as the Straddle, the Scissors, the Western Roll and the notorious Fosbury Flop. Our Olympic dream will soon be a reality! Rock on Sammy!

Wilf picked up a PowerPoint presentation entitled 'Proposed Olympic hedge styles', with computer-generated illustrations bearing various captions such as – BOX-SHAPED, A-SHAPED, CHAMFERED, TOPPED A and ROUNDED HUMP. These categories were broken down further into hedge species – holly, blackthorn, hazel, beech, etcetera.

'Do you know, young Vicky,' Wilf said, 'it takes five hours to lay twelve feet of hedge and just a few minutes to destroy it.' He shook his head. 'I must admit I don't altogether support this barbaric sport, but it attracts readers, and that's what the *Gazette* is all about. *Readers*. We'll put it on Page One, Pete. Good work, Vicky. Oh! And good work on Scarlett Fleming's obit, too.'

'Thank you, sir.'

Pete glanced at his wristwatch. 'Bollocks. We've got to go.'

'Speaking of Mrs Fleming,' I said, trailing after them onto the landing, 'I have a few questions about her accident and wondered if I could contact the Spanish authorities.'

'The *authorities*?' Wilf stopped and swung round to face me. His good eye seemed to bore into my skull. 'Good God, girl.

Have you no feelings?' Wilf glowered at me with such displeasure I felt my face begin to burn. 'The *Gazette* doesn't want the gruesome details. Our obituaries are a celebration of life. Have you any idea how upset Dougie would be? The man is prostrate with grief.'

'The obituary will be in tomorrow's edition,' Pete scolded. 'You're asking Wilf to pull it so you can add more *details*?'

'No. I just thought . . .' I bit my lip. 'Sorry. You're right. I was just curious.'

'Your time is better spent investigating these rogue funeral outfits,' said Wilf. 'I want a full report on my desk next Thursday.'

'And photos. Don't forget the photos,' Pete said with a nod, gesturing for Wilf to go ahead of him down the stairs. 'Sorry about that, sir. Vicky tends to be overenthusiastic.'

'Keep her away from Dougie,' I heard Wilf say as he descended into the gloom of the hall. 'That man's heart is broken.'

I slunk back to the reporters' room more frustrated than upset. Wilf's schoolboy friendship was clouding his judgment. *Idiot, Vicky!* I should have kept my concerns to myself. Now I wouldn't be able to make *any* international calls to Europe because the *Gazette* always received an itemized phone bill. Wilf had hauled everyone over the coals once for abusing the system and making too many personal calls – except for me of course. Dad had warned me of the dangers of caller ID.

I stifled the urge to kick the wastepaper basket under my desk. Wilf's orders meant I could only make inquiries abroad via e-mail and the Internet. It might take weeks to get any sort of answer.

The reporters' room was empty. I could hear sounds of merriment seeping through the floorboards from the reception down below. No doubt Tony had got waylaid downstairs and was helping Barbara out.

After leaving a fourth message on Neil Titley's answering

101

service suggesting the day-in-the-life feature would obviously give him free advertising, I got cracking on the Internet.

How on earth did journalists ever manage without it? Presumably, they spent their lives in libraries or on the road. These days information was readily available at the touch of a button. Frankly, I still believed in old-fashioned journalism and human contact.

Despite Wilf's *and* Melanie Carew's claims that Douglas Fleming was 'prostrate with grief', he'd reacted very strangely to some of my questions. I saw something in his manner and reactions and that *something* could never be detected from a phone conversation.

I spent the rest of the morning searching Google for anything and everything connected to dying abroad. I trawled through the Foreign and Commonwealth Office's website and discovered that 'repatriating the deceased' was a complicated and expensive process. It seemed that every country throughout the globe had different rules and regulations.

Money was key, and from what gossip I'd gathered, the Flemings hadn't had much of it. If a person travelled with the correct insurance or similar, the body *could* be transported home within five to seven days – but only if death was from natural causes. If the police were involved – say a traffic accident or murder, in fact, anything suspicious – the process took much longer. Sometimes *months*! And as I suspected, the local authorities worked closely with the FCO and the UK police.

Fleming said he heard the news that his wife had died on the Sunday. She was buried at St Peter's first thing Thursday morning. Mary told me the coffin was already at Headcellars, which suggested it must have arrived sometime on Wednesday. Even if Scarlett had died of natural causes – and not a traffic accident – that had taken only four days. I knew for a fact that Fleming didn't go to Spain himself to get the body, so he must have made a lot of phone calls or perhaps had friends in high places.

I e-mailed the Information Commissioners Office citing the Freedom of Information Act and requested passenger manifests at Barcelona and Perpignan airports. It was a long shot, made even longer by an automated reply informing me of a twenty-business-day wait to process my request. Of course, I could have called in a favour from Topaz's cousin, DS Colin Probes who most certainly owed me a few, but that was something I would rather die than do.

My thoughts turned to the redheaded copper. It was a pity he was a policeman. We'd nearly gone out for dinner once, but having heard my father say countless times, 'The only good copper is a dead copper,' I bolted out at the last minute.

I made myself a cuppa and carried on with my research. It appeared that a plethora of legal documents were needed to accompany a body: a death certificate, embalming certificate, 'no objection' certificates, and a 'sealing of the coffin' certificate undertaken in the presence of an embassy official from the country receiving the body, to name just a few.

If the person had died in France – perhaps Scarlett's car had veered down a ravine in the French Pyrenees – she would have been given a police tag and the local mayor's approval before being embalmed and placed in a wooden coffin. But was it France, or Spain? I didn't know the exact location. Yet.

Following 9/11, new rules stated that the coffin had to be lined with zinc, not lead – supposedly too dense for security X-rays – and hermetically sealed. Scarlett's coffin must have been incredibly heavy, but somehow Fleming and Neil Titley managed to navigate St Peter's the Martyr cemetery and the heavily overgrown Albert Square using nothing but a flimsy hospital gurney.

I called at least a dozen funeral companies who said it was highly unusual to sell a coffin separately. Those coffins available online – and there were some beauties – took several weeks to build because they were all custom-made.

Using Google Maps for names of towns, I turned my

attention to yoga retreats, health farms, spas, and meditation centres across the northeast coast of Spain and southwestern France. I fired off e-mails to all and sundry pretending that Scarlett Fleming was my aunt and I wanted to send her something for her birthday. A few replies came back immediately saying they had no record of anyone ever staying there by that name.

As the day wore on, my obsession with Google Earth satellite sky map grew. *Good grief!* I could zoom right in on San Feliu, the small town where I sent my letters to Mum and Dad in care of the El Matador pub. What if I could actually see them? Of course, I knew it wasn't in real time, but it was a strange sensation having access to other people's lives. Again, I wondered if the new CCTV surveillance systems were a good idea.

'Oh, is that Spain?' Annabel said, leaning over my shoulder. Startled, I practically jumped out of my chair. I hadn't heard her sneak up behind me.

Instinctively, I hit the 'back' button, but my computer didn't respond. The street plan of San Feliu and its high-rise hotels was frozen in time. 'No. I mean, yes. I think so.' *How long had she been standing there?*

'If you're thinking of going on holiday, I wouldn't go to the Costa Brava,' Annabel declared, perching on the corner of my desk. 'I'm told it's full of ghastly British ex-pats and criminals.'

'I was doing a bit of research on Scarlett Fleming's yoga retreat,' I said quickly. 'It's amazing what you can find out from these maps. Her car ran off the road and into a ravine.'

'What are you looking for? Wreckage?'

'You should include this kind of thing in your CCTV report,' I said, ignoring her remark. '"Is THE WHOLE WORLD UNDER SURVEILLANCE?" There's a great headline for you.'

'Why are you bothering about Scarlett Fleming, anyway?'

I shrugged. 'Something feels off, that's all.'

Annabel leaned in even closer and whispered, 'Maybe she never even *got* to Spain?'

'I already thought of that,' I said. 'I'm waiting to hear from the Foreign and Commonwealth Office.'

'You'll wait forever,' Annabel said with a smirk. 'Why don't you ask the cops for help? I'll put in a word if you like. I've got a few contacts with the boys in blue. As a matter of fact, they're helping me on this exposé I'm working on.'

'Don't worry. It's not urgent,' I said quickly. 'In fact, I'd rather you didn't. Wilf thinks I should leave Fleming alone.'

'They're pals, that's why. I already told you I think Fleming did it. She was such a pretentious woman, driving around in that flashy Range Rover.'

'Look, no offence,' I said, 'but why don't you just work on your exposé and let me work on mine?'

'I was just trying to help. I thought we were friends.' Annabel sounded hurt. 'Look, I don't want to force you to come tonight—'

'Sorry. I've got a lot on my mind.' I felt guilty. 'Of course I want to come.'

'Would you like me to do your makeup?'

'Yes, please!' I immediately brightened up. It was good to have a friend.

'That's settled then. I'll come to your place around five thirty.' Annabel got to her feet, gave a catlike stretch and sauntered back to her desk.

After having to reboot my computer twice before I could shut it down, I put on my safari jacket and got ready to leave. Annabel was tapping away on her computer.

I caught her muttering to herself, 'God! Fancy that' and 'Clever, clever me.'

'Bye,' I called out. 'See you later.'

Annabel looked up from her computer screen. 'Did you know that Wormwood Scrubs was featured in that film, *The Italian Job*?'

'Why the sudden interest in Wormwood Scrubs?' I said lightly.

Annabel shrugged. 'Just curious.'

I decided to leave the building through the side entrance, which opened directly onto the High Street. Judging by the number of voices, laughter, and Frank Sinatra singing 'Fly Me to the Moon', Barbara's pre-Gala party was still going strong.

Back at Factory Terrace I took a long hot bath and did some thinking. Annabel's interest in prisons had unsettled me this afternoon, but I was positive it was just my own paranoia at work.

To my joy, Neil Titley finally returned my call, full of apologies. Apparently he'd spent all day transporting six ladies from Plymouth's Purple Hat Club to Windsor Castle for a sixtieth birthday celebration. I offered to buy him a pint at the Three Tuns but he said that he worked a second job at weekends and suggested we meet outside the Banana Club on Plymouth Hoe the following night at nine p.m.

Just-call-me-Neil was very excited about the possibility of a feature and already had two full-page ads he'd like to take out – 'free, per your voice mail', which was slightly worrying. Like all independent newspapers, the *Gazette* relied on paid advertising to exist. I knew I'd never be able to slip a freebie past Barbara, let alone Wilf.

By sheer fluke, the Banana Club was where Sadie, my landlady's daughter, performed as a pole dancer. I made a mental note to mention this to Mrs Evans. She was always sending Sadie care packages and it would save her a trip to the post office.

Tonight's Gala should prove interesting. If the 'prostrate with grief, widower actually showed up at all, I resolved to watch him like a hawk.

15

'What an adorable little room!' Annabel bounded through the door carrying a Gucci evening bag and a red oval vanity case. Not only was she early but, much to my chagrin, she was also wearing the cobalt blue halter-neck dress.

'How did you get in?' I was filled with panic. A postcard from Mum and Dad lay on top of a book next to my bed. 'I thought Mrs Evans had already left.'

'I stopped their car at the end of the road.' Annabel glided around the room, inspecting my desk and examining the titles on the bookshelf. 'She told me the front door key was under the mat.'

'You should have called. I might have had no clothes on!' I tried hard not to look over at the nightstand. In my imagination, the postcard seemed to grow into a giant poster calling out to Annabel as if to say, 'Vicky's a liar! Her parents are alive! They're hiding in Spain!'

Annabel drifted over to the chest of drawers and peered into the wooden bowl that held moped, office and house keys. She picked up a hideous porcelain clown that I had inherited when I took the room saying, 'What an ugly little thing,' examined my camera, and finished up by taking the last tissue from the box. 'No photos of your parents?'

Annabel turned to face me. I gave a cry of surprise. 'What have you done to your eyes?' They were a piercing electric-blue. 'And your hair! It looks different.'

Annabel smirked, 'You like?' She gave a dramatic twirl and ended up admiring her reflection in the mirrored wardrobe.

'You look . . . well . . . amazing.' Envy and resentment surged through my body. Not only had she decided to wear the cobalt blue dress that she'd implied she disliked, Annabel had even stolen my eyes as well.

'Contact lenses, obviously,' Annabel said, looking over at me via the mirror. 'And frankly, I've been bored with Nice 'n Easy's natural copper red for ages. This is a new shade. It's called burnished eggplant. I don't think I've ever looked more beautiful.'

The effect really *was* mesmerizing and I just knew – *knew* – that my handsome lieutenant would only have eyes for her tonight. It was too depressing for words.

'I've brought my makeup case.' Annabel pouted seductively at her own reflection. 'I can't make any promises but – good heavens!' She spun around. Her eyes zeroed in on my chest. 'What's happened to my dress? You didn't let Mrs Evans get hold of it with her needle, did you?'

'Of course, not.' Instinctively, I clamped my arms across the bodice. 'It's just a padded bra.'

The strapless black dress had looked fine as long as I stood still. Any sudden movement caused the elasticized bodice to fall down. Mrs Evans had found an old crimson whalebone bustier belonging to Sadie and laced me into that. She'd then sewn the black dress to the bustier. Up until Annabel's unexpected entrance, I'd been pleased at the effect. It pushed what little I did have, upward. I even had cleavage!

There was a downside. It was horribly uncomfortable. I knew I'd have welts by the end of the night because part of the whalebone was visible through the fraying material but I was sure it would be worth the pain.

Luckily, Sadie and I were the same shoe size. Mrs Evans had loaned me a pair of silver strappy sandals with four-inch heels – Sadie's 'old dancing shoes'. Once I got used to the height, they were surprisingly comfortable and made me feel tall and sexy – up until now.

Annabel grabbed my desk chair and moved it over to the mirrored wardrobe with the back facing away from her – supposedly so she could stare at herself while she worked on me. As I sat down, a searing pain from my bustier shot through my rib cage. It felt as if I'd been stabbed.

'Mrs Evans makes the costumes for the Gipping Bards,' Annabel said. 'Once those costumes are on and she's done her so-called finishing touches, they are impossible to get off without scissors.'

'Well, she didn't touch it,' I lied. I couldn't dwell on being surgically removed from my bustier right now and changed the subject. 'I'm afraid I don't have a hair dryer.'

'I guessed as much. That's why it always looks a mess.' Annabel opened her little case on my bed and retrieved a small travel hair dryer. 'I suppose you go to Dorothy's Coiffeur?'

'It's convenient.'

Annabel shook her head with despair. 'Well, as long as you don't let her talk you into getting a lavender perm.'

I laughed, and so did Annabel and, for the next half an hour, while she blow-dried my hair with her round styling brush and made up my face, I was happy we were friends – though I reminded myself that leopards never changed their spots. Even so, it felt nice being fussed over.

Annabel didn't stop talking about cosmetic brands and skin care. I wondered what on earth possessed her to become an investigative reporter and was just about to ask, when she ordered me to stand up and turn to face the mirror.

'Omigod!' I hardly recognized myself. I looked incredible!

Annabel had dried my hair into a neat bob and trimmed my fringe. My eyes were heavily rimmed with kohl pencil. She must have done something to my cheekbones because they looked chiselled and, as for my lips! What a deep luscious red!

'Now for the jewellery.' Annabel helped me put on the necklace and earrings. 'You look just like Cleopatra.'

'I love it!' I just couldn't stop staring at the new me. It just goes to show what the right makeup and hair can do for a girl's self-confidence.

Compelled to give her a heartfelt hug of gratitude, I turned around. I swear my heart practically stopped beating. Annabel was standing by the nightstand reading that wretched postcard. I knew what it said by heart. 'Weather good. Wish you were here.' Luckily, Dad always took precautions in any form of written communication and now I saw why.

'Who are "M & D"?' said Annabel.

'Marie and Derek. Old friends of my parents.' I tried to sound calm but my mouth went dry. Thank heavens I'd given Mrs Evans the same names when I caught her nosing through my mail once. 'Godparents actually.'

'You never mentioned you had *godparents*.' Annabel's voice was heavy with accusation. 'I thought you were completely alone.'

'That's because I hardly see them. I feel alone.'

'I thought you didn't know anyone in Spain.'

'I don't. They just love travelling,' I said smoothly. 'They send me postcards from every country they visit. Last year they were in the Sahara Desert. Did you know that every sand dune is different? They sent me some great photos. Would you—?'

'No thanks.' Annabel dropped the postcard onto the bed. 'Come on, we'll be late.'

As we got into Annabel's BMW I felt a heady sense of euphoria. Whether it was because I'd handled her questions about my parents so neatly – I even believed the sand dune story myself – or maybe for the first time in my life, I knew what it felt like to have confidence in my appearance. I didn't even care about the stupid cobalt-blue halter-neck dress and Annabel's bionic-woman eyes anymore.

I looked fantastic and Robin was going to fall madly in love with me. I just knew it!

16

It was just after six thirty when we turned into the car park of the Gipping Manor Hotel.

Located on the outskirts of Lower Gipping, the term *manor* was somewhat of a euphemism. Built in the late seventies, the two-story cinderblock structure was no more a former manor house than I was travelling royalty.

I'd been here before, of course. The Manor – as it was known by the locals – was the venue for all committee and indoor sports meetings ranging from the Rotary Club; Boy Scout, Girl Guide, and Brownie packs; Gipping Ballet School; the Women's Institute; and naturally, the Gipping Snail Racing Federation. Even the Gipping Bards had been known to perform here when the old theatre at the bottom of the High Street had been closed for fumigation.

The car park was packed. People were even fighting over parking spaces. I noted Jack Webster – dressed in a tuxedo – had stepped out of his Land Rover and was close to blows with Hilda Hicks who was threatening him with her riding crop.

'There are so many people here,' I said as I spied a coach from Totnes disgorging its occupants in all their finery.

Annabel slammed her foot on the brake. 'My God!' she squealed. 'I've just seen a naval officer!'

My stomach flipped over. It had to be Robin. 'Where?' A car horn blared behind us. I swivelled around to see the front of a minivan practically in our rear seat. Annabel ignored it.

'Was he in a silver Fiesta?' I said.

'Who cares? If there's one, there'll be more.' She turned to me, eyes alive with hope. 'What if there is a crowd of sailors here in uniform! Can you imagine?'

I could. And did. But I was only interested in one. It was hard not to get caught up in the excitement. I cracked my window open and heard the distant sounds of salsa music. For some reason I'd been expecting something old-fashioned.

Annabel gave a seductive wriggle. 'I just *love* Cuban music. It's so sexy.'

Unfortunately, the sexy Cuban music was short-lived. By the time we'd been forced to park on the street and walk a good quarter of a mile in high heels, the starring band – Hogmeat, Harris and the Wonderguts – had begun to play Tony Orlando's 'Tie a Yellow Ribbon'.

'Ugh. A cover band.' Annabel shuddered as we walked through the pseudo-Tudor porch and into the foyer. Barbara was standing at the door to the ballroom-cum-gymnasium, collecting tickets. She wore her grey hair down. A diamante Alice band sparkled on her head matching a tight, glittering Lurex skirt and black chiffon blouse with trumpet sleeves.

'Tickets please – goodness Vicky.' Barbara's jaw dropped. 'You look stunning.'

I felt myself blush. 'Thanks. Annabel did my hair and makeup,' I said, adjusting the whalebone corset with a wince.

'Trust me,' Annabel said, handing over two flimsy pieces of green paper stamped GASTROPOD GALA! ABSOLUTELY NON-TRANSFERABLE. 'It took a *lot* of work.'

'Oh! Heavens!' said Barbara, staring at Annabel. 'I thought I was talking to the bionic woman for a moment. Your eyes . . .'

'Thank you. I bought these on the Internet.' Annabel widened them for Barbara's benefit. 'I have several different colours.'

With an ill-concealed snigger, Barbara stamped our wrists with a snail-imprinted seal so we could 'come and go as we wanted'.

'You look just like Cleopatra, Vicky,' Barbara said suddenly. 'Can the Bards borrow that jewellery? Pam Green and I are drawing up a list of next season's plays and of course, *Antony and Cleopatra* is always a favourite.' Barbara stepped closer and lowered her voice. 'Now that Scarlett Fleming is dead, it will give someone else a chance to play the lead role. You'd make a *lovely* young queen.'

'I hadn't considered acting,' I said modestly. Perhaps I'd give it a try. I could imagine Robin sitting in the front row, captivated by my Oscar-worthy performance.

'She hasn't got time for all that nonsense,' Annabel declared. 'Anyway, I thought you said someone had broken into the storage unit and stolen the pyramid.'

'It wasn't the pyramid,' Barbara said. 'A costume from *Robin Hood and the—*'

'Excuse me,' came a familiar voice. 'You're blocking the entrance.'

I stepped aside and came face-to-face with Topaz. Her expression was one of pure jealousy.

'Hi, Topaz. You look—' I struggled to find the right word – 'striking.'

Topaz was dressed for the scaffold. She had on a long black wig, a black turtleneck, and a black mid-calf-length wraparound skirt. She even wore thick black leggings. I saw them peeping under her hemline. In her arms Topaz carried a small fluorescent orange rucksack.

'You can't take that in there, dear,' said Barbara. 'We're very tight on security this year. Al-kye-doe.'

'Al-Qaeda.' Annabel rolled her eyes at me. 'I don't think we need to worry about terrorists here.'

'Here let me carry that.' Steve Burrows, Gipping's paramedic, materialized by Topaz's side. He had a pink cherubic face, cropped blond crew cut and sparkling blue eyes. Mrs Evans called him 'Sexpot Steve' because he was a notorious womanizer. Given his enormous size, this was surprising yet even I – who wasn't remotely attracted to him in the slightest – found that every time he came near me, I felt a strange tingling sensation in my nether regions. And tonight was no different.

'No. I'm fine.' Topaz clutched the bag to her chest.

'Love the hair band, doll. Very Alice.' Steve handed Barbara two green tickets, but kept hold of her hand. He kissed it gallantly. 'Go on, let Topaz take it in, Babs. I'll vouch for her.'

'Goodness. How can one say no to such a charmer?' Barbara giggled. 'All right, just this once.'

'Oh. My. God. They're *together*!' Annabel whispered in my ear. 'I thought Topaz was a *lesbian*!'

One could never tell with Topaz – though I hoped she knew what she was in for. I'd been alone with Steve before and somehow found myself kissing him passionately minus my top.

'Perhaps you could keep an eye on Olive Larch this evening, Steve?' Barbara said. 'With all the excitement . . .' She gestured toward the ballroom that was heaving with people singing and dancing to 'Do the Funky Chicken'.

'Happy to,' he said with a wink.

'Take me to the bar, *darling*,' Topaz said, throwing me a look I could only describe as defiant.

'Your wish is my command, doll.' Steve took her arm and froze. 'Blimey. I didn't recognize you, Vicky. Jesus. You look *hot*!'

I felt *hot*! All these compliments were going to my head. 'Hi, Steve. You don't look so bad—'

'Oh no! Quickly, we've got to go. *Now!*' Annabel hissed, seizing my arm and dragging me into the melée.

The ballroom-cum-gymnasium was decked out in green,

115

white and silver bunting. Striped paper streamers fell from the lighting fixtures. A thick layer of green and silver helium balloons covered the entire ceiling.

Annabel propelled me toward the corner of the room and behind a shoulder-high stack of plastic chairs. She looked scared. 'Walter Rawlings is here with his wife.'

Rumour had it that Christine Rawlings's dislike of the 'young tart who slept with my husband', would result in 'the next time I see her she'll wish she hadn't been born.'

I pried Annabel's grasp from my arm. 'You're hurting me.'

'Don't leave me alone.'

'We'll just avoid them,' I said. 'Come on, let's get a drink.'

We pushed our way through the crowd to a long trestle table covered in a green paper cloth that served as a bar. I noted it was positioned next to a giant amplifier. Fortunately, the three-strong band was taking a break up on stage.

I was surprised to see that the lead singer, Hogmeat, was actually Barry Fir, owner of the organic Pick-Your-Own. He was decked out in leather and wore his jacket open exposing a heavily tattooed chest. I had seen Barry Fir's naked torso before when he donned a Speedo to enter the Farming Competition a couple of months ago. It was tattooless then.

'Those are fake,' Annabel declared, answering my unspoken question. 'I saw him buying three packets of transfers from This-and-That Emporium yesterday. 'How stupid!'

No more stupid than your false eyes, I wanted to say, but thought better of it.

Barry's sidekick, Harris, was none other than Bill Harris, our local postman. He played bass and reminded me of an older version of Keith Richards – if that were possible. The third member of the band was on drums. With heavily oiled slicked-back hair, he wore a tight T-shirt emblazoned with the logo GRAB THE GUT and sported the most enormous beer belly I had ever seen. Wonderguts wasn't one of my mourner regulars but I knew him to be a member of the Gipping Bards since his lead performance in *Equus* had prompted one of Eunice's petitions on indecent exposure.

There wasn't much choice in the drinks department: champagne – I saw the label and it was something I'd never heard of – and Tesco sherry.

Annabel picked up two glasses of champagne. 'Here, you try it.'

I took a sip. It was horribly sweet. 'I've had worse.'

Her response was drowned in a cacophony of ear-splitting electronic whistling followed by an explosion of frantic drumming and cymbal thrashing.

The band was back with a vengeance.

We were swept up in the wave of revellers retreating from the bar and the amplifier. Since it was a hospitality bar, I couldn't help wondering if this were some ruse by the organizers to discourage too much drinking.

'Where's Mr Casanova?' Jack Webster elbowed me aside and stood glaring at Annabel. 'I've got a bone to pick with him.'

'Don't Jack! Please,' cried his wife, Amelia, dressed in a full-length navy ensemble with a rhinestone paste brooch.

With a bright red nose and a map of capillary veins stretching over his cheeks, Jack Webster bore all the signs of a heavy drinker. He peered blearily into Annabel's face. 'What the bloody hell is wrong with your eyes? You look like the bionic woman.'

'If you're talking about Dr Frost,' Annabel said haughtily, 'he's working tonight, Mr Webster.'

'Working? Hah!' He turned to Amelia. '*Working?* Breaking up someone else's marriage more like. While the husband's away, the wife will play. And him out risking his life in the North Sea.'

Annabel turned pale. 'I don't know what you're talking about.'

'He doesn't mean anything by it,' Amelia said desperately. 'Come along, luv. Let's go back to the bar.'

Jack swayed unsteadily on his feet, shouting, 'You can bloody well tell him from me and the cutters, this is his last warning? Understand?' before allowing Amelia to drag him away.

'Why would he say a thing like that?' Annabel said. 'Horrid man.'

My suspicions as to Dr Frost's extramarital activities had just been confirmed and poor Annabel didn't have a clue. I wondered who it could be.

'Let's find where we're sitting,' said Annabel.

The seating plan comprised of circular tables for eight people, with a raised celebrity table for GSRF officials complete with neatly labelled place cards. CHIEF MARSHAL – DOUGLAS FLEMING, SCRUTINEER – TONY PERKINS, SECRETARY – OLIVE LARCH and BOOKIE – MC – LEONARD EVANS.

I noted that Mrs Evans had already taken her place at the top table, looking very done up with her newly coiffed tight perm and wearing a buttercup yellow dress.

On the wall behind her, a framed portrait of Queen Elizabeth II was flanked by enlarged photographs of past snail champions. A handwritten card gave a brief description of each snail's athletic achievements. It would appear that no snail had yet to beat Archie who competed in the World Snail Racing Championship in 1995. Archie made the *Guinness World Records* on completion of the thirteen-inch sprint with a staggering time of two minutes and twenty seconds.

The revellers were already dividing into groups. Jack Webster and his hedge-cutting friends – Errol Fairweather, Eric Tossell, John Reeves, Larry Green and all their wives – occupied two full tables; the Gipping Bards, two more. There was one for the Women's Institute, Pennymoor Morris Dancers, Gipping Riding Club, Eco-Warriors – even the juvenile gang, the Swamp Dogs, was dressed up in rented tuxedos and sitting with their parents.

On the far side of the room sat the hedge-jumpers, who had

brought in an art easel on which to prop a huge placard SUPPORT
YOUR OLYMPIC 2012 TEAM. Dave Randall was demonstrating
a new style of jump – presumably the Larch Leap – using a gym
horse that he must have dragged from the games equipment
cupboard.

'There's our lot,' I said, spotting Wilf who was joined by
Edward, Paige – Edward's very sweet wife – and Pete at the
Gazette table close to the stage. Barbara pushed past them and
snagged the empty seat next to Wilf, for whom she'd held a
crush for donkey's years, obviously forfeiting her place at the
Gipping Bards table of which she was a key member.

We headed over – I lost count of the number of compliments
or the amount of times that Annabel told everyone, 'Trust me,
Vicky took a *lot* of work' and 'Do you like my eyes?'

'Don't our girls look pretty, sir?' Barbara touched Wilf's arm
and leaned into him slightly but he was too preoccupied studying
the *Mollusc Monthly* newsletter that had been left on every chair.

'Hi, Pete.' Annabel wriggled behind Wilf and squeezed into
the spare seat next to our unusually dapper-looking chief
reporter. She gave him a kiss on the cheek. 'I'm looking for a
place to sit. Any suggestions?'

'I'm afraid you can't sit there,' said a pleasant voice behind
me. I turned and saw a dainty blonde with a snub nose in a
simple black gown. 'You must be Annabel.'

Annabel leapt to her feet, while Pete stared down at his plate
and mumbled something that sounded like, 'Bollocks.'

'I'm Pete's wife, Emily,' the blonde said with a smile. 'And
I'm sorry to say that it seems all the chairs at this table are
snapped up.'

'Hello, Emily,' I said quickly, offering my hand. 'I'm Vicky.
Pete's spoken so much about you.'

'Really? That does surprise me.' Emily smiled again, but I
saw the coldness in her dark green eyes. 'What a pity you two
lovely girls will have to sit elsewhere.'

'But there are two empty seats,' Barbara protested.

'I believe they are already spoken for,' Emily said coolly. 'Isn't that right Peter?'

Pete mumbled something again, and opened his copy of the *Mollusc Monthly* saying, 'Seabiscuit is looking good, Wilf.'

'No worries!' I said brightly. 'We thought we'd just come by and say hello. Hello. See you all later. Bye.' I took Annabel's arm and steered her back toward the bar. Fortunately, the band was on another break.

'My God. What a bitch!' Annabel downed two glasses of cheap champagne in quick succession. 'Poor Pete. How awful to be married to her.'

'We'd better find another table,' I said, scanning the room, which was rapidly filling up with guests.

'Not near the Rawlings, okay?' said Annabel. 'Or Quentin Goss. I saw him with his wife, too. Oh! And definitely not by the Women's Institute. They all hate me.'

Sounds of 'testing-testing-one-two-one-two', squawked from Mr Evans's microphone signalling that the evening programme was about to begin. 'Ladies and gentleman, pleeeeease take your seats!'

There was a panicked rush to the tables for those left standing – rather like musical chairs. Annabel and I searched for two seats as Ronnie Binns barrelled toward us, firing off photographs from a surprisingly professional-looking camera. He must be making extremely good money as a garbologist.

Suddenly, the opening chords of 'God Save the Queen' blasted through the room. Ronnie stopped dead in his tracks and pulled himself up to his full height, shoulders thrust back. There was a screeching of chairs as everyone scrambled to their feet and turned to face the portrait of Queen Elizabeth at the top table.

'Back to the foyer,' I shouted over the noise. 'Let's regroup.'

We were almost out of the ballroom-cum-gymnasium when Annabel pointed to a table in the far corner. 'Four seats at two o'clock! Oh! *God!*' She gave a cry of delight. 'There's that *sailor*!'

Unfortunately, Topaz and Steve were also sitting there. I hesitated, torn between wanting to be close to my darling Robin. I didn't relish being next to the new lovebirds – though it seemed Annabel wasn't bothered. I distinctly recalled that she had once succumbed to Steve's charms, too. Annabel obviously had a very short memory or deliberately chose to forget about it.

Robin was standing to attention in a full, regimental salute. He looked so handsome in his white dress uniform I thought I'd died and gone to heaven. Next to Robin, Eunice was belting out 'God Save the Queen' in a powerful soprano.

While I hesitated, Annabel moved fast. She scuttled over to the table and tried to introduce herself to Robin during the second verse but he just stared stoically ahead.

In the end, Annabel sheepishly gave up and took the empty chair on Eunice's right.

I was surprised that the proceedings had started without Douglas Fleming or Olive Larch. Their two places stood empty at the top table. I hoped she hadn't had another of her episodes, or perhaps Fleming had changed his mind about appearing in public so soon after his wife's death.

I kept wondering who could have made that mysterious phone call. Every time I glanced around the room – mainly to get a glimpse of Robin on my left – I met Steve's blue eyes staring steadily at me. Twice, he blew me a kiss and mouthed the words, 'You look *hot!*'

'*God*, this is endless,' Annabel muttered, as the anthem ground on to a third verse, and then a fourth. The singing became less strident as voices dropped off, one-by-one. Only the Women's Institute, who knew the words to all six verses, gamely carried on.

An unexpected trip around the drum kit, punctuated by a crash of the cymbals all but drowned out the final verse, followed by thunderous applause that grew even louder when Douglas Fleming walked in with Olive Larch on his arm. She looked very nice in a sparkling pale blue ensemble and tiny tiara in her cropped hair.

It would appear that the widower was not prostrate with grief after all.

'Please welcome your hosts. . . .' Mr Evans paused, cupping his ear for *another* drum roll from the band. 'Douuuuglas Fleming and Olllllive Larch!'

More applause followed. A bread roll sailed across the room and landed in the middle of the dance floor. Unfortunately our table was tucked in the corner so I couldn't see who threw it though I noted that Topaz leapt to her feet, eyes darting left, right and centre. It would seem she had been right to expect trouble.

When I turned to Robin again, I realized he was fussing over Eunice who sat rigidly upright, clutching a butter knife. Her face had turned an unattractive mottled red. Beads of sweat were accumulating on her brow. Annabel grabbed a copy of the *Mollusc Monthly* and started to flap it at Eunice's head.

'She doesn't like that,' Robin snapped, and snatched the leaflet from Annabel's hands.

'I was only trying—'

'Don't panic!' Steve hoisted himself out of his chair. His bulk seemed to get tangled up in the tablecloth. Fortunately, Topaz managed to hold the hem and save the place settings.

'Medic coming through!' Steve cried. 'Keep breathing, doll.' He knelt beside Eunice. 'I'll take over now. Head between the knees, luv.'

'Thank you. I'll go and fetch her wrap from the car.' Robin turned to me. 'Vicky, a word in private, please.'

Robin wanted to talk to me, *alone*! I stood up to follow.

'I'm coming, too,' said Annabel.

'I think you'd better stay and save our seats,' I said quickly. 'The event was overbooked and there'll be latecomers.'

Leaving Annabel to pout, I hurried after Robin and found him waiting for me in a small alcove at the bottom of the stairs.

Even though the circumstances were highly inappropriate, I couldn't help hoping that Robin would sweep me into his arms saying, 'Vicky, I can't stand it any longer.' He'd pull me close to his manly chest, uttering, 'You're so beautiful. Much more beautiful than Annabel. Say you'll be mine.'

'We've got a problem,' he said.

I came back to earth with a bang. 'We have?'

'Are the rumours about Douglas Fleming and Olive Larch, true?'

'I haven't heard anything.'

'Perhaps your pretty friend might know?'

'The one with the bionic woman contact lenses?' I heard myself say, then wished I hadn't sounded so catty.

Robin smiled at that remark – *I love making him laugh* – but his expression quickly changed to one of concern. 'Mum told me she filled you in on Auntie's health problems so I don't need to tell you what might happen if Fleming doesn't keep his promise.'

A worm of foreboding began to grow in the bottom of my stomach. 'What promise?'

'Auntie told me you'd insisted that Fleming never stopped loving her.' Robin's voice held a hint of accusation. 'Is that true?'

'Not . . . not . . . in those exact words.'

'She only needs the *slightest* encouragement,' Robin said, exasperated.

'I didn't know.' I felt slightly annoyed. Surely he wasn't blaming *me* for Eunice's state of mind?

'If he marries someone else . . .' Robin took a deep breath. 'I'm afraid of what she might do.'

Suddenly, I saw Eunice at St Peter's again and her euphoria at Douglas Fleming's eligible status; the way she had shown up at his office with a plateful of biscuits all dressed up like a dog's dinner. The phone calls she claimed Fleming had made and her jealous reaction to Olive Larch.

Good grief*! What if she tried to get rid of Olive?*

I looked at Robin's face. It was etched with anguish. 'Sorry,' he said. 'I shouldn't be burdening you with my troubles.'

'You're not at all. Really,' I said, trying hard not to look thrilled. I *wanted* to be burdened by Robin.

'I'm away so much and Mum and Auntie don't really get along.' Robin reached out and took my hand. 'And then she's always in trouble with the police. Don't you reporters know people in the police force who could occasionally pull in a favour?'

'Well, it depends what it is,' I said.

'I just wish someone would keep an eye on her. Do you know of anyone who might?'

'Me!' I cried. The words had tumbled out of my mouth before I could stop them. *Idiot, Vicky, idiot!* When I'd originally thought of offering my services, I'd had no idea that Eunice had some form of mental problem.

'You really mean that? I don't know how to thank you.' Robin lifted my hand to his lips and kissed it. I'd expected to feel a frisson of *je ne sais quoi*, but felt absolutely nothing. I was obviously still in shock at the gargantuan task I'd just let myself in for.

'Just check on her every day and make sure she *always* takes her medication.'

Medication! 'Of course.'

'You'll have to get that from Dr Bodger in Newton Abbot.'

'But, that's miles away,' I said. 'What's wrong with Dr Frost?'

'She can't stand him.' Robin dropped my hand. 'I'm going back to the table but you wait here for a few moments. I don't want Auntie to think we were talking about her.'

'What about her wrap?'

'She didn't bring one.' And with that, Robin was gone.

It was with a mixture of optimism and dread that I counted to twenty before returning to our table. True, I loved the fact that

Robin felt indebted to me and that we would be in daily contact when he went back to HMS *Dauntless*. But I was deeply uncomfortable about this so-called keeping an eye on Eunice that I had promised so rashly to do. I was an investigative journalist, not a nanny. Somehow, I felt just a tiny bit taken advantage of. Perhaps this was what it was like to be in a relationship? *Love me; love my family.*

With that happy thought, I walked back to join my man.

17

The ballroom-cum-gymnasium was in virtual darkness when I stumbled back to my chair. A projector was trained on the only blank wall available above the makeshift bar.

An air of restless expectancy filled the room as someone onstage fiddled with a portable CD player – presumably the same machine that initially blasted out Cuban music – in an attempt to find a specific track from a Dionne Warwick CD.

I could have slipped quietly into my chair had it not been where Topaz had dumped her rucksack, which fell to the floor with a loud thud. 'I didn't want *him* sitting next to me,' she said in a low voice.

To my astonishment, the 'him' in question was none other than DS Probes. It certainly explained Topaz's childish gesture with her rucksack. The two were very distant cousins and had enjoyed a brief fling for which Topaz seemed to feel nothing now but disdain.

I stole a glance at Probes and, even in the poor light, had to admit he was one man who *did* look very handsome out of uniform, especially with his ginger hair fashionably coiffed in stiff spikes.

Accompanied by Dionne Warwick's tearjerker, 'That's What Friends Are For' the slide show finally stuttered into action. Of course, I'd written Sammy Larch's obituary, but even I wasn't prepared to see just how big a role the old boy had played in the Gipping community during his ninety-five years on this earth.

From discovering his first snail in a Devon hedgebank at age five, we witnessed not just Sammy's accomplishments in the snail world, but his dalliance with other Devon country pursuits – pole climbing worm charming, the highly dangerous flaming tar barrel racing, and even a brief flirtation with hedge jumping.

As the show ended and the lights went up to tumultuous applause, a quick glimpse around the room showed there wasn't a dry eye in the house. Even Topaz had streaks of black mascara running down her cheeks.

Given Sammy Larch's unpopularity when alive, I was once again reminded of how even a cantankerous old man, previously reviled in life, could assume a saint-like status after death.

Olive, Fleming and Mr Evans made their way on stage to stand alongside the band. Mr Evans handed Olive the cordless microphone but she stood there, frozen.

Several moments dragged by. Someone in the audience coughed. Another bread roll sailed through the air and landed at her feet. A voice called out, 'Get on with it, luv.'

Fleming threw his arm around her shoulder and took the microphone. 'I know that Olive joins me in thanking you all for coming here tonight.'

I glanced over at Eunice and saw her stiffen. Robin patted her hand.

'It's a strange feeling being up here without my dearly departed Scarlett . . .' Douglas Fleming paused, seemingly close to tears. 'But I'm sure, knowing her as you all do, she would have wanted us to carry on and have a good time.' He bit his lip and closed his eyes as if reliving some painful memory. Olive gently squeezed his arm in sympathy.

The room was silent. You could have heard the proverbial pin drop until a voice cried, 'When's the funeral?'

'Scarlett's obituary will be in the *Gazette* tomorrow,' said Fleming. 'Tonight is very—'

'I heard she'd been buried already,' came another voice from the floor. This prompted cries of disbelief and outrage. I heard 'open casket!' 'London caterer!' and 'thirteen-pan steel band.'

'It's a travesty!' shouted Phyllis Fairweather seated at the Women's Institute table as the other members started banging on the table with their spoons.

Hadn't I warned Douglas Fleming there would be trouble?

'It's what she wanted!' Fleming's voice cracked with anguish. 'Who am I to take away her last dying request?'

Unfortunately, I was too far away from the stage to really see Fleming's expression. He certainly sounded upset but if you ask me, he seemed to be putting on quite a performance. His audience certainly bought it, but I wasn't sure if I did.

'Ladies and Gentlemen. *Please!*' Mr Evans took back the microphone. 'Some respect. This is a very tragic situation but as Scarlett would have said, "Let the party go on", and it must, because tonight we have a very special announcement. Barry?'

The words 'Larch Legacy' flew around the room creating mass speculation on who was going to get the award. I looked over at Dave who had already got to his feet and was straightening his bow tie.

Barry Fir, aka Hogmeat, retrieved an enormous fake cardboard cheque the size of a small table from the side of the stage. Wonderguts began an enthusiastic – but short – drum roll as Ronnie Binns, crouching low and snapping photos, darted toward the stage. He promptly collided with Tony who had set up his tripod in the corner.

Olive pulled out a sheet of paper and began to read, 'It is with great pleasure—' her hands were shaking, 'That I am able to award the Larch Legacy and a check for five hundred pounds to—' Another crash of drums, 'The Hedge-cutters of Gipping-on-Plym!'

The cutters tables exploded with cheers and whoops of joy. I thought I'd misheard and turned to Topaz. 'What did she say?'

'Sssh,' Topaz hissed. 'I'm trying to listen.'

'My father was always grateful to the cutters for preserving the beauty and heritage of our Devon hedgerows,' Olive said in a halting voice. 'For helping keep the hedgerows safe for God's small creatures and in particular, the snails we love. For the little red berries . . .'

As Olive droned on, my heart plunged further and further into my boots. I felt incredibly sorry for Dave who held his face in his hands, but more sorry for myself.

I had committed a journalistic snafu of monumental proportions.

I had taken a story given to me at face value.

My career was ruined.

Thank God we were seated at the rear of the room so I couldn't see the reaction on the *Gazette* table, but I could definitely see Dave's growing despair. Comforted by his cronies, there was a lot of alcohol being passed around – and a rain of bread rolls being thrown at Jack Webster as he swaggered to the stage.

It was all too much for Dave. He leapt to his feet. 'You bloody thief!'

Topaz grabbed her rucksack and stood up, too, but promptly sat back down when Mr Evans grabbed the microphone again shouting, 'Thannnnk you, Olive. Ladies! Gentlemen! The buffet is ready in the next room. Load up your plates and let's get this show on the road!'

The spattering of applause was swiftly drowned out by the mass exodus to the adjoining dining room and the promise of food provided by Helen Parker, who had taken over my former landlady's catering business, Cradle to Coffin Catering.

'Vicky?' said Steve. 'Can I bring you a plate of something?'

'No, I'm fine, but thanks.' My appetite had completely gone.

'You've got to eat, doll. Just a few nibbles?'

'Yes, *please*,' said Topaz pointedly. 'And you'd better be fast. I'm told it was frightfully under-catered.'

Steve needed no further encouragement and set off in the direction of the dining room. Robin followed suit, leaving Eunice staring stonily into her lap.

I sat there in a stupor. I dreaded going anywhere near the buffet table where I was bound to bump into Wilf.

'I *told* you there would be problems!' Topaz gloated.

'What's she talking about?' muttered Annabel.

'Nothing,' I said miserably. 'Aren't you going to get some food?'

'We're waiting for the stampede to be over,' Annabel said, leaning in to Probes. 'Aren't we, Colin?'

Colin?

'Evening, Vicky,' said Probes. 'Ms Potter.'

I tried to speak but was overcome by an inexplicable attack of shyness.

'Oh, hello. I didn't recognize you out of uniform,' Topaz said with a sniff. Other than myself, Probes was the only person who knew Topaz's true identity. Why he kept her secret was one of life's great mysteries.

'Well?' Annabel gestured to Robin's empty seat. 'What's going on with the sailor?'

'Sssh,' I said, quickly pointing to Eunice who now had her eyes closed.

'She's not listening. Everyone saw you follow him out into the foyer.' Annabel gave an indulgent laugh. 'Colin said you were huddled cosily together under the nook at the bottom of the stairs.'

'I d-d-didn't say it quite like that.' Probes had the grace to blush. 'Ms Lake asked if I'd seen you and I said I had.'

'Personally I think you're wasting your time.' Annabel

glanced over at Eunice again and lowered her voice. 'He's a bit of a mummy's boy.'

'He's just attentive and kind,' I said, though I was beginning to think Annabel might be right.

'Colin has very kindly offered to help me with my exposé.' Annabel picked up a bread roll and began to pull it apart. 'He's with the Drug Action Team in Plymouth.' Of course, I already knew that.

'As a m-m-matter of fact, one of the reasons I am here tonight is because—'

'You should ask him about *Spain*, Vicky.'

My mouth went dry. 'Spain? Why? What for?'

'You know, silly.' Annabel rolled her eyes. 'Scarlett Fleming?'

'Oh, yes. Scarlett Fleming. No. Actually, I'm fine.'

'Vicky e-mailed the Foreign and Commonwealth Office,' said Annabel, as if I wasn't sitting right next to her. 'She'll wait forever, won't she Colin?'

'If I can be of assistance—'

'You'd better get to the buffet, quick.' Steve materialized at our table with two plates laden with steak and kidney pie, creamed mashed potatoes, and carrots. 'The food is running low already. Where's Topaz?'

'I thought she was with you.' I hadn't noticed her slip away. 'She's probably in the ladies' loo.'

'Her food will get cold.' Steve took Topaz's empty chair next to me and edged it close. 'Do you want some of mine, doll?'

'We're off.' Annabel dragged Probes to his feet. 'Come on, Colin.'

'Spain, you say?' said Probes thoughtfully.

I began to rise. 'Wait for me—'

'Hang on, doll. I want to talk to you.' Steve put his hand firmly on my knee. His touch was electric and sent shivers down my spine. I was acutely aware of the smell of Old Spice and antiseptic. 'God, you look gorgeous tonight.'

131

'Your food is getting cold.'

'Maybe I don't care,' he said, staring at me with lust in his eyes.

'Honestly, Steve, you're incorrigible.' I couldn't help laughing. 'You're here with Topaz and hitting on me. Don't you have any shame?'

Steve shrugged and gave me an impish grin. 'She invited me and who am I to turn a lady down but' – his lips brushed my ear – 'if you want the honest to God truth, she frightens me. She's the one woman I would never want to be alone with. Unlike you.'

'And what about Annabel?' I said, reminding him of his swift liaison with her not so long ago and one I only knew about because Annabel bore the telltale morning after signs of stubble burn on her face.

'She forced me,' he said in deadly earnest. 'But *you're* different.'

'Because I'm not interested.' I tried to stand up but Steve kept hold of my knee.

'Dinner. Tomorrow night. I'll pick you up.'

'I'm busy.'

'Sunday! Come on, doll! You're breaking my heart.'

'Somehow I doubt it.' I removed Steve's hand from my knee. 'Enjoy your pie.'

'I won't give up,' he called out, as I headed into the dining room.

There was quite a feast. In addition to the usual Marks & Spencer cook-from-frozen nibbles provided by Cradle to Coffin Catering, the Women's Institute had contributed homemade salads and baked goods. Naturally, each contributor's name was written on a small white flag and stuck into the relevant dish. I noted that no one had touched Amelia Webster's anchovy and gherkin piccalilli.

Apparently the delicious steak and kidney pie – served in commercial-sized stainless steel chafer dishes – was actually made from scratch by Gillian Briggs, who used to be a cook in the Women's Royal Navy back in the 1970s.

The queue was a long one. As I tried to find the end, snatches of conversation drifted toward me: 'Don't eat the piccalilli,' 'I heard Scarlett had plastic surgery,' and 'It didn't take Fleming long to get his feet under the table.'

At this last provocative remark coming from Pam Green, director of *all* Gipping Bard productions, I pretended to readjust my right sandal – no mean feat given the stabbing pain I endured from my whalebone corset in trying to bend over.

'That's an unkind thing to say, Pam.' Barbara had her back to me. 'Dougie has always been fond of Olive.'

'Fond of her money, you mean,' said Pam darkly. 'I heard he was handling the Larch millions.'

'I doubt it, dear,' Barbara said. 'Olive is my best friend and I'm quite sure she would have told me.' She paused for a moment, '*Who* said that? Was it Ruth?'

'I'm afraid I can't say,' Pam said somewhat smugly. 'But Scarlett told me Dougie wanted them to be friends with the Larche's even though she couldn't stand Sammy.' Pam lowered her voice. 'He used to pinch her bottom, you know.'

'That's not true—'

'He was *determined* to reach his one hundredth birthday and get a telegram from the queen,' Pam forged on. 'How *convenient* that Sammy died when he did.'

'I'm sure he didn't *plan* on falling down the stairs. Pam.' I detected a note of irritation in Barbara's voice.

'And Dougie losing his wife so soon afterward . . . well . . .' Pam turned to stare at Fleming who was posing arm in arm with Olive for Ronnie Binns – *since when had he become the official photographer?* 'He's hardly the grieving widower, is he?'

I had to admit she had a point. Fleming seemed to have made quite a recovery after his emotional breakdown on stage as he laughed and joked for the camera.

'I really don't believe in idle tittle-tattle,' sniffed Barbara, the queen of gossip. 'Excuse me. I must get some trifle.'

She drifted off leaving Pam Green to corner Florence Tossell with her speculations.

'Vicky! Over here!' Probes was holding three empty plates. 'I've saved you a place.'

Surprised and delighted – the queue was long – I squeezed in beside him, ignoring grumbles of 'The end of the line is around the corner' and 'You can't push in.'

'Where's Annabel?' I said as Probes handed me a plate.

'She went to make a phone call.' Probes stared down into my eyes – I didn't remember him being so tall. His eyes were a very dark blue with unusually long, brown lashes. I'd always thought natural redheads had sandy coloured eyelashes and wondered if he wore mascara or even had them dyed.

'You look l-l-lovely tonight,' he said, turning red.

'Thank you.' Even though I'd heard this compliment many times, I actually blushed, too. 'It's Annabel's dress and she did my makeup.'

'I know. She told me.' He grinned. His dimples really were quite charming. 'You're very difficult to pin down,' Probes went on. 'I was hoping—'

'What are you doing here?' Robin stood in front of me holding two plates of steak and kidney pie. He looked horrified. 'You didn't leave Auntie alone, did you?'

'Of course not,' I said quickly. 'Steve was there.' Frankly, I hadn't realized my keeping-an-eye-on-Auntie duties had already begun.

Robin scanned the room anxiously. 'Where's Olive Larch?'

I looked, too. There seemed to be no sign of her. 'I'm sure everything is all right,' I said, more for my own benefit. Robin's panic was contagious.

'Is there a problem, sir?' Probes switched into his concerned police officer mode.

'No. Why would there be?' Robin said rather rudely. 'I

thought Vicky had volunteered to keep an eye on my aunt but obviously I was wrong.'

'I'm sorry.' I really didn't know what else to say.

'Excuse me.' And without even his customary nautical salute, Robin charged off.

'What was all that about?' said Probes.

'Nothing.' I actually felt upset. Barbara walked past us with a bowl of trifle. 'Hold my plate,' I said. 'I'll be right back.'

I caught up with Barbara in the doorway. 'Olive went to powder her nose,' she said, in answer to my question. 'Why?'

'Just wondered.' I tore after Robin but when I reached our table, Steve was by himself. There was no sign of Eunice or Topaz. Even her rucksack was gone.

Robin was practically hyperventilating. 'Where the hell can Auntie be?' He turned to Steve – whom I noted had almost polished off Topaz's pie as well as his own. 'You!' Robin barked. 'What was your name again?'

'Steve,' he said placidly. 'Keep your hair on. No need to fret. Mrs Pratt went to powder her nose.'

Robin and I looked at each other in horror and chorused, 'Ladies!'

We'd barely moved an inch when a deafening Klaxon horn exploded into life. It was the loudest alarm I'd ever heard. For a moment, no one moved, everything dissolved into chaos. Plates laden with steak and kidney pie splattered to the ground to join the trifle and other items on the menu.

Steve snapped to attention. Whipping a white headband emblazoned with a red cross from his tuxedo pocket, he tied it around his forehead. With no one near enough to grab the tablecloth, place settings, glasses, and bread rolls followed Steve in his wake as he dived into the action shouting, 'Medic! Make way for the Medic!'

Then, just as suddenly, the horn stopped. A series of loud spits and pops was followed by a hissing noise. Throughout the ballroom-cum-gymnasium, dozens of sprinklers began to discharge torrents of rank smelling water. There were screams from the ladies and a variety of colourful curses from the menfolk. Several yelled, 'Fire!' and – along with yours truly – slithered their way toward the foyer on a floor slick with buffet detritus.

On stage Hogmeat, Harris and the Wonderguts hastily packed away their electronic equipment – including Mr Evans's public announcement system.

'Do *not* panic. Stay calm.' Probes stood on top of a chair clutching a megaphone – obviously taken from the gym closet. 'There is no fire. I repeat. There is no fire.' But no one seemed to pay any attention.

Ronnie Binns dashed about taking more photographs. Clearly, his expensive camera was waterproof, too.

We reached the foyer only to find it was blocked by a massive brawl between cutters and jumpers who seemed oblivious to the fact that they were getting soaked to the skin.

In a large pool of water, Dave Randall was straddling Jack Webster, smearing his face with trifle. I had the stray thought that Tuxedo Temptations were going to be very unhappy tomorrow morning when ninety per cent of their suits were returned damaged.

I scanned the room for Robin, but it looked like he'd got to dry land before the alarm bell went off.

'Please make your way to the dining room,' Probes boomed through the megaphone, as he advanced toward the bottleneck by the foyer. 'I repeat. Make your way to the dining room.'

We duly turned around and trooped off to the dining room to find Mr Evans and lanky Simon Mears, leader of Gipping Boy Scouts, directing everyone through the open French doors and into the car park. There, Simon's wife Nicola – Brown Owl of First Gipping Brownie pack – was taking a roll call of sorts. Steve dashed about, administering what appeared to be smelling salts – judging by the violent reaction and swift recovery of each lady in need.

136

The shock that had ripped through Gipping Manor was now replaced by relieved laughter. I heard, 'the evening's still young' and 'wet T-shirt competition'. Several of the ladies' gowns, when wet, became transparent – much to the delight of the menfolk.

I spied Robin talking on his mobile phone. There was still no sign of Eunice. I was about to join him, but he pointed at the French doors and mouthed some kind of order. Presumably, that meant I was supposed to go back and find his wretched aunt. I was wet, cold, and beginning to have second thoughts about a future with Lieutenant Robin Berry.

Barbara hurried toward me. 'Have you seen Olive?' She was shivering and looked like a drowned rat. 'Dougie's worried sick. She never came back from the bathroom.'

My stomach flipped over. I'd seen the mixture of despair and envy on Eunice's face. After forty long years of unrequited love, who knew what she'd do to her rival? 'Wait here, Barbara. I'll find her.'

I set off in search of Olive Larch and prayed she had come to no harm but in truth, I feared the worst.

18

I ran as fast as my high heels allowed around the outside of the building and back into The Manor front entrance. Fortunately the sprinkler system had been switched off. Also, it had not extended to the corridor leading to the loos, which was bone dry.

I heard the shrieks even before I opened the door.

'What on earth's going on?' I cried, trying to make sense of what I saw before me.

Olive was sprawled on the floor in what I prayed was just a dead faint. She was clutching a pair of nail scissors in one hand. In the other was a crumpled brown paper bag.

Inside the stall I heard Eunice screaming as Topaz – fake cat's ears perched atop a black balaclava – gleefully wound a length of orange nylon binder twine around the stall door grab handle, presumably to prevent Eunice's escape.

Furious, she rattled the door yelling, 'Let me out. Let me out!'

'Shut up or you'll be sorry!' shouted Topaz. The hammering stopped. Eunice began to whimper.

I knelt down beside Olive and was relieved to find she had a pulse – and a surprisingly strong one, too.

'We've got to find Steve,' I said.

'Not we. *You.* My job is done.' Topaz had discarded the black skirt she'd worn to the gala. Around her waist was a wide handyman's belt that had several compartments bulging with all sorts of tools and gadgets.

'You're not going anywhere,' I said firmly. 'I want to know exactly what happened here.'

'Vicky? Is that you?' said Eunice in a tremulous voice.

'Sssh!' Topaz whispered. 'No names.'

'Yes, it's Vicky,' I said. 'Hold tight Eunice. Everything is going to be okay.'

'Take this.' Topaz retrieved a can of mace from her handyman belt. 'She might get violent. Wait.' She cocked her head. 'Can you hear a siren?'

'Probably the fire brigade. Was it you who set off the alarm?'

'Of course not,' Topaz said. 'But I told you there'd be trouble.' She removed her belt and thrust it back into the rucksack. 'I have to go.' She pulled out a small cylindrical object with a red tag. 'I was never here.'

'What's that?'

'It's a flare to mask my exit.' Topaz walked over to the bathroom window, which already stood wide open.

'No one will see you. They're all in the car park,' I said. 'And besides, using a flare will only attract attention.'

'You're right. Good point.'

'Vicky, Vicky,' Eunice whimpered from behind the stall door. 'Let me out. Please!'

'The Caped Kitten never takes chances.' Topaz said in a low voice. She pointed to Olive who had managed to sit up. Olive took one look at Topaz, let out a pathetic squeak, and promptly fainted away again.

And, with a swirl of her cape, Topaz clambered out of the open window and vanished.

Seconds later, DS Probes appeared in the doorway followed

by Robin, Steve and Barbara. 'What's going on here then?' he said.

'Auntie!' shouted Robin. 'Where are you?'

'Robin! Oh! Help!' Eunice became hysterical.

Barbara flew to Olive's side. 'Oh, oh! She's dead.'

Steve promptly dropped to his knees and skidded across the tiled floor to Olive in an impressive *Saturday Night Fever* move. 'I've got her, doll.'

'She fainted,' I said helplessly.

'What the *hell*?' Robin swung around to face me, his eyes flashed with anger. 'Who locked Auntie in the lavatory?'

'I don't know,' I lied, inwardly cursing Topaz and her stupidity. 'I just got here myself. Let's—'

'I'll do it.' Robin fumbled with the binder twine on the stall door but to no avail. Clearly, Topaz had not used a nautical knot.

'Allow me.' Probes stepped forward with his Swiss Army penknife and effortlessly sliced through the orange nylon cord.

Freed at last, Eunice burst out of the stall and tumbled into Robin's arms. 'Auntie! Thank God you are all right,' Robin said.

'I was trying to help her,' Eunice said feebly. 'But she attacked me.'

'Olive Larch *attacked* you?' Robin shot Olive a glance of pure venom.

'She would say that, wouldn't she?' Barbara shouted defiantly from Olive's corner.

'Are you calling my aunt a *liar*?' Robin seethed.

Probes caught my eye and I could have sworn I saw a flash of amusement. 'Did you see anything, Vicky?' he said, pulling out a small notebook from inside his drenched tuxedo – yet another tragedy for Tuxedo Temptations.

'When I got here Eunice was already locked in.' This was true. *Blast Topaz!*

'But, wait . . .' Probes frowned and returned to the stall door. He inspected the dangling piece of twine with his pencil and flipped it over. 'Who did this?'

'Well, Olive certainly couldn't,' said Barbara hotly. 'She was practically left for dead on this cold floor.'

'Hardly,' Robin snorted. 'She tried to kill Auntie with scissors! Look! She's got them in her hand!'

'I don't think Ms Larch is strong enough to lock anyone in the bathroom,' Steve said as he bathed Olive's forehead with a damp paper towel.

'If she didn't lock Auntie in,' said Robin contemptuously, 'who did?'

What was I to do? Even though Topaz's disguise was ridiculous, I just couldn't bring myself to blow her cover. It could lead to all sorts of complications. Knowing the citizens of Gipping-on-Plym as I did, they wouldn't forgive being taken for fools by stuck-up Ethel Turberville-Spat from The Grange. Much as I was tempted to tell Probes, I didn't want to get involved.

Olive began to tremble. 'I saw a dark creature,' she began. 'I think . . . I think . . . it was that thing that lives on the moors.'

'The what?' I said.

'It's a phantom wild cat rumoured to roam the moors,' said Steve.

Robin rolled his eyes. 'Nice try.'

'She's not the first person to have seen the Beast of Bodmin,' said Steve. He turned to Olive, adding gently, 'Was it a catlike creature, luv?' Olive nodded, her eyes filled with tears.

'On Bodmin *moor* in Cornwall,' Robin said with scorn. 'Not in the middle of Gipping-on-Plym.'

'But, I saw it,' she protested.

'I'm afraid we're going to have to press charges for assault,' Robin said.

'Assault? *Assault?*' Barbara shrieked.

'I'll get my solicitor on it first thing tomorrow morning.'

'This is a very serious allegation, Lieutenant Berry,' Probes said.

'I am aware of that,' said Robin. 'Of course, we might be willing to discuss an out-of-court settlement but—'

'Okay, okay, enough of the macho talk for one day. Let's get these ladies home,' Steve said firmly. 'It's all right for you sailor, you're not cold and wet. But Barbara and Vicky are. Whatever you say, Miss Larch and Mrs Pratt have suffered a nasty shock.' He clapped his hands. 'Let's go. *Now*.'

Robin scowled but to my surprise, followed Steve's orders. Taking Eunice's arm, they paused at the door. 'You'll be hearing from us, officer.'

'I was only trying to help,' whispered Eunice.

The foyer was swarming with firemen and uniformed police officers that were leading the brawlers away in handcuffs. Probes strolled over to greet familiar faces and lend a hand while I watched Olive's tearful reunion with Douglas Fleming. I had to admit he looked genuinely concerned.

'Vicky, you've got to help me!' Dave Randall called out, as a young constable with acne escorted him toward the exit. Seeing Dave brought back the full impact of the Larch Legacy snafu that I'd conveniently forgotten about.

I hastened to join him. 'Whatever happened?'

'I'm afraid I can't allow you to talk to the prisoner, Ms,' said the constable who looked as if he couldn't be more than twelve.

'It was all agreed. Sammy promised.' Dave shook his head with disbelief. 'You've got to believe me.'

'I do.' And, to my surprise, I really did.

'*She* did it,' Dave said. '*She* never liked me and *she* made him change his mind.'

'Who? Olive?'

Dave stopped walking. 'No. Scarlett Fleming.'

Scarlett Fleming? But before I could ask him why and how the dead woman could possibly be involved, the young constable bundled Dave into one of two waiting custody vans and the doors were slammed in my face.

As I watched the convoy peel out of Gipping Manor car park,

I realized I hadn't seen Annabel after the fire alarm went off. Surely she wouldn't leave without me?

Apart from one of those ridiculously tiny Smart cars that had slipped effortlessly into a narrow space reserved for leaving baby strollers, it looked like everyone had left.

I began to worry. Perhaps Annabel was waiting for me in the warmth of the BMW? I hurried back into the street where we'd parked earlier but to my growing fury, saw her car had gone.

I couldn't believe it. I had no money. No mobile phone. No coat. Annabel had left me stranded! It was at least a two-mile walk back to Factory Terrace and my feet were killing me in Sadie's shoes. *Blast Annabel!*

I burst into tears and started to hobble home but had only gone a few yards when I heard a car behind me.

Without giving a thought to my safety, I turned and flagged it down.

The Smart car pulled up alongside. The electric window purred open and a familiar voice said, 'Can I give you a lift?'

It was DS Probes.

19

With the heater on high, the car smelled of Probes's distinctive musky scent. Wrapped in a green tartan blanket, I slowly began to thaw – though the pain in my rib cage was becoming unbearable.

'Factory Terrace, isn't it?' he said, as the little car sped along the narrow country roads with surprising speed.

'Thank you.' I hoped he wouldn't start to grill me about the bathroom incident. I was determined to speak to Topaz first.

He handed me a hip flask. 'This will warm you up.'

I took a sip. It was cherry brandy and burned a path from my throat to my stomach. I felt better instantly.

Probes turned on the radio. The sound of soothing jazz music filled the car. Perhaps he didn't feel much like talking, either.

The evening had been an unmitigated disaster in every way. I wasn't sure what had upset me the most. Annabel abandoning me; my handsome Robin turning out to be such an idiot and – *God* – how could I have allowed myself to get talked into keeping an eye on his dreadful aunt – though I had to admit, I did feel a little bit sorry for her. And then there was Topaz-the-vigilante

144

leaving me to hold the proverbial baby. All this paled into insignificance as I imagined my reception tomorrow morning at the *Gazette* over the Larch Legacy snafu. Wilf's fury! Pete's scorn! Annabel's glee!

I forced myself to think of something else, something trivial, and turned my attention to studying Probes's car.

The Smart car inside was even smaller than it appeared on the outside – if that were physically possible. My knees were squashed against the glove compartment but Probes had to drive with his legs open embracing the steering wheel. His spiked hairstyle brushed the roof causing him to hunch over in the driver's seat.

'My other car is a Porsche,' he joked.

I was startled. He must be telepathic. 'This car is *small*,' I said.

'True. But let's say I've had a few *improvements* made to the engine.' Probes gave a chuckle, instantly changed down to third gear and we accelerated to sixty miles an hour in seconds. 'Handy when pursuing suspects down narrow country roads,' he said, navigating the twisty lanes with ease, 'And of course, no one expects a plainclothes copper to drive one.'

'You got a promotion?'

'Detective Sergeant,' Probes said. 'Thanks to you. Don't you remember?'

Of course I did. Even though it hadn't been intentional, I suffered the usual pang of guilt about helping a copper in any shape or form. Dad would be so disappointed.

'Congratulations,' I said. 'Does this mean you've been transferred back to Gipping?'

'I'm still with the Drug Action Team in Plymouth.' Probes cleared his throat. 'I came because . . . I was h-h-hoping you'd be here tonight.'

My stomach filled with butterflies. Out of uniform, Probes was very attractive – quite sexy actually – but he was *still* a copper.

'I really wanted to thank you properly,' Probes went on. 'I've been trying to take you out for a curry for weeks but you're so busy, I can never pin you down. And I'd really like to.'

'What, pin me down?' I said, and then wished I hadn't. 'That came out wrong. Sorry.'

He laughed. 'Freudian slip, perhaps?'

'Of course not,' I said quickly, but an image of Probes doing just that popped into my head. I felt my face turn red and was grateful that it was too dark for him to see it.

'Pity,' he muttered.

We drove on in an awkward silence until Probes said, 'What's all this about Scarlett Fleming and Spain?'

'It's nothing really.' *Blast Annabel and her big mouth!*

'It's no trouble.' I could sense his eyes on me and wished he'd keep them on the road. 'Annabel mentioned a yoga retreat on the Costa Brava.'

'Not the Costa Brava,' I said firmly. *Never the Costa Brava!* 'I believe it was closer to the Pyrenees Mountains. That's in *France.*'

'Yes, I know. Annabel said that you'd already contacted the Foreign and Commonwealth Office,' Probes said. 'Do you think there is something fishy about Mrs Fleming's death?'

Yes, of course I did! *But, not if it meant Probes would start to ask awkward questions.* 'Not at all. A few ladies were interested in taking up yoga and were curious as to where it was. Mr Fleming said he didn't know.'

'He seemed to be enjoying himself this evening,' Probes said. 'All things considered.'

'He was putting on a brave face. Stiff upper lip and all that.' Of course, I agreed with Probes one hundred per cent but he was still a policeman – no, now a *sergeant* – and that was even more of a reason why I didn't want him nosing around in Spain or France, for that matter.

'Can't hurt to make a few inquiries.'

'No need for that,' I said quickly.

'Why?' Probes said. 'Is it because of Lieutenant Berry?'

'Of course not,' I said, astonished. 'What's he got to do with yoga?'

'I know these naval chaps get jealous when they're away at sea.'

Surely Probes didn't think Robin and I were an item? The funny thing was that twenty-four hours ago, I would have been happy with that possibility. Now, I couldn't care less.

'We're just friends,' I said. Maybe not even that.

'Look, Vicky . . .' Probes took a deep breath. 'Your personal life is your own business, but just be careful, that's all.' When I didn't comment, he went on. 'Eunice Pratt is trouble. When I worked in Gipping, she was a nightmare. It wasn't just the endless petitions, either. And now I've met the nephew . . .'

He didn't finish his sentence, but he didn't need to. Much as I hated to admit it, Robin and Eunice were like two peas in a pod. 'Mrs Pratt is not well,' was all I managed to say.

'But it's her nephew who wants to press charges.'

'I'm sure he didn't mean it.' But I knew Robin had. It wasn't the first time I'd heard him threaten legal action for monetary gain.

'It looks like the party has continued here,' said Probes. We had pulled up outside Factory Terrace where the street was lined with cars. Many were double-parked.

Probes turned off the engine. 'Do you want me to escort you inside?'

'No thanks.' I suddenly felt nervous. The atmosphere between us seemed charged with electricity. With a jolt, I knew exactly what it was – the same kind I'd felt with Steve only a hundred times more intense. Alarmed, I lunged for the door handle but Probes leapt out and – given the size of the car – was opening my passenger door before I had time to blink.

'Keep the blanket.' He took my arm and helped me out.

147

His touch felt warm and firm. 'Vicky, there *was* just one more thing.'

I knew it! Probes had used that sneaky *Columbo* ploy. I braced myself for the Spanish inquisition – no pun intended.

'If there is something you aren't telling me about tonight at Gipping Manor, for whatever reason, I'm asking you to reconsider.' He gently readjusted the tartan blanket over my shoulders. 'Remember, setting off a fire alarm is a punishable offence.'

'I know.'

Probes bent down and kissed my forehead. 'Goodnight.' My skin felt on fire. Horrified, I tore into the house without a backward glance though I sensed he was still watching me.

Fortunately, I managed to sneak upstairs without being seen. As with most parties, the guests all tended to congregate in the kitchen and Chez Evans was no different. I could hear good old Frankie belting out 'New York, New York'.

In my bedroom I struggled to get out of Annabel's dress. She had been right about Mrs Evans's sewing efforts.

Still furious with Annabel's selfishness, I grabbed a pair of scissors from my desk and savagely cut the material from bodice to hem.

Thinking of scissors, my mind flew to Olive Larch. The pair she'd clutched in her hand – although small – were still lethal. I couldn't imagine her attacking Eunice but I certainly could see her trying to defend herself.

As I climbed into bed, sleep refused to come. My rib cage had nasty welts from Sadie's bustier and I still could not get warm despite being wrapped in the tartan blanket, which smelled of Probes.

My mind drifted to Dave's parting comment. How could Scarlett Fleming have changed old man Larch's mind, and why? With both Sammy and Scarlett dead, he'd better have concrete proof that the Legacy was meant for the jumpers.

I was also struck by the fact that Scarlett Fleming was

now the subject of yet another mystery to say nothing of her grieving husband's behaviour at the Gala tonight. It was quite obvious there was something going on between him and Olive Larch.

I closed my eyes. I wasn't done with Fleming. Yet.

20

Having spent a restless night, haunted by dreams of Probes covered in trifle playing the drums, I got up early and crept downstairs.

Fortunately, Mr and Mrs Evans were still fast asleep. I peeped into the open sitting room door and saw a mass of empty glasses and bottles of half-drunk gin, wine and a keg of beer. There were going to be a lot of hangovers this Saturday morning.

The kitchen wasn't much better. There was no bread left in the stoneware pot and only enough milk to make a cup of tea. In the end I ate dry cereal.

Scribbling a note to Mrs Evans, I mentioned I was off to Plymouth that night and if she wanted me to give Sadie a parcel, I'd happily deliver it.

I had a slight headache but that was nothing compared to the feeling of utter dread that had settled in the pit of my stomach at the prospect of seeing Wilf.

The *Gazette* looked the worse for wear, too. In the window the inflatable snail's shell lay limp and puckered. In reception, the remnants of yesterday's all-day party were still in evidence.

Tony was jumping childishly on the semi-collapsed helium balloons, trying to pop them. Every time there was a loud bang, Barbara clutched her head in pain.

'Where is today's *Gazette*?' I said anxiously.

'Wilf took them all upstairs,' said Barbara. 'Dreadful snafu on the front page, dear.'

Tony strolled over and thrust a copy in front of me. 'Kept this one back for you,' he said with a smirk. 'Nice photograph of Randall.'

Written in bold in gigantic font was LARCH LEGACY NAMED! Under more headlines – TIRELESS PETITIONER TRIUMPHS AT LAST and LARCH LEAP IS NEW JUMP FOR OLYMPIC HOPEFULS – a grinning Dave stood in front of a flourishing yew hedge wearing a moleskin jacket emblazoned with the logo,

Team GB
Let's Jump
London Olympics 2012

'Looks like someone is going to be writing retractions and apologies today,' Tony went on. 'The phone hasn't stopped ringing all morning with indignant cutters and baffled readers.'

'It's not ringing now,' I said defensively.

'That's because I had to take it off the hook,' said Tony.

'Oh, be quiet, Tony,' Barbara snapped. 'Haven't you got something better to do?'

'I'll tell Wilf you're here.' Tony sauntered out of reception.

'If you want my opinion,' said Barbara. 'I'd stick to your guns. I've known Dave since he was a nipper, and if he said Sammy Larch promised him the money, then he did just that.'

'Did Olive say there had been a mistake?' I said hopefully.

'Olive doesn't bother herself about money.' Barbara rubbed her forehead. 'I really must take another aspirin.'

'Are you feeling all right?' I said noting the dark rings under her eyes.

'I was up most of the night with Olive,' Barbara said with a sigh. 'Poor thing was very shaken up. I don't care what that *dreadful* sailor said, the Pratt woman tried to suffocate Olive to death. Her health isn't good – and now she's begun to hallucinate . . .'

'The Beast of Bodmin?'

Barbara nodded, but wished she hadn't. Clutching her head again, she sank down into one of the two brown leatherette chairs. 'It sent her over the edge. I'm very worried about her state of mind. Douglas seems to be the only person who she feels safe with and if that *dreadful* sailor presses charges . . .'

'Pssst!' came a voice from the nook. Barbara rolled her eyes. 'Sorry. I forgot to mention Topaz has been waiting for you, though why she thinks there is any privacy in that nook is anyone's guess.' Since Barbara liked to maintain that the flimsy plywood structure built across the far corner of reception was extremely private, it just showed how severe her headache was this morning.

Topaz peeped out of the brown-spangled curtains. 'Over here. Hurry.'

'I suppose I'd better put the telephone back on the hook,' Barbara grumbled, taking a silver hip flask out of her cardigan pocket. 'There is only one way I am going to get through today. Would you like some?'

'No thanks.' I slipped inside the nook. Topaz was sitting on one of the plastic chairs dressed in her medieval serge uniform and white-lace mop cap.

'*Good grief!* What happened to you?' I said. Her face was covered in telltale red splotches. Despite Steve's protests that he never wanted to be alone with Topaz, he'd clearly changed his mind. *Men!*

Topaz frowned. 'What are you talking about?'

'Your face? It's all red.' I bet she'd try and deny it.

Topaz thoughtfully touched her chin. 'Oh, *that*.'

'A food allergy, perhaps?'

'No. I kissed that Steve chappy,' Topaz said with a dismissive wave of her hand. 'Why? Are you jealous?'

'Of course not.'

'For a man, he's a frightfully good kisser but I have to say that pillow talk is a complete waste of time,' said Topaz. 'He refused to tell me a thing. Are you going to sit down?'

'Can't stop. I've only got a few minutes. What kind of information were you hoping to get from him?'

Topaz shrugged. 'Just snippets really. In my new role as the Caped Kitten it's frightfully important that I'm ahead of the game.'

'What game?'

'Being in the loop,' said Topaz. 'Steve hears lots of snippets but he said he'd only tell a real reporter.' She slumped back in her chair and scowled. 'I told him I worked for the *Gazette* but he didn't believe me.'

'I'm sure if it's a life-or-death situation, we'll soon know about it.'

'Aren't you a tiny bit curious?'

'About snippets? No,' I said. 'But I *am* curious about what really happened in the ladies' loo last night.'

Topaz fell silent. She began to twiddle with the lock of hair that always seemed to dangle out of the front of her mop cap.

'Look, I don't mean to be rude,' I said. 'But I really have to go upstairs.'

'I was trying to think,' she snapped. 'All right. I'll tell you what happened in the ladies' loo if you tell Steve that I'm a real reporter.'

'An undercover reporter,' I corrected her.

'Sssh.' Topaz jabbed her finger at the brown-spangled curtains. 'I bet Barbara is listening.'

'Barbara already knows.' I sat down at the table and took out my notebook and pencil. 'Start from the beginning.'

'You promise, you *swear* you'll tell Steve?' Topaz extended her hand. 'Shake on it.'

'I promise.' I took it – taking care to keep my other hand hidden behind my back with my fingers crossed. Where Topaz was concerned, I didn't want to promise anything. 'You've got five minutes to tell me what happened in the ladies' loo.'

'Well, it all started with Annabel.'

'*Annabel*? What's she got to do with it?'

'You think she's your best friend, but she isn't.'

'Go on.'

'Remember when that sailor was in such a fizz over his missing aunt?'

How could I forget? 'Yes. Go on.'

'Well, I thought I'd go and look for her, too,' Topaz said. 'I'm not *just* a vigilante, I like to do nice things for old people.'

'So you went to the bathroom . . .'

'That was afterward. On my *way* to the ladies, I overheard Annabel talking to you'll never guess who.'

'Topaz . . .' I said in a threatening voice. One of my pet peeves was her insistence on playing childish guess-who games.

'Ronnie Binns.' Topaz beamed.

'I'm sure she wasn't happy about that.' I already knew that Ronnie had been trying to corner Annabel for days.

'But she *was*!' Topaz said triumphantly. 'There was a funny alcove covered by a heavy dark blue curtain outside the gents. I saw her drag him behind there.'

'*Drag* him.' I laughed. 'Behind a *curtain!*' Like everyone who'd experienced Ronnie's personal hygiene problem, the idea was ludicrous.

'So I crept up to the curtain to listen and you'll never guess—'

'Topaz!'

'Sorry. They were talking about you.'

I went very still. Why would Annabel be talking to Ronnie Binns about *me*? 'What were they saying?'

Topaz shrugged. 'I only heard snatches because her mobile phone rang and she said something about Plymouth and a photograph tomorrow night – that must mean, *tonight*. They both came out and I had to dart around the corner and *that's* when I saw Eunice going into the ladies.'

I'd lost interest in Eunice and the ladies' loo. 'Why didn't you find out who Annabel was talking to?'

Topaz frowned. 'Don't be silly. I could hardly go up and *ask* her.' But all I could think was why Plymouth? What photograph? 'I hear lots of gossip at the café,' Topaz went on. 'Everyone knows that Eunice was frightfully in love with Douglas Fleming. My vigilante instincts knew she was going to pick a fight with Olive. And I was right!'

'How did you know that Olive was in the ladies' loo?'

'I saw her go in.'

'So you set off the fire alarm.'

'Of course I didn't,' Topaz said. 'I heard the two women screaming at each other and knew it was a case for the Caped Kitten, which was why I never go anywhere now without my equipment.' She pointed to her orange rucksack under her chair.

'Tell me exactly what you saw in the bathroom.'

'I came in through the bathroom window.'

'How?'

'I'd opened it earlier in case I needed a getaway plan. The Caped Kitten always plans ahead,' said Topaz. 'That awful Pratt woman was sitting on top of Olive Larch holding a brown paper bag over her face,' Topaz said. 'It was frightfully exciting. Olive was thrashing about trying to stab her with a pair of scissors.'

'Couldn't you have just separated them?'

'In my line of business, you have to act fast,' Topaz said. 'I just pulled the Pratt woman off Olive – incidentally, I have been weight training – bundled her into a stall and then you turned up.'

'You are going to have to tell this to the police,' I said, closing my notepad.

'No way.' Topaz shook her head vehemently. 'Are you kidding? The Caped Kitten never deals with the cops.'

'Then, I'm not telling Steve you are an undercover reporter.'

'But you promised!' Topaz wailed. 'All right. All right. I'll tell Colin – but no one else.'

Barbara's head poked in between the curtains. 'Wilf is asking for you, Vicky.'

'I have to go,' I said to Topaz, and got to my feet. My heart began to thump disconcertingly in my chest at what lay ahead.

'Just one more thing . . .' Topaz paused at the entrance to the nook. Was everyone stealing my *Columbo* technique? 'You absolutely *swear* that you're no longer friends with Annabel?'

'We just work together, Topaz. Okay?' Frankly, I couldn't be bothered to argue. I had far more important matters on my mind.

'Goody.'

Leaving Topaz seated in the nook to write up her report, I approached Barbara behind the counter in reception.

'What sort of mood did Wilf sound in?' I said.

Barbara shrugged. 'It's hard to say, but remember, follow your instincts, dear. That's what I always do.'

And with that in mind, I thrust back my shoulders, held my head high, and mounted the steps to the scaffold.

21

'**D**ave was just as shocked as we were, sir.' I'd been standing at Wilf's desk watching him clean out his Dunhill pipe for a full three minutes and he hadn't even acknowledged my presence.

The front page of the *Gazette* lay accusingly before me. In the bottom left-hand corner was a photograph of Scarlett Fleming dressed as Cleopatra holding a Victoria sponge cake with the caption: ON THE STAGE OR BEHIND THE STOVE: GIPPING MOURNS LOCAL CELEBRITY and, TURN TO PAGE 11 FOR THE FULL STORY.

I hated being in Wilf's office even more than Pete's. It was so claustrophobic. That was the problem with these old Queen Anne buildings with their small, square rooms and high ceilings.

Piles of newspapers towered on every available surface – floors, filing cabinets, and even under Wilf's desk. The only reason there were none on the windowsill was because when the stacks got too high, Wilf would open the window and toss them into the backyard below where they slowly decomposed over time.

I glanced over at Pete who was lounging against a dry-erase

board that was divided into fourteen sections – each representing a page in the newspaper. Since today marked the start of a new week, it was currently blank.

'Dave really *was* shocked,' I said again.

Pete yawned. He looked tired. 'Shocked doesn't cut it.'

Wilf still said nothing. He just carried on scraping the bowl with a small penknife, tipping the caked tobacco onto a small mackintosh square on his desk. Finally, he looked up. 'I'm disappointed in you, Vicky. Taking Randall's claim at face value without checking the facts smacks of amateurism at the lowest level.'

I cringed with embarrassment. I knew Wilf was right. 'Perhaps someone forced Sammy Larch to change his mind?'

'In the spirit world?' Pete sneered. 'Larch died weeks ago – in case you forgot.'

'The decision was made before he died, Pete.'

'But can you prove it?'

Of course I couldn't! It was just *a. feeling* I had and Barbara felt the same way, too. 'There's too much at stake for Dave to make it all up,' I said. 'We need to save Dave's Olympic dream, not get on the bandwagon with everyone else.'

'It's too late for that.' Pete handed me a copy of the *Plymouth Bugle*. 'Seen this?'

I hadn't. My heart sank.

'The GSRF is a laughing stock,' muttered Wilf, savagely thrusting a pipe cleaner into the stem.

Splattered on the front page of the tackiest tabloid in the West Country were photographs of the Gala fiasco with the headline GARCON! THERE'S A SNAIL IN MY TRIFLE!

Several hand-drawn cartoons of garden snails accompanied snaps of various brawling tuxedo-clad gents covered in various delicacies from the buffet table. Another photograph showed Gillian Briggs screaming under a water sprinkler – OH LA LA ! FUN AND FROLICS AT THE MANOR. Her white dress had become indecently transparent and clung to her ample form in unattractive folds.

But nothing was as bad as Dave Randall being bundled into a waiting custody van: HEDGEROW HOOLIGAN: DO YOU WANT THIS MAN IN OUR OLYMPICS? A telephone hotline number followed so readers could call in and vote.

I threw the newspaper down in fury. 'No wonder Ronnie Binns can afford a new camera. This is his doing.'

'Ronnie Binns?' Wilf's jaw dropped. 'Well, I'll be damned.' His one good eye zeroed in on Pete. 'I thought he was one of ours?'

'Defected, sir,' said Pete. 'We can't afford his prices.'

Wilf grunted and began to pack fresh tobacco into his pipe – Sir Walter Raleigh's – *It smokes as sweet as it smells.* 'The *Gazette* doesn't give in to paparazzi terrorists and we're not starting now.'

'Do we care about this drivel anyway?' I cried, leafing through the paper. 'I mean . . .' *Good grief.* A blurred out-of-focus shot of a catlike creature was caught behind the kitchen dustbins in Gipping Manor car park – BEAST OF BODMIN HUNTS FOR NEXT VICTIM. Of course it was Topaz. I stifled a snort of laughter.

'This is hardly a laughing matter,' Pete scolded.

'You *have* to laugh,' I said quickly. 'Anyone who takes the *Bugle* seriously is beneath our contempt. It's sensationalism. Not journalism!' Wilf looked up in surprise. 'As a journalist, my mission is to tell the *truth*!' I was actually getting quite heated about it all. 'If there is a conspiracy, we should expose it.'

'Conspiracy?' Pete seemed to perk up. 'Bloody hell.'

'Please let me make some inquiries before printing apologies, sir,' I appealed to Wilf then turned to Pete. 'Honestly, if I'm wrong, I'll take full responsibility. You can blame it all on me.'

'We would,' said Pete.

'All right.' Wilf nodded. 'I must say you've always proved to be thorough in the past. Not every trainee reporter snags two national scoops in her first year on the job. You'd better make a start. Off you go.'

'I thought I'd go to the snail meeting at the Tuns tomorrow,' I said. 'See what I can find out.'

'Isn't tomorrow your day off?' said Pete.

'It'll give me a chance to have a word with Ronnie Binns, too. See why he defected to the *Bugle*.'

'I was going to go to the Tuns to cover the first snail meeting,' said Pete. 'Thing is, Emily's parents are in town and—'

'Don't worry. I'll take care of it,' I said. 'Oh, and tonight I've got a meeting with one of those guerrilla undertakers. Go-Go Gothic.'

'I like your enthusiasm, young Vicky.' Wilf made a strangled chuckling noise before adding, 'You'd better watch out, Pete, or she'll have your job.'

I left Wilf's office feeling euphoric. Sauntering over to Tony's desk I leaned over his shoulder and whispered, 'Thought you'd like to know that Wilf and Pete are backing up Dave's story.'

'Those bloody jumpers are environmental barbarians,' Tony snapped. 'The sport should be banned. Oh! Someone looks in a bad mood this morning.'

I spun around. Annabel was standing at the door dressed in jeans and a baby blue sweater dress with a face like thunder. 'You've got some nerve,' she said. 'Call yourself my friend?'

'I could ask *you* the same,' I said hotly. 'Thanks for leaving me stranded.'

'*You* stranded? Where the hell were you?' I noted that Annabel's eyes were red-rimmed and bloodshot. Had she been *crying*?

Tony made a silly *woooh* noise and said, 'Now, then, children.'

'Oh shut up,' we chorused.

'I want to talk to you,' said Annabel. 'In private.'

160

22

I followed Annabel to the usual venue for private conversations – the ladies' loo. Her face was flushed an ugly red. 'I looked for you everywhere last night!'

'Was that after your little assignation with Ronnie Binns?'

'I don't know what you mean,' Annabel fumed. 'I told you, I've got nothing to say to the wretched dustman.'

I couldn't believe why she still persisted in lying to me. 'You were seen going behind a curtain with him.'

'That's utter rubbish. Whoever said that is blind!' Annabel sank onto the wooden chair and wailed, 'If you must know, it's a miracle that I'm not lying dead in the gutter.'

'What are you talking about?'

Annabel's bottom lip began to quiver. 'It was after the fire alarm went off,' she said. 'I'd gone somewhere private to make a phone call—' At least that part of her story was true – 'Suddenly Christine Rawlings and her friends appear out of nowhere and wouldn't let me pass.'

'Oh, dear.' I'd always assumed Christine Rawlings's threats to be just that – threats.

'It was more than "oh, dear".' Annabel's eyes began to

161

water. 'They started calling me horrible names and were rude about my contact lenses. I have to wear contacts. I can't see without them. And then they attacked me. Look!' She pushed the sleeve of her sweater dress up to the elbow. There was a nasty purple bruise. 'And here, too.' Annabel bent over and rolled up the bottom of her jeans to reveal more bruises. 'Quentin Goss's wife kicked me with her Prada shoes. Why are they so cruel? It's not my fault their husbands fancy me.'

'How did you manage to get away?'

'The fire exit was open.'

A light went on in my head. 'You mean, the one behind the curtain where you had that rendezvous with Ronnie—?'

'I don't remember where!' Annabel shouted. 'I had to get out. They were going to kill me.'

'Oh, dear,' I said again. 'Dr Frost must have been furious.'

Annabel burst into tears. 'Jack didn't come home last night. *Again.* I called the police station and the hospital in case he had an accident but . . .' She shook her head in despair. 'I found him at the surgery this morning.' She looked at me with such misery in her eyes I actually felt sorry for her. 'Jack told me he had to pick something up from his office last night and must have fallen asleep.'

'Perhaps he had.' If she couldn't see the obvious, I certainly wasn't going to tell her.

'I know Jack can't be having an affair.' Annabel pulled a tissue out of a fake Coach handbag and blew her nose. 'I'm young and beautiful. Aren't I? I mean, look at me, Vicky. Aren't I?'

'Yes. Of course you are.' I was more concerned about why she wasn't coming clean about Ronnie Binns. Unless . . . *Good grief!* It came to me in a flash. Hadn't Topaz heard Annabel talk about 'Plymouth' and 'photographs'? Was Annabel in cahoots with Ronnie and flogging pictures to the *Bugle*? 'You're not working with Ronnie on the side, are you?'

'For heaven's sake,' Annabel said crossly. 'Of course I'm not. I'm a serious investigative journalist and besides, he stinks and gives me the creeps. Oh, Vicky.' She let out another wail. 'What am I going to do about Jack? Maybe he was punishing me for going out?'

'Maybe.'

'I'm going to make him jealous.'

'That kind of thing never works.' At least, that's what Mum always says.

'What do you know about relationships?' Annabel said with scorn. 'No. You and I are going clubbing tonight in Plymouth and I'm going to collect lots of telephone numbers.'

'I'm working tonight.' I wasn't sure if I wanted to be out with Annabel in her current reckless mood. What if she went off with a sailor and abandoned me down at the docks?

'On a Saturday night?'

'A reporter never sleeps.'

'Neither does Plymouth. Never mind, I'll pick you up after whatever it is you're doing,' said Annabel. 'Where is it?'

'Actually, I have to go to Plymouth,' I said reluctantly. 'I'm meeting the chap who drove the rented hearse for Scarlett Fleming's funeral at nine.'

'You can't go all the way to Plymouth on your funny little *moped*.'

'I've done it before.'

'Don't be silly.' Annabel went to inspect her reflection in the mirror, all tears forgotten. 'I'll pick you up at seven.'

I returned to the reporters' room with mixed feelings. I was pleased we'd cleared up last night's misunderstanding. I did feel a little guilty about Annabel's run-in with the wives – though it was hardly my fault.

Driving to Plymouth with Annabel would give me another chance to try to find out why she was fascinated with Ronnie Binns. Annabel was already flogging fake handbags on eBay to make some extra money. Why not cash in on Ronnie's sideline, too? If she still wouldn't come clean, I fully intended to corner him – figuratively speaking – at the Tuns on Sunday.

Fortunately, the reporters' room was empty. Tony had already left for an action-packed Saturday of soccer and rugby matches before the season ended and cricket began.

Back at my desk Tony had scribbled *Call Lieutenant Berry. Urgent!* on a Post-it.

Even though I was having serious second thoughts as to Robin's romantic viability, dialling his number still gave me the butterflies.

Robin picked up on the second ring. 'You'll need to go to Dairy Cottage and pick up Auntie's statement,' he said briskly.

My heart sank. 'She's written one already?'

'It's very detailed. I want you to read it and add what you saw, too.'

'I. Can't. Hear. You,' I said, bursting into a series of guttural sounds simulating radio static – a trick I'd learned from Dad. Of course I could hear Robin but I needed time to think.

'Hello? Vicky, are you still there?'

'Hello? Robin? Yes. Awful line.'

'I took photographs of Auntie last night,' he said. 'She's got a nasty bruise on her shoulder and practically cracked her skull open on the toilet bowl. We'll go for a charge of aggravated assault.'

'Sorry. Didn't. Catch. That.' I launched into the static routine once more and slammed the phone down. *Blast!* He couldn't be serious! It rang again immediately but I let the call go through to the answering machine.

After counting to sixty, I tentatively replayed Robin's message. It was a long one.

Basically my instructions were to drive to Dairy Cottage 'on the double' and collect the statement and a series of photographs illustrating Eunice's 'injuries'. Apparently Eunice was expecting me. I was then to call on Olive Larch and, showing her the

164

evidence – but 'don't leave the photographs or statement' – suggest she consider making an offer so the charge would all 'go away'.

I was to stress that aggravated assault was a 'very serious offence' and imply that it was distinctly possible Olive might go to prison. I wasn't to worry about the specifics of monetary compensation since Robin would be home next Saturday. He then rang off without so much as a thank you.

Frankly I was disgusted and had no intention of doing his dirty work. I was also bitterly disappointed. I'd wasted *weeks* of my life, yearning after a man who turned out to be nothing like Prince Charming after all. On the bright side, at least Robin was out of circulation all week, which gave me some time to sort out the mess Topaz had left in the ladies' loo that night.

Of course, I'd have to question her again. Caped Kitten or not, she was going to have to come clean but first things first.

Since Eunice was expecting me this afternoon. I'd have to start with her.

I phoned Dairy Cottage armed with the very real excuse that I couldn't come over today because I was working.

'Don't bother,' said Mary. 'She's asleep and I can't wake her up.'

My stomach turned over. Robin mentioned Eunice had cracked open her skull. *Good grief!* What if she died? Should I call 999? I tried to keep my voice steady. 'Mary, Robin said she had a head injury. It's important she's kept awake.'

'I gave her a sedative,' said Mary calmly.

'Her medication, you mean?' I said. 'From Dr Bodger?'

'No. The vet.'

'The *vet*!' I shrieked. 'What was it?'

'Acepromazine,' said Mary. 'For the cows. Don't worry, dear. I pop it in Eunice's bedtime cocoa all the time. Goodbye.' And with that, she put down the phone.

A quick Google revealed acepromazine's principal values lay in 'quieting and calming frightened and aggressive animals'.

Perhaps Mary had the right idea, after all. At least she hadn't mentioned the statement or photographs. That was something to be thankful for.

I bit my lip, perplexed. I was beginning to think Probes had a point. The entire family spelled trouble.

Speaking of trouble, I needed to track down Dave Randall. I knew he'd been held at the station overnight and couldn't reach him on his mobile. In the end I left a message to the effect that the *Gazette* was one hundred per cent behind him.

Dave called me straight back. 'I've got caller ID,' he said gloomily. 'I recognized the *Gazette* number and thought your editor was going to give me a bollocking.'

'No. I got that. We need to talk.'

'I can't face anyone. Did you see the *Bugle?*'

'You're jolly well going to see me,' I said firmly. 'I've really put my job on the line for you and this wretched Larch Legacy. I'm coming over now.'

'I'm in hiding,' whined Dave.

'Nonsense!' How could someone who showed such bravery out in the field, be such a coward! And to think I'd considered him as my once-in-a-lifetime seducer! 'Where are you?'

Dave gave a heavy sigh. 'Do you know the Nobody Inn in Doddiscombleigh, near Exeter?'

'That's miles away,' I said with dismay. It would take me at least an hour by moped. I really *must* buy a car. 'I'll meet you somewhere in the middle.'

'I can't drive,' he said. 'I've been drinking.'

'You do have definite proof?'

'In writing. Signed by the great man himself.'

'I'm on my way.'

I'd no sooner put the phone down when it rang *again.*

'Vicky? Colin here,' said Probes. Little butterflies fluttered around in my stomach. 'Any chance of a drink tonight?'

'Can't. Sorry. I'm working.'

Probes laughed. 'Okay. I get the hint.'

'No. Really. I am.' I found myself grinning, too.

'Look, I made a few inquiries about Spain—'

Blast! No! 'You didn't have to.'

'It was just a few phone calls,' Probes said. 'Scarlett Fleming never left the country.'

'Are you positive?'

'I checked with all the port authorities and passenger manifests. Over the past few weeks there has been no record of any car accidents – fatal or otherwise – within a one hundred mile radius of Perpignan in the Pyrenees or Barcelona and the Costa Brava.'

'That's very thorough,' was all I managed to say as I struggled to make sense of this astonishing development.

'What's happening? Is this a police matter?'

'I'm not sure . . .' I said slowly. My heart was doing all sorts of funny leaps and jumps. 'I need to check a few more things out first.'

'Let me know if I can be of any more help. Remember, you owe me a favour now.'

I put the phone down and grabbed my moped keys, trying to make sense of what I'd suspected deep down, but hadn't really wanted to believe.

Mild-mannered Douglas Fleming had murdered his wife. He'd picked a time when Whittler was away, fabricated a bogus trip to pretend she was out of the country, killed her, and then organized rent-a-thug to transport her body into the family vault.

How unbelievably convenient and to think that nobody would have been any the wiser had it not been for that phone call I received on Thursday morning.

The problem was, how could I prove it?

I hurried to fetch my moped and began to curse Dave. I really didn't have time to trek all the way to Exeter. My thoughts were consumed with Neil Titley – not the Larch Legacy.

Yet, I reminded myself, as things now stood, it was

imperative that Dave and I salvage our tarnished reputations. Dave had better have proof and it had better be good.

As I sped north on the dual carriageway toward Exeter, I hoped the Nobody Inn was still serving food.

I was absolutely starving.

23

It took me nearly three hours to find Doddiscombleigh. Tucked away near Belvedere Castle on the outskirts of Exeter, it was a tiny hamlet nestling in acres of forestland.

Devon was famous for its lack of signposts. At crucial crossroads and T junctions, picking the right road was more a case of trial and error. As the afternoon wore on, I began to worry that Dave would be plastered by the time I found him or thrown out for drunk and disorderly behaviour. Fortunately, when I finally pulled into the car park, I was relieved to see his old Land Rover was still there.

A traditional Devon longhouse with whitewashed walls and a slate roof, the Nobody Inn had been built around the mid-sixteenth century. Despite the May afternoon, a log fired burned merrily in the grate. The public bar and lounge was still packed thanks to the all-day drinking hours.

Dave was seated on a stool slumped over the counter at the end of the bar. He was nursing a pewter tankard and stared moodily ahead. At least he was still conscious and hadn't passed out. That was something to be grateful for.

Grabbing the empty stool next to him, I sat down.

'I thought you weren't coming,' he said.

'It's not the easiest of places to find.'

Dave turned to me, bleary-eyed. His dark curls were flattened against his head. He smelled rank and clearly hadn't bothered to wash, let alone shave, after a night in the cells. 'It's all over, Vicky. I'm finished.'

'What'll you be having, my lovely,' said a buxom woman in her fifties. She had sparkling brown eyes and wore her long grey hair piled on top of her head. 'The kitchen's open all day. Fancy some homemade soup?'

'Yes please.' I realized I was starving.

'You're Vicky, aren't you?' the woman said. 'I'm Hilary. Dave told me you were coming. Soup is on the house.' She leaned across the counter, lowering her voice. 'He's in a dreadful state.'

'We'll sort it out.'

'Awful business, old Larch reneging on the deal,' she said. 'I know all the details, dear. Dave and my lad Toby used to go to school together. He's like a son to me. I'll get your soup.'

'Tell me what happened,' I said.

Dave drained his pewter tankard and slammed it on the bar followed by a highly unattractive belch. How could I ever have found him sexy? He fumbled in his moleskin jacket pocket and brought out a crumpled scrap of paper. Carefully, he smoothed out the creases and gave it to me.

Written in spidery scrawl, I carefully read the contents. *This confirms my agreement with Dave Randall of Cricket Lodge, that the Gipping Hedge Jumping Society will receive the Larch Legacy for 2010 and a sum of five hundred pounds. It is understood that a new jump, the Larch Leap, will be named in my honour.* The paper was signed Sammy Larch and dated a full month before he died.

'This is fantastic!' I impulsively gave Dave a hug and then wished I hadn't. He clung to me and his foul-smelling breath literally took mine away.

'It's still too late,' he said. 'Webster has the money now. There will never be another Larch Legacy. It's over.'

'Who cares about Webster,' I said waving the paper at him. 'This is all the proof we need.'

Hilary returned with two bowls of chicken soup and homemade crusty bread. 'One for you, too, my lad,' she said, removing Dave's pewter tankard. 'No more ale.'

Dave and I tucked in. It was delicious. He began to perk up. 'What are we going to do?'

'As I told you on the phone, the *Gazette* is behind you, so let's see what we can salvage.' I took out my notepad. 'You mentioned you'd drummed up some corporate sponsorship.'

'Leviathan tractors said they'd chip in some cash but only if it tied in with the Larch Legacy.' He slumped over once more. 'See? It's all her fault.'

We were back to Scarlett Fleming *again*. 'Why did you think Mrs Fleming made Sammy change his mind?'

'Let's just say we had a falling out a few months back over her maze.'

'Not the one in the formal garden, surely?' Headcellars boasted a magnificent miniature box-hedge maze that always drew a crowd at the annual Gipping Garden Open Day.

Dave had the grace to blush. 'One of the lads was getting married and we'd had a few pints.' He stared wistfully off into space. 'Rows and rows of neatly clipped privet. Beautiful – green and tight.' He sighed. 'You couldn't possibly understand.'

'I daresay she didn't, either.'

'She went spastic,' Dave recalled. 'Ran out of the house screaming and hit me behind the knees with a cricket bat. It's a miracle I can still jump. I'm telling you, she might seem all Ms Nice on the outside, but she's got a vicious temper.'

Perhaps Fleming killed her in self-defence?

'I'm surprised she didn't sue for damages,' I said.

'She did. But the magistrate's a jumper and chucked out the charges.'

'So you think it was revenge?'

'Yep,' Dave said. 'I had a feeling she'd try something when I went to Sammy's the night he died.'

A peculiar tingle came over my nether regions and it had nothing to do with sitting close to Dave Randall. I liked to call it my Romany alarm. Mum claimed we had gypsy blood and I believed her. 'Go on.'

Dave shrugged. 'I got there around seven and Scarlett answered the door. I'd written a list of sponsors for Sammy and wanted to go over the new jump but she just snatched the paper and slammed the door in my face.'

'Maybe you interrupted something?'

'Yeah. Exactly.' Dave leered. 'Old Scarlett looked all flustered. Her hair was a mess and her shirt was torn. If you ask me, there was a bit of hanky-panky going on.'

'Don't be silly. He was ninety-five and besides, weren't Olive or Douglas Fleming there, too?'

'That's what I thought until I went to the Nag and Bucket afterward,' Dave said. 'Guess who was up there hiding in a quiet corner having a basket of scampi?'

'Please don't play guess who with me, Dave.'

'Olive Larch and Douglas Fleming.'

'*Alone?*' I said sharply. This did seem odd. Why would Olive and Douglas be alone? Why would Scarlett want to stay behind with Sammy? Hadn't Pam Green said Scarlett refused to be on her own with him because he was such a lecherous old sod? If Dave's claim were true, it sounded like the two could be indulging in a bit of hanky-panky, after all. I tried hard not to think about it. On the few occasions I'd met Sammy before he died, he never wore his false teeth.

'I went over and said hello,' said Dave. 'Told Olive I'd just popped in to see her dad. She got all jumpy but Fleming pointed out that Scarlett would take good care of him. When I left around ten, they were still there.'

Catching sight of the time, I realized I had to leave if I was to get back to Gipping in time for tonight's adventure with Annabel. 'Can I keep this paper for a few days?'

'Will you print it on the front page?' said Dave hopefully.

'That's Wilf's call but I suspect he'll want to talk to you first.' I got to my feet. 'Don't worry. We'll sort it out.'

Dave jumped up – somewhat unsteadily – and pulled me into a bear hug. 'Thanks, Vicky. You've saved my life. You know that, right? Any time you're in trouble, just come to me, right?'

'Right. Thanks. Bye.' Extricating myself, I thanked Hilary for the soup and headed home.

Yet again, I took a wrong turn and ended up practically in the next county of Somerset, mainly because I wasn't paying attention to the road. I couldn't stop thinking about Scarlett Fleming's unsavoury tryst with Sammy Larch – the tryst that ended with him lying dead at the bottom of the stairs with a broken neck while her husband and his daughter ate a basket of scampi at the Nag and Bucket.

Perhaps there had been some weird foursome going on? Maybe Douglas Fleming was content to turn a blind eye to his wife's dalliance with Sammy because he had already started his affair with Olive? It would certainly explain his sudden romantic interest in her.

According to the coroner report, there had been nothing suspicious about Sammy's death but, if something fishy had been going on, I knew just the person to ask: Steve Burrows. I was positive he would have been called to the scene first and much as I hated to admit it, he had proved to be a very astute informant in the past.

As I turned into Factory Terrace, my heart plunged into my boots. Annabel's BMW was parked outside number twenty-one. How long had she been there? *Please God don't let her be snooping in my bedroom.*

I practically hurled my moped into the carport and hurried indoors.

Mrs Evans was covering a small box with brown paper.

'You're late. We were just getting worried,' she said. 'This is for Sadie and—'

'Where's Annabel?'

'She wanted to wait in your room.'

Even though my laptop was password protected and I always made sure I hid anything distinctly incriminating, I still felt consumed with an irrational fear. Would Annabel find the photographs of my parents and their postcards in a shoebox under the floorboards?

There was only one way to find out.

Heart in mouth, I raced upstairs.

24

Annabel was lying on my bed with her eyes shut. She was wearing low-rider jeans, a black tube top and high-spiked strappy sandals. Gold chains and heavy bangles completed her ensemble.

She threw her arms over her head, yawned, and gave a seductive wriggle. 'Where have you been?'

'Sorry, got held up.' I looked anxiously around the bedroom for any signs of disturbance.

Dad used to play 'Trenchers' with me after dinner. He'd place a dozen small objects – thimble, matchbox, trinket and etcetera – on a wooden tray for me to study. Then, whisking it away for a few moments, he'd return it and demand to know what was different. Sometimes, items were missing. Sometimes, he just rearranged the order.

Tonight, my room was different. One wardrobe door was ajar; my nightstand drawer wasn't closed properly. My laptop lay open, too.

Annabel had been snooping.

'I'm afraid I was a bad girl,' she said, getting to her feet and went straight to my wardrobe. 'I had a look through and honestly, you've got no clothes at all.'

'I'm not great at shopping.' I said heaving a sigh of relief.

'We'll go soon, I promise. But right now—' she checked her watch. 'We need to leave in ten minutes. No time to shower.'

'I'll just change.'

Annabel pulled out a cornflower blue shirt from my wardrobe. 'Put this on. It brings out the colour of your eyes and while you are doing that, what's the password to your computer? I need to check my e-mails.'

'I don't have the Internet here.' This was true. It meant that if I needed to work in the evening, I had to go back to the office.

'Why do you keep it password protected anyway?' she said with a laugh.

'Don't you?'

'Of course not.' She cocked her head. 'You're such a funny thing. I often wonder what's going on in that little head of yours.'

'Well, while you are wondering away, I'll change.' I refused to let her wind me up.

'Oh, where's my black dress?'

'At the dry cleaners,' I lied, glad that Annabel's snooping can't have spread to delving under the duvet at the bottom of my bed.

Ten minutes later, Mrs Evans followed us out to the BMW clutching a heavily taped, brown-paper parcel. 'Sadie's expecting you,' she beamed. 'You have to go to the stage door and ask for Sadie Sparkles. You are such kind girls, thank you.'

'We're happy to do it,' Annabel said, taking the credit. 'Any other message for her?'

Mrs Evans's eyes watered a tad. 'Just tell her I love her.'

As the BMW left Factory Terrace behind, Annabel scoffed. 'Sadie *Sparkles*! God! What a pain. How did you manage to get talked into that? We'll have to park twice now and it's expensive.'

'It makes Mrs Evans happy and will only take a few minutes.'

'You're right,' Annabel said. 'Don't you wish you had a mum that gave you care parcels?'

'What you haven't had, you'll never miss,' I said lightly, though inside I felt wretched pretending my parents were dead.

'Gosh. I wish I could be like you,' said Annabel. 'I think about my mum all the time. I was eight when she left. How old were you when your parents had that car crash. Spain, wasn't it?'

'No. It was in Africa.' I refused to tell the parents-eaten-by-lions story again. 'Actually, I'd rather not talk about it. It makes me sad.'

'I thought you said what you haven't had you'll never miss?'

'That's because I don't think about it to miss it,' I said quickly.

'You *have* to think about it – especially on your birthday and at Christmas. You've got no brothers or sisters. No one to buy you presents apart from your godparents in Spain.' She gave a peculiar laugh. 'Marie and Derek?'

'I told you, they don't live in Spain,' I said.

'Am I upsetting you?' Annabel reached out and patted my knee. 'We're friends. We should be able to tell each other everything.'

'I will,' I lied. 'But not today. To be honest, I'm far more worried about *you*. You've seemed so unhappy recently. Is everything all right with Dr Frost?'

'Oh, what do you know about relationships?' said Annabel.

'Probably not as much as you, but I'm a good listener.' *Bravo Vicky! Get her to talk about herself.* 'He'll regret it if he lets you go.'

'I know!' Annabel cried. 'That's just it! He doesn't realize what a catch I am. All he does is work, and one day he'll come home and I won't be there, and then he'll be sorry.'

'Perhaps you need to spice up your relationship a little bit?'

I suggested. Mum always maintained it was important for a woman to be unpredictable. That way, a man never got bored – though in Mum's case, Dad couldn't handle her volatile moods and sought solace in the arms of Pamela Dingles.

'I do! I try to make him as jealous as possible,' said Annabel. 'But he doesn't seem to notice.'

'Maybe he doesn't trust you anymore so he's pulling back?' Into another woman's arms and I couldn't say I'd blame him! Annabel must be a handful.

'I'm very trustworthy.' Annabel sounded hurt. 'I've been one hundred per cent faithful to Jack.'

'That's not true,' I said. 'What about Steve Burrows? I know you spent the night with him a few weeks ago.'

'It was business and besides, I never go all the way, so it doesn't count. Wait . . . . What the hell?' She leaned forward, peering closely into the rearview mirror. 'I *knew* it! We're being followed.'

I swivelled around to look out the rear window and, to my dismay, recognized the Mark II Capri practically riding our bumper. *Blast!* It was Topaz and she was in disguise! I know it sounded childish but I felt really guilty. Hadn't I sworn that Annabel was no longer my friend? Topaz had caught me red-handed.

'Omigod! I think it's a farmer!' said Annabel.

Topaz was wearing a flat, tweed farmer's cap, wire-rimmed spectacles and a false moustache. 'Looks like it,' I said. 'But why do you think she— he's following us?'

'There is only one way to find out!' Annabel slammed her foot down on the accelerator. The BMW surged forward. We tore along the dual carriageway, reaching seventy miles an hour in seconds.

'Omigod!' said Annabel as her eyes flicked back and forth from the road to the rearview mirror. 'He's really keeping up.'

I held on to the sides of my seat. 'Don't get caught for dangerous driving,' I said as we cut between two slow-moving trucks and swerved onto an exit ramp. Annabel hit the brakes. 'I think we've lost him. No! *Blast!*'

I turned around again. Topaz waved and flashed her headlamps. We sped off once more along an old highway that ran parallel to the dual carriageway. 'Omigod,' cried Annabel for the third time. 'We're really being chased!'

Suddenly it occurred to me that Topaz would not want her cover blown. I began to relax.

'I hope you know where you're going.'

'It's the back road to Plymouth. Watch this.' She started slamming on the brakes, then flooring the accelerator.

I was beginning to feel carsick. 'If he'd wanted to run us off the road, he would have done so by now.'

'Good point, but this is fun.'

'*Please*, let's just ignore him,' I begged, after nearly being thrown through the windshield for the umpteenth time. 'We'll get caught for speeding. Oh! There's a police car!' There wasn't, but it had the desired effect. Annabel instantly slowed down.

We passed the WELCOME TO PLYMOUTH sign and merged into the Saturday-evening traffic. The Capri sat firmly on our tail, until we turned into Plymouth Hoe itself – a natural cul-de-sac since it ended at the edge of a cliff overlooking the English Channel.

'Looks like we've lost him,' said Annabel. 'What a weirdo.'

I had to agree with her there. 'The Banana Club is at the end of the Hoe.'

Annabel sniggered. 'Don't you mean the *Hoe* is at the end of the Banana Club?'

'Sadie is an exotic dancer.' Annabel could be so unkind. 'And anyway, the word *hoe* derives its name from Anglo-Saxon times and actually means a sloping ridge shaped like a foot.'

'Okay, Ms Prim,' Annabel said. 'It was just a joke.'

The Banana Club was easy to find. The former lockup, built literally into the cliff face, was painted in browns and greens to simulate jungle foliage. Devon is one of the few counties in

England with a climate mild enough to grow palm trees. A pair of genuine Torbay palms flanked the main entrance – although the bananas that nestled in the fronds were clearly plastic.

Despite the relatively early hour, cars lined the streets. Parking was going to be a problem. People were strolling along the bluff enjoying a sunny May evening. In the distance I saw several gunmetal grey ships anchored in the port and knew one would be HMS *Dauntless*.

My thoughts turned to Robin. How strange that only twenty-four hours earlier I had been fantasizing about spending the rest of my life with him, but now I prayed we wouldn't run into him. He was bound to ask if I'd picked up Eunice's statement and probably order me back to Dairy Cottage 'on the double' to do so.

Annabel zipped into a parking space with a large blue handicapped sign.

'We can't park here,' I said. 'It's for disabled motorists. The fine is huge.'

'Stop worrying.' Annabel opened the dashboard, pulled out a disabled placard, and stuck it on her rearview mirror. 'When I broke my ankle, Jack gave me one of these and I kept it.' She laughed. 'Why? Surely *you*, of all people, aren't going to report me?'

'What's that supposed to mean?' I said. Annabel didn't answer, merely smirked. Taking out a compact mirror, she reapplied her lipstick, then handed both to me. 'Here. Use mine.'

'I'm fine without it.'

'Nonsense. We're going out clubbing. Here, I'll do it.' Annabel cupped my chin in her hands and deftly applied the lipstick. 'Very pretty. Come on. Let's go.'

Outside, the air was brisk. We walked the few yards to the Banana Club. A smoked glass booth was located to the right of the main entrance. Alongside a placard – LADIES, THIS COULD BE YOU – were posters of scantily clad girls in animal skins clinging to vines and poles in extremely ambitious positions.

'Some of these look impossible,' Annabel said, peering closely at a young girl executing a vertical inversion.

'Now, *that* would spice up your sex life,' I said. 'You should try it.'

Annabel turned to me, 'Omigod. You're right! I should!'

'Can I help you?' Came a disembodied female voice from behind the smoked-glass window.

I leaned down to speak into the small microphone at the base of the screen. 'We're here to see Sadie Sparkles.'

'Stage door is down the alley on your right.'

Since the Banana Club was the last building on the Hoe, the stage door was easy to find. Tucked down a side alley that reeked of sea salt and urine, a neon light marked STAGE ENTRANCE flashed above a yellow door that was several steps below street level.

'It's disgusting down here,' said Annabel as she kicked what looked like an empty packet of condoms out of our path. 'There's more than dancing going on if you ask me.'

I had to admit the thought had crossed my mind, too. I hammered on the stage door. It opened instantly, revealing a heavy-set man with oily, slicked-back hair dressed in a tattered navy blue sweater and jeans. He held a clipboard under his arm and was eating a hamburger.

'We've got a package for Sadie Evans . . . Sparkles, I mean,' I said holding up the box. 'She's expecting us.'

He consulted his clipboard. 'Vicky Hill and Annabel Lake?'

We nodded. He stepped aside and waved us in.

'I'm Bert,' he said through a mouthful of burger. 'Follow me.'

'God!' Annabel whispered as we entered a narrow corridor lit with red-tinted lightbulbs. 'It feels like a brothel.'

'I didn't know you'd been in one.'

'I haven't.' We both began to giggle. It felt as if we were doing something illegal.

A door marked MANAGER opened and a man in his early

181

sixties stood before us. He had a pencil moustache and wore his grey hair in a neat ponytail. 'Are you girls auditioning?'

'No. Visiting Sadie Sparkles,' I said, brandishing Sadie's parcel once again.

'I'm interested,' piped up Annabel, thrusting out her boobs.

I stared at her with horror. 'She's joking.'

'No. I'm serious.'

'Very nice,' he said, giving her an appraising look that made Steve's leering bland by comparison. 'Name's Liam.'

'I'm Annabel.'

'Let's go somewhere quiet and I'll take your particulars.' He took her arm before I had a chance to intervene.

'I'll come and find you later,' Annabel said with a wink.

Liam steered her back into his office saying, 'Have you danced before?' and closed the door.

'She'll be all right. Liam looks after his girls,' said Bert. 'Let's go and find Ms Sparkles.'

Bert led me down a second corridor. Above, I could hear the beat and muffled applause. We had to be right under the stage. We stopped outside a door clad in red velvet and emblazoned with dozens of glittering stars. The nameplate, SADIE SPARKLES, was embossed in large silver letters.

Bert knocked. 'Someone to see you, luv.'

Sadie greeted me with a big smile. I'd met her before. Although she was only two years older than me, she seemed much more worldly.

'I expected this last week,' Sadie said, snatching the box from my hands. She wore her waist-length blonde hair down, heavy kohl-rimmed eye makeup, thick false lashes and a full-length pink silk robe decorated in sequins.

Sadie opened the door wider. A silver pole was bolted to the ceiling behind her. 'Come in and tell me about Mum. How is her arthritis?'

I followed Sadie inside, glad of her genuine concern for her mother and, at the same time, suffering a mixture of feelings for my own. I rarely spoke to Mum so would never know if she had any ongoing ailments. The postcards I received from my parents were more a statement to say 'we're alive' rather than a warm personal letter filled with 'we miss you'.

Sadie pointed to a daybed covered with a fake fur leopard-skin throw. 'Make yourself at home. I'll get some scissors.'

I sank down on the bed and took in my surroundings. A large mirror hung on one wall framed with naked lightbulbs. Stacks of makeup littered the countertop beneath along with half-used tissues, brushes, and perfume bottles. Sadie had plastered the other walls with photographs of Hollywood celebrities – notably Catherine Zeta-Jones – and fellow showgirls executing pole dancing climbs, spins and inversions. Above the daybed was a shelf of books with lofty titles such as *Jonathan Livingston Seagull* and *The Way of the Peaceful Warrior* by Krishnamurti.

Pointing to a photo of Catherine Zeta-Jones playing Velma Kelly in the hit show *Chicago*, Sadie said, 'I really want to get into musicals like Catherine. Get out of Plymouth. Move to New York, you know?'

'At least you got out of Gipping-on-Plym,' I said.

'Yeah. What a dump. I can't imagine why you're there.'

My thoughts exactly. 'I'll be a full-fledged journalist in July,' I said defensively. 'Then I'll be off.'

'Mum said you fancy yourself as the next Christiane Amanpour.'

I felt my face turn red. 'Well . . . not really.'

'You've got to visualize it. Know what I'm saying?' Sadie said. 'I'm very spiritual. You have to act like you already *are* Christiane Amanpour.'

Clutching the scissors in her beautifully manicured hands, Sadie joined me on the daybed and started stabbing at the brown paper. 'I don't know why Mum always has to do it up like this.'

Sadie's robe gaped open. Beneath was a minuscule halter-neck, one-piece leopard-skin cave-girl costume. It was hard not to stare, especially since her voluptuous breasts were barely restrained by the flimsy top. I couldn't help wondering how everything stayed in place when she was hanging upside down.

'Here, you try.' Sadie thrust the box at me. 'I don't want to ruin my nails. These are acrylic tips and cost me a fortune.'

Finally, we got the paper off. Sadie tipped the box upside down onto the bed. Two packets of Marks & Spencer digestive biscuits came tumbling out, followed by some homemade raspberry jam, a pair of brand-new pink pyjamas still with the price tag on, and an envelope. Sadie ripped it open and pulled out five ten-pound notes. 'Good old Mum,' she said grinning. 'Your parents are dead, aren't they?' I must have looked startled because Sadie added, 'Mum told me. I'm sorry. Must be hard.'

'It doesn't get any easier.' I had to change the subject. 'Your mum seems quite happy at the moment.'

'Snail season,' Sadie said, getting up and moving to the countertop. She stuffed the money into her handbag. 'Dad's always nice to her in the summer. I wish he'd be nice to me.'

It was common knowledge that Leonard Evans heartily condemned Sadie's chosen profession. I knew what it was like to have a dad who disapproved. 'I'm sure when you're dancing on Broadway he'll come around.'

'Do you think so?' Sadie said hopefully. 'It's hard for Mum to put up with him sometimes. That's why she likes to keep busy. I couldn't believe it when Mrs Fleming gave her the boot.'

'I heard about that.'

Sadie sat in front of the mirror and began to backcomb her hair. 'She had it coming. It's Karma. Know what I'm saying?'

'Really? Why?' My pulse began to quicken. I'd never thought to ask Sadie about Scarlett Fleming.

'I told Mrs Fleming, "What goes around comes around."'

'You *spoke* to her? When?'

'Just before she went off on her holiday. We get our nails done at Polly's in the Barbican.' Sadie held up her hand and inspected her nails for a moment before continuing to backcomb her hair. 'Mum worked for the Flemings for twenty years. She worked hard. They just bought a brand-new Range Rover and next minute, Mrs F. tells Mum they can't afford her anymore. Bugger.' Sadie winced as her hair got caught in the comb and she yanked it from her scalp. 'Then, I hear she's going on a fancy yoga retreat in Spain. If you want to get rid of someone, be honest about it, know what I'm saying?'

'I bet she didn't like that.'

'She was a bitch. Told me to mind my own business,' Sadie said. 'She even got the locks changed! Mum went back to get her feather duster and couldn't get in. Yeah. Mum was upset. She didn't even like cleaning there because it gave her the creeps. I didn't like it there, either.'

'Why?'

'Everyone knows Headcellars is haunted.' Sadie shrugged. 'Something to do with a dead monk. Mum used to take me there in the school holidays. It had a secret passageway, you know.'

It seemed everyone except the man who lived at Headcellars knew the place was haunted. I made a mental note to tell Topaz she was right. 'Did you run into Mr Fleming much?'

'Haven't seen him since I was a kid.'

'What about Neil Titley?' I said suddenly. 'He runs a company called Go-Go Gothic.'

'Neil? Yeah,' Sadie said. 'Works here part-time as a bouncer. Sometimes I put a little business his way. Why?'

My first thought was, *Great! The missing link!* Douglas Fleming must have met Neil Titley here at the Banana Club. My second was acute disappointment. I'd never imagined Douglas Fleming to be the kind of pervert who would frequent these establishments, especially to see someone he'd known as a child perform.

'I thought you said Douglas Fleming never came here?' I said.

185

'If he did, I didn't see him. We get a lot of blokes sneaking in here wearing disguises. Wives don't like it, you see.'

There was a tap on the door and Bert poked his head in. 'Another visitor, Ms Sparkles.'

'Hi!' Annabel burst in, eyes wide with excitement. 'You must be Sadie. Wow. How great to meet you.'

'You're the Annabel who is living with that old doctor, aren't you?' said Sadie. I thought I detected a hint of malice in Sadie's tone but couldn't be sure.

It hardly mattered. Annabel appeared not to hear and made a beeline for the vertical pole. She swung around it, flicking her hair this way and that.

'Liam said I was a natural, but I needed practice,' said Annabel as she wrapped both legs around the pole and tried to shin up. Instead, she slid down, landing hard on her bottom. 'Ouch!'

'It takes a *lot* of practice,' said Sadie, stifling a snort of laughter. I had to look away so as not to laugh, too.

'Of course, I'm in jeans,' said Annabel. 'It must be easier with bare legs.'

'Ten minutes, Ms Sparkles,' said Bert from outside the door.

'I've got to warm up now,' Sadie said. 'But you should stay for the show.'

I looked over at Annabel who was nodding her head with great enthusiasm. 'We'd love to,' she gushed. 'Can we watch you now?'

'Whatever.'

Annabel flung herself next to me on the daybed, practically bouncing with excitement.

Sadie removed her robe. She flipped her head forward, ruffled her hair, and tossed it back. I had to admit, it looked authentically messy, as if she had just stepped out of prehistoric times – although the red acrylic nail tips added a twenty-first-century flair.

Annabel's jaw dropped. 'Are those hair extensions?'

'Yeah,' said Sadie. 'But it's real hair. Polly on the Barbican imports it from Mumbai.'

'I didn't know there were blondes in India,' said Annabel.

'She dyes it,' I whispered.

Sadie started with a few stretches and lunges followed by a perfectly executed cartwheel. Her breasts did not move once. I studied Annabel out of the corner of my eye. She seemed utterly enthralled.

'Tell Bert to give you house seats,' Sadie said, as she finished her warm up routine with sideways splits. 'See you out there.'

As Annabel and I settled into our seats three rows back from the stage, I reflected that the evening was going well.

Sadie had provided another piece of the puzzle. Fleming must have hired Neil Titley to do his dirty work. I was a little nervous about confronting Titley and would have to tread carefully. I didn't want to frighten him off – or worse – give him reason to alert Fleming that I'd been here asking awkward questions.

I looked at my watch. 'I have to slip away to meet this Go-Go Gothic chappy in a few moments,' I said to Annabel.

'I'll save your seat,' she said. 'The place is really filling up. There are a *lot* of sailors here tonight.'

I scanned the audience but there seemed to be no sign of Robin, thank God.

'Isn't the set amazing!' gushed Annabel.

She was right. It was. Among fake palm trees festooned with thick green vines was a series of vertical poles set into the floor.

Mechanical parrots squawked and model monkeys chattered from the treetops. In front of a thatched hut, a large cauldron big enough to hold three people simmered over a fake fire. African drums began to beat.

'Compliments of Sadie Sparkles,' said a young waitress,

handing us two plastic pineapples liberally adorned with paper umbrellas. 'Banana Coolers. Enjoy!'

We both took tentative sips. It nearly blew my head off. 'Jeez!' I cried. 'It's practically neat rum.'

'Omigod!' Annabel nudged me. 'Over there! Isn't that the farmer who was following us?' She squealed and ducked down. 'Oh! He's looking over!'

Fortified by rum, I waved. Annabel hid behind me, giggling. 'Don't encourage him!'

Topaz stuck up her middle finger and turned her back on us just as the lights dimmed. The African drumbeat grew louder and the audience began to stir with restless anticipation. There were a few wolf whistles.

Suddenly, there was a loud crash of simulated thunder and lightning. People screamed. A statuesque black man dressed in a loincloth wheeled an animal cage onto the stage. Someone was inside.

'Oh! It's Sadie!' Annabel grabbed my arm, trembling with excitement.

Sadie rattled the bars and pretended to be scared. The drumming became more frantic as the black Adonis did a series of leaps and jumps around the cage before letting her out. She began a seductive dance around him. Unfortunately, I couldn't stay any longer to see who ended up in the pot as I realized it was nearly nine.

'I have to go,' I whispered in Annabel's ear. 'If I'm not back in half an hour, you'd better call the police.'

'Okay,' she said, mesmerized by the black Adonis who was spinning Sadie above his head on one hand. I got the feeling that if something did happen to me, Annabe wouldn't notice until the club shut. By then it would be too late and my body would be discovered in an alley behind a Chinese restaurant in a dumpster.

For a moment I hesitated about meeting Neil Titley alone but reminded myself that Christiane Amanpour must have interviewed far more dangerous people than I – African despots, Middle Eastern tyrants to name just a few.

Plymouth Hoe was a busy place at night. As long as we stayed firmly in the public eye, I felt sure I'd be safe.

25

I recognized Neil Titley and his flattened nose immediately. He was standing with a man with a shaved head under a Torbay palm in front of the main entrance. The two were dressed alike in the black-suited uniform of the nightclub bouncer. Both wore earpieces and looked very American Secret Service.

'Here she is!' Neil broke into a huge smile and engulfed me in a bear hug that was so friendly it took me completely off-guard. 'Were you inside watching the show?'

'I came with my friend,' I said, extricating myself from his embrace. 'I also know Sadie Sparkles very well.' Despite Neil's warm welcome, I wanted him to know I hadn't come to the Banana Club alone.

'Sadie is a darling. The punters love her,' said Neil. 'This is Tyler.'

'You say you brought a friend?' Tyler leered. On closer inspection, it looked like he had misguidedly shaved off his eyebrows as well as his hair.

'Yes,' I said. 'Why?'

'Maybe we could make a foursome later on tonight?' said Tyler. 'Are her eyes a beautiful as yours?'

'I'm here on business, actually.' Even though the answer would have been no, I felt flattered. With all the hot dancers in the Banana Club, it felt good to be singled out.

'Don't take any notice of him,' said Neil. 'He asks every woman out and keeps a score. How many was it last night? Eleven?'

'Twelve, man.' Tyler gave Neil a playful punch.

So much for being singled out.

'As I say, I'm here on business, Neil, so can we get on with it?'

'I snagged the small conference room,' he said, and turned to Tyler. 'We'll be about twenty-five minutes.'

Neil led the way back into the club and up a narrow flight of dimly lit stairs. Judging by the sound of the African drums vibrating through the floorboards, I suspected Sadie was still trying to avoid being boiled alive.

We entered a windowless, soulless room, containing nothing but a round table and four chairs. A titanium briefcase stood in the corner.

I began to feel nervous again. Did Douglas Fleming know I was on to him and tipped Neil off? What was in the briefcase – instruments of torture? Why had he brought me up here? If I screamed, no one would ever hear my strangled cries for help.

Gallantly, Neil pulled out a chair for me then sat down opposite. He snapped open the briefcase, withdrew a spiral bound document and slid it toward me. 'For your newspaper.'

I glanced at the title page. *Go-Go Gothic Business Plan – Our Passengers Go All The Way!* 'Goodness. You've put a lot of work into this.'

'I've done my research,' said Neil in a pompous voice. 'Now you keep your part of the bargain and we'll both get rich.'

'Of course,' I said weakly. 'I do have a few questions—'

'I'll be taking questions after the presentation.' Neil got to his feet and stood with his hands clasped behind his back. Looking me directly in the eye, he launched into a highly

191

impressive presentation of his long-term goals for Go-Go Gothic. Neil spoke of profit and loss calculations, projected sales over a five-year period, an interactive presence on the Internet, and – the ultimate – a Go-Go Gothic Global empire. 'After all, Virgin's Richard Branson started with just one airplane.'

I applauded politely and couldn't help wondering if taking money to dispose of a body was also in Neil's business plan.

'I want to make Go-Go Gothic a household name,' Neil went on enthusiastically. 'And with your newspaper behind me the world is our oyster.'

'I have to talk to the editor, first,' I said hastily, kicking myself for not mentioning that the *Gazette* was just a little weekly newspaper. 'Let's talk about you.' I took out the small notepad that I always carried with me. 'How did Go-Go Gothic begin?'

Neil pointed to the spiral-bound document. 'It's all in there.'

'Great. I can't wait to read it,' I said. 'But how do you attract your clients? I couldn't find you on the Internet.'

'Technical difficulties,' Neil said. 'I'm using a virtual consultant in Mumbai. Should have the website up and running next week.'

'So you've been relying on word of mouth? Referrals?'

'Sadie puts a lot of business my way. Stag nights, hen parties, that kind of thing. I give her an intro cut.'

'Why don't you take me through a typical booking?' I said slyly. 'How about the Fleming funeral last Thursday?'

'That was a favour,' Neil said. 'I don't like doing coffin transfers – that's what we call them in the business.'

At last I felt I was getting somewhere. 'Really? Why?'

'Coffins are heavy—'

'Because they're lined with zinc?' I put in. 'Hence the hospital gurney?'

'That's right,' Neil nodded. 'You have to hire extra people. Pushes the cost up.' Neil pointed at the spiral bound document again. 'You'll see on page nine—'

'So Sadie referred Douglas Fleming to your company?'

'No.' Neil shook his head. 'It was a woman who made the booking.'

'A *woman*?' This was puzzling. 'Was her name Eunice Pratt? When did she call?'

Neil reached into his jacket pocket and brought out an iPhone. His hands were the size of hams. 'Here we are, April twentieth. Melanie Carew. She called me at nine-oh-five.'

Melanie Carew? Good God! I found that hard to believe although Melanie hadn't seemed too bothered about Scarlett's demise. 'Did Go-Go Gothic supply the coffin?'

'Too much trouble. A custom-made one will set you back a few thousand and if you buy one on the Internet, you don't know what you're getting.'

'So you're saying that Fleming supplied the coffin?'

Neil shrugged. 'Must have done and I'll tell you something else, it was a very fancy coffin. Egyptian looking. Covered in hiero-whatever.'

'Hieroglyphics?'

'That's it. And a snake was carved into the lid.'

'That *does* sound fancy.' *And expensive.* My Internet research had also revealed that so-called fancy carved coffins took weeks to build.

Fleming was guilty all right. A prebought custom-made coffin! A prebooked car! A premeditated murder!

'Bollocks!' Neil said looking at his watch. 'They'll have my guts for garters. I've got to get back on the door.'

Thanking Neil for his time and promising him to call should I have any further questions about Go-Go Gothic, I picked up the PowerPoint report and followed him out of the room.

I found Annabel wandering around the corridor downstairs looking agitated. 'For God's sake! I've been looking for you everywhere,' she cried. 'Where the hell have you been? We'll be late!'

'I thought the clubs didn't close until two.'

Rather than answer, Annabel merely grabbed my hand and dragged me out of the Banana Club. I tried to say goodbye to Neil but he was handing out his business card to a bunch of young women waiting to get in. I heard snatches of 'discount for parties of six or more' and 'yes, we can provide a Chippendales stripper.'

Annabel walked briskly along the Hoe. I only just managed to keep up and was surprised that she hadn't bombarded me with questions about my meeting.

Suddenly, Annabel stopped next to the illuminated statue of Sir Francis Drake, famed Elizabethan circumnavigator of the world.

'I'm tired,' she said, and promptly sat down on a stone bench at the base of the statue.

'I thought you wanted to go clubbing.'

'I've changed my mind,' she said irritably. 'I want to sit here for a minute.

Annabel closed her eyes, which was just as well because Topaz's Capri cruised slowly on by. Even though Topaz kept her eyes firmly ahead, I knew she'd seen us. Twenty yards further on, the car mounted the pavement and Topaz cut the lights. She was beginning to give me the creeps.

'Can we go back to the car?' I said. 'I'm getting cold.'

Annabel's eyes snapped open. She glanced at her watch and looked toward the end of the Hoe. A tall man in a leather trench coat was walking toward us. 'Wait . . . I don't believe it.' Annabel got to her feet and waved. 'Dino! Is that really you?'

The man drew closer and smiled. He had thick, wavy hair, a hooked nose, and wore heavy-framed spectacles. 'Annabel Lake. Well I never! What are you doing here?'

They exchanged a stiff hug. 'We were just leaving,' she said. 'This is my friend Vicky Hill.'

'Hi,' I said, looking from one to the other suspiciously.

'You've got beautiful eyes,' said Dino.

'Everyone tells her that,' Annabel laughed. 'Don't you think they're an unusual sapphire blue?'

'Very unusual.' Dino nodded thoughtfully. 'Why don't I take a photograph of you girls together and e-mail it?'

'Oh, lovely.' Annabel clapped her hands. 'Would you?'

'It won't come out.' I hated having my picture taken. 'It's too dark.'

'Stand closer together. Under the light . . . and smile!' Dino withdrew his iPhone from his jacket pocket and took a snap. 'I'd suggest a drink but I've got a meeting.'

'I think we're off home. Aren't we, Vicky?' Annabel gave a dramatic yawn. 'Gosh. I can't believe I am so tired! Bye, Dino – oh! And don't forget to send the photo!'

Once we were on the road home, I couldn't stop thinking about Annabel's bizarre exchange with this so-called Dino. Why had he wanted to take our photograph? Did Annabel think I'd been born yesterday?

I *knew* it was a prearranged meeting – I'd witnessed plenty of those with Dad – and yet money had not changed hands.

'Dino seems a nice guy,' I ventured. 'Have you known him long?'

'Actually, he's an informant,' said Annabel. 'It's always awkward to bump into one's informants. I never know what to say!'

'I thought you were having a rendezvous,' I said lightly. 'Meet me by the statue at ten, kind of thing. I wouldn't have minded.' I could have begged Topaz to take me home.

'What an extraordinary thing to say,' Annabel laughed. 'You are funny.'

'You were all excited about going clubbing and suddenly – poof – you're tired.'

'Guilty as charged,' said Annabel. 'The truth is, seeing those pole dancers has got me thinking.'

'You're going to change your job?'

'No silly. I'm going to perform for Jack. Didn't you say I

should spice up my sex life? Well, I'm going to start tonight and can't wait to get cracking.'

'Oh, lucky Jack,' was all I managed to say.

Annabel had neatly changed the subject, which meant she was up to something, but I couldn't think what.

The journey home was spent listening to Annabel's colourful account of what Sadie endured at the hands of her handsome captor. I decided against telling Mrs Evans about her daughter's raunchy performance – although recalling Mrs E.'s steamy afternoon trysts, I concluded that the apple did not fall far from the tree.

As I lay in bed later that night, my thoughts turned to Fleming and Melanie Carew. An affair with the secretary was such a cliché. Was it possible he was leading two women up the garden path while courting Olive Larch?

Armed with Neil Titley's startling revelations, I couldn't wait for tomorrow to come. Douglas Fleming would be attending the GSRF first race of the season at the Three Tuns and I had a lot of questions to ask him.

26

'Wakey, wakey, rise and shine!' came a cheery voice. I opened my eyes and bolted upright. Topaz was standing over my bed holding two mugs of tea.

'What are you doing here?' I looked at the clock. It wasn't yet eight. I'd been hoping for a lie in. 'It's Sunday morning!'

Topaz looked a wreck and was still dressed in her farming gear – though I was glad to see she had removed the heavy moustache. Even so, a faint line of grey glue was visible on her upper lip.

'What a night!' She passed me a mug.

It would appear I was back in her good books again – though I did eye the nightstand for a handy blunt instrument in case she got any funny ideas.

'How did you get in?' I pulled the duvet up under my chin.

'Mrs Evans was up making the tea.' She took a sip. 'I say, this is frightfully good.'

'You didn't come here to bring me my morning cuppa,' I said grumpily. 'And if you expect me to apologize for going out with Annabel last night, it was all work. I had a meeting.'

'That's why I'm here. This *is* about Annabel.' Topaz was so excited she sat down and bounced on the edge of my bed.

'Careful!' I shrieked as tea slopped onto the sheets.

'Sorry. I've been up all night and you'll never guess what I saw.'

'No games, Topaz. It's too early and can you move? I can't breathe.'

Topaz shifted a few inches away. 'I'll tell you, on the condition that I get a front-page exclusive and a real job.'

'It depends what it is, and you know I can't promise anything. It's not up to me.'

'All superheroes are newspaper reporters,' Topaz declared. 'I'll go elsewhere and then you'll be sorry.'

'If you're thinking about the *Bugle,* don't bother,' I said. 'It prints nothing but rubbish.'

'True.' Topaz gave a peculiar snort, half chuckle, half snicker. 'They thought the Caped Kitten was the Beast of Bodmin!'

'Quite,' I said. 'So what's this about Annabel?'

'Remember the man you met by the statue of Sir Francis Drake?'

'Yes,' I said. 'He's one of Annabel's informants.'

'Goody. I thought as much.' She beamed. 'I followed him *all* night.'

'And?'

'His name is Dino DiMarco. He's got a huge warehouse down by the docks and—' she paused dramatically, 'You'll never guess what's in there.'

'Handbags?'

'Yes!' Topaz screamed with excitement. 'Yes! Handbags! Boxes and boxes of them! I found a place to hide and watch. People were coming and going all night long. Money was changing hands. She's a criminal. Don't you see?'

I did see, but I needed to think. Annabel had a room full of handbags that she openly admitted to flogging on eBay but this sounded like a whole other operation. I also realized that Annabel had been telling the truth and that made me feel conflicted. I didn't agree with what she was doing, but I just couldn't snitch on my friend.

'Annabel will go to prison, and I'll have her job,' said Topaz happily. 'Let's go to the police. Let's call Colin now!'

'It doesn't quite work like that,' I said. 'We have to catch her in the act of physically receiving the stolen goods. You need to get hard evidence. Photographs.'

'Bother. You're right.' Topaz gave a heavy sigh. 'There is always so much to learn.'

'Did you get a look at the handbags?'

'Not close up. Why?'

'Just wondered.' There was a world of difference between dealing in fake handbags and selling stolen merchandise. I thought of a potential problem. Dad's friend and my godfather, Chuffy McSnatch, dealt in the latter – among other things. The criminal world was small. Everyone knew everyone and I certainly didn't like the idea of Annabel being in it. 'Maybe you *should* keep an eye on things, Topaz.'

'Golly! You mean, go undercover for real? Stake out the warehouse? Write reports?'

'Well . . . yes, I suppose I do.'

'Ha-ha,' Topaz sang childishly. 'You'll *have* to tell Steve I'm a real reporter now!'

'Okay. I will.'

'Really?' Topaz's eyes bugged open. 'When? Today?'

'I've got the GSRF meeting at the Tuns,' I said. 'How about this evening? Ask him to come to the café at six thirty.'

Topaz put her mug down on the nightstand. 'Thanks, boss.' She was bursting with excitement and leaned over to give me a hug. I tried to avoid her touch but was utterly trapped in my bed.

'Oh, I wish I could snuggle in with you right now,' she said. 'I'm so tired.'

'We work together, remember?' I said, shoving her roughly away. 'There is just one more thing.'

'I'm all yours.'

'As an *undercover* investigative reporter, there can be absolutely no scandal attached to your reputation.'

'You're right.' Topaz sighed. 'I won't touch you again, I promise.'

'I'm not talking about us . . . not that there is an us,' I said hastily. 'I was talking about setting off the fire alarm on Friday night.'

'But I didn't!' Topaz's eyes filled with tears. 'I promise on my aunt's grave.'

'Remember that side door you found behind that curtain?' I said. 'It was a fire exit.'

'How was I to know?' she said sulkily. 'Are you going to punish me?'

'I won't, but the police might,' I said sternly. 'Take my mug downstairs when you leave.'

Topaz did as I asked and fairly skipped out of my bedroom. As I heard her Capri – and several car alarms being triggered by the powerful V-8 engine – roar out of Factory Terrace, I slid back under the duvet for a snooze.

Unfortunately, mere moments later my mobile rang. With a groan, I recognized the caller ID. It was Robin. Didn't he realize it was Sunday morning? I hit 'ignore' and let it go to voice mail but couldn't go back to sleep.

Pushing Annabel and her handbags, and Steve and Sammy Larch's fatal fall aside, I tried to focus on Douglas Fleming and the day ahead.

Questioning a killer without arousing suspicion was no easy task and required tact, skill and nerves of steel. I'd done it twice before, surely I could do it again.

27

The first race of the season was held in a gloomy annex at the rear of the Three Tuns.

Part skittle alley, part games room, today's venue had been vastly brightened up by the GSRF's signature green and silver bunting hanging from the rafters. Even though it wasn't quite eleven, the car park was packed and the place was rapidly filling up with competitors and fans alike, all wearing green sweatshirts emblazoned with the letters GSRF.

To the right of the front entrance Olive Larch sat at a trestle table marked REGISTER SNAILS HERE. Registration cost twenty pounds per snail for the entire season with an additional five pounds entry fee per race. Personally, I thought that a bit steep but since GSRF offered cash as prize money, could see the reasoning behind it.

A dry-erase board listing the locations of all the upcoming twice-monthly meetings stood on an easel next to the trestle table. Local pubs took turns hosting the event. Some publicans liked to throw in plates of sandwiches and fruit punches on the house. Since I was partial to Cornish pasties, I was particularly looking forward to next month's venue at the Nag and Bucket.

A long line of eager entrants clutching shoeboxes or holding palm-sized saucers snaked around the outside of the annex. I drifted over, notebook in hand to ask a few general who, what, when, where, how and why questions. There were a handful of first-timers – 'not from these parts', but willing to 'give it a go just this once.' Most of the competitors were simply taking part because 'that's what we've always done.'

Everyone seemed in excellent spirits although the general consensus was that the secretary was unbelievably slow. I had to admit they were right. Olive Larch sat in front of a large leather-bound ledger and painstakingly entered each snail's details in her spidery scrawl. Next, she fixed a tiny numbered plaque to the snail's shell with glue. The snail was then passed on to the Scrutineer – Tony – for slime testing and, if necessary, assigned a minute weight cloth. This strip of silk had small pockets – sewn by Olive – specifically for lead weights and was fastened to the plaque with cotton. Champions such as Seabiscuit, Bullet and Rambo would be among the select few to be allocated a handicap.

I took a pale green leaflet from a pile entitled *GSRF-Everything You Need To Know But Are Afraid To Ask* and skimmed the contents.

Basically, snails were run in heats of six on any of the three circular cloth-covered tables placed along the floor of the alley itself. These tables looked like four-ring archery targets. Six snails were placed in the bull's-eye and, on starters orders, made their way to the outside perimeter. The first two to cross the line went through to the finals, which was held at the far end of the annex on a specially adapted billiard table, covered with a waterproofed wooden insert. Flanking the billiard table were three-storey bleachers, affording an excellent view for spectators.

Scoring was as follows – six for a win, five for second place, four for third, and so on. These points went toward the Larch Legacy Supreme cup awarded to the best overall champion of the season. Naturally each race meeting had its own champions of the day.

Spying the Barker brothers from Gipping's notorious gang, the Swamp Dogs, I noted each lad carried a glass plant-mister filled with water and demanded to know why.

'Snails like damp conditions,' said Mickey who was the oldest and tallest of the four. The boys' job was to make sure every racetrack was well spritzed prior to each heat.

I spotted Mr Evans standing on an upturned orange crate next to a blackboard. As the official bookie, he was taking bets for major races including the Half-Yard Sprint, the Three-Yard Endurance and the One-Yard Steeplechase. Mrs Evans – looking very fetching this morning in a green velour jumpsuit – took the money from eager punters, recording each transaction in yet another ledger.

Catching my eye, her face lit up and she beckoned me over, much to the chagrin of one of her customers, a man with mutton-chop whiskers and bad teeth. I hadn't seen him before. No doubt he was an out-of-towner.

'Did you see Sadie last night?' she whispered, keeping one eye on Mr Evans in case he overheard. 'Did she like the care parcel?' Assuring her that yes, I did see Sadie and yes, she did like the care parcel, I was about to ask her not to allow *anyone* to enter my bedroom whether I was there or not, but didn't get the chance. Mr Evans announced that bets were about to close for the first race – The Maiden Half-Yard Slide.

Leaving Mrs Evans to her duties, I saw Wilf chatting to Fleming and strolled over. Fleming seemed perfectly at ease. I still found it difficult imagining him as a coldblooded killer.

'The Gala was an utter fiasco,' I heard him say. 'Not helped by that rabble rouser Randall. Those jumpers are a destructive lot.'

'Morning gents,' I said.

'Ah, just the person I want to see,' said Wilf. 'Make sure you get plenty of tidbits today, young Vicky.'

'At least Randall isn't here,' Fleming remarked. 'We don't want any more bad publicity.'

'Actually, I saw Dave Randall yesterday, and he has written proof that the Larch Legacy should have gone to the jumpers.'

'Do you have proof?' Wilf swung around to face me and fixed me with his one good eye.

'Yes, a signed document. Dave said he felt someone made Sammy change his mind at the last minute.' I was about to mention it had been Scarlett but remembered that hearsay was one of Wilf's pet peeves. Instead, I said, 'Don't you handle the Larch estate now, Mr Fleming?'

There was a slight pause before Fleming gave a pleasant smile and said, 'Whoever told you that was misinformed.' He glanced over at the clock on the wall. 'Goodness. Is that the time? You'd better get My Girl settled on table two, Wilf. I'll be starting your race in ten minutes.'

As Wilf hurried away I called out, 'Good luck! Break a shell!' before turning to Fleming. 'Can I have a quick word?'

'Perhaps later, dear,' said Fleming. 'I need to run to my car. I left the starter pistol there.'

'I'll come with you. We can talk on the way.'

'Of course,' he said, but a flicker of annoyance crossed his face.

Outside in the car park, Fleming withdrew a small case from the boot of his black Audi RS Avant. 'What was it you needed to ask me?'

'I wanted to apologize about missing out on some key details in Mrs Fleming's obituary.'

Fleming looked surprise. 'It is me who should apologize for the rather sparse information I gave you. You did a lovely job. I've had a few people come up and tell me they had no idea Scarlett was such an accomplished actress.'

'Funerals are a specialty of mine,' I said modestly, 'which is why I am so persnickety about details. Where on earth did you find an Egyptian coffin at such short notice?'

'I'm sorry?' Fleming turned white. 'I don't follow.'

'I'm sure a lot of my readers would be interested to know.'

'The funeral company did everything,' Fleming said quickly. 'I really must get back.'

'And obviously, they arranged for the body to be transported from Spain, too?'

'Of course. Really, Vicky, is this necessary? Scarlett is gone. *Gone!*' Fleming's eyes grew watery, but this time crocodile tears would not fool me. 'I cannot believe these questions coming from *you* of all people. You have always shown such kindness. Scarlett called you a journalist with a heart, but now . . . I don't know what to think!'

'I'm just doing my job,' I faltered. 'I was only—'

'Stop!' He held up his hand. 'Enough! Let's forget we ever had this conversation. I don't want to tell Wilf that you are harassing me. Good day.' And with that, he stormed back to the annex.

You idiot, Vicky! I could have kicked myself. My interrogation skills left a lot to be desired. What had I expected? That he would just cave in and admit that he preordered the coffin himself?

I trooped back to the annex thoroughly disheartened until I spied Ronnie Binns placing a shoebox on the windowsill. Oh well. My day was already ruined. Why not just finish it by insulting Ronnie Binns, too?

Ronnie cupped Rambo – wearing a plaque with the number five and a dark purple weight cloth – in the palm of his hand.

'Rambo seems shy this morning,' I said, peering closely at a brown shell. 'Oh! Excuse me.' I took two steps back as the full force of Ronnie's foul body odour hit me. Once again, I marvelled at how Annabel survived behind that curtain in Gipping Manor with this smelly little man.

'He's resting, aren't you, my boy.' Ronnie lovingly ran a grimy forefinger across the snail's shell. 'Saving his strength for the steeplechase.'

205

'What extra weight is he carrying?'

'Half an ounce.'

'That's a lot.'

'Aye. I don't expect him to win today, but I'll be happy if he gets placed third.'

'I saw your work in the *Bugle*,' I said. 'You really should have offered those photographs to the *Gazette* first.'

'The *Gazette* doesn't pay,' Ronnie said flatly.

'I'm surprised—' I gave him a playful nudge. 'Given your relationship with Annabel.'

Ronnie turned pink to the tips of his ears. 'She told you we had a *relationship!*'

Careful, Vicky. I could see I'd have another Fleming-Eunice love disaster on my hands if I didn't watch out.

'She tells me everything,' I said, crossing my fingers behind my back. 'It sounds like you are quite the romantic.'

Ronnie beamed with pleasure. 'She calls me her angel. Said if it hadn't been for me, she would have died that night.'

I bit back my retort. If it hadn't been for *me*, both of them would have been burned to a crisp! 'How sweet,' I said. 'That was a *big* night.'

'She likes to talk about it,' said Ronnie.

'Really?' This was puzzling. The night in question was one I knew Annabel still suffered nightmares over and surely Ronnie Binns was the last person she'd ever want to relive those memories with.

'Aye, she likes to talk about the weather.'

'The *weather*?'

'I hear you want to do some acting with the Bards,' said Pam Green elbowing her way between us. 'Barbara mentioned it.'

'Oh! Right.' I was momentarily distracted by Pam's silly hat – a snail antenna hair band. 'Ronnie, wait—' But it was too late. Ronnie had shuffled off in the direction of table three.

'Such a smelly man. Barbara thought you needed rescuing.' Pam pointed to the bleachers and waved at Barbara who gave me the thumbs up. 'I'll be auditioning for our autumn programme next month.'

She handed me a Gipping Bards flyer printed in medieval typeface. I glanced at the list. It seemed alarmingly ambitious with productions ranging from Ibsen's A *Doll's House* to Andrew Lloyd Webber's rock musical *Starlight Express* performed entirely on roller skates. 'I don't care what Barbara told you,' she said. '*Antony and Cleopatra* will *not* be in the programme this season.'

'Scarlett Fleming's Cleopatra would be a hard act to follow,' I said.

'Nothing like that. Someone broke into the Bards storage unit on the industrial estate and stole the coffin.'

I swear my heart stopped beating. 'Was it an *Egyptian* coffin?'

'Of course. The Bards prides itself on being authentic,' said Pam with a sniff. 'Excuse me, I must snag Ruth Reeves. She'd make a perfect Nora if she'd lose ten pounds.'

It all fell into place. I looked over at Douglas Fleming standing with the starter pistol in his hand, wondering how he'd killed his wife. Was it by a single shot to the head? Strangulation? Poison? Suffocation? Electrocution? The methods were endless but would I ever be able to prove it?

'You look like you've seen a ghost,' whispered a voice in my ear.

I came back to earth with a jolt. Dressed in jeans and a teal Guernsey-knit sweater, Probes had a pint of shandy in each hand. 'I thought you looked thirsty. Don't worry. I know you're driving. Yours is a weak one.'

'Thanks.' Frankly I could have done with a nip of brandy from Barbara's hip flask.

'I've been thinking about Scarlett Fleming,' said Probes. 'Maybe she used a pseudonym?'

'I've been thinking about her, too,' I said slowly. 'How easy is it to exhume a body?'

28

'Exhuming a body is a very complicated process,' said Probes, offering me a salt-and-vinegar crisp. 'There's a lot of red tape.'

'I'm not hungry,' I said.

Probes took a sip of shandy. 'You'd need Mr Fleming's permission, of course.' *I could just see myself asking for that!* 'And *all* the relatives, naturally. Wasn't she American?' He took out his notebook. 'If I can help, I will.'

'Yes. As far as I know, Mrs Fleming had one relative in Atlanta.'

Probes duly wrote *Relative in Atlanta. Name?* on his pad. His writing was small and neat. 'You'd have to obtain permission from the coroner's office or get a licence from the Home Office,' he went on. 'I take it Mrs Fleming was buried in sacred ground?'

'St Peter's the Martyr.' I frowned as I recalled how Fleming had invited me to step inside the family vault to view the coffin. Surely he wouldn't have suggested it if he were guilty? I might have said yes! What if I was wrong about everything?

'In that case, you'll need a Bishop's Faculty, too,' said Probes. 'Permission from the church.'

'Whittler's away on holiday and not back until Tuesday,' I groaned.

'And of course, official grounds for *requesting* an exhumation,' Probes said sternly. 'A hunch just will not cut it.'

We both fell silent. 'What if the actual coffin itself was a bona fide reason for an investigation?' I said suddenly. 'Don't all coffins have to be lined with zinc and hermetically sealed?'

'A danger to public health, you mean?' Probes nodded slowly. 'That's a possibility. The smell would be quite dreadful—'

'And the Fleming vault is above ground. I might even be able to produce a witness – someone who handled the actual coffin.' I wondered if I could persuade Neil Titley to come forward. Wasn't it said that even bad publicity was good publicity?

'You'll still need to go through all the official channels,' said Probes. 'It would take some weeks. Maybe months.'

Unless I broke into the vault myself!

'You're not thinking of doing anything rash, are you?'

'Of course not!' *Was the man a mind reader?* 'Like what?'

'It's a criminal offence to exhume—'

'Everything is a criminal offence to you, Colin,' I laughed. My face burned with embarrassment having never addressed DS Probes by his first name before.

'Sorry,' he said ruefully. 'I tend to say that a lot, don't I?' He shot me a boyish smile. I'd always thought his teeth were like sharks but actually they were just small and neat – rather like his handwriting. 'Speaking of offences,' he went on, 'I'm afraid Gipping Manor Hotel is going to press charges on the GSRF because of Friday night's fiasco.'

I had to admit I wasn't surprised. I took out my own notebook. This was a story the *Gazette* had to snag first. 'Any details?'

'Thousands of pounds worth of water damage. Broken furniture. Smashed glasses. Someone had vandalized the portrait of our queen by smearing trifle over her crown.' He shook his head. 'What's wrong with people?'

'I knew about the bread rolls being thrown, but not the trifle.'

'It all started with the fire alarm going off,' said Probes. 'There was a fire exit behind a curtain next to the ladies' toilets. The alarm was activated when the door opened and automatically set off the sprinkler system.' *Topaz was going to have to come clean.* 'Mrs Pratt obviously used the fire alarm as a decoy so she could attack Olive Larch in the bathroom.'

'She said she didn't,' I said.

'And you believe her?' Probes cocked his head. 'Were you aware that the Flemings had filed a restraining order on Mrs Pratt several weeks ago?'

'Yes. But the two incidents are completely unrelated,' I said. 'This is England and everyone is presumed innocent until found guilty.' At least that's what Dad always says.

Probes looked taken aback. 'True. But in this case we have proof.'

'How?'

'The Manor car park has a surprisingly sophisticated CCTV system,' he said. 'The footage is being examined as we speak.'

I went completely still. Why hadn't I thought of that! 'The CCTV footage,' I whispered. 'Of *course!*' The Gipping Bards storage unit was on the industrial estate behind Fleming's office. I had to look at that footage! What's more, Melanie Carew had it running around the clock. Given I had more than a few questions to ask her about her boss and their relationship, I'd pay her a visit first thing Monday morning.

'Speak of the devil,' said Probes, 'Mrs Pratt's got some nerve!'

I looked up. Eunice had just entered the lounge. Dressed in her pale lemon suit and pillbox hat, she carried a canvas bag emblazoned with BAN CCTV! NO PRIVACY! She marched purposefully toward the door marked TO ANNEX.

I leapt to my feet. 'I'll go after her.'

'No! Don't! She could be dangerous,' said Probes. 'That handbag looks bulky.'

But I was already halfway across the room shouting, 'Eunice! Wait!'

Eunice spun around. To my surprise, her face registered relief. 'Vicky! I was coming to find you.'

Probes joined me. 'Mrs Pratt, I'm afraid I'm going to have to ask to look inside that bag.'

'Why?' She clutched the bag to her chest. 'I know my rights.'

'If you prefer, we can always talk about this down at the station,' said Probes coldly.

'New GSRF policy, Eunice,' I said quickly. 'Mind if I have a peep?'

'I don't mind *you* looking,' she snapped, passing me the bag. 'But not *him*.'

Probes rolled his eyes and stepped aside. 'Please, be my guest.'

I opened it to find a navy collapsible umbrella, a rolled up plastic raincoat, and an envelope. It was addressed to me. 'I think I know what this is,' I said with a sinking heart. Eunice's wretched signed statement. 'Why don't you give it to me later?'

'Robin needs you to read it and make sure it's in order,' Eunice said, shooting a defiant look at Probes. 'Don't worry, Officer, you'll see it soon enough.'

Probes opened his mouth and shut it again. Drawing Eunice to one side, I said, 'Why don't we go and have a chat about it?'

'I have to talk to Olive first.'

'Not a good idea,' I said in a low voice. 'Not in front of the policeman.'

'I don't care.'

'I think Robin wouldn't be very happy if you got into trouble with the police. *Again!*' Eunice didn't answer. 'Did you drive

211

yourself here today?' She nodded. 'Why don't you wait outside in your car until the officer has gone and then we can go and talk to Olive together?' Of course, I had no intention of doing any such thing.

She scowled and said, 'All right,' before tossing Probes one last defiant glare and stomping out of the bar.

'You certainly seem to know how to handle her,' Probes said. 'I'm afraid I have to go in a few moments. I've got to be back on duty in Plymouth by three.'

'I'd leave by a different exit if I were you,' I said. 'As long as Eunice thinks you're in here, she'll stay away from Olive Larch.'

'Vicky, there is something I want to ask you.' Probes gave a cough and made a great deal of clearing his throat. 'Tuesday is my night off. W-w-would you have dinner with me?'

A frisson of *je ne sais quoi* passed between us. My mouth went dry. 'I might be working.'

'Didn't you say Whittler was back on Tuesday?' Probes said. 'We could talk about exhuming Scarlett Fleming's body.'

'That sounds romantic.' *Blast!* What on earth made me say that!

'Did you want to be romantic?' Probes's eyes twinkled.

'No,' I mumbled but my stomach turned over. I looked down at my shoes.

'Why don't I pick you up at seven?'

'Is she resisting arrest, Officer?' shouted Arthur the barman from behind the counter. 'Shall I call for back up?'

'No, need.' Probes whisked out a pair of handcuffs from under his jacket. 'I've got these.' The two men cracked up with laughter. 'Just kidding.'

I turned scarlet as the unwanted vision of Probes handcuffing me to a bed flashed through my mind. 'I must go,' I said hastily. 'Mrs Pratt is waiting for me outside.'

'Just one more thing,' said Probes.

'No more copper jokes, please,' I begged.

'Can you tell Annabel I don't have an answer for her yet,' he said. 'She'll know what I mean.'

I nodded, dying to ask exactly what he *did* mean but far more desperate to make my escape. Leaving the two men talking – no doubt about me – I steeled myself for a strong dose of Eunice Pratt.

29

Eunice's Ford Fiesta was parked in front of someone's garage door under a sign that said DON'T EVEN THINK ABOUT PARKING HERE.

Putting on my best smile, I strolled over and got into the passenger seat only to be greeted by a curt, 'You took your time.'

'Sorry,' I said pleasantly. 'I'm covering the snail racing today.'

Eunice handed me the envelope with a scowl. 'It's all in there.'

Bracing myself for the worst, I tore it open and pulled out two typed pages. Skimming the contents, I noted that Robin had obviously done this sort of thing before as he used all sorts of professional jargon like *unlawful attack* and referred to Olive as the *perpetrator*. There was no mention of Topaz – or should I say, the Beast of Bodmin. Eunice had signed her name at the bottom stating the contents were 'true, so help me God.'

'You're quite sure it was Olive who locked you in the stall?' I said.

Eunice snapped an indignant '*Yes.*'

'You didn't see anything strange, at all?'

'Are you calling me a liar?'

'I only ask because of the *Bugle*, which, by the way is a dreadful newspaper.'

'It's utter filth. I won't have it in the house.'

'Glad to hear it. As I was saying, the *Bugle* carried a photograph of a huge catlike creature stalking the car park on Friday night. Several of the guests claim they saw it, too. Apparently, the newspaper is offering a reward for any further information.'

Eunice was quiet for what seemed like a full two minutes until she asked, 'What kind of reward?'

'I can probably find out,' I said, encouraged by the glint of greed I caught in Eunice's eye. 'Olive Larch was convinced she saw something jump in through the ladies' loo window and we'll soon find out what it was.'

'How?'

'There are CCTV cameras everywhere.' I pointed to one located under the eaves of the garage roof above us – although I happened to know it was a fake. 'Whatever went on in the bathroom was filmed. As a matter of fact, the police are checking it right now.' This was sort of true. 'That was why I was talking to Detective Sergeant Probes earlier.'

Eunice's face crumpled. 'I knew there was something there!' she wailed. 'But Robin didn't believe me.'

'Well, *I* believe you. Let's forget about the assault charge for now.' With a huge sigh of relief I took out my notebook. 'Why don't you tell me exactly what happened?'

'I really *was* trying to help that stupid woman but she panicked,' said Eunice. 'Even at school she was pathetic, claiming she couldn't do games because of her nerves. Dougie didn't—'

'You said you were helping her.'

'Something horrible *did* climb in the window.' Eunice's eyes grew wide at the memory. 'I've never seen anyone so frightened before. All the colour drained out of Olive's face. She grabbed a pair of nail scissors from her handbag and started doing this.'

Eunice made stabbing motions, mirroring those – rather too well – from the shower scene at the Bates motel in *Psycho*.

'What happened next?'

Eunice dropped her hand. 'Olive started to hyperventilate. When Robin was little, he used to do that if he didn't get his own way so I knew what to do.'

Yet another strike against Robin as potential husband material. 'Did you actually see the . . . creature?'

'It came in the window behind me but—' Eunice shuddered. 'I felt its evil presence.'

'Go on.'

'Olive collapsed. She was gasping for breath.' Eunice began to tremble. 'There was a paper bag in the rubbish bin – that always worked on Robin. I got on top of her and tried to hold the bag over her nose and mouth.' Eunice grabbed my arm, her voice urgent. 'She fought me. Screaming. Thrashing around with those nail scissors and then—' Eunice licked her lips. 'The c-c-creature . . . it picked me up. Shook me and threw me into the stall. I thought it was going to eat me alive.' With another agonizing wail, Eunice let go my arm and slumped forward over the steering wheel.

'How awful,' I said, gently rubbing her back. I know it sounded unkind but I had this urge to laugh my head off. The idea of anyone thinking Topaz was the Beast of Bodmin was ludicrous. 'It must have been a dreadful shock.'

'Robin is going to be very angry,' she whimpered.

'He doesn't need to know for now. Let's just wait and see what the CCTV cameras reveal.'

'Yes. Good.' Eunice seemed to magically perk up. 'Are you ready?'

'For what?' I said warily.

'To talk to Olive,' said Eunice. 'I don't want her getting hurt.'

'The officer will be there all day,' I lied. 'Why would Olive get hurt?'

'She needs to know that Dougie loves me,' Eunice said earnestly. 'He told me that if anything ever happened to Scarlett we would be together forever. He made me promise that nothing would stand in our way.'

My heart sank. This was seriously alarming. 'You haven't told anyone this, have you?'

'Dougie didn't even bother with Olive until recently.'

'You said you all went to school together.'

'We were all at the *same* school. Different years. Everyone had a crush on Dougie but he never gave Olive the time of day. Why now? *Why?*'

I knew exactly why. Money – the oldest motive for murder in the book. With Sammy Larch dead, Olive had inherited millions of pounds.

'She needs to know he's mine,' Eunice went on. 'She needs to know he's still calling me *every* day.'

'I think you *should* tell her,' I said smoothly 'But in private. Not in front of that lot in there.'

'Yes, you're right,' Eunice nodded. 'She'd be embarrassed, wouldn't she?'

'As for your statement,' I said, changing the subject. 'Just tell Robin that we're waiting to see what turns up in the CCTV footage. I must go now. Bye.'

As I watched the silver Ford Fiesta leave the car park, I realized I was no further forward in my Fleming-has-an-accomplice theory.

My mind returned to Pam Green's words about Sammy Larch's death being convenient. Even though Dr Frost had signed the death certificate, it was Steve who'd arrived first on the scene. I hadn't thought about it at the time, but maybe he did have a good reason to want to talk to a *real* reporter.

With Topaz present tonight, too, there would be safety in numbers. I only hoped this wasn't a case of out of the frying pan, into the fire.

30

Topaz was waiting outside The Copper Kettle. 'You're late.'

'Goodness,' I gawked. 'I almost didn't recognize you.'

Even though I was used to Topaz's many disguises, tonight she'd really gone to town. For a start, it looked as if she had used a garden trowel to plaster on her makeup – heavy black eyeliner, thick blue eye shadow, and scarlet lipstick. She wore a black halter-neck top that was practically transparent and no bra. An indecently short black skirt exposed sturdy thighs, which were clad in fishnet stockings. The whole effect was somewhat risqué and made me nervous. 'Where's Steve?'

'Change of plan,' she said. 'We're going to Badger Drive.'

The phrase *ménage à trois* flew instantly to mind. 'No. I don't think so.'

'But you promised!' Topaz stamped her foot. 'If you don't come, I'm going to tell Annabel that you asked me to spy on her.'

'Don't be childish,' I said, irritated.

'Steve really wants to see us,' said Topaz. 'He said he had

something very important to talk about and wanted to tell you – me, really – in person.'

The problem was, I really *did* need to talk to Steve.

While the afternoon had dragged on at the Three Tuns, I'd been able to watch Fleming and Olive for all four heats of the Three-Yard Endurance – *and* the Finals. It was clear he was fond of her – unless he'd been putting on an act for everyone to see, which was possible. He did perform with the Bards, after all.

Given the fact that Fleming was newly widowed, I was astonished that no one seemed to think his lovey-dovey behaviour unusual. But Barbara claimed that, 'when you get to our age, you take love when you can.' She certainly wasn't the only one holding that opinion. Many thought the new couple 'sweet' and 'darling'.

Olive being worth millions troubled me. If Fleming was capable of knocking off his wife of forty years, I was quite sure he'd have no problem doing the same to Olive.

'All right. I'll come with you,' I said to Topaz. 'But I can only stay an hour and I'm taking my moped.'

'Suits me.' Topaz gestured to her rucksack on the floor in the doorway. 'I might end up staying overnight anyway.'

'You probably will – looking like that.'

'Like what?'

'I'm only saying we're supposed to be professional news-paper reporters. If you want to be taken seriously, you need to dress for the part.'

'I *am* dressed for the part,' Topaz said, puzzled. 'It's you who isn't.'

I had deliberately removed what small trace of makeup I usually wore and picked a grey moth-eaten poloneck sweater and jeans. My plan was to look as unattractive as possible. I wasn't taking any chances with either of them.

'Let's get this over and done with,' I said. 'I'll meet you there.'

Moments later, Topaz roared past in her Capri, hand firmly

on her DeLorean *Back To the Future* themed horn. When she gunned the V-8 engine the customized double exhaust set off all the car alarms parked along the High Street. I was very glad I'd decided to travel under my own steam judging by the stares and fist waving from many disgruntled motorists and pedestrians alike.

Steve lived in a four-storey Victorian house in Badger Drive, which had been converted into flats. I left my moped next to the empty Capri and went inside where I found Topaz chattering to Hilda Hicks who was holding a green canvas bag emblazoned with the logo PINGIRL PONIES.

'I take it the snail crowd have gone by now?' Ms Hicks said in her loud, strident voice. Sunday night was bowling night at the Three Tuns skittle alley.

'They were putting the tables away when I left an hour ago,' I said. 'Though I expect many will still be drinking in the bar.'

'Better be off then,' she boomed. 'Ms Potter, should I telephone Ms Turberville-Spat to firm up the details?'

'Don't worry,' said Topaz, giving me a sly wink, 'I talk to Ethel all the time. I'll make sure she sends over the paperwork.'

'Jolly good. Jolly good.' Ms Hicks smiled again and, with a curt nod, strode out of the house.

'What was all that about?' I said, as we began the endless, tortuous climb to Steve's top-floor flat.

'I'm leasing out the stable block and grounds to the Riding Club for their summer camp,' Topaz said. 'It's funny how the old bat doesn't know who I really am.'

Neither did I. I often wondered if Topaz even knew who she was herself.

The next time we spoke was outside Steve's front door. I rang the bell.

'Wait a moment.' Topaz panted as she dumped her rucksack on the floor. There was a loud, metallic-sounding clunk. Pulling out a pair of high, strappy dancing shoes, she took off her black pumps and slipped the shoes on. They looked very similar to those I'd borrowed from Sadie.

My heart sank. 'You haven't got a collapsible pole in that rucksack by any chance?' I said, half joking. It would certainly explain Topaz's racy ensemble.

'It's supposed to be a surprise. Don't say anything.'

'I won't, as long as you promise to keep that pole in there until I leave.'

Steve threw open the door with a broad smile, which instantly evaporated. 'Topaz!' he said horrified. 'What are you doing here?'

'Hello darling.' She kissed him on the cheek and swept imperiously inside. 'Oh, how frightfully sweet. You're playing our song.' The sound of ABBA's 'Take A Chance On Me' filled the air.

Hadn't Steve played the very same song to me the first time I came here? Amused, I raised a quizzical eyebrow to our host for the evening.

Steve looked mortified. 'The song is for you, doll, not her,' he protested. Somehow, I didn't believe him.

Steve was dressed in neatly pressed khakis and a crisp white – and tight – short-sleeved shirt. His usual twinkling blue eyes looked troubled as he corralled me into the tiny space behind the front door and grabbed my hand. 'What's *she* doing here?'

As always, a frisson of electricity surged through my body at his touch. I was acutely aware of his scent – Old Spice and antiseptic – and looked for an escape. 'Apparently, you invited us both.'

'Hey!' Topaz shouted from within. 'When do I get my Steve Special?'

'Not tonight,' Steve called out, then in a low voice added urgently, 'I swear I only invited *you*.'

'Topaz said you had something important to tell me.'

He looked sheepish. 'The truth is, you looked so hot at the

Gala on Friday, doll. I just had to see you again and I knew you'd say no.'

'So this was just a trick to entice me into the badger's den?'

'Don't hate me, doll.'

Topaz suddenly appeared, towering above us in her high-heeled shoes. 'What are you two doing?' she demanded.

Steve dropped my hand and sprang aside. Even I felt guilty.

'I was about to help Vicky off with her coat,' he said smoothly.

'Goodie.' Topaz jumped forward. 'Let's take it off together.'

'Don't touch me!' I said, waving them both away. 'I'm not staying. I just got a text message on my mobile. I have to go.'

'Oh! What a frightful shame.' Topaz did not sound disappointed. 'Can you just tell Steve that I work for the *Gazette!*'

I turned to Steve who now looked seriously worried. 'Topaz secretly works for me. Her position is so secret that not even our chief reporter knows.'

'You *see*! I told you so!' Topaz gave Steve a playful punch. 'It's just as well you *are* leaving, Vicky,' she said, 'The table is only laid up for two people. There's champagne and everything.'

'Just stay for one glass,' said Steve in a small voice. 'Just one. Please.'

He looked so desperate I relented.

Steve led the way into the sitting room and jumped when Topaz mischievously pinched his bottom.

'I've got to go to the kitchen,' he said. 'Make yourselves at home.'

It was clear that Steve had gone to a lot of trouble this evening. The sitting room was spotlessly clean and smelled of Pledge lemon furniture polish – Mrs Evans's favourite brand. Fake flames leapt in the fireplace; I lost count of the number of candles that flickered from every available surface, casting a romantic glow around the room.

A huge arrangement of red roses sat on the pine coffee table along with a bottle of champagne in a silver ice bucket and two cut-crystal tulip glasses. Two china plates, two silver knives and forks atop two red linen napkins sat next to a platter of Marks & Spencer canapés, a cheese board, and a bowl of grapes.

Steve had done all this – just for me! Frankly, I was touched.

'There are strawberries dipped in chocolate in the fridge,' said Topaz, flopping onto the sofa. Her skirt rode up even higher but she didn't seem to care. Taking a salmon pinwheel, she added, 'Steve's an ABBA fan. Look.' She pointed to a large framed vintage poster of the Swedish musicians in white bell-bottom trousers that hung on one wall. 'He collects vinyl records, too.'

Of course, I already knew all this having been to Chez Steve before. In fact, seeing Topaz lounging on the sofa, it was hard not to relive that moment when Steve kissed me and—

'Why are you looking at me like that?' said Topaz coyly. 'You've gone all red.'

'I was just thinking about work,' I lied. 'There are a couple of loose ends in the Sammy Larch death I need to clear up for my report.'

'Why? He died weeks ago. Who cares now?' said Topaz, cramming an entire shrimp vol-au-vent into her mouth.

'That's just where you are wrong,' I said. 'As a professional investigative journalist, a case is never closed until all the *i*'s are dotted, and the *t*'s crossed.'

'I see, boss,' Topaz said eagerly. 'What's this got to do with Steve?'

'Did I hear my name?' Steve sauntered in with the plate of chocolate-covered strawberries, a tea cloth and a coffee mug emblazoned MEDIC MEN ROCK! 'Champagne anyone?'

He popped the cork and expertly managed to pour the bubbling liquid into each glass and his mug without spilling a drop. 'Cheers ladies!'

I had to admit Steve's choice in champagne was surprisingly good and far superior to the stuff that was served at Friday's Gala.

'Sit down everyone.' Topaz patted the sofa beside her and said in a seductive voice. 'Plenty of room for three.'

'I'm fine standing,' I said quickly.

'I've got a beanbag.' Steve retrieved a brown leather beanbag from behind the sofa and dragged it around to the opposite side of the coffee table.

He sank down heavily to ground level, reminding me of a beached whale. It looked very uncomfortable and he certainly wasn't able to reach the canapés.

'Let's get down to business,' said Topaz. 'Steve, you mentioned you had something frightfully important to tell me.'

'Did I?' Steve looked startled. 'Right. Yep. Maybe later.'

'Oh! You mean after Vicky has left.' Topaz shot me a look of triumph. 'Steve only wants to tell me, not you.'

'Well, I have a couple of questions for you, Steve.' I said taking out my notebook.

'Anything, doll,' he said miserably.

'I say,' said Topaz, 'does anyone have a pencil and piece of paper?'

'Here.' I ripped out a page and handed her one of my spare pens – I always carry extra in my pocket. 'I want to talk about the night Sammy Larch died.'

'I got the 999 call just after the pubs shut,' Steve said. 'Of course, the poor old bugger was dead when we got there.'

'Because it was a busy night and you arrived too late?' said Topaz, pencil poised.

'No. We didn't arrive too *late*.' Did I detect a hint of annoyance in Steve's usually mild-mannered voice? 'Gipping paramedics have a reputation of reaching any accident scene within ten to fifteen minutes of a call. When Tom and I got there, Larch had been dead for hours.'

'Hours?' I said sharply. Dave had mentioned he'd called round at seven. 'How many?'

'Yes, how many?' echoed Topaz.

224

'Rigor mortis had set in,' said Steve. 'That usually happens between two and four hours after death.'

'Rigger-who?' said Topaz, licking the end of her pencil. 'What's that?'

'I'll explain later.' This meant Scarlett could have been in Sammy's house at the time of his fall. 'Weren't you suspicious?'

'Happens occasionally with the old folk,' said Steve with a shrug. 'Larch was ninety-five. Family members don't like to have the body taken away too soon.'

'It's true,' said Topaz. 'My aunt's cousin twice-removed kept her husband in the bath for three days before she called the ambulance.'

'I'll ask the questions just for tonight, okay?' I said.

'Sorry. It's just so *exciting*!'

'The death certificate stated that Sammy had fallen down the stairs and broken his neck,' I said.

'That's right.' Steve nodded. 'It was quite a tumble. Poor old bugger was covered in bruises.'

'I fell down the stairs once,' Topaz declared.

'And there was something weird,' said Steve. 'I found three tiny plastic red triangles stuck in the old boy's sweater. I've got them somewhere.'

'Who made the emergency call?' Topaz said.

'Thank you, Topaz. Let me ask the questions. Steve? You were saying.'

'Scarlett Fleming made the call. Told me she went into the kitchen to make them a pot of tea and heard a loud thump.'

'So, when you arrived, Olive and Douglas Fleming were there, too?'

'Dougie was brilliant. Both ladies were in a dreadful state. In fact, Olive had one of her episodes and we had to sedate her.'

'By *we*, I take it you mean Dr Frost?' I said.

'No. My partner Tom and I. Frost . . . well . . . can someone pass me the very *last* canapé and some grapes?'

'I'll get it. I don't like mushrooms.' Topaz jumped up,

making sure that Steve got an eyeful of thigh as she bent over to put the solitary vol-au-vent and bowl of grapes straight onto the carpet. 'Would you like me to peel you a grape?'

'No, I can manage. Thanks.'

Topaz flung herself back on the sofa.

'What did Dr Frost make of it all?' I said.

'Took five minutes to examine the body and rushed off,' said Steve. 'As a matter of fact, he didn't show up until gone one in the morning. We thought we'd have to call out a locum. Of course, the following morning we knew why.'

'Why?'

Steve blushed. 'No reason.' He suddenly found the bowl of grapes absolutely fascinating.

'Come on, Steve,' I said sternly. 'What aren't you telling me?'

'Us, you mean,' said Topaz. 'I'm a reporter, too.'

'Frost is my boss,' Steve sounded unhappy. 'Annabel is your friend.'

'She's not Vicky's friend,' Topaz chipped in. 'You can tell us anything. We won't repeat it.'

Steve looked at me. I shrugged. 'Please go on.'

'The next morning, I get a call from a friend at Plymouth General who had treated his wife to a romantic night at The Imperial—'

'Oh! That five-star hotel on the quay?' said Topaz.

Steve nodded. 'He saw Frost in reception picking up a room key.'

'Dr Frost was staying the night in a hotel?' Topaz frowned. 'How frightfully odd. I wonder why.'

I knew why. Further proof that Dr Frost was having an affair.

'Wait!' said Topaz. 'The Imperial Hotel is close to those warehouses!'

'Warehouses?' said Steve.

'I bet they're in it together,' shrieked Topaz. 'Frost is flogging handbags, too!'

'Handbags?' Poor Steve looked bewildered.

'Remember what I told you, Topaz,' I said sternly. 'Now is not the time to discuss this.'

'Well, I need more champagne.' Steve attempted to rise off the beanbag but collapsed. 'Can someone pour me a glass?'

'Not for me,' I said, polishing off my own. 'I have to go.'

'Okay. Bye,' said Topaz, jumping to her feet. 'Stay right there, Steve. You and I have some unfinished business.' She reached down for her rucksack. 'I'm just nipping to the loo.' Topaz skipped out of the sitting room. I heard a distant door slam.

'Don't leave me with her, Vicky,' said Steve, struggling to get up from the beanbag. In the end he rolled onto the carpet and staggered to his feet. 'She's a nutter.'

I had to agree with him. 'The problem is that she's easily encouraged,' I said. 'You just have to say a firm no.'

'I tried that the other night but she kicked me in the goolies.' Steve looked up sharply. 'What's that clunking noise?'

We turned to see Topaz trying to jam a long pole vertically in the doorway. She'd changed into a long transparent negligee through which I saw the outline of a leopard-skin costume. Her lips were painted a garish red.

All the colour drained out of Steve's face. 'Bloody hell,' he said, and sank onto the sofa whispering, 'I'm a dead man.'

'Change of plan, Topaz. Steve just got an emergency call and he has to leave, *now*.'

'That's right! I did!' Steve instantly brightened up.

'What rotten luck.' Topaz grinned from ear to ear. 'Are you sure?'

'I'm *positive*,' said Steve happily. 'Multiple pile-up on the road to Pennymoor.'

Minutes later, Steve had blown out all the candles, turned off the fire, and put on his white coat. With equal speed, Topaz had collapsed the pole, switched outfits, and tipped the remaining food from the coffee table – including the chocolate-dipped strawberries – into her rucksack without uttering a single complaint.

It was only when we reached her Capri, she said, 'Golly! That was a close one.'

'What do you mean? I thought you liked Steve.'

'Me?' Topaz's eyes widened. 'Why would I?'

'You certainly seemed to like him on Friday,' I pointed out. 'And . . . well . . . tonight with all that Banana Club pole dancing palaver.'

'You can't be serious.' She regarded me with utter horror. 'He's a man! Really Vicky, you are funny. It's part of being a reporter. Pillow talk. Making a man feel you fancy him in exchange for information.'

'Reporters do not need pillow talk,' I said firmly. 'They need to know how to ask the right questions.'

'You can think what you like, but if I hadn't got all dressed up like this, I'm positive Steve wouldn't have told us about Frost and the Imperial Hotel.'

There was no point arguing with Topaz's logic. 'Pity he got that call though. He never did tell me what was so important,' she said.

Topaz unlocked the Capri and threw in her rucksack. 'Do you want to drop off your moped and we'll go in my car?'

'Go where?'

'To Plymouth,' she said. 'I want to stake out the warehouse again. See if I can catch Annabel and Frost in the act. I've brought a camera.'

'Can't. I've got the snail racing results to write up, and besides, I'm tired.'

'An investigative journalist never sleeps, remember?' Topaz slid into the driver's seat. 'I'll give you a full report tomorrow, boss.'

As Topaz roared out of Badger Drive I wondered if I was wrong in allowing her to go off on a wild goose chase to Plymouth. I was positive Frost had nothing to do with selling

228

handbags and had been simply having an affair. I didn't even care with whom.

All I could think about was Steve's revelations. Why would Scarlett kill off Sammy Larch? How fortunate for her that Frost was too preoccupied with getting back to his mistress in Plymouth to notice anything awry? What if Fleming had known that Scarlett was going to knock Sammy off and made sure Olive Larch was out of the way at the Nag and Bucket? Nothing made sense.

I didn't want to wait for Whittler to come back and go through all the red tape of gaining access to the vault and exhuming the body. It could take months.

Maybe I *should* break into the vault. I recalled that all property belonging to the Gipping Bards bore an identifying stamp. *Somehow* I had to get hold of the key. *Somehow* I had to persuade Melanie Carew to let me look at the CCTV cameras and have a little chat with her about her so-called phone call to Go-Go Gothic.

If Fleming really was after Olive Larch's fortune, he could only get it after they were married. Since Scarlett had been dead less than a week, surely I had time.

Olive was perfectly safe. For now.

31

Mrs Evans burst into my bedroom and slammed a mug of tea down on my night table. 'They've eloped!'

She thrust back the curtains sending the metal runners screeching along the rusty rails. Sunlight streamed through my window as I tried to shake off a bad night's sleep.

'Didn't you hear what I said?' she cried. 'They've eloped!'

'Who?'

'Olive Larch and Douglas Fleming, of course!' Mrs Evans perched on the edge of my bed. Her dentures clicked into overdrive. 'My Lenny was in on it. He said Dougie swore him to secrecy.'

'It's a bit sudden, isn't it?' I sat up, instantly awake, and reached for my morning cuppa.

'They were all over each other at the Gala,' said Mrs Evans. 'Didn't you notice?'

'Yes, but even so,' I said, 'his wife's hardly been dead a week.'

'Frankly, dear, when you reach a certain age, you have—'

'To take love when you can. I know.'

'Exactly!' Mrs Evans unnecessarily lowered her voice.

'Though I daresay he'll be widowed again soon and then he'll be sitting pretty. No more money problems for him.'

'Why do you say that?' I said sharply.

'Olive Larch is very rich . . . and very ill.'

'I know she suffers from panic attacks.'

'She's very, *very* ill.' Mrs Evans folded her hands in her lap and gave me a knowing look. There was a pregnant pause.

'How ill?' And how strange that Barbara had never implied Olive's poor health was *that* serious.

'I'm not one to gossip, dear but . . .' Another pregnant pause.

'You can't tell me anything I don't already know,' I said, trying one of Dad's brilliant tactics for getting information. Reverse psychology.

'You didn't hear this from me . . .' Mrs Evans lowered her voice again. 'Olive Larch has a potentially lethal ventricular arrhythmia.'

'A *what*?'

'If she gets an emotionally mediated adrenergic surge, she could die.'

Any doubts I'd harboured as to why Mrs Evans had been fired from Dr Frost's employ for going through patients confidential files, now vanished. 'You're saying she has heart problems?' I wondered if Fleming knew this. Was it possible he was even more of a cold-blooded killer than I first feared?

'Exactly!'

A cunning plan began to form in my mind. 'Have they actually gone *away* to get married?'

'Oh yes. There's a place in North Cornwall that does quickie weddings.'

'That's quite a drive. Do you think they might stay overnight?'

'Oh yes. Lenny told me Dougie had booked a night at the Castle Hotel in Tintagel. Four-poster bed and all the trimmings.'

'That's great,' I said, realizing it really *was* great. My prayers had been answered. With Fleming away, it gave me the perfect opportunity to head down to Gipping-on-Plym Power Services office. 'As you said, Mrs E., everyone has a right to happiness.'

'Let's hope she gets to enjoy some of it,' Mrs Evans said darkly. 'My friend Joan had a bad heart and died when—'

Fortunately my mobile rang. I could see that my landlady was eager to settle in for a long gossip about medical ailments but I was anxious to get cracking. Snatching the phone off the nightstand, a quick glimpse showed the number was from Dairy Cottage. *Blast!* I really did not want to talk to Eunice Pratt right now.

'I'd better answer this, Mrs Evans. Sorry. It's important.' Instead I hit the 'ignore' button saying, 'Vicky Hill speaking. Yes. No. Yes. Oh really,' and scrambled out of bed.

'I'll leave you to it,' Mrs Evans mouthed dramatically and tiptoed toward the door.

Once I was out of earshot, I checked my voice mail. As I feared, it was Eunice saying she hadn't had the courage to tell Robin about the CCTV and 'would you do it, Vicky because he likes you.'

How ironic that a mere three days ago I would be crying with happiness upon hearing those very words. Now I wouldn't mind if I never saw him ever again. Or her. The thought of telling Eunice that Fleming and Olive had eloped filled me with dread. I resolved to deal with that problem tomorrow.

Half an hour later after devouring a boiled egg on toast – and hearing more details on Joan's fatal heart attack – I left Factory Terrace. As I passed The Copper Kettle I noticed the picture window blinds were down. A sheet of paper was pinned to the door.

Curious, I stopped. Apparently, Topaz was closed until further notice for 'personal business'. Much as I appreciated her assistance in spying on Annabel, I didn't think it a good idea to turn away what few customers she actually had.

Resolving to talk to her about her business acumen later, I

set off for Middle Gipping and reached the GOPPS office shortly before ten.

To my surprise, the trademark blue-and-white-striped barber-styled revolving pole was not revolving and the GOPPS Venetian blinds on the front door were down, too. Was everyone away on personal business?

Puzzled, I double-checked the sign and yes, opening hours *were* between nine and three and the office closed for lunch from twelve to one thirty. Melanie should definitely be there.

How typical and infuriating. *While the cat's away, the mouse will play.* I hammered on the door but there was no reply.

Taking the narrow path alongside the building, I trotted toward the car park to the rear where a familiar silver Saab 9.3 sat next to Melanie Carew's dark red Vauxhall Astra. One thing I made a point of knowing was who drove which car in Gipping-on-Plym.

I had no idea that Dr Frost paid his electricity bills personally.

Returning to the front door I pulled out my mobile and dialled the main number. *Blast!* My call went straight to the answering machine. I was beginning to get worried and called a second time, then a third. On the fourth try, a breathless female voice gasped, 'Good morning. Gipping-on-Plym Power Services.'

'Is that you, Melanie?' I said. 'The front door is locked. Are you all right?'

'I'm fine.' I could hear some sort of rustle in the background. 'I'm stocktaking.'

Stocktaking what? Electricity? 'I need to talk to you.'

'Can you come back later?'

'I'm sure Mr Fleming wouldn't be happy if he knew you weren't opening on time.'

More rustling in the background, then, 'I'll be right there.'

After some fumbling, Melanie opened the door. Her eyes were bright and her red hair looked distinctly dishevelled. I noticed that her floral blouse had been wrongly buttoned up. 'Sorry,' was all she said.

I may still be a virgin but I wasn't born yesterday. *Good grief!* Was the Rubenesque Melanie Carew Dr Frost's mystery woman? It just goes to show that Annabel's *Cosmopolitan* pout, long legs and big boobs didn't automatically guarantee fidelity.

Once inside, I looked for signs of illicit hanky-panky, but there was none – nor was there any sign of Dr Frost. No doubt he'd sneaked out the rear exit like the coward I knew him to be.

Melanie sauntered back to her desk and sat down. She picked up her handbag and began rummaging around inside. I recognized it as one of Annabel's – a fake Chanel. It looked like Dr Frost was a cheapskate as well as a cheater and had probably filched it for his new lover.

Melanie took out a compact mirror and lipstick and began to repair her makeup. 'I'm afraid Mr Fleming isn't here today.'

'It's you I want to talk to,' I said, sliding into the seat opposite.

'About what?'

I tried to sound casual. 'I saw Dr Frost's car outside.'

'No, you didn't,' she said quickly.

'He's caught on camera.' I gestured to the CCTV monitors behind her. Perhaps they were a good idea after all. 'Look, I know about you and Dr Frost and honestly, it's none of my business.'

'It's just a bit of fun,' said Melanie, but she looked worried. 'If my husband finds out, he'll kill him.'

'Where is your husband?'

'On an oil rig out in the North Sea,' she said. 'His friends call him Pit-bull Pete.'

'*Your* husband is Pit-bull Pete?' I looked at Melanie with sympathy. Pete Carew was renowned for picking fights in pubs just for the fun of it.

'You were seen at the Imperial Hotel in Plymouth on Thursday April the second.' The first was a bluff, the second, was true. I'd double-checked my notebook for the date Sammy died.

'I don't see how.' Melanie frowned. 'I took the service elevator.'

'Doesn't it bother you that Dr Frost has a live-in girlfriend who actually happens to be my friend?' I realized I was beginning to feel angry and didn't know why. I didn't like Dr Frost and I didn't particularly like the way Annabel exploited her boyfriend but it wasn't as if they were married. However, Melanie was.

'Jack told me he's been trying to end their relationship but she just won't let go.'

I, too, had suspected as much. 'If he's not faithful to Annabel,' I said, 'I'm afraid he's not going to be faithful to you.'

'Faithful? Who said anything about wanting him to be faithful?' Melanie gave me a look as if I'd just suggested she cut off both her legs. 'Jack and I meet every Thursday at the Imperial for a bit of slap and tickle. More often if he can get away. Besides, he's helping me lose some weight.'

'Okay. Right.' I tried – but failed – to push the image of a naked Melanie slapping and tickling Dr Frost in a five-star hotel bed.

'You won't tell anyone, will you?' she said. 'I don't want Pete to serve time again. He'd lose his job.'

'I'll you what,' I said, 'let me take a look at those CCTV monitors and we'll call it quits.'

'Why?' she scowled. 'You don't believe I'm having an affair with Jack, do you? You think I'm too fat.'

'I don't think anything of the sort,' I said firmly. 'I'm trying to help Pam Green and Barbara Meadows find out who broke into the Bards storage unit. Those cameras cover part of the industrial estate as well as your car park.'

'Sorry. I'm just a bit sensitive about my size,' said Melanie.

'I'm sensitive about having a flat chest,' I said. 'I don't think any woman is happy with what she looks like.'

'Except Annabel Lake,' Melanie said ruefully. 'And even she

can't keep her man.' We both laughed at Annabel's expense, which oddly enough, made me feel disloyal.

'It's going to take you a long time to go through all that footage,' said Melanie. 'Can I make you a cuppa?'

I sat down with a delicious mug of tea and a plate of digestives – Melanie abstained, claiming, 'Jack has me on a no-carb diet,' and started going through all the footage.

There were far more comings and goings in Gipping-on-Plym Services car park than I'd expected, mainly because customers patronizing next-door's building supplier tended to use it as an overflow car park. As for the Gipping Bards' storage unit, no one went near it.

Shortly after lunch – Melanie had kindly run out and brought me back a chicken salad – I hit 'stop'. Pressing 'play-rewind-play' over and over again, I tried to make sense of what I saw.

The time code on the footage said eleven thirty p.m. and it was dated two weeks ago. Even though it was night, the halogen lighting installed throughout the industrial estate – the subject of much controversy by Gipping's Eco-warriors – clearly showed the arrival of a Range Rover with the number plate, SCLTT.

Mesmerized, I watched the car pull up to the Bards, storage unit and two figures get out. Fleming from the front passenger side, and a woman – dressed in a coat and woollen hat – from the driver's.

Fleming went around to the rear of the car and opened up the boot. He clambered in – presumably to fold down the rear passenger seat – while the woman unlocked the unit door and vanished inside. Fleming followed.

Both returned carrying the coffin between them and slid it into the rear of the Range Rover. The woman got back into the driver's seat while Fleming closed the car boot then locked the storage unit door. He returned to the front passenger side, slid in, and the Range Rover sped away.

I began to feel light-headed. Surely, the mystery woman

couldn't be *Scarlett Fleming!* The footage was recorded well before she died. Was Fleming so heartless that he tricked her into stealing her own coffin?

'Are you all right?' said Melanie, standing over me holding two mugs of tea. 'You're as white as a sheet.'

'It's a bit hot in here,' I said. 'Can you take a look at this for a moment?'

Melanie put the tea down. I replayed only the part where the couple got out of the car and unlocked the storage unit.

'That's Mr and Mrs Fleming,' she said.

'Are you positive?'

'Oh yes. She won't let anyone drive her Range Rover. Not even Dougie,' Melanie said. 'Isn't that the Bards' storage unit?'

'Looks like they had a key,' I said. 'Mind if I borrow the tape to show Pam and Barbara there was no break-in, after all?'

'Is Jack on that tape, too?' she said suspiciously. 'You're not going to try and blackmail me, are you?'

I hadn't been planning on it. 'I won't, if you wouldn't mind answering a few questions. Truthfully.'

Melanie gave a heavy sigh. 'I can't refuse, can I?'

'Did you book Go-Go Gothic for Mrs Fleming's funeral?'

'No. I don't do personal stuff. Once you start down that road, you'll soon be picking up their dry cleaning and feeding the dog.'

'You've worked for Douglas Fleming for years,' I said. 'What was their marriage like?'

'I know you shouldn't speak ill of the dead, but' – Melanie thought for a moment – 'Scarlett was a bossy cow. She always put on the lady-bountiful act around other people but she bullied poor Dougie. I don't know how he stood it.'

A shiver ran down my spine. Perhaps he hadn't? Perhaps she pushed him to his absolute limit.

'Did you know that Mr Fleming is marrying Olive Larch today?' I said.

'Olive *Larch*? I don't believe it!' Melanie's jaw dropped.

Since she hadn't been at Friday's Gala – nor had Dr Frost for that matter – she wouldn't have seen Fleming and Larch together. 'I always thought if he ever remarried, it would be that awful Eunice.'

'What about the restraining order?'

'That was Scarlett's doing.' Melanie retrieved a plastic bag of celery from her desk drawer. 'A couple of months ago – right out of the blue – Eunice started coming here a lot.' I cringed knowing full well this would have been after I'd implied Fleming still had feelings for her. 'They'd been school sweethearts, you know,' Melanie went on. 'Eunice made him laugh. I knew he liked her, but God knows why. Still, takes all sorts. Then one day, Scarlett got wind of what was going on and put a stop to it.'

'This is great. You've been really helpful.'

'Oh! It's nearly three. I must close up,' said Melanie. She paused. 'Funny he should end up marrying Olive, though. I never saw Dougie as the gold-digging type. Just goes to show you never really know someone.'

On that score, I couldn't have agreed with her more. Popping the tape into my pocket I thanked her and left.

The next few hours dragged as I waited for darkness to fall. Even though I knew Headcellars was empty, it would be foolish to attempt a daytime break-in.

I spent my time thinking about the Douglas Fleming I thought I knew and liked. Dad, too, said no one really knows anyone. As I heard giggles and 'You are a devil, you are,' coming from the Evans's bedroom, I was beginning to think he was right.

32

Headcellars was located at the bottom of a dell and reached via a long, twisty narrow lane flanked by overgrown hedgerows.

I'd never been spooked by the darkness. I wasn't superstitious nor did I believe in ghosts, but I had to admit as I came upon the Tudor house silhouetted against the night sky, it was definitely creepy.

Clouds scudded across the sky showing glimpses of a three-quarter moon, which illuminated Scarlett's famous – and now tortured – maze garden. I could quite see why she'd been furious with Dave and his jumping friends. Although the carefully clipped sculptured animals remained untouched, the neat box hedges in geometrical shapes lay in ruins across the front lawn.

Leaving my moped next to the stone wall on the left side of the house, I was struck by the utter stillness of the night. All I could hear was the sound of a few cows munching, along with the occasional moo coming from the field next door. On the horizon I could see the lights of Dairy Cottage.

My thoughts flew back to Mary Berry and the morning she claimed Fleming gave her a cheery wave as he loaded his wife's coffin into the American Cadillac. Why did he want Eunice to know that Scarlett was dead if he already planned on marrying someone else? It didn't make sense.

I turned my attention back to the house and breaking in. Under the gables was a fancy alarm unit. I'd expected as much and had come prepared, silently thanking Dad for all those hours of training. Naturally, I was also dressed for the part in black leggings, black polo sweater, black balaclava and thin, black gloves. I wore a bum bag around my waist holding a Mini Maglite, Swiss Army penknife, screwdriver and a wire coat hanger.

I started off by walking around the perimeter hoping to find a stray window open. Often with listed buildings, there were so many nooks, crannies, and windows dotted here and there, not all could be alarmed.

At the rear of the house was a forecourt in front of a converted barn that now served as a two-car garage. A decorative wishing well formed a centrepiece. Its tiled pitched roof covered in honeysuckle.

Fleming's black RS Audi Avant was gone – presumably he'd taken that to Cornwall – but Scarlett's expensive Range Rover stood outside. Considering she was the only one who drove it, I was surprised it was not in the barn.

Retrieving my Mini Maglite from my bum bag, I played the beam along the redbrick walls and up the side of the house. A nightlight burned in an upstairs window then suddenly went off, only to reappear in another part of the house a few moments later.

I stopped dead in my tracks. Prickles went up and down my spine. Every sense in my body switched to high alert. Hadn't Topaz, Sadie *and* Mrs Evans claimed the place was haunted? The notion was stupid.

I waited for what seemed like eons but the light remained where it was. It was probably one of those new timer switches. There had been a crop of burglaries recently and perhaps

Fleming thought word of his absence might reach the wrong ears. By leaving Scarlett's Range Rover outside and the inside lights on, it would give the appearance that someone was home.

Satisfied with my logical explanation, I made my way to the far side of the house and came across a small frosted bathroom window on the ground floor. The top hinged section was latched open. I always marvelled at why the general public usually decided not to alarm these little buggers. They *always* provided a way in – especially for someone like me. Hadn't Dad nicknamed me The Little Rat when I used to help on the occasional night job?

I clambered up onto the windowsill, stuck my arm through the narrow opening, and, using my specially adapted wire coat hanger, reached down to lift the lever. The lower window popped open. It was tiny, but I squeezed through without any problem.

Once inside, I was glad to find the bathroom door was open. This was extremely lucky, since it was often the actual act of opening that door into the rest of the house, that triggered the alarm.

I peered into the corridor and to my surprise, noted the Flemings did have a motion and heat-sensored alarm system – I could see the units built into the coving – but those telltale green and red lights were flashing and therefore, not alarmed.

I thought about turning the overhead lights on but decided against it. Even though the house was isolated, if I could see Dairy Cottage, they could certainly see Headcellars and of course, there were other farms in the neighbouring area, too.

After several futile tries – one door led down to a cellar – I found Fleming's study. It was the last room at the end of a long corridor. Glad to see heavy velvet curtains drawn tight across a large casement window, I went over to his oak desk and decided it was safe to switch on the green banker's light.

The room was more of a library than a study. There was a large inglenook fireplace filled with dried flower arrangements.

Two entire walls were covered from floor to ceiling with books. A tapestry stretched across a third. On top of a long wooden cabinet stood a glass, framed display case filled with earth, leaves, and what looked like hamster furnishings. I went to take a closer look.

There was a miniature house, exercise wheel, and tiny jungle gym. Two large snails and several babies were nibbling on lettuce leaves. Presumably one of them was the famous Seabiscuit. It was hard to tell. To me, all snails looked alike.

I pulled out Fleming's chair and sat down. The drawers were locked but easily opened with my Swiss Army penknife. The first had the usual pencils and sticky notes. The second was filled with unopened bills. Many envelopes were stamped FINAL NOTICE. I pulled out bank statements and discovered all carried hefty overdrafts. I opened a manilla envelope. It was Douglas Fleming's life insurance policy and had been cashed out six months ago.

Basically, the Flemings were practically bankrupt. Dad always said that money was often the main cause for divorce – and murder. It was no wonder Fleming had wanted to marry wealthy Olive Larch and not poverty-stricken Eunice Pratt.

My eye caught a British Telecom envelope. Withdrawing the itemized statement, I recognized the phone number of Dairy Cottage immediately having seen it on my caller ID enough times these past few days.

I stared at it for several moments. Eunice had been telling the truth. The time of each call was registered as early morning or late afternoon.

Working in a farming community, I'd learned a few things about a typical farmer's day. With a jolt, I realized that those calls coincided with the daily milking schedule when Mary was bound to be outside with her cows. No wonder she had scoffed at Eunice's claims! Yet, why would Fleming call from home when his wife was bound to be around? Even though Mary said she often saw Scarlett doing her yoga in the garden, making secret phone calls seemed a bit risky. Why hadn't Fleming phoned Eunice from his office?

Unfortunately the statement cut-off date was the week prior to Scarlett's death. But I was sure the calls must have continued. Eunice had said as much.

I made a final search of the third drawer and pulled out an old tobacco tin. Inside were several keys – presumably spare house, office, cars – and, thankfully, the heavy ornate clef key to the Fleming vault. Slipping it into my bum bag, my eyes were drawn to a dark blue vinyl wallet stamped BRITISH AIRWAYS. Inside was a one-way economy ticket – paid in cash – from London Heathrow to Rio de Janeiro in the name of Sydney Pember. The departure date was this coming Thursday!

I was seriously baffled. Was Fleming going to flee the country under an assumed name? Surely, he couldn't be planning on getting rid of Olive so quickly?

Good grief! Olive already suffered from a weak heart. What if the physical exertion on her wedding night was too much for her? Or worse – what if Fleming had decided to get rid of her on their honeymoon? The cliff paths along the north Cornish coastline were treacherous. All it would take was one little push.

There was a sudden loud clunk. A violent shudder started under the floorboards and continued up the wall in front of me, ending in a mind-numbing groan. A series of gurgles! The whoosh of rushing water! Had the house not been empty, I would have sworn it was a toilet being flushed.

I leapt to my feet, paralyzed with fear. Every hair on my neck stood up. Goosebumps coated my arms. Directly above my head came the sound of slow, heavy footsteps. My heart hammered so hard in my chest I thought I was going to die of fright.

My God. It was true. Headcellars *was* haunted!

I shoved everything back into the drawers and slammed them shut, switched off the banker's lamp, and tore out of the study. I raced along the corridor as if the hounds of the Baskervilles were hot on my heels, flew into the bathroom and scrambled out of the window, not even bothering to relatch it.

I didn't look back until I stopped my moped at the top of the drive to catch my breath.

My hands were shaking so much I could hardly hold the handlebars. I did *not* believe in ghosts. I did *not*. There had to be some logical explanation. *Think Vicky think!*

And then it hit me. Maybe Scarlett Fleming wasn't dead, after all. Perhaps it had been *her* footsteps I'd heard upstairs? Was it conceivable that the two of them were in this scam together?

Scarlett never went to Spain. Neil Titley had sworn that it had been a woman who had booked Go-Go Gothic's services and Melanie had denied any knowledge. Scarlett got Neil's number from Sadie Evans when the two used to chat while having their nails done at Polly's on the Barbican. Scarlett must have booked her own funeral!

As I'd suspected all along, Fleming's grief – despite a couple of dramatic performances – had seemed incredibly short-lived. There was the sudden friendship with Sammy Larch – despite everyone knowing that Scarlett couldn't stand him. What about the night the old boy died? Fleming took Olive to the Nag and Bucket while Scarlett may well have pushed her father down the stairs but I could never prove it. It was pure fluke that Dr Frost had been too preoccupied with getting back to the Imperial Hotel in Plymouth to examine Sammy's body properly.

But where did Eunice fit in? Why would Fleming keep calling her?

Despite telling myself otherwise, I was thoroughly spooked by this evening's developments and would have preferred a visit to St Peter's churchyard in broad daylight.

There was no time for nerves. With that one-way ticket to Brazil a mere two days away, I had to move fast.

33

I'd be lying if I didn't say that cemeteries gave me the creeps. A part of me almost wished I'd persuaded Topaz to accompany me tonight. She seemed to suffer no qualms about ghost hunting and her mindless chatter would have steadied my nerves.

A fox's strangled cry made me jump. It was all I could do not to turn tail and flee.

I took the main pathways through the graveyard and up to Albert Square. The wrought-iron gate seemed unnecessarily noisy when I pushed it open. A rustle of wind through the leaves and the hoot of an owl only made me jittery. A ghostly moon peeped behind the clouds.

Arriving at the Fleming vault, I retrieved my Mini Maglite from my bum bag and switched it on. The beam lit up the narrow stairway, which led down to the heavy iron doors.

Dad says, *'There's nothing to fear from dead people'* and that *'It's the living you have to watch out for.'* Even so, my hand shook as I slipped the key into the lock and turned it.

With a click, the door swung open and I stepped down into claustrophobic gloom.

The vault was deep and not how I imagined at all. On both

sides, marble plaques marked the final resting places of Fleming's ancestors stacked three high. My heart sank. I'd assumed I'd see coffins nestling in alcoves, not sealed in individual tombs. If Fleming had already sealed up Scarlett, I was doomed.

Moving in deeper, I played the flashlight over ancient walls – 'Cuthbert F. Fleming 1801–1895' and 'Florence W. Fleming 1775–1856' to name just a few – and marvelled at the sense of history here. I could only trace my family tree back two generations.

Suddenly, my stomach flipped over. A hollowed out section toward the rear lay empty and gaping – presumably these three shelves were ready to receive the next generation of Flemings.

On the top shelf was a new coffin. Heart pounding, I moved closer.

Just as Neil Titley had said, it was decorated with Egyptian hieroglyphics, but I couldn't find the Gipping Bards stamp of ownership. It had to be on the bottom.

I had to see it. I had to know. But what if I was wrong? A horrific vision of Scarlett's disfigured remains tumbling out made me pause for thought. But wait! Hadn't Probes said that decaying bodies smelled dreadful?

Taking a deep breath I inhaled deeply. It was just dank, stale air. Wedging the flashlight in a gargoyle's mouth opposite, I grabbed the corner of the coffin and tried to move it. Without warning, the shelf crumbled away. I leapt aside as it – and the coffin – crashed onto the ground, shattering into pieces.

To my joy, not only was the cavity jammed with newspapers and sandbags, my flashlight illuminated PROPERTY OF THE GIPPING BARDS stamped in red ink.

I leaned against the cold walls, exhausted.

At last I had proof. Scarlett Fleming was very much alive. But the future sure looked bleak for Olive.

34

To my dismay, as I drew close to 21 Factory Terrace, Topaz's Capri was parked outside. It was past midnight. She was the last person I wanted to see tonight.

My thoughts were consumed with Scarlett Fleming. She must have been hiding at Headcellars all the time. Had she known I'd been there and rifled through Fleming's desk?

I stopped a few yards away and cut the moped engine. All I could see was the top of a flat cap. Topaz must have reclined the driver seat. Hopefully she was still asleep.

A cowbell sounded the moment I pushed my moped into the drive. All too late I saw the black nylon thread that Topaz had stretched between the gateposts and fed back through the car's rear window. *Damn and blast!*

Topaz sat bolt upright and flung open the driver's door. I gave a start. She was dressed in her farming disguise.

'I was waiting for you,' she said. 'Why are you dressed like that?'

'Keep your voice down,' I whispered. 'I could ask the same of you. Get back into the car.'

Leaving my moped on the kickstand, I got into the passenger

seat and narrowly missed sitting on a thermos flask. 'Is there any hot chocolate left?'

'No.' Topaz pulled the driver's door shut. 'Well? Where have you been?'

I was about to tell her to mind her own business when I suffered one of my brilliant flashes of genius. 'I have a confession to make,' I said. 'I think you are right about Headcellars being haunted. Didn't you mention something about a priest hole?'

'You went ghost hunting *without me*?'

'I came by the café to get you but it was closed.' This was true. 'Where did *you* go?'

'You'll never guess.'

'You're right. I can't. Surprise me.'

'I followed Annabel to Dartmoor prison.'

I went very still. 'The *prison!* What on earth was Annabel doing there?'

Topaz grinned. The light from the street lamp illuminated her teeth. Together with the false moustache, she looked like a caricature of Groucho Marx. 'Guess.'

'I really can't. Please, Topaz.'

'She was seeing someone!'

'Who? How do you know?'

'I followed her inside but they wouldn't tell me. It was visiting hours and she was gone a long time. But that's not all. Guess what happened next?'

'Get on with it,' I snapped.

'Annabel drove all the way to London. Have you heard of Wormwood Scrubs prison? It's very famous.'

'No. Why?' I was beginning to feel light-headed. Of course I knew Wormwood Scrubs! I knew it very well. Dad had been in and out for years.

'She visited someone there, too!' said Topaz. 'Don't you see the obvious?' When I couldn't answer, she gleefully went on, 'Annabel's handbag operation is *huge*. She's obviously got dealings on the inside. She might even have some handbag ring going on.' Topaz seized my arm, nodding manically. 'This is the biggest scoop ever, isn't it? Have you any idea what the fall-out might be?'

I most certainly did and I had to do something about it. I *had* to get hold of Dad's great friend and partner-in-crime, Chuffy McSnatch. Since he dealt in handbags, he might be implicated. Surely Annabel wasn't stupid enough to visit her suppliers or informants openly in prison?

'Good work, Topaz.'

'You said we needed to catch her red-handed. I took some photographs.' Topaz opened the glove box and retrieved a disposable camera. 'I'll get them developed at This-And-That Emporium tomorrow.'

'Pity you couldn't get the names of who Annabel was visiting at those prisons,' I said.

'Of course I did.' Topaz pulled up her rucksack and unzipped it. She retrieved a scrap of paper. 'It was frightfully good fun. I just joined the queue of people and must say blended in very well with the crowds. No one took any notice of me, at all. When I came to sign the visitor book, I just looked at who Annabel went to see, pretended I didn't feel very well and just left. Here—' She handed me the paper. I glanced at the names – Wayne Henderson in Dartmoor, and Nigel Keeps in Wormwood Scrubs. I'd never heard of either.

'I've also got the address of the warehouse,' she said. 'I wrote it on the back. It's close to the Imperial Hotel, just like I thought.'

'You've done really well, Topaz. Thank you.'

'She'll go to prison, won't she?' Topaz grinned. 'Do I get to share a byline?'

'Yes, yes, of course.' I was only half listening. 'We still need to catch her physically receiving stolen goods.'

'All in good time, boss,' said Topaz. 'I'm going back to the warehouse every night until I catch her on camera!'

Promising Topaz I'd be in touch the next morning, I bid her goodnight.

Sleep wouldn't come. For some reason I just couldn't buy Annabel's handbag endeavour. Hadn't she dreamed of her first front-page scoop? She wanted to be a serious reporter! Why jeopardize her career? Whatever Annabel was up to, she was a fool to fraternize with known criminals.

My thoughts turned to poor, gullible Olive. Fleming wouldn't be the first husband who knocked off his wife on their honeymoon for monetary gain.

I tossed and turned for hours. I couldn't help feeling that I should have tried harder to stop Fleming because I'd suspected him all along. Even though the police would never act on a hunch, if Olive died it would be all my fault.

35

I grabbed my moped and raced out of the house early the next morning, anxious to get to the office. If there was any bad news, Barbara was bound to hear it first.

At the end of the road Mrs Evans was waiting at an empty bus stop. I had a sudden thought and pulled up alongside, cutting the engine.

'The Reverend Whittler is back from Disney World tomorrow,' she said, before I had a chance to bid her good morning. 'I'm just popping in to give the rectory a quick spit and polish.'

'Does the name Sydney Pember ring any bells?'

Mrs Evans frowned. 'It does seem familiar.'

'Perhaps you saw it on an airline ticket somewhere?' Fleming's desk drawer had been locked but that would never have deterred my nosy landlady.

'No. Not there,' she said slowly.

'Maybe at Dr Frost's surgery?'

'Are you suggesting I look in confidential files?' Mrs Evans sounded hurt.

'Of course not,' I said smoothly. 'It's terribly important. My editor asked me to ask you. He said you knew everyone in Gipping.' He hadn't.

Mrs Evans turned pink with pleasure. 'I've never thought of myself as an informant,' she beamed. 'Now, let me think.'

I looked at my watch praying she'd hurry up – not that getting to the *Gazette* any earlier was going to change Olive's fate. 'Perhaps he's someone in the Gipping Bards?'

'That's it!' Mrs Evans snapped her fingers. 'It's not a he, it's a she. Scarlett didn't like the name Sydney. Said it was too manly. Pember was her maiden name before she got married.'

'You see! You do know everyone!' Thanking her profusely, I went on my way deeply troubled. If I'd needed further proof that Scarlett was alive, I had it now. There must have been a second airline ticket in that desk drawer and I'd missed it.

Convinced that Olive must now be dead, I steeled myself for scenes of grief in reception. When I arrived I couldn't believe my eyes.

Olive Larch was very much alive. She and Fleming – holding a bottle of champagne – were chattering to Barbara. All three were holding green plastic cups – no doubt left over from Friday's pre-Gala party.

'Just in time. We're celebrating.' Barbara waved me over. 'Olive's got her wedding photos.'

I was overjoyed. 'Congratulations!' I said, engulfing her in a warm hug.

She stiffened and tried to push me away. 'I can't breathe, dear.'

'Sorry! I'm just so surprised . . . I mean, *pleased* to see you.' I looked over at Fleming who had the nerve to smile and looked perfectly at ease.

'Goodness, Vicky,' said Barbara. 'You only saw them on Sunday! What a romantic you are.'

'We're having a glass of champagne.' Fleming hastened over to the counter to fetch me a plastic cup. 'We insist you have one, don't we Olive?'

I said yes despite the early hour, though what I really needed was a stiff brandy.

Barbara and I toasted their health. 'I thought you would be gone for ages,' I said. 'No honeymoon?'

'We'll take a proper holiday at the end of snail season,' said Fleming, moving over to Olive and rubbing her shoulders. 'Olive fancies a cruise, don't you dear?'

Olive blushed. 'I've always wanted to go to Greece.'

'A *cruise*?' said Barbara shooting me a knowing wink. 'All that time cooped up in a cabin. Whatever will you two do with yourselves?'

'I like playing Scrabble,' said Olive.

'Me, too,' I chipped in, anxious to steer Barbara away from her pet subject. Sex.

'We would have stayed a few days longer,' said Fleming. 'Unfortunately, Gipping Manor demands an inquiry into what happened at the Gala. As Chief Marshal I've called for an extraordinary committee meeting to get to the bottom of it all.'

'It's tonight at the Evans's,' said Barbara.

Excellent! The meeting was bound to run late. It would give me a chance to sneak back to Headcellars and find that other airline ticket.

'Perhaps Vicky should help Olive with the minutes, Dougie,' Barbara suggested.

'What a good idea,' said Fleming. 'We'd like the *Gazette* to print our side of the story – although I have to admit, I was very disappointed in this week's lead.'

'I'm afraid I can't comment on that at the moment,' I said firmly.

'Trust that hooligan, Randall, to concoct such a story!' Fleming declared.

I longed to say, 'It was Scarlett's doing! The Legacy belongs to Dave!' but fortunately Olive intervened. Putting her hand on Fleming's arm she said, 'Please, Dougie. Let's not spoil this happy day.'

'Quite right. Sorry.'

'It's very kind of you to help with the minutes, Vicky,' said Olive.

'I'm happy to.' I smiled. *Blast!* Still, at least I could keep an eye on her.

Leaving the revellers drinking the rest of the bottle I went upstairs. Olive may be safe for now but I had come to realize I was out of my depth. I needed help and decided I'd have to confide in Pete.

I'd come clean about breaking into the Fleming vault and finding the empty coffin. I'd tell him I was convinced that Scarlett was still very much alive and had the evidence to prove it. We could go to the police together. This was no longer about my career. This was about saving Olive's life.

Upstairs in the reporters' room, Annabel was already seated at her computer and feverishly typing away. 'You're in early. Is Pete here?'

'Can't stop. Got to do this,' she said with a dismissive wave of her hand.

Pete emerged from his office and handed me a sheet of paper. 'Just got this in from Ripley and Ravish.'

'Do you have a minute?'

'Not now,' he said. 'Whittler is back tomorrow. You're going to have your work cut out for you with this lot,' Pete went on. 'They'll be a few back-to-backs. I suggest you get a head start and visit a few families before the services. Maybe Gipping needs Go-Go Gothic, after all. Ripley's swamped.'

'Speaking of Go-Go Gothic,' I said, 'I really want to talk to you about this Scarlett Fleming business.'

'Later.' He checked his watch. 'Ready for action, Annabel?'

'Absolutely.' Annabel got to her feet and grabbed her notebook. I was struck by her appearance. For once she was dressed conventionally in a black round-neck sweater, black tailored trousers, and black leather pumps. Around her neck, a yellow scarf was tied in a neat knot. Her hair was pulled back in a ponytail and she actually wore *pearls* in her ears. The whole effect exuded professional competency.

Annabel gave me a cursory nod as she passed my desk and followed Pete into Wilf's office. Pausing in the doorway, she turned, saying, 'See that we're not disturbed for the next fifteen minutes, Vicky. I'm on an important conference call.'

Conference call? With whom?

The moment the door closed I darted over to eavesdrop. The conversation was difficult to follow with Annabel talking in a low voice, Pete interjecting with suggestions, and whoever it was on the other end shouting. But what I could make out shocked me to the core.

Annabel was talking to a television producer from Westward Television. She was on the trail of a wanted criminal, someone who had a hefty reward on his head. Yes, she could produce witnesses, facts, evidence and photographs, and yes, she was certain that her story had the potential to become a real life docudrama that could 'guarantee high ratings' and appeal to a 'mass demographic audience'.

Appalled, I went straight to Annabel's desk and sat down. Her computer was password encrypted despite her earlier assurances to the contrary. I was undeterred. Another of Dad's after-dinner games involved the psychological study of passwords – dates of birth, favourite pets, colours, boyfriends, childhood nicknames or special interests.

After many false starts of typing in the boyfriends I knew about, and the colours she wore, I started on handbag brand names. I got to *M* for Mulberry – Annabel's all-time favourite – and I was *in*!

Keeping one ear acutely trained on Wilf's door – I could hear several voices talking at once now – I went straight to the Internet and selected 'history' from the menu bar.

I swear my heart stopped beating.

The same phrase came up over and over again.

The Fog.

My fingers were trembling so much I could hardly type. How could Annabel have known about Dad? How had I given myself away?

I hit 'Find' and typed in The Fog. What seemed like millions of folders popped up on screen: Prisons/Time Served, Rap Sheet, Extradition, Press Clippings, Personal Details and Actors Wish List.

I clicked open PERSONAL DETAILS and was faced with a bullet point list of odd snippets all about my family. From the notorious colour of the Hill sapphire blue eyes to the damning fact that he had one daughter called Victoria Ada Hill.

There was a subfolder labelled KNOWN ACCOMPLICES. Two names jumped out at me straight away – Wayne Henderson and Nigel Keeps, men that Annabel had visited in jail.

I moved the mouse down and opened REWARD.

The good news was that no one knew of Dad's exact whereabouts other than that it was rumoured to be in Spain. The bad news was that there was actually a huge hundred-thousand-pound reward 'for any information that would secure The Fog's extradition back to the UK where he was expected to face charges of armed robbery.' A security guard had been accidentally shot during a hold-up in Tiffany's in Bond Street. He was still in a coma.

I remembered the incident vividly. It had been all over the news but I never connected it to my dad. Days later, my parents fled to Spain.

I felt sick to my stomach. My dad was a loveable rogue: a glamorous Pink Panther-style thief. He wasn't a killer.

I'd never bothered to read the stories written about my dad in the newspaper – though I suspected Mum kept a scrapbook. I lost count of the number of times she told me how the wrong men were often put in jail and that the British justice system was a travesty. It was one of the reasons that I had wanted to become a professional journalist – to find and report the truth – but there was no time to dwell on that now. I *had* to see Chuffy McSnatch.

Hitting 'sleep' on Annabel's computer, I slipped out of the *Gazette*, through the side entrance, and took the alley to the one private place I knew I couldn't be overheard.

Huddled under an elder bush in the backyard behind the office and surrounded by piles of rotting newspapers, I dialled Chuffy's pager 'only in an emergency', and waited. I used to scoff at all the precautions that Chuffy took, but not anymore.

Within minutes, my mobile rang. 'It's Vicky Hill, Harold's daughter,' I said, suddenly seized by the urge to cry.

There was a long pause and the sound of shallow breathing, then, 'Saturday. Seven o'clock. Paddington Station. Clock. Code Columbo.'

'I can't, I can't!' I wailed. 'It's urgent. They know about Dad. I've got to see you *now*!'

Chuffy didn't answer. It was all I could do not to scream his name aloud – an absolute no-no. 'Please say you're there.'

'Calm down, luv,' said Chuffy quietly. 'I've got business in Taunton this afternoon, can you meet me there?' Taunton was an hour and a half up the Penzance-to-London Paddington line.

'Yes.'

'Find your way to the Railway Inn,' Chuffy said. 'I'll see you in three hours.' There was a click, and Chuffy was gone.

Three *hours*. The wait seemed unbearable. Tears stung my eyes. I had to get a grip. I couldn't fall apart now. There was too much at stake.

Chuffy would demand the details. It was vital I understood how Annabel had found out about my dad.

I'd been tricked. Annabel had deliberately set out to be my new best friend when all the time she'd been intending to betray me.

Retrieving my moped, I made a quick stop at Factory Terrace, relieved that Mrs Evans was out at work. Chuffy might order me to leave the country immediately. In my bedroom, I lifted up the rug and loose floorboard to retrieve what cash I had,

257

my passport and the bundle of postcards from Mum and Dad that I kept hidden.

As I stuffed them in a rucksack, I reflected how pathetic it was that my life could fit in such a small bag.

I had to wait for over an hour at Gipping Junction for the next Inter-City 125 to London Paddington. Retreating to the platform café with a cup of tea – no cake, I wasn't hungry – I took out my notebook and started to put the pieces of the puzzle together.

How had all this begun?

I wrote down, *sapphire blue eyes.* Annabel had made a big deal of them – she'd even photographed them with her mobile. The photo was obviously used as some kind of identification. *But wait!* So did that strange Italian-looking man – Dino – whom Annabel and I had 'bumped into' at the Hoe last Saturday night. Hadn't he done the exact thing? There was something familiar about him that I just couldn't quite place.

There were Annabel's visits to Dartmoor and Wormwood Scrubs prisons. Even though I hadn't had time to look at the PRISONS/TIME SERVED folder, I knew they'd be listed. How foolish was I! How blind! Annabel's exposé had never been about fake handbags at all!

As for Ronnie Binns – I should have known that she wouldn't willingly seek him out. Annabel hadn't been interested in the weather. She was asking about The Fog – two words that were meaningless to Gipping's garbologist, but promised fame and fortune for wretched Annabel Lake.

It hadn't taken her long to work it out – the incriminating postcard from M & D, the satellite map of San Feliu on the Costa Brava, and of course the ultimate giveaway, my sapphire blue eyes.

I boarded the train with a heavy heart. My thoughts turned to DS Probes. Annabel had been talking to him at the Gala. Hadn't she said she had friends in the police force? *God!* What if Probes was on my trail, too. Yes, he talked of wanting to pin me down, but perhaps he had a warped sense of humour and meant – in handcuffs!

As I stared out the window at the passing countryside, I thought of poor Olive Larch and felt utterly wretched. I could never protect her now or go to the police.

It looked like we were both doomed.

36

'**B**ut I've been so careful,' I said miserably to Chuffy.
I'd found him tucked in the corner of the Railway Inn
public bar nursing a pint of Guinness. He always looked
shifty. Dressed in a shabby trench raincoat, Chuffy bore a
striking resemblance to Peter Falk from the Columbo detective
series.

Apart from a mismatched couple – a businessman and a
brassy blonde – canoodling in the opposite corner, the bar was
empty.

This was not surprising.

As its name suggests, the Railway Inn was a mere stone's
throw from the rail tracks. Every few minutes, a train either
arrived or departed or just tore through the station at such speed
that the walls and grungy furniture literally moved. The sound
was so deafening that all conversation had to stop.

'I hide everything under the floorboards,' I went on after the
third train had flown by in as many minutes. 'I only use cash.
How was I to know that Annabel had overheard Dad's nickname
and put it all together? It's the blasted Internet, too.'

'That's why you've got to be careful, Vicky,' Chuffy scolded.

I pointed both forefingers at my eyes. 'These are the culprits! People recognize them!'

'Your dad told you to change your identity,' Chuffy said, 'but you wouldn't have it.'

'I don't want to live a lie.'

'You already are.'

My protest was lost in the backwash of another Inter-City 125 tearing past, horn blaring. Mutinously, I stared at the canoodling couple. What on earth was a distinguished-looking businessman in suit and tie doing with such a vulgar-looking woman? He had to be at least thirty years her senior.

'Let's go through this again,' said Chuffy. 'You're positive this Annabel only visited Dartmoor and Wormwood Scrubs?'

'That's what my informant told me and she's been tailing her this week,' I said. 'Do the names Wayne Henderson and Nigel Keeps ring a bell?'

Chuffy looked startled and muttered what sounded like a curse, under his breath. He nodded gravely. 'They worked for your dad in the old days. Used to meet in your kitchen in Riley Lane. You'd have been about fourteen.'

'So they'll remember me.' Naturally, Annabel would have shown them my photograph. 'What about Dino something-or-other?' I said suddenly. 'Annabel introduced me to him in Plymouth. Has he been in our kitchen, too?'

'Dino DiMarco,' Chuffy said with distaste. 'He owes me a favour.'

'My informant followed him. He deals in handbags and I'm convinced Annabel sells them on eBay out of her house. She's such a thief.' All too late I realized my huge faux pas and hastily tried to backtrack. Chuffy dealt in stolen merchandise.

My face burned with shame. 'Not that there's anything wrong in flogging handbags,' I mumbled.

'There's a lot wrong in flogging *fake* handbags,' Chuffy declared. 'I wouldn't touch 'em. My stuff is genuine Hoat cootur.'

Haute couture! 'Exactly!' I said. 'Because according to the Anti-Counterfeiting Group, there's a big clamp-down on fake anything. The authorities are positive the proceeds go toward funding terrorism.'

'I read the papers,' said Chuffy.

'We should notify the authorities and get Annabel arrested!' I cried.

'Notify the *authorities*?' Chuffy's expression turned ugly. 'Snitches are the scum of the earth,' he hissed. 'I'll pretend I didn't hear that.'

Mortified I looked away, wishing that the floor would swallow me up. In the uncomfortable silence that followed three trains passed by. Across the room, the young woman caught my eye and mouthed the words, 'Are you okay?' I nodded. Her unexpected kindness brought a lump to my throat.

'Don't pout,' said Chuffy finally. 'It doesn't suit you. Does this Annabel live alone?'

'No, with a doctor.'

'Write down her address and make sure you get them both out of the house tonight. I don't care how you do it,' he said. 'And give me the address of Dino's warehouse, too.'

I scribbled down both and gave him Topaz's report. He slipped it into his pocket.

'I want you to go back to Gipping and clear out your stuff,' Chuffy said. 'I'm talking computer. I'm talking laptop. Delete all files. I'll get new papers for you. Keep your mobile turned on until I give you instructions, then destroy it.'

I nodded mutely. Even though I suspected this would happen, knowing my dream as an investigative journalist was coming to an end was utterly devastating.

Chuffy stood up and bent over to gently kiss me on the forehead. 'Chin up,' he said. 'Everything is going to be all right.'

'Is it true about the security guard being in a coma?' I said quietly.

Chuffy nodded grimly. 'It was an accident. Best forget it.'

But I knew I couldn't.

I was ordered to wait a full fifteen minutes while Chuffy left the Railway Inn so we wouldn't be seen leaving together.

My spirits plunged even further. How on earth would I get Annabel and Dr Frost out of the house? I sat gloomily watching the clock. The businessman whispered sweet nothings in the brassy blonde's ear, then got to his feet. 'Ten minutes,' he said, and left.

The woman took out a small compact mirror and began to touch up her makeup and comb her hair. She opened a raggedy clutch bag and took out a pink business card.

To my horror, she sauntered over to me. 'Here,' she said, laying it on the table. 'Give me a call sometime. We get nice punters. No creeps.'

'Thanks.' I watched her leave before examining the card. *Good God!* Could my day get worse? EDWINA'S ESCORTS: WOMEN WITH CLASS stared up at me. Had she honestly thought I was a hooker and Chuffy was my client? The thought was repulsive.

My indignation turned to excitement. That was it! I knew exactly how I was going to deal with Annabel and Dr Frost. *Thank you Edwina!* All it would take was one clever phone call.

It was only during the return journey to Gipping Junction that my thoughts returned to Olive Larch. I'd write to Pete. Taking out pen and paper I wrote a detailed account of all my suspicions, taking care to include Scarlett's part in Sammy Larch's tragic fall. I told Pete where to find the key to the vault, the incriminating CCTV tape – in my bottom drawer at Factory Terrace – and gave him Neil Titley's contact number.

As I reread my report, another wave of misery hit me afresh. It didn't seem fair that I had to leave Gipping-on-Plym because of my dad. Chuffy said he was going to make it all go

263

away and I knew he'd do just that. Did that mean I had to go away, too?

One piece of advice that Dad had always given me was to deny everything. Even when Mum caught him in flagrante with Pam Dingles in a hotel room in Shoreditch, he swore he was helping her change a lightbulb.

The only connection I had to Harold Hill was my name and my eye colour. I'd looked myself up on Google once and discovered there were dozens and dozens of Vicky Hills in existence. As for my sapphire blue eyes – hadn't Annabel purchased her own coloured contacts on the Internet? The postcard she'd seen in my bedroom was just a postcard. It was all circumstantial evidence. Nothing could be proved.

My spirits began to lift.

Thanks to a signal failure, the train was an hour late getting into Gipping Junction. I made my untraceable phone call from the pay phone on the platform station. By the time I reached Factory Terrace it was after six.

The members of the Gipping Snail Racing Federation were already in full cry in the sitting room. Tony was taking photographs, Mrs Evans had laid out nibbles on the coffee table, and Barbara was handing round paper plates. I was about to take off my safari jacket when I realized there was no sign of Olive.

'Where's Olive?' I asked Fleming.

'She was feeling very tired,' he said. 'I persuaded her to stay at home. She said she knew the minutes were in good hands. Do sit down, Vicky.'

I stared at him with mounting horror. 'I'll be back in a moment.' Dragging Mrs Evans out in the hall, I whispered urgently, 'Some emergency has come up. I can't stay.'

'That's all right. Barbara's taken the minutes before.'

'I'm going to leave something in an envelope for Tony to give to Pete,' I said. 'It's really important you don't forget.'

Reassuring me that she wouldn't, I dashed upstairs to

grab an envelope and stuffed the report inside, scrawling CONFIDENTIAL: PETE CHAMBERS and left it on the hall table.

I got back on my moped and tore off toward Headcellars, praying I'd get there before it was too late.

37

The gravel drive was flanked by thick woodland on one side and a hedge on the other, behind which was a field of cows. Presumably, they were the same cows that Mary Berry had put out to pasture on that fateful morning when all this began.

Being May, the evening was still relatively light. I prayed that whatever Scarlett had planned for Olive's demise would happen under cover of darkness.

Spying a five-bar gate, I left my moped in a concealed spot and continued on foot. Having no idea what lay ahead, I didn't want to announce my arrival. I'd seen enough movies where the friendly neighbour or a lone cop shows up unexpectedly. It always ended badly.

Keeping to the field side of the drive behind the hedge, I crept stealthily toward the house. Unfortunately, the cows followed me en masse. Each time I paused, they stopped, snorting and stomping their hooves. When I continued, so did they. It was most unnerving and it was all I could do not to run.

To my dismay, the hedge had been stock-proofed. The only exit from the field to the house was a second five-bar gate, a good fifty yards farther on. *Idiot, Vicky!* I was losing valuable time!

The cows suddenly made a wild dash and congregated around the gate – presumably expecting to be fed. *Blasted cows!* It was a good five or more precious minutes of careful negotiating around piles of cow manure, before I could clamber over.

I found myself in the courtyard behind the house. Scarlett's Range Rover stood outside the converted barn.

Praying no one was watching from a window, I darted over to the car and ducked down behind it. Retrieving my Swiss Army penknife, I plunged the blade into the front and rear passenger tires. If Scarlett were planning on a hasty exit, two flat tires would certainly slow her down.

I made another dash toward the back door and that's when I heard them. Chilling screams were coming from inside and the sound of smashing glass and china. I went to turn the handle but the back door had been locked.

Frantic, I recalled the tiny bathroom window I'd climbed through before. It was open. I scrambled inside as Olive's screaming grew louder and more hysterical.

Jumping down into the bathroom, I ran into the hallway toward the dreadful noise and stopped dead. Horrified.

A brown-robed monk was grappling with Olive at the top of the cellar stairs.

For a split second, I thought it was the ghost of Father Gregory until I realized the figure was dressed as Robin Hood's Friar Tuck, complete with full face mask and monk's pate.

'Scarlett!' I yelled. 'Let her go!'

Startled, Scarlett turned toward me, loosening her grip on Olive for a second. It was all Olive needed. She kicked Scarlett in the shin crying, 'Help, Vicky! Help!' But it only made Scarlett more furious.

With one final determined push, she flung Olive away and through the open cellar door. There was a sickening series of thuds and screams as Olive tumbled down the stairs. Then, silence.

I was so shocked I could hardly breathe. 'You've killed her,' I whispered, backing away, hardly able to believe what I'd seen. *Please God don't let Olive be dead.*

Scarlett swiftly moved toward me. She looked grotesque and utterly terrifying in her ill-fitting mask especially as it looked like she'd added some touches of her own. Friendly Friar Tuck's face had black-rimmed eye sockets and fake blood streaked down grey cheeks.

Surrounded by broken vases and smashed picture frames, I cast around for a weapon of any kind but fell over a fallen chair. Scarlett lunged forward with astonishing speed. She grabbed my wrists and hauled me to my feet, slamming me hard against the wall. Through the mask, her eyes were yellow with rage.

'Please Scarlett, don't,' I protested feebly. 'It's not too late to talk.'

She didn't answer, simply propelled me toward the open cellar door. 'Yes, let me go to Olive,' I begged. 'She might still be alive.'

Instead Scarlett kicked the door closed. I tripped and fell on my back again, dragging her down with me, only just managing to roll out of her way as she hit the floor, loosening her grasp.

I spied an abandoned cricket bat yards away and stood up, only to pitch forward as Scarlett took hold of my ankles; her acrylic nails digging deep into my flesh.

I went down again, hitting my chest on an overturned chair and my head on the corner of an oak dresser. Severely winded, I lay there, eyes closed, unable to move. I'd forgotten that among her many accomplishments, Scarlett held a red belt in Tae Kwon Do.

Was this how it would end for me? I steeled myself for a final beating but nothing happened. All I could hear was a loud click, retreating footsteps, and the sound of my heart pounding in my ears.

I hauled myself into a sitting position. My head hurt. My ribs were sore. The house was eerily silent. My thoughts flew to Olive. I had to get to her yet I knew Scarlett would be back at any moment. I'd seen enough horror films to know there had to be a grand finale.

I longed to call out to Olive, to reassure her that she wasn't alone, but I daren't utter a sound. Wait! I could call 999! I didn't need to speak. They could triangulate my bearings! I pulled out my mobile but my hands were shaking so much I couldn't hit the right numbers. Then, a blinding pain in my arm as the phone was kicked out of my grasp.

'I wouldn't do that if I were you,' said Scarlett calmly, as I watched my mobile skitter away.

She stood over me holding Fleming's starter pistol. She had discarded her monk's costume for a navy velour jogging suit, anorak and trainers. Her blonde hair was scraped back in a ponytail. Except for a slash of bright red lipstick, she was devoid of makeup and sported just four acrylic nails.

'The phone lines have been cut,' she said and, without taking her eyes off me, snatched up my mobile and put it in her pocket.

'The police are on their way,' I bluffed. 'They know your real name is Sydney Pember.'

'Really? How clichéd!' Scarlett said. 'I was expecting something more original from the *Gazette*'s star reporter. Oh! By the way, I liked my obituary. You did a nice job.'

'Thank you,' was all I managed to say but my hopes rose a little. Scarlett was beginning to talk. This was good. Dad always said that keeping your abductor talking was the key to survival.

'It was a bold plan, but if I must say, not very well thought through,' I said, then wished I hadn't.

'I beg your pardon?' A tide of red flew up Scarlett's face. 'It was very well thought through. How dare you!'

'What I meant was, there were things I'd have done differently.' I tried to sound calm but my stomach churned with fear.

'Really,' she said, her voice hard. 'Like what?'

'Hiring Go-Go Gothic was a mistake.'

'I wasn't to know Titley's outfit was a gimmick,' Scarlett snapped. 'Sadie told me he had a very classy Cadillac.'

'And pretending to be Melanie Carew when you made the booking,' I said. 'You must have known someone would check.'

Scarlett's jaw hardened. 'Go on.'

'The phone call you made to me on Thursday morning at that ridiculously early hour and not bothering to leave your name.' It was a wild guess but the expression of surprise on her face confirmed I was right.

'You had to be involved. You write the obituaries!'

'Why go to all that trouble of faking your own death?' I said. 'Couldn't you just get divorced or disappear?'

'It takes seven years for a missing person to be declared officially dead,' said Scarlett. 'Seven years! Dougie and I don't have that kind of time and nor does Olive, besides—' she drew herself up to her full height, 'I'm a *very* important person in the community. Someone like me can't just be buried *quietly*.'

'The funeral *was* quiet,' I said. 'No one came.'

'Ah! But you wrote about it. My photograph was even on the front page!' said Scarlett. 'As a matter of fact, I rather enjoyed Dougie telling me how everyone was devastated that I'd died in such tragic circumstances.'

'I think they were more disappointed that they missed out on the slap-up meal and thirteen-pan steel band,' I said dryly. 'You had a preneed funeral plan, remember?'

'It was never paid for.'

'And of course, an open casket is a rare sight in Devon.'

'Hah! But I'd suffered horrific injuries in that car crash,

270

dear,' said Scarlett. 'An open casket would have been so gruesome.'

'Why pick a yoga retreat? Why Spain?'

'Could have been the Pyrenees,' she said. 'I wanted to create confusion. By the time the Foreign and Commonwealth Office collaborated and got through all the paperwork, Dougie and I would be long gone.'

'Not if the Fleming vault was exhumed.'

'Why would it be?'

'To inspect the coffin,' I said. 'You and your husband were captured on CCTV stealing it from the Bards' storage unit. Along with Friar Tuck's costume.'

Scarlett smirked. 'Nice try, dear but it would never hold up in court,' she said. 'I was wearing a disguise and by the time the police get permission to exhume my body – so strange to think I'm dead – it'll be too late.'

I knew she was right. 'You'll be far away in Rio.'

'Exactly.' A slow smile spread across Scarlett's face. 'You see, Dougie and I thought of everything.'

'Not quite,' I said. 'You might have got away with murdering Sammy Larch, too, had you not had a witness.'

'You're bluffing.' Scarlett laughed. 'You can't prove it and you can't prove I was here, either. Olive is lying dead and Dougie and I inherit *all* her money!'

'Fleming is already suspected of murdering you. He married Olive too soon. Everyone will think the worst!'

'In case you forget, Dougie has an alibi tonight,' Scarlett said. 'I do believe he's at your house as we speak.'

'You really have thought of everything,' I said incredulously. 'Everyone knew that Olive suffered from poor health – and a fright, such as an encounter with an imaginary ghost, could kill her.'

'Correct.'

'You push Olive down the stairs, Fleming discovers her body, and calls the police,' I went on. 'Reeling from the recent

271

deaths of two wives, he decides to leave Gipping-on-Plym and start a new life.'

'Almost. But not quite.' Scarlett smirked. 'You've forgotten all about Eunice Pratt.'

'You're right! I have!' I tried to sound intrigued but a sick feeling came over me. 'What about her?'

'A woman obsessed with a man who doesn't want her,' said Scarlett dramatically. 'A woman who stalks the object of her desire. A woman who already has a restraining order on her head. What do you think such a woman would do to her rival in love?'

Suddenly, the penny dropped. 'You set her up! You made sure Fleming waved at Mary Berry the morning of the funeral knowing full well she'd tell Eunice.' I shook my head with amazement. 'And the phone calls!' I recalled the itemized phone records made to Dairy Cottage and Eunice's increasing distress and confusion. 'You used her. How unbelievably cruel.'

'As a matter of fact, I'm expecting her here at any minute. So it's time for you to go.'

I came back to reality with a jolt. Scarlett would never have told me all this if she planned to let me live.

Pressing the pistol muzzle against my temple she said, 'Get up and walk.' I stumbled to my feet. She frog-marched me past the closed cellar door and into the library.

Astonished, I saw the tapestry on the far wall had been drawn aside. Behind the oak wainscoting was a small, low door. It was open.

'The priest hole,' I said horrified. Too late I guessed what was in store for me. I lashed out at Scarlett's legs but she slapped me hard across the face with the pistol. 'Believe me, this might not be a real gun but I can assure you a bullet at point-blank range will kill you.'

Defeated, I crawled through the low doorway and into darkness. 'And don't bother to scream,' Scarlett said, peering through the opening. 'These secret hiding places have walls several feet thick. No one will ever hear you.'

Scarlett closed the panel shut. I heard a final click. I was alone. No one could help me now.

38

I sat without moving for what seemed like hours, numbed by the very real possibility that I just might die.

I still couldn't believe I was trapped. I couldn't believe that Olive Larch was probably lying dead at the bottom of the cellar stairs, and I'd soon be joining her in the hereafter.

If, by some miracle, she had survived the fall I jolly well hoped she'd tell the world that I'd tried to save her but couldn't save myself. Other than Olive, no one knew I was here. I didn't even have my mobile – Scarlett had made sure of that.

But, *wait*! Hope soared in my breast. Chuffy promised he'd call me with instructions. Wouldn't he realize that Scarlett's voice wasn't mine? Of course, she wouldn't answer and besides, Chuffy had no idea I was on the trail of a killer. My spirits plunged.

What about Mrs Evans? Hope soared again! Perhaps she'd been her usual nosy self and opened the confidential envelope. She'd get help, wouldn't she? My spirits rose again. Even if help came, they'd never find me. No one found Father Gregory, either.

But, *wait*! My moped! *Blast!* Even if it were discovered in the undergrowth, Annabel's exposé would soon put paid to that. I could see the headline now. DAUGHTER OF NOTORIOUS CRIMINAL, THE FOG, VANISHES! No one would care. They'd *expect* me to disappear – just like my parents had.

I drew some comfort from knowing that Chuffy would protect Dad's identity. He'd tell my parents that I had followed his advice and taken a new name and moved to a new location. It would be months before they wondered why I hadn't been in touch. I'd be dead in three weeks or less!

Oh, God! It could be *years* before the truth was discovered – most likely when old houses like these were no longer valued and torn down. I stifled a sob of self-pity. My skeletal remains would be found lying on the floor and the superstitious locals would believe they'd finally located their missing medieval monk.

Tears welled up in my eyes. I recalled Mum's stern words, *'Crying won't help.'* She was right. It wouldn't. I couldn't just sit here waiting for the grim reaper to call.

At the thought of the Reverend Whittler another wave of self-pity hit me anew. There would be no funeral or after-service party for me. Not even a headstone at St Peter's the Martyr commemorating the short life I had lived. It would be as if I had never existed.

I wiped a tear away from my cheek. There had to be some way I could let the world know what really happened. Then, when my bones were found, the truth would be out. I'd get my front-page scoop all right. I'd be on every newspaper in the world – just like the famed Lindow Man who was murdered in the first century A.D. and discovered lying facedown in a peat bog.

Lindow Man's murder remained a mystery – but mine would not. Wasn't I journalist? All I needed was paper, pencil and a little bit of light.

I'd been reluctant to use my Mini Maglite only because of

my fear of enclosed spaces. Who knew how tiny this place really was?

'Courage, Vicky!' I said aloud, and pulled the flashlight out of my pocket.

Thankfully, the room was a little bigger than I expected. At least I could stand up.

A quick sweep around the walls revealed a narrow camp bed, a pillow, two chenille blankets, an oil lamp, and a box of matches. I also discovered three bottles of water and a granola bar.

I struck a match and lit the oil lamp. There was a pop and puff of acrid smoke. I turned up the flame, grateful for the yellow light. It made the tiny room a little friendlier.

Throwing a blanket around my shoulders, I sat on the camp bed and ate the granola bar. I wondered what small comforts Father Gregory had enjoyed all those years ago. How long had it taken him to die?

The oil lamp flickered, casting eerie shadows across the walls sending a shiver down my spine. The hairs on the back of my neck stood up and I had to admit I sensed some kind of presence.

'I don't believe in ghosts,' I said aloud. Anyway, hadn't Topaz mentioned that when the priest hole was finally discovered, the old man had vanished?

I went very still as my mind grappled with the remote possibility that perhaps, just *perhaps*, he'd escaped.

Hadn't Sadie mentioned secret *passages!* What if Father Gregory hadn't vanished? What if he'd dug his way out?

Casting the blanket aside, I fell to my knees and began the painstaking process of checking over every inch of the floor and walls.

At an early age Dad had trained me in the art of opening combination safes, so my hearing was finely tuned for any tell-tale clicks or subtle changes in depth and sound.

I'd been tapping away on solid walls for what seemed like forever when I struck gold. The tone became hollow.

Like most old houses in Devon, the walls were made of cob – a mix of earth and clay. Relieved, excited and utterly exhausted, I pulled out my Swiss Army penknife and stabbed manically at the plaster.

The blade went straight through. There was a cascade of stones and pebbles as part of the lower wall began to crumble. I lay on my back and with both feet, kicked as hard as I could.

I'd discovered Father Gregory's tunnel.

39

The secret passage was so low I could only wriggle forward a few inches at a time on my elbows. It was so narrow my shoulders scraped the sides. I couldn't have turned back even if I'd wanted to.

I tried to grasp the Mini Maglite between my teeth but it was too heavy. I felt my safari jacket tear. My mouth and eyes were full of grit and dirt. I couldn't breathe. I felt suffocated. Had Father Gregory really escaped this way or would I come across his bones right here in this hellhole?

Crawling through the tunnel was the most horrifying thing I'd ever had to do. I prayed as I had never prayed before and my prayers were answered.

Finally, I felt cool air on my face and saw a pinprick of light in the distance, growing larger inch by inch.

Sobbing with relief, I came to the end of the tunnel only to discover that it opened into a vertical, cylindrical shaft. I was halfway down a well but all was not lost.

Iron rungs covered in green moss and slime were embedded into the curved walls. Below me was dank water – I had no idea how deep – and above, light.

I'd lost track of time and had been under the impression I'd been stuck here for hours. It had only been twenty minutes.

Reaching across the void, I grasped the nearest rung and rattled it to see if it was rotten. It held firm. With joy and gratitude in my heart, I began my climb to freedom.

At the top I took in deep breaths of air but was dismayed to see my exit blocked by a metal grill and padlock. I couldn't believe it! All this way and still trapped.

Wedging my body on either side of the well's walls, I pulled out my Swiss Army penknife once more. The lock was rusted and easy to pick. It snapped open and fell, tumbling into the water, landing with a faraway plop. I tried not to think that could have been me.

With all my strength, I heaved the metal grill up and over the lip with my head and shoulders. It fell with a deafening crash.

Clambering onto the stone ledge, I emerged from the old wishing well in front of the converted barn.

There was no sign of Scarlett's Range Rover. Eunice's silver Ford Fiesta stood in its stead. Fleming can't have wasted any time in summoning her to Headcellars.

With dread, I raced around to the front, but Fleming's Audi wasn't there.

I hesitated. Perhaps he was actually *bringing* the police? But that wouldn't make sense. If the plan *were* to frame Eunice, he'd have to catch her red-handed and then call for help.

I made my way to the front door. It was unlocked. I pushed it open and stepped inside, catching a glimpse of my reflection in the hall mirror. Startled, I had to look again. I was covered from head to foot in mud and my beloved safari jacket was in shreds.

The house seemed deathly still and unfriendly. Broken vases, smashed picture frames and upturned chairs lay scattered about the long hallway.

'Eunice?' I called out. 'It's Vicky. Where are you?' There was no reply. I hoped she wasn't hiding.

Hastening to the cellar door, I expected to see it wide open but it remained locked. Olive must be still down there. I rapped on the door, 'Olive, are you all right?' Harder still, 'Olive! It's me, Vicky!'

'Thank heavens,' said a familiar voice. I turned to find Mary Berry hurrying from the library with an opened bottle of Courvoisier in her hand. Her face was ashen. 'Something bad has happened,' she cried. 'The phone lines are cut. There must have been a break-in.'

'Is Eunice with you?'

Mary shook her head, 'I can't find Olive.'

'She's in the cellar.'

'*Cellar?*'

'We must get an ambulance. I think she's hurt.'

'Cellar steps are lethal,' said Mary, taking a swig of brandy. 'She's probably dead.'

'Where's Eunice?'

'I don't care what you think, she didn't do it,' she said. 'Why are you covered in mud?'

'Yes. I know,' I said. 'There's no time to explain. Fleming will be here any minute.'

'Not until eight he won't,' Mary said grimly.

I looked at my watch. We had fifteen minutes. 'You must tell me where Eunice is,' I said urgently.

'That *scoundrel* phoned and wanted Eunice to meet him here at eight o'clock.' On sensing my confusion, Mary took another nip of brandy adding, 'He rang around five. I'd normally be out with the cows but didn't want to leave Eunice alone.'

'Fleming thought you were *Eunice*?'

'I had a mouthful of chocolate cake. He said it was urgent that I come over to Headcellars at eight o'clock.' A disgusted expression came over Mary's face. 'He told me that he *loved* me and at last we could be together.'

'So you came here to confront Fleming?' I was incredulous. I'd always thought Mary detested her sister-in-law.

'I know what you're thinking,' she said. 'I can't stand the woman but family is family. For weeks Eunice claimed he'd been calling her and swearing undying love, but I refused to believe her.'

'Where is she now?' I asked for the umpteenth time.

'Acepromazine,' said Mary. 'Eunice will be out cold for days. The moment she learned that her precious Dougie had eloped with Olive Larch, she went to pieces.' Mary frowned. 'Wait . . . if Olive is in the cellar and Dougie wanted her to come here . . .' She clapped her hand over her mouth in horror. 'He was going to frame her,' Mary said appalled. 'But *why*?'

'Scarlett is still alive,' I said. 'They both wanted Olive's money.'

'I thought I saw her Range Rover on my way over here. She won't get far. She's got two flat tires.'

'Listen!' My heart turned over. A car door slammed outside. 'It's Fleming!'

'He must be stopped!' Mary declared. 'There are two of us. We'll confront him.'

'No! He's too clever,' I said. 'Fleming has a cast-iron alibi. Scarlett has vanished. Olive could have fallen. Somehow we have to get him to confess.'

'Eunice?' called out a familiar voice. 'Where are you?'

The blood drained out of Mary's face. 'It *is* him! He's *here*!'

'Quickly,' I hissed. 'The downstairs loo.'

We darted inside. I threw open the window. 'Can you climb out and get help?'

Mary was trembling. 'I don't know. It looks a bit small.'

Through the crack in the door, I watched the hallway.

'Eunice? Hello?' Fleming came into view. 'I know you're here. Darling?' he cooed. 'Where are you?'

'What's he doing?' whispered Mary.

'Sssh!' I felt sick with nerves. Fleming was standing by the

281

cellar. Glancing up and down the corridor – presumably to check the coast was clear – he withdrew a key from his pocket, unlocked the door, and disappeared inside.

I flew down the hallway and slammed it shut. *Blast!* Fleming had kept the key!

Fleming began hammering and rattling on the door. 'Eunice let me out! I know you're there!'

I threw my body weight against the door but with each thump, knew I couldn't hold him off indefinitely.

Mary raced out of the bathroom, dragged an upturned chair toward me, and we wedged it under the handle.

'That'll hold,' she whispered. 'I'll go for help.'

'Eunice, please!' Fleming was growing more desperate. 'This isn't funny. Let me out. I know what you've done. Olive is alive. She needs a doctor!'

Was he lying? Was it a trick to make me open the door? I didn't know what to do. Mary could be ages.

Fleming had gone quiet. Fear began to bubble up once more. Was he administering the killer blow while I stood helpless only feet away? I closed my eyes and whispered a prayer to God, begging him for help.

When I opened my eyes, I thought I was dreaming. Mary was walking toward me grinning from ear to ear. Behind her was DS Probes making bizarre hand gestures that I guessed meant for me to stay quiet and do nothing.

In silence, he handed me a note. *Pretend Eunice is here. Let him out.* I nodded my understanding. Mary took Probes by the hand and led him away to the downstairs loo.

In a flash, I guessed their plan.

Taking a deep breath, I kicked the chair away from the door and opened it. Fleming charged out, utterly furious. '*Eunice!* What the hell—?'

'Mr Fleming!' I feigned astonishment. 'What happened? Are you all right?'

His expression switched to anguish. 'Vicky! Thank God. It's

Olive . . . she's alive, but unconscious. Eunice threw her down the stairs.'

'You saw her do it?'

'Yes but I couldn't stop her,' he cried. 'I hurried to Olive's side and that's when Eunice locked me in. Where is she?'

'Her car is still outside,' I said. 'I think she's hiding.'

'We must get an ambulance. The police.' He sounded close to tears. 'I can't believe it. My poor Olive!' *Nice performance.*

'Why aren't you at the Evanses?' I said.

'I was worried about Olive and quite rightly so. Wait—' Douglas looked at me with suspicion. 'What are you doing here?'

Careful, Vicky. 'Same reason as you. When I saw Olive wasn't at the meeting, I began to worry. I knew she'd be alone. Dairy Cottage is only a few minutes away.'

'Yes, yes.' Fleming looked relieved. 'You know Eunice is insane. She's been stalking me for months. She's a dangerous woman. She failed to kill Olive today but I know she'll try again.'

'I don't think so, dear,' said Mary, stepping out of the shadows. 'Eunice has been tucked up in bed for the past two days.'

'Mary! The Fiesta . . . I . . .' Fleming turned pale.

'I drove it here. You say you actually *saw* my sister-in-law push Olive?'

'I didn't say that,' he said quickly. 'I just saw *something* push her. The house is haunted. Did you know we have a ghost here?'

'That's strange,' said Mary, turning to me. 'Because Vicky says she was positive it was Scarlett who threw Olive down the stairs.'

'That's not possible. Scarlett is dead,' Fleming said wildly. 'You must have seen the ghost! It was a monk, wasn't it?'

'You mean the ghost in a Friar Tuck costume?' I said dryly.

'I don't know what you're talking about.' Fleming was becoming angry. 'We're wasting time.'

'I know Scarlett Fleming is alive,' I said.

'You can't prove it.'

'I'm afraid we can, sir.' Probes emerged from the bathroom. 'I'm arresting you on suspicion of bigamy, fraud—'

'You can't!' Fleming said horrified. 'I'm innocent.' I had to admit, Fleming's stubbornness was impressive.

'I've had enough of this! Tell the truth, you *cad*!' I hadn't noticed Mary slip away but now she stood before us holding a snail in the palm of her hand.

'What are you doing?' said Fleming, turning white. 'That's Seabiscuit!'

Without a word, Mary gently placed the snail on the floor. A little grey head peeped out of its shell.

My heart went into my mouth. 'Mary,' I whispered, 'don't do it.'

'Just watch me.' Mary slowly lowered her heavy work shoe over Devon's reigning champion for three seasons running. As her foot hovered mere inches above Seabiscuit's shell she said, 'I'm told it's a quick death, but who knows?'

'No! All right!' Fleming gave an anguished sob. 'I'll tell you everything.'

The next half hour was chaotic. Steve's ambulance turned up at the same time as police backup – Probes had alerted both the moment he arrived and Mary had given him the scoop.

As Fleming was handcuffed and bundled into the back of a police car, a call for 'All cars' was launched on the police radio to apprehend a Range Rover, registration number SCLTT.

'She didn't get far,' said Probes, as we waited outside anxiously for Steve and his partner Tom to emerge with Olive from the cellar. They'd been down there for ages. 'Traffic stopped her on the M5 at Junction 8. It's a criminal offence to drive on the motorway with a flat tire.'

'I'm still worried we won't be able to prove she pushed Olive,' I said anxiously. 'If Olive doesn't pull through, it will be Scarlett's word against mine.'

Probes nodded gravely. 'Did she fall or was she pushed.'

'Exactly. Just like Sammy Larch's so-called accident.'

'You look exhausted,' Probes said. 'We'll go out another time.' On seeing my surprise he added, 'Our date? Tonight? How else did you think I knew where to find you? I went to Factory Terrace to pick you up.'

It turned out that Mrs Evans *had* opened the confidential letter addressed to Pete and was in a 'terrible dilemma'.

'I'm happy to say she made the right choice in handing it over to the police,' said Probes. 'I suspected you'd try to handle this mess yourself and came here straightaway.'

Tears sprang to my eyes. I turned away.

'What's wrong?' Probes touched my arm. 'I know it's all been a terrible ordeal.'

The truth was I felt overwhelmed and confused. Seeing Probes arrive with the police and all the flashing lights and sirens brought back the reality of the other 'mess' I was still in.

In all the excitement, I'd forgotten about Chuffy, my parents, and Annabel's exposé. Annabel had mentioned she had connections with the boys in blue. She and Probes were on first-name terms. Did Probes already know my true identity? Would I be the next to be taken down to the station for questioning and he was simply biding his time?

'I'm just tired,' I said.

'I didn't see your moped. Do you want me to take you home?'

'It's in the undergrowth.' I tried to smile and offered him my hand. 'Thanks for everything. See you around sometime.'

Probes shook it, but a hurt look crossed his face. 'Congratulations on your exclusive,' he said stiffly. 'Goodbye, Vicky.'

I walked back into the house alone just as Steve and Tom emerged from the cellar carrying Olive on a stretcher. To my relief, her face wasn't covered with a sheet – though she looked as white as one.

I trailed after them to the waiting ambulance and watched as they slid the stretcher inside and closed the doors.

'She's unconscious but she'll live,' said Steve gravely. 'Broken hip, broken leg, but her heart is as strong as an ox.'

'Really?' I said recalling Mrs Evans's extremely detailed diagnosis on the state of Olive's health. 'I thought she had some sort of heart problem.'

'Not Miss Larch.' Steve lowered his voice. 'I know all about her little episodes. If you ask me, they're a form of attention seeking, often the result of an overbearing parent. I did a course in behavioural therapy in Plymouth.'

'I'm just glad she'll be all right.' Mrs Evans must have read the wrong patient file and mistakenly told Scarlett all about Olive's 'potentially lethal ventricular arrhythmia'.

'You feeling all right, doll?' said Steve, his expression filled with concern. 'Looks like you've been through the mill.'

'Through a tunnel and down a well, actually.'

'Why don't you come around to my place?' he said. 'You need a hot bath and a massage. I've had a Jacuzzi installed, too. You can relax. Listen to music. I'll cook—'

'You just don't give up, do you?' I said dryly.

'On you? Never.' Steve thumped his chest dramatically. 'As long as there's breath in Steve's body, doll. Oh! There was one more thing.'

He pulled a plastic bag out of his pocket. Inside were two tiny oval-shaped red pieces of plastic. 'These were stuck in Olive's woollen cardigan.'

I was ecstatic. 'It's one of Scarlett's acrylic nails!'

'Yeah, that's what I found on Sammy Larch's body, too,' said Steve. 'I've got them at home somewhere.'

'You're amazing!' I threw my arms around him and kissed Steve on the cheek.

He turned pink with pleasure. 'Are you sure you won't change your mind about the Jacuzzi? I've got bubbles.'

Later, as I sank into my own bubble bath, I knew that

although the Flemings were in custody and Olive was safe, my problems were far from over. Without my mobile, there could be no news from Chuffy. Had he foiled Annabel's plan? Was the Hill clan safe?

I wasn't out of the woods. Yet.

The next few days would be crucial.

40

The first sign that Chuffy had succeeded came the very next morning when Gipping police turned up at the *Gazette* and arrested Annabel on suspicion of dealing in stolen merchandise.

Following a tip from a certain Dino DiMarco, police raided her bedroom in Blundells Court and discovered a box full of Birken handbags. Barcodes confirmed these items had been taken from a Hermes factory break-in several weeks before.

'I swear I only sell fakes on eBay,' Annabel sobbed. 'I don't know where those handbags came from, I swear it.'

Only too willing to help police with their inquiries, a tearful Annabel produced the address of a warehouse in Plymouth. Astonishingly, by the time the cops arrived, it had been cleared out. According to Barbara, Annabel had appealed to Probes for help but he 'regretfully' declared that 'stolen property was not within his jurisdiction' and urged her to 'come clean'.

If that weren't bad enough, Annabel's biggest blow came when her so-called witnesses – Wayne Henderson and Nigel

Keeps at Dartmoor Prison and Wormwood Scrubs respectively – suddenly changed their tune. Claiming they'd never heard of The Fog, they admitted they'd do anything for money and that the 'lady reporter told them what to say.'

Since it was only their word against hers – tape recorders and mobiles were banned during prison visiting hours – Wilf was predictably furious and demanded Annabel explain herself.

She did – by insisting I was the daughter of a notorious wanted criminal called Harold Hill, nicknamed The Fog. Everyone laughed.

Luckily they believed my staunch denial and feigned outrage that she should accuse me of faking my poor parents' death. Of course, the newly purchased contact lenses in several different colours certainly helped. Barbara said she always thought my sapphire blue eyes were 'too blue' to be real.

When the *Plymouth Bugle* found its way onto Pete's desk, it would seem heaven would not be smiling on Annabel Lake for some time to come.

Chuffy had demanded I made sure Blundells Court was empty that fateful night and I had obliged. Splashed across the front page was the headline FROST BY NAME NOT FROST BY NATURE. A photograph taken inside the Imperial Hotel showed Dr Frost lying on the lobby floor as Annabel beat him over the head with her handbag.

The article went on to say that Edwina's Escorts insisted that Dr Frost had been a client but naturally, he denied it.

True, I did feel a twinge of guilt at impersonating the concierge at the Imperial Hotel. The suggestion that personal items had been left in his room was hardly a crime but I had never expected the ruse to go public. The scandalous scoop bore the stamp of Topaz Potter but since The Copper Kettle had been closed for days, I wasn't able to confront her.

Deep down I was devastated by Annabel's betrayal but threw myself into work – and there was plenty of it. Apart from catching up on a huge backlog of funerals, Gipping-on-Plym

289

was gripped by a fever of disbelief on learning that Scarlett Fleming was very much alive and kicking.

I detected a certain admiration from the members of the Gipping Bards who could talk of nothing else – 'I never guessed in a million years' and 'If anyone could pull off being dead, Scarlett could do it.'

The duo faced a long list of charges ranging from theft (captured on CCTV), bigamy (Fleming now had two wives), and first-degree murder. Thanks to the urging of DS Probes and Steve producing the acrylic nails he'd found in Sammy Larch's woollen cardigan, the old boy's body was immediately exhumed. The autopsy revealed that he had Scarlett's DNA under his fingernails. Case proven and closed.

Scarlett pleaded temporary insanity. She insisted she had not been herself since being prescribed a new form of HRT, which was suspected to have been the cause of two domestic stabbings in Wales.

Unfortunately, Dr Frost could not back up her claim, having taken a leave of absence due to personal reasons.

For a third time, I basked in the glow of being the *Gazette*'s star reporter. My phone was on fire with curious readers filled with questions on how I unravelled the Fleming's elaborate plan. I was happy to tell them.

NO MORE TOMORROWS FOR SCARLETT!
SAYS VICKY HILL IN EXCLUSIVE!

The four-page exposé that followed included a firsthand account of my escape from Headcellars. Photographs of the priest hole and a publicity shot of me emerging from the wishing well provoked several visits from the Gipping Spiritualist Society, all eager to know if Father Gregory had telepathically shown me the way out. I said 'no comment' although admittedly, I had sensed *some* kind of presence that night.

Naturally I gave Mary Berry the credit she was due – PLUCKY

Pensioner Saves the Day. Without her courage and quick thinking, we may never have trapped Fleming into making a confession. Mary became a mini-celebrity and was deluged with invitations to speak of her experiences to the Women's Institute nationwide, all of which she declined, stating, 'My cows are more important.'

Eunice slept for four days straight. There was a nasty moment when she visited Olive in hospital but it turned out she wanted to discuss the Beast of Bodmin. According to hospital staff, the two women bonded and all assault charges were dropped prompting a flurry of phone calls from HMS *Dauntless* – all of which I ignored.

Olive made good progress. She revealed that while she lay close to death on the cellar floor, her father had come to her in a vision to insist the Larch Legacy continue.

To Dave's joy, Olive confirmed that the note was indeed written in her father's hand and the wrong team had won. Rather than remove the Legacy from Jack Webster's cutters, Olive created an honorary award called Daring to Dream along with a cheque for three thousand pounds, enabling Dave to build an Olympic training course at Pennymoor Jump. In a rush of generosity, Olive also settled an 'undisclosed' sum of money on Gipping Manor in compensation for the damage caused at the GSRF Gala.

As for Go-Go Gothic – true to my promise Neil got far more free publicity than even he dreamed possible. With quotes on the front page, 'The coffin *had* felt a bit light,' and a short day-in-the-life feature on page eight, Neil showed his gratitude by giving me a one-year free pass to the Banana Club.

By late Saturday afternoon and with still no sign of Topaz, I was beginning to think she might have gone away for good. I felt a pang of loneliness. I realized I missed my strange little friend.

Marching to the rear of the café, I rapped smartly on the door. The kitchen curtain moved. I caught a glimpse of a face.

Moments later Topaz stood before me dressed in a smart tweed skirt, twinset, and pearls, looking every inch a lady of the manor. Her own dark hair was pulled back from her face and secured with a tortoiseshell barrette.

'Where have you been?' I demanded.

'I've just got back from London,' she said with a sniff. 'I do have another life, you know.'

'So I see, your ladyship. Mind if I come in for five minutes?'

'If you have to.'

Inside the kitchen I showed her the *Bugle*. 'It looks like you've been busy.'

Topaz turned red. 'The *Bugle* pays,' she said defensively. 'I've got my ancestral home to support. I've got responsibilities.'

'The *Gazette* would never have printed that story anyway,' I said. 'How did you find out?'

'You told me to follow Annabel, so I did.' Topaz scowled. 'It's so annoying. While I was at the Imperial Hotel, someone must have tipped off her dealer. All the handbags were moved out of that warehouse. We'll never catch her now.'

Knowing full well that all charges would be dropped against Annabel eventually, I decided against telling Topaz about her arrest.

'Actually, I'm frightfully busy. Can we talk another time?' Topaz said. 'I'm working tonight.'

'I thought you might have given up this idea of being a journalist.'

'Are you kidding? Actually' – Topaz took a deep breath – 'if I tell you something will you promise you won't be cross?'

'I'll try.'

'The *Bugle* is offering a reward for anyone who has seen the Beast of Bodmin. They want photos of the big cat. I told them I had first-hand experience and you'll never guess what—' she started to hoot with laughter. 'They're going *to pay* me!'

I was incredulous. 'For taking photographs of *yourself*?'

'Yes!' she shrieked. 'That's why I'm off to Bodmin tonight. I need to be authentic. I say – do you want to come?'

'Maybe another time,' I said.

'Wait!' Topaz stepped closer. 'You're wearing contact lenses.'

'Of course,' I said quickly. 'You didn't think sapphire blue was my real eye colour, did you?'

'I much prefer the sapphire blue,' she said. 'Where did you buy them?'

'The Internet.'

'Really? I wonder if they do a red werewolf version?'

Leaving Topaz to her nighttime plans, I left the café. A FedEx truck was parked outside the *Gazette*.

'I'm afraid we're closed,' I said to the young driver who was trying to peer through the blinds at the front door. He held a slim envelope in his hands.

'I work there. I can sign for it.' I flashed him my press card. 'Here's my ID.'

With a quick glance he said, 'It's for you, anyway.'

My stomach turned over. Even though the return address was fictional, I knew it was from Chuffy. For some stupid reason, I'd assumed all was forgotten and that life would just go on.

I let myself into the side door and went through to reception to find some scissors. As I snipped open the tamper-free package, I realized my hands were shaking.

Inside was a one-way airline ticket from Plymouth to Barcelona – the irony of which did not escape me – with the following Monday as my departure date. There was also a fake passport in the name of Laura Fort James.

I stared at the new me – a photograph taken at Mum's birthday dinner one carefree day last year. My eye colour was noted as brown. There was no note.

I had to sit down. The reception walls were filled with framed 'exclusives', some dated back to the Second World War. Mine were on there, too.

I'd grown to love Gipping-on-Plym and its citizens. I even enjoyed writing obituaries. I knew I'd leave one day, but not like this.

Resentment flared in my breast. I had dreamed of being a reporter ever since I was a child. I was doing what I loved. Why should my life be ruined because of what my parents had done? I needed to think. If only I had someone to talk to. If only I had a sign as to what I should do? Stay – or go.

Tucking my passport and ticket inside my tattered safari jacket, I headed back to Factory Terrace with a heavy heart, which plunged even deeper when I saw Annabel's BMW parked outside number twenty-one. The few words we'd spoken since she accused me of being Harold Hill's daughter – wait, I *was* his daughter – were terse and unfriendly. The last person I wanted to see was Annabel yet what could she be doing here?

In the hallway a pink suitcase stood on the floor alongside a red cushion with huggable arms. *Thank you God!* Annabel must be leaving Gipping for good! She must have come to say good-bye!

Annabel and Mrs Evans were sitting at the kitchen table drinking tea and eating a Victoria sponge cake. A pink business card lay on the table. I recognized it instantly – Edwina's Escorts.

'Here she is,' said Mrs Evans. 'Annabel is going to stay here with us until all this business is sorted out.'

'She's *what*?' I said with horror.

'I hope you don't mind,' said Annabel coldly.

I gave a bright smile. 'Of course not. It'll be lovely.' *Blast! Goddamit! Bugger!*

'I've made room for her in the sewing room,' Mrs Evans chattered on. 'She and Dr Frost are having a trial separation after that . . . incident.'

Annabel fingered the Edwina's Escorts business card. 'I just don't believe he'd pay someone.'

'What's that?' I said innocently.

'I found this tucked under my windshield wipers.' Annabel gave a shudder. 'I don't want to talk about it anymore.'

Of course I knew what the card said because I'd written it. *Wonder where your boyfriend goes at night? Try the Imperial Hotel.* I'd signed it, *A Friend.*

'Do you think it was Jack Webster?' I said.

'He's no friend to anyone,' Mrs Evans chipped in.

'What about that farmer chap in the Capri who tailed us to the Banana Club last Saturday?' I suggested. 'He's obviously infatuated with you and just the type to cause trouble.'

'Yes,' Annabel nodded slowly. 'He *has* been following me a lot.' She shuddered again. 'Oh, it's all been so horrible. The photos in the newspaper, people laughing behind my back, being suspended and without *pay*!'

'At least Wilf kept it out of the *Gazette*, dear.' Mrs Evans patted Annabel's hand.' Why don't you take a long bath? That'll make you feel better. Vicky will show you to your room.'

Out in the hallway, I picked up the cushion with huggable arms but Annabel snatched it out of my hands. 'You think you're so clever, don't you,' she hissed. 'Nice try with those contact lenses, but I know who you really are, Victoria Ada Hill.'

I looked her steadily in the eye. 'I don't know what you're talking about.'

'Someone got to my witnesses, and I *know* you had something to do with it.' She was close to tears of rage. 'And those Birken bags in my bedroom—'

The doorbell rang. 'Answer the door,' shouted Mrs Evans from the kitchen. 'I'm on the phone.'

'Will do!' I called back. 'The sewing room is the third door on the right.'

Muttering, 'It's not fair' and 'I'll prove it', Annabel stomped up the stairs with the cushion under one arm, carrying her suitcase.

I was far more shaken by Annabel's desire for revenge than

I cared to admit, but when I discovered DS Probes standing on Mrs Evans's doorstep I thought I was going to die.

'I'm sorry,' he said as he whipped out a pair of handcuffs. 'You're under arrest.'

'No!' I whispered. My head began to spin. My knees went weak. Strong hands grabbed my shoulders. The next thing I knew I'd fallen into Probes's arms.

He looked worried. 'It was a j-j-joke, silly. I only wanted to take you to dinner.' I was speechless. 'I've never made a woman faint before,' Probes said wryly. 'No strings attached. Just friends.'

I looked up into his eyes, searching for any signs of insincerity but found none.

Suddenly, there was an ear-splitting scream from upstairs. 'Omigod!' shrieked Annabel. 'My black dress! My lovely dress is cut to shreds!'

Blast! Mrs Evans was supposed to have repaired it.

At the sound of Annabel thundering down the stairs yelling, 'Vicky! You ruined it!' I took Probes's arm. 'Let's go!'

As we sped out of Factory Terrace it occurred to me that I couldn't leave Gipping quite yet. There were still a few unanswered questions – most notably, with DS Probes for starters.

At the pub last Sunday, I distinctly remembered him mentioning he was finding something out for Annabel.

Given the recent developments, it was vital I discover what that might be. I couldn't risk another exposé. As Dad says, '*Keep your friends close, but your enemies closer*', and that was exactly what I proposed to do.

With Annabel ensconced in Factory Terrace, and Probes pursuing me for reasons that weren't yet clear, I didn't want to make any hasty decisions.

Probes looked across at me and smiled, and I smiled back. I'd managed to outsmart Annabel, I was sure I could outsmart Probes, too.

I'd have to delay my flight but why worry about leaving Gipping today. I'd worry about it tomorrow. After all, tomorrow is another day.

Scarlett O'Hara was on to a good thing.